The story of Josephine Cox is as extraordinary as anything in her novels. Born in a cotton-mill house in Blackburn, she was one of ten children. Her parents, she says, brought out the worst in each other, and life was full of tragedy and hardship – but not without love and laughter. At the age of sixteen, Josephine met and married 'a caring and wonderful man', and had two sons. When the boys started school, she decided to go to college and eventually gained a place at Cambridge University, though was unable to take this up as it would have meant living away from home. However, she did go into teaching, while at the same time helping to renovate the derelict council house that was their home, coping with the problems caused by her mother's unhappy home life – and writing her first full-length novel. Not surprisingly, she then won the 'Superwoman of Great Britain' Award, for which her family had secretly entered her, and this coincided with the acceptance of her novel for publication.

Josephine gave up teaching in order to write full time. She says, 'I love writing, both recreating scenes and characters from my past, together with new storylines which mingle naturally with the old. I could never imagine a single day without writing, and it's been that way since as far back as I can remember.' Her previous novels of North Country life are all available from Headline and are immensely popular.

'Bestselling author Josephine Cox has penned another winner' *Bookshelf*

'Hailed quite rightly as a gifted writer in the tradition of Catherine Cookson' *Manchester Evening News*

'Guaranteed to tug at the heartstrings of all hopeless romantics' *Sunday Post*

'Another

Also by Josephine Cox

JOSEPHINE
COX

Whistledown
Woman

headline

First published in Great Britain in 1990 by
Macdonald & Co. (Publishers) Ltd.

First published in paperback in 1991 by
Futura Publications

This edition published in 2014 by
HEADLINE PUBLISHING GROUP

1

Cataloguing in Publication Data is available from the British Library

ISBN 978 1 4722 2690 7

Typeset in Times by Avon DataSet Ltd,
Bidford-on-Avon, Warwickshire

Printed and bound in the UK by Clays Ltd, St Ives plc

Headline's policy is to use papers that are natural, renewable and recyclable
products and made from wood grown in well-managed forests and other
controlled sources. The logging and manufacturing processes are expected to
conform to the environmental regulations of the country of origin.

HEADLINE PUBLISHING GROUP
An Hachette UK Company
338 Euston Road
London NW1 3BH

www.headline.co.uk
www.hachette.co.uk

Dedication

Planning and writing *Whistledown Woman* was a unique and wonderful experience, and one which I hope will be relived by the reader, as the words, images, love and adventures are brought alive on the pages.

Throughout the creation of this story, I had a very special friend by my side. He has been beside me through thick and thin for over thirty years, and I pray he will be for many more to come. His name is Ken. He's my beloved husband and friend. Often, in the small hours, I would wake him up to discuss some part of the plot, but he never turned away or complained. Instead, with bleary eyes, he would listen patiently, then, both of us growing too excited to sleep, we would go downstairs, drinking gallons of tea and discussing *Whistledown Woman* until the dawn came.

Thank you, sweetheart. God gave me something very special when he gave me you. Would that everybody at some time in their lives could have such a warm companion.

Acknowledgements

My thanks to the following:

Gypsy Lore Society, America.
Appleby Information Centre (historic details and maps).
Bletchley Library – members of staff, for uncovering archaic and valuable books – relating to old Romanies.
Maritime Museum, Liverpool Docks.
Maritime Museum, Greenwich.
Mr and Mrs Gardener (for their true-life account of a great liner going down).
American Embassy, London.
USAF Duty Officer, Chicksands.
Law Society, London.
Her Majesty's Prison, Manchester (Archives).
Professor Taylor, Hull University (authority on North End, Boston).
Ken (my husband), for ceaseless efforts and thorough research.
Sergeant Jones, United States Air Force Base, Shefford, Beds.
(Anonymous) learned gentleman at Jesus College, Cambridge University, on a point of law, regarding murder trial procedure.
Peter Yourell.

Part One

1921
Starlena Accused

How can this shameful tale be told?
I will maintain until my death
I could do nothing, being sold;

Muir

Chapter One

'You'll be hanged! Make no mistake about that!' The words were emblazoned on Starlena's heart.

In her mind's eye, she could still see the malice in Freya Judd's snake-green eyes, then the merest glimmer of a smile as she'd added in a voice vibrant with hatred, '. . . You'll not be so high and mighty when they bring *that* sentence down on you, my beauty!' At which, Freya Judd had been taken from the court. But her grim warning was not so easily removed. It hung in the air with dark menace, striking fear into Starlena's heart.

During these past six months, since that bright autumn morning when the police had taken her into custody on a charge of murder, Starlena had thought on many things: loves and passions; hatred and fear. Into her choked and weary mind had come all manner of recollections, some pleasant and soothing, others of a very different nature and with which even now she could not come to terms, for they had shaken her to the very core of her being. So many things had happened, so much had come about to turn her life upside-down, that at times in the darkness of her prison cell, the uncanny stillness of the night gave her to wonder whether the whole thing had not been a dream – a nightmare from which at any moment she might be awakened.

But it was no dream! A nightmare, yes – but not one from which she could escape, for Starlena now knew without doubt that even before her wretched mother had birthed her, the shape and direction of her destiny was so strongly defined that in order to have changed it, heaven and hell would have needed to merge! And yet in all truth, had not that very phenomenon taken place through the enactment of her life?

'Come on! Come on! Look sharpish, there!' The uniformed escort leading the way, twisted her neck to look behind and address the others following. At once, Starlena felt the prod of stiff fingers in her shoulder blades as the officer immediately behind urged her on. 'Pick your feet up!' came the curt instruction. So with one impatient representative of the law in front, the other close on her heels and no place to go but forward along the narrow stone-floored corridor, Starlena pushed ahead. And as her feet carried her on in all urgency to the place where her fate must be decided, she thought again on Freya Judd's warning and an involuntary shiver ran through her. *Would* she be found guilty and executed? And back came the answer to her own question: yes! It was likely!

A look of resignation settled in Starlena's dark eyes. If today her own life became forfeit, then in all truth it would be a fitting justice, for she would not deny that she was guilty of many things, and, were it not for her, at least one innocent soul would not now be lying in the churchyard.

Time and time again in that place where the final chapter of her life was being played out, Starlena had listened passively during the revelations which had made the jury gasp and had written a look of desperation on the face of the man defending her. She had witnessed also the smile of triumph on the faces of her enemies. And in that moment, Starlena was ready to meet the consequences of her actions, however terrifying they might be. Her only regrets were for the pain she had caused those who loved and prayed for her.

Throughout every minute of this long tortuous trial, Starlena had felt their despair, and in spite of the fact that she could have drawn a measure of comfort from their darling familiar faces, she had stopped herself from looking towards where they were seated, lest she might see the pain in their eyes, choosing instead to focus her attention on the young, unfortunate barrister who had for many wearying hours put forward her case, a case which, he claimed, 'in all humanity demands the mercy and leniency of this court!'

Of a sudden, the corridor narrowed and darkened, and the little party drew to a halt at the foot of a steep flight of wooden steps. In minutes, the hatch above was flung open and the two enclosing doors swung back to reveal the grand carved ceiling of the court-room, where, high on the wooden-panelled wall above the elevated judiciary bench, was mounted a magnificent bird, its great body encrusted with patches of iridescent colours and the awesome spread of its mighty wings seeming to envelop all below.

Starlena felt herself propelled forward. Going now onwards then upwards, she emerged into the courtroom, where as before she walked briskly across the enclosed area to place herself by the small wooden chair, this flanked by two fresh-faced officers and facing the vast interior of the room which Starlena thought was cold and forbidding, and which somehow put her in mind of Freya Judd, a thing without a heart.

Since the start of this trial, countless thousands throughout Lancashire and beyond had been fired with curiosity at the nature of Starlena's crime, and at the unfolding of her story. And in those months following her arrest great numbers of people had crowded into the Manchester courtroom so as to follow the proceedings on a more intimate level.

Today was of special importance, for now the trial was drawing to its close. The presentation of both defence and prosecution would be concluded, the summing-up would take place, after which the jury would be directed on the law and called upon to retire for the finding of a verdict.

The silence throughout the courtroom was ominous, as all concerned waited for that moment when proceedings would begin. All eyes were on the proud bewitching figure of the woman known as Starlena; for it was in her and the uniqueness of her story that every man and woman here – every onlooker, loved one and enemy alike – found fascination. And now, as one and all gazed upon her, they were made to recall the words of the man defending her, for what he had said directly to the jury, and in tones of reverence was this:

'I want you, *all* of you, to look long and deeply at this woman.

Upon the evidence you have heard you must now decide whether in her you see a cold and calculating fiend – or a woman of remarkable warmth and courage, an innocent victim of such curious circumstances as to be unparalleled in your experience.'

Throughout, not once had Starlena betrayed any sign of her inner turmoil. And even now, as she stood, chin high and gaze unwavering, not a soul there could tell what was on her mind. The dark prison garb took nothing away from the slim youthful strength of her frame which, together with the rich dark eyes and hair shining blue-black as a raven's wings, gave her the charisma of a magnificently beautiful woman! She had a pride about her that was startling, and a confidence that took hold of the heart.

But for all that, the woman Starlena had offered nothing in the way of her own defence, seeming to have already carved an end to her extraordinary life.

So, the outcome seemed inevitable. The sentence would be extreme – of that no-one had any doubt.

In no time at all, the judge drew to an end of his summing-up, the jury retired to chambers, and the prisoner was ordered back to cells to await recall on the jury's return.

Leaving the railed enclosure, Starlena would again have averted her eyes from the gaze of her loved ones. But now, in this final hour, she could not. In that swift moment before she was turned away, her gaze lifted to embrace those who were ever in her heart, alive in her every thought, waking or sleeping. They were all here, those darling people, whose aching hearts reached out to console her. And only now, when her pained gaze fell on those stalwart and precious friends did her eyes sadden and begin to swim with tears so long suppressed. In their faces she saw the joy and laughter of times gone by and now so vital in her memory. Oh, how she loved them all, these dear ones who were intricately woven into her life, etched on her soul for all time. Briefly now, Starlena looked on them, her gaze moving lovingly from one to the other.

There, in the nearest row, was the oldest and wisest of them all, a small wizened figure wrapped head to toe in a dark fringed shawl, with only the gnarled brown hands visible on her lap, and a roguish lock of stark grey hair struggling out from the edge of the shawl which was draped about her face and shoulders in that comforting and familiar manner which had always distinguished her. The eyes alone were the live essence of her wise old soul, being darkly brilliant, and holding as they did a wealth of life's experience. They held also, as they gazed on the prisoner, the greatest love one woman could ever have for another.

To Starlena, this wonderful woman, now physically hampered by the onset of arthritis and worn down by life's cruel adversities, was the mountain peak of her own existence – for this was her beloved Rona, once gypsy of the road and teller of fortunes, and the warmest, boldest friend a body could ever hope to have on this earth.

Beside the old woman was seated Celia, the gypsy queen, still in her younger flush of womanhood and who, with her brown plaited hair, hazel eyes and ordinary features, could not be described as beautiful. But there was about her a handsome, eye-catching arrogance and, in those defiant amber eyes, more than a hint of deep resentment towards Starlena.

The boy she had grown up with was also here – Anselo had been here for every punishing moment of Starlena's trial, his rich dark eyes gleaning her face for something – a smile, a look. Starlena knew not what. She knew only that through his desperate eyes there shone a deep abiding love which sought to give her comfort, but which, by its very nature, could not. Starlena had fought to keep her gaze from meeting his. Yet, of a sudden, a great loneliness came over her, and it took every ounce of her control to draw her gaze along, until it came at last to rest on him. Anselo! The very name was like a song, like a sure-footed gazelle wending its way through the bracken, like the wind whistling through the treetops or the warmth of a summer sun on her upturned face. Anselo was wildly magnificent, with his shoulder-length black hair and dark passionate eyes.

Hardly daring to look at him, Starlena's thoughts were drawn back to when she was little more than a child, and Anselo just a man. Paramount in her memory was a night of illicit love, when passions had blossomed beneath a star-studded sky on a beautiful and sultry evening when, in Anselo's tender arms, she had become a woman.

He was no longer the impressionable young man she had once given her deepest heart to, for so many years had come between. Yet, the passage of time had been kind to him, and now he was a proud and strapping figure of a man, his black eyes afire with passion, his dark and handsome appearance accentuated by the familiar deep-scarlet jacket which had been Starlena's favourite.

Now a renewed boldness flooded into her heart, as she returned the intensity of his gaze. As they looked, each into the other, the same forceful emotion shook their hearts and both were saddened by it.

Looking beyond the familiar faces, Starlena's gaze came to rest on a man much older – a man whose image had the effect of freezing her to the core. An uncommonly offending fellow he was, with stiff unyielding features – one dead eye-socket covered by a crimson patch which could not disguise the jagged scars which ran from beneath it. The one good eye was of the most startling royal blue, whose probing glare could deeply unnerve a body, as it attempted to do now, with Starlena. His sandy-coloured hair was thick and undisciplined, his entire manner arrogant and threatening.

In all his forty years and more, this man had never known the joy of giving – had never once been moved to gladly share his possessions, or himself. He was a fiend, corrupted by an insatiable appetite for power and damned by his crippling greed. As far as Starlena herself had been concerned, this man above all others had wreaked on her the devil's own mischief. His name was amongst those most revered and respected throughout the whole of Lancashire, for the Wymans were immensely rich and for generations had been part of a tradition which gave them the right to rule like lords in their own little kingdom. But this particular Wyman was not liked. He was feared and held in contempt by many. His name was Redford. Redford Wyman – brother of Starlena! And, as sure as the earth turned on its axis, he was here to see her hang.

8

Beside him, and equally vindictive, was Freya Judd. A harsh-faced woman with light brown hair drawn severely back and piercing green eyes which never once left Starlena's face, she also was determined that Starlena should lose her life.

These two, Redford Wyman and Freya Judd, stayed close one to the other. There were never spawned two more ungodly creatures than these!

Yet, if those two were the devil's own advocates, the two seated behind them were like a ray of sunshine in Starlena's troubled world. Her dark trembling gaze came now to meet that of a man, an American whom she had known for only a short while, but who meant so very much to her. Instantly, Starlena's heart was moved with a great surge of warmth and love for this man, Jackson Grand, for if Anselo had stirred memories of illicit passions and forbidden emotions, this man touched her heart more deeply. Theirs also had been a love which had brought pain in its wake, a love which was not theirs to take – yet it had been a love so compelling that it would not be denied. They were drawn together now, just as they had been in the past. And now, as then, it would seem that Fate was against them. Yet, as they gazed at each other, there grew between them a uniquely silent understanding – a belief in God and in that eternal hope which surely was their right. In the magnificent beauty of Jackson's dark green gaze, there shone for Starlena a wonderful strength, and such aching love that made her want to run to him and fling herself into his arms. But such comfort was not to be. Not at this moment in time, and maybe never.

As Starlena looked upon the gentle features of Elizabeth Judd, she would not have been surprised to see there a look of loathing. Instead, the soft blue eyes smiled reassuringly and, knowing how cruelly this woman had been treated with Starlena believing that she herself was not entirely blameless, it was then she had to turn away, the tears filling her dark eyes, her heart sore within her.

Now, after sweeping one last glance over the old woman, Rona, whose lingering gaze needed no words to convey the love in her heart, Starlena was led away to follow the familiar route back to

9

the confines of her cell; where for a while she would welcome the enforced solitude and employ the time reflecting on her fate.

'I'll see you're brought some food!' The officer had secured her prisoner, then, after turning the key in the lock, she had showed her face at the grill, adding, '. . . there's no telling how long the jury are likely to be out.'

Starlena made no reply, for there was need of none. She knew in her bones that the jury would not take too long, for they had little choice but to find her guilty of murder as charged. How could there possibly be any other verdict?

Of a sudden she felt the trauma of these last months, and as though pressed downwards by the weight of the devastating events which had brought her here, her body sank wearily onto the stiff narrow bed, her shoulders upright against the wall, its damp coldness striking with a shock against the back of her head. With a great sigh of relief that, come what may, it was now almost over, Starlena closed her eyes. As she did so, a surging emotion akin to glory swelled her heart and lifted her faith. Gone was the uncertainty, the fear and the darkness which had cloaked themselves about her like a mantle. The darling face of the old gypsy came into her mind, bringing with it memories of summer days, open fields and running brooks teeming with fish – of wild horses, proud black stallions and newborn foals still wet from birthing. The song of a bird and the sharp dry smell of an open charcoal fire. She could feel again that special joy when holding a tiny helpless babe in her arms – and even now, after all that had happened, there murmured deep in her loins that trembling warm urgency of a passion which could not be denied, for she was only a woman, with the heart and emotions of a woman – both of which might soon be silenced forever.

She thought of her darling girl-child, Ronalda, at this moment in the care of others, and her heart was pained. Had the child been either Anselo's or Jackson's, she would at least have had a father to love her. But Ronalda would have no-one to watch out for her – other than beloved Rona, the gypsy woman.

Deliberately Starlena dwelt on all things comforting, forcing out of her mind those thoughts which saddened and frightened her – and as God was her witness, there had been too many of those. Far too many!

Paramount in her recollections was Rona, not as she was now, slow and aged, but as she had been, a handsome young woman with the strength of a bull and a heart as big as the open countryside she had once called home. This was how Starlena remembered her, the woman she had always believed to be her own flesh and blood; and who in every way had encouraged Starlena, first as a child, then as girl and woman, to believe that she too was of the dark gypsy blood, and that Rona was her own true mother. In all those eventful years, there had been no call for Starlena to think otherwise.

Life had been wonderful, an exciting adventure that could never end. Until the truth of Starlena's birth and background became a threat to her very life. At this point, the free spirit became the hunted, and the nightmare began.

Starlena thought on the story revealed to her only in the final moments of inevitable tragedy. And even though Rona had deceived her for a lifetime, she must still think of her as her own mother, for the love between them had been forged stronger than any blood-ties. Now, as she was drawn into a strange restless sleep, Starlena recalled how Rona had explained the untoward circumstances which had led to a lone gypsy-woman taking Starlena the newborn child to raise as her own.

In remembering how it had been, and the events which followed it, it was to Rona that her heart went out.

Part Two

1898
Starlena born

'Our life is turned out of her course
Wherever man is made . . .'
                              Wordsworth

Part Two

Chapter Two

'You've med a few bob then, Leum, you ol' bugger!' The big man gave a weary groan as he straightened up from the cluttered space beneath the market stall. From here he withdrew a wooden crate, then with his free hand he tipped back his chequered flat cap, mopped the glistening sweat from his brow and grinned a broad toothless grin. 'Every blessed week, I fotch *my* vegetables to market and you fotch yourn. An' sure as the sun'll come up tomorrow, at the end o' the day *I'm* left wi' crates o' stuff to trundle back 'ome – an' you're sold out to the last parsnip. I'm telling you, Leum – you shall 'ave to give us yer secret afore we're all made bloody paupers!' Swinging the crate up onto a neat display of prime cabbages, he rammed his two sizeable fists into the depths of his overall pockets, leaned back against the stall and let out a great earth-shattering roar of laughter, the gusto of which caught the attention of the few market-traders still loading their unsold goods onto flat-wagons. One man in particular, no more than a few feet away from the fat man, not so engrossed in harnessing up his faithful old horse that he hadn't been made aware of the conversation, laughed also.

Pausing in his labours the fat man nodded towards the lean brown-haired man with dark intense eyes, the man called Leum. Then, smiling warmly at the olive-skinned woman attired in a long flowing dress of dark material, her black hair tucked into a gypsy-type blue linen square and her whole manner showing her impatience to be off, he said in his light-hearted way, 'There's yer secret, Leum, wouldn't you say? Sitting up on yon cart – that magnificent wife o' yourn. By! What a woman to 'ave working alongside you, eh? Better than any man when it comes to tilling the ground an' persuading the earth to give of its best – an' there's nary a soul to touch 'er when it comes to horses! Knows their ways like the back of 'er hand, she does. An' wi' folks going to no other when they're in need o' buying a new horse or pairing off a mare – why, I reckon you've got a bloody goldmine in yon woman!' Smiling into the woman's eyes, he said in a quieter voice, 'You're a grand eye-catching creature, Rona Parrish – an' no mistake!'

'An' you're a man wi' too much of a roving eye for the women, fat Joe!' the woman retorted with a twinkling smile. ''Appen I should let yer wife know of yer randy ways, eh? Yer a for'ard bugger, that ye are!' On the last word she broke into a soft laugh and shaking her dark head plied her attention to the old cob up front, who was beginning to fret from the waiting.

'All the same, Leum's a fortunate man, an' if I didn't know that the rascal treated both you and the bairn like the jewels you are – well, I'd 'ave the pair of you away, you can reckon on that!' the fat man insisted.

'Oh aye! Happen so, but it'd need to be over my dead body, you old sod!' Leum called out with equal good nature. Then, climbing onto the cart beside his wife, he looked away from the men who, quietly laughing, had already returned their attention to loading up their unsold wares.

For a long moment Leum Parrish sat quiet, looking into his wife's smiling face and taking stock of her. She was not beautiful, for her face was too large and her lips too thin. Her dark skin was too weathered by the elements they both must needs fight, and her clothes were not fanciful or flattering – for how could fine garments be suited to drawing out a living from the earth, or breaking in a filly possessed with the spirit of a mountain lion! No, his Rona was not of the beauty such men might seek; although there was indeed a handsomeness about her that struck the heart, her teeth being even and startlingly white, and her large dark eyes having depths that seemed to magnetize a body. Strange also, how those eyes had that same effect on the horses she handled. Yes, there was a

16

degree of magic about his woman, and he loved her fiercely!

Stirring beneath her husband's loving gaze, Rona was moved to reach out her hand, clasping long strong fingers over his work-worn fist. She too loved with a fierceness which sometimes frightened her, for to love so immensely and with all of one's being, was a dangerous thing! It swelled up inside you, sucking in every other emotion until there was nothing left but this consuming and wonderful love, without which there would be nothing left but a great empty void.

For now, though, Rona's life was complete. It was a hard life, yes – but while she had Leum; and now a beautiful girl-child of such tender age that she had not yet been given a name, Rona wanted nothing more.

Without words, the two of them kept their gaze locked each into the other, the love which moved them alight in their eyes. Bending to kiss her, Leum would have lingered, but Rona spoke now, saying, 'Will you take the reins, Leum? I'll check the bairn afore we move off.'

As he did so, she slid down from the high seat on the front of the cart, and in a moment was on her knees beside a small wooden cradle, this securely wedged behind the flat panel situated beneath the seat. With great tenderness, Rona reached her hand into the cradle and with careful fingers lifted the cover from the sleeping child's face. The girl-child was beautiful! Although only a few weeks old, already her black hair was inches long, and when for a fleeting moment she opened her eyes, they were of the same dark colouring as her mother's.

'Ssh, my bairn,' whispered Rona, waiting to see the eyes closed again in sleep before softly replacing the cover. Then she climbed into her place and with Leum keeping the rein they started the old grey cob away from the Blackburn market and out upon the long tiring journey which would take them home. The familiar route would lead them through the district of Church, then on over the hills to the outer fringes of Shillington Hamlet, where stood the smallholding of twenty acres which they had rented these past fifteen years, ever since Rona had turned her back on a gypsy

17

culture she had passionately loved. And all for a gorgio, a man who knew nothing of the gypsy way of life. But if Rona had a passion for the wandering ways of her ancestors, it was as nothing compared to the intensity of her adoration of this man. She had come to him as an innocent young girl and for fifteen years had toiled beside him, giving him everything a man could ask – loyalty, comradeship, comfort and love. Yet the one thing needed to make their joy in each other complete was ever elusive, until in the summer of her thirtieth year Rona had conceived the child they both longed for. And when in this year of Our Lord 1898, on a blustery bitter day in February, the little miracle had come into the world screaming her protest, Rona knew that whatever happened for the rest of her life, *nothing* would compare with the magnitude of emotion which had rushed through her – and which to this day she could not recall without the greatest feeling of humility.

Somewhere in the distance a clock struck five, prompting Leum to say, 'I should wrap that there blanket about yer legs, my beauty. It'll be late afore we get 'ome – an' this March wind's striking a bit chilly!' He gripped both reins into one hand as with the other he collected a rough grey blanket from the floor between his legs. Gathering it onto her lap, he instructed, 'Tuck it well over, lass. Don't want you catching pneumonia!'

Rona did as he bade, for she knew only too well that they would feel the bitter cold winds once they were headed out of Blackburn and onto the exposed open road. And as she wrapped the blanket around her own legs, so she covered Leum's; after which she drew herself up tight to him. Now so close to him that the warmth of their bodies merged, she laid her head on his shoulder and hoped they might get safely home before the dark set in.

It was over an hour later, as Leum drove the old cob on over the moors, that the black, fancy brougham came speeding towards him from round a blind narrow bend, the large bay horse pushed hard and flaring at the nostrils, forcing Leum up and into the bank.

Rona cursed, and would have turned to shake her fist at the high-born lady inside. But Leum chided her, shook his head and remarked, 'They're gentry, my beauty. 'Appen down from the rush o' London an' don't know no better!' Then, slapping the reins gently against the old cob's rump to drive him on, he added with a chuckle, 'Let's be thankful it weren't one o' them new-fangled motor-car contraptions! Old Treach from the market was telling me a while back that they've done away wi' the red flag, an' raised the speed limit to fourteen miles an hour! Can you credit that, my beauty? Fourteen miles an hour! Won't be long afore *nobody's* safe on the roads, I'm tellin' yer!'

Rona made no acknowledgement, being too incensed at the incident. Now, after quickly checking that the child was safe, she gave an angry toss of her dark head and made a sharp retort.

'Ach! You're too easy, Leum Parrish! Allus ready to turn the other cheek!' Her temper, however, was swiftly subdued by the patient smile on his kindly face, and laughing aloud she snuggled herself back into the warmth of his body. 'Aye! Too easy altogether, my man!' she murmured with affection.

Kathleen Wyman descended from the carriage, her cheeks flushed from the haste of these last few miles in a long and tedious journey from London. She regretted the near-collision with the horse and cart back there on the road, but an hour from home she had felt the unborn child quickening inside her. Fearing its untimely arrival in the middle of nowhere, with only the driver to give assistance, she had been panic-stricken to get to the relative safety of her home – although even the prospect of returning to Accrington and Bessington Hall gave small comfort, in the light of her husband's increasing possessiveness and the subsequent inevitable rows that caused.

Now, straightening her aching back, she turned to face the house, a great sprawling residence, whose whole structure was bound together by monstrous wooden beams which, at the four gables, created an attractive criss-cross design. The chimneys were numerous, grouped into sets of four and topped by heavy decorative collars which seemed to curl outwards like flowers on the verge of opening. There were bay windows made up of small leaded panes, which trapped and reflected what remained of the light of a dull

March day. Nestling up to the staunch stone walls and stretching invading fingers across the windows, were many spreading shrubs and creeping ivy. Like a bright green carpet, the curved lawns spread either side of the house and across its front, skirting the broad gravelled drive and walkway to the entrance, which in itself was a beautifully constructed archway, adorned overhead by substantial fluted strips of stone, and approached up a curving flight of some eight wide steps.

For a moment longer, the lady of the house gazed upon this magnificent dwelling, thinking how like a prison it had become of late. And all the while she was mentally preparing for the inquisition which she sensed was imminent. By no stretch of the imagination could she be described as a strong-willed woman, as she herself would be the first to admit.

With a deep sigh, she squared her shoulders, gathered the flowing taffeta skirt into two hands, dismissed the driver and the carriage to the stables and took herself across the gravelled forecourt, up the steps, then on through the great wooden doors and into the panelled hallway. Here she paused just long enough to take off her waist-jacket and bonnet, which she handed to the maid who had rushed to greet her; then her large round eyes looking into the oval mirror above, she patted neat the coiled loops of black hair piled high on her head, after which she went with nervous steps into the drawing-room, where she knew her husband would be impatiently waiting. The elaborately panelled room was his favourite, a quiet place encumbered with great lumbering furniture of dark oak. It was not a room which Kathleen liked. But it was a refuge of sorts for her husband – the 'den' where he did most of his thinking.

As the door opened to admit his wife, Edward Wyman got up from the deep brown leather armchair, where for the best part of the day he had been brooding, incensed by the effrontery of his wife in disobeying his orders. Going now to the fireplace, he stood before the flames, looking down into them just long enough for his wife to shut the door behind her. Then, upon the click of its closing, he swung round to face her, his dark blue eyes almost iridescent in their fury. Drawing himself up to his full considerable height, he stuck out his barrel chest, stroked the thick brown beard which covered the lower half of his face, and in a low heavy voice he hissed the word, 'Well!' instantly drawing his lips tightly together and with his large hand snatching undone the small bow-tie at his neck, all the while with his eyes riveted on his wife's anxious face.

Kathleen Wyman folded her hands before her in a nervous gesture, and try as she might to dispel the feeling she could not. She was afraid! Beneath the hostile glare of those unwavering eyes, she *was* afraid! He could do that to her. And he knew it. This husband of hers who would also be her jailer and who had kept her buckled down in all the twenty years of their marriage – he was no fool. He had long discovered that the love she had borne him in the early years had withered away soon after the birth of their only son, Redford, now eighteen, a man ready to be shaped in the hard ways of his father – and already showing the same unyielding, domineering traits in his character, although, unlike his father, he had not yet learned to exploit their full potential. Of the two men, Kathleen recoiled more from her husband, for he, like a predator, fed on the weakness in her.

Edward Wyman was a man of little forgiveness, unable to tolerate in others any shortcomings excluded from his own nature. He came of hard and arrogant stock. His father had won a knighthood – an honour which ceased when he himself did, but in any case Edward Wyman would neither have wanted a title nor have worn it well. For the better part of his adult life he had been a doctor – a good doctor it was said – but now early retired from it since his father's demise some four years back. No, such a man as he had no need of titles nor of the privileges that went with them. His diverse interests did not embrace political matters. His great abiding passion was the inheritance of extensive land and property situated in the outer parish of Accrington, Lancashire. Oh, there was money too – a substantial fortune by *anyone's* standards! But that in itself was not of paramount importance, because money begets money, seeming to look after itself and multiplying by the hour. Whereas the land needed attention lavished upon it. And if

Edward Wyman starved his family of love and tenderness, he did not stint of it where his land was concerned. One thousand acres of finest prime earth! He coveted it, as he did the magnificent mansion, which had been the Wyman ancestral home for close on three hundred years.

With his vast inheritance had come certain responsibilities: a community comprising of a scattered village and isolated hamlets, some eighty cottages in all, these tenanted by the employees of Bessington Hall and kept in good condition under the eagle eye of Edward Wyman himself; as was the land, which was superbly maintained. Edward Wyman was renowned for being a man of meticulous and rigid habit, a man not afraid of hard work and who expected the same of his men. In return he paid them well and kept their homes in good repair. The men for their part respected him for the employer he was – hard, demanding and brutally forthright; his greatest failing was his possessive nature – of his men, his heritage, and more obsessively, of his wife, the lovely timid Kathleen. There his jealousy bordered on madness itself. It was said that the greatest irritant to him was the age difference between them, Kathleen now thirty-six and he some twelve years older. In spite of her assurances to the contrary, he would insist that she felt attracted to men nearer her own age – one in particular. This was a man by the name of Durnley, a lawyer based in London, and on whom Edward Wyman had called from time to time in the course of business transactions. Not any more, though! Not for some time now – since he had come to suspect the man's blatant attraction to his wife, and she doing nothing to discourage him. All along his wife had denied it. But, by God, he'd get to the bottom of it and no mistake!

'Answer me, woman! Have you nothing to say?' he demanded now, his mounting fury exploding on his last words and seeming to carry him forward physically until his face was no more than inches from his wife's anxious features.

'What would you have me say?' she asked, surprised at the calm in her voice when all inside her was trembling. Oh, how she prayed that this child she carried might be a girl – for the Edward Wymans of this world had little time for the female of the species, while she herself would *dote* on a girl-child – she would make amends for her unappealing son and make it her business to raise this child in the knowledge of graciousness. Her daughter would be a lovely, noble creature – unselfish and loving of spirit! Kathleen Wyman had promised herself so and having done that, there seemed little else to live for.

For now, surprisingly, she did not flinch beneath her husband's anger. Indeed, as Edward Wyman stared long and hard on her dark beauty, his own face a study of suspicion, it was *he* who first turned away. Now, throwing his fists together behind his back, he crossed to the great open fireplace, his manner deliberate and menacing. Here he paused, his broad back to his wife and his bright downcast eyes piercing to the heart of the flames. In the silence of the ensuing few moments, when the only interruption was the dull rhythmic ticking of the majestic old grandfather clock which stood against the long casement windows like an appointed sentry marking the passing of time, Kathleen Wyman would have left the room, hopeful – yet perhaps not fully convinced – that the master of the house had said his last word on the matter.

Yet even as the thought crossed her mind, he seemed aware of it, for without turning round, he again spoke, this time in a thick flat voice which instantly quickened the anxiety in Kathleen Wyman's heart – for she knew of old that such a tone of voice must herald the furore to come.

'Stay where you are! I have *not* yet dismissed you.' Now he turned. Sucking in a breath which flared his nostrils and swelled his chest to frightening proportions, he said in the same level voice, 'I want the *truth*! This tale I was told about you taking yourself off to London to consult a physician – was it not all lies? A pack of lies! Presumably to throw me off the *real* reason – and that being one devious solicitor by the name of Durnley!' At this point his breathing had quickened and his eyes were like two searchlights which now fixed themselves on to the woman's pale features, as though to force out some manner of confession which would satisfy his dark suspicions. 'Well I'm waiting! You took yourself off to London to see this fellow, Durnley! You have no need of any doctor but me – there *is* no better, I can assure you. And well you know it. So! We'll have the *truth* – for you'll not leave this room until I have your admission!'

In the face of her husband's mood, Kathleen Wyman instinctively knew better than to argue. It was true – she had *not* gone to consult any physician, for she felt secure in the knowledge that when her time came, both she *and* the child could not do better than be entrusted to Edward, whose medical skills were well known and who excelled in the practice of delivering life into the world.

The truth was that she had felt the need to get away from here – if only for a day and a night. And yes, she *had* spoken with George Durnley. That had been her main reason for taking the uncomfortable trip to London. Their discussion had been strictly professional, concerning, as it did, the possibility of her seeking first a legal separation from Edward Wyman, then hopefully a divorce. These very matters had been paramount in her thoughts for a long time now – postponed only by the state of her pregnancy, and the anxiety that she should not lose her newborn babe to him. When she finally went from this house, it would be with the child in her arms. And she would take any measure necessary to keep it from his clutches!

Thinking now on the child inside her, Kathleen Wyman found a measure of courage which surprised her. Facing squarely the man before her, she said, 'Very well, I did *not* go to see any physician. You were right. But if you entertain notions of some *romantic* alliance between Mr Durnley and myself you are *not* right – you are very much mistaken. And if I *do* have occasion to consult a man of his profession – *any* man employed so – then I have every right to do so!' This had been the very first time she had stood up to her husband's bullying, and somewhat shaken by the experience, Kathleen seemed to shrink visibly. But spurred on by the thought of her child and the not too distant prospect of their escape from this unbending man, she stood her ground and waited, for she knew that her outburst would surely unleash that vicious temper of his – a black consuming passion over which, of late, he had little control.

As the row raged on, she was thankful at least that with the exception of an ageing cook, one maid, together with two orphans, Freya Judd and her younger brother, Lester, the servants had been dismissed for the weekend. As for Redford, the son she had already lost to his father's ways, no doubt he would be hidden away in some safe corner, unable and unwilling to come to her aid.

Upstairs, a slim fair-haired young man in all his nakedness gave a moan of impatience as with swift angry strides he rose from his large comfortable four-poster bed and went to the window which he pulled tight to close out both the noise and the dusk. Then he crossed the richly patterned carpet to the door, and closed that also – all in an effort to shut out the angry voices of his parents. He had been somewhat amused by his mother's retaliation and defence of herself – for as a rule, on such occasions, it was his father's voice that prevailed.

Having effectively banished the intrusion that threatened to curb his enjoyment, Redford Wyman returned to his immense bed, and to the source of his present pleasure. This was an attractive young woman with light brown hair and hard green eyes, who, being in her twentieth year, was some two years older than her master's son.

For a long moment Redford Wyman stood by the bed, his narrow blue eyes greedily roving the taut nakedness of the woman lying on the softness of his sheets, a woman of insatiable passions, a woman who made love with more vigour than all his previous gentle females put together! She was a woman of rough and ready stock who gave him a deal of fornication – the like of which he would not get elsewhere. Freya Judd was an eager giver who knew just what was wanted and who had so far asked for nothing in return. She was for the moment a plaything, a vessel of amusement which, when he had taken his fill, could easily be discarded!

Stooping now, he spread out the fingers of his right hand and gently stroked the tips of her small stiff breasts, then ran down over the firmness of her abdomen and finally, with the greatest tantaliza-tion, he let the tips of his fingers creep between the soft whiteness of her inner thighs. Then when her whole body was trembling and her eyes pleading with him, he lowered himself onto the bed, where in a moment he had slithered into her open nakedness, his low

25

whispers growing quickly feverish. The two were now one, each devouring the other. In his exquisite anguish, the man called out her name over and over. 'Freya . . . *Freya*!'

Downstairs, the noise had abruptly ceased. There was a long painful measure of silence, which weighed upon the air far more ominously than had the fury of angry attacking voices. Then there came the soft thud of a door being thrust back, immediately followed by the muffled sound of hurrying footsteps. And in another moment, the authoritative voice of Edward Wyman demanded 'Freya! Where the hell are you, woman? Freya! Freya!'

In the throes of her mounting ecstasy, it took a moment for Freya Judd to distinguish the one voice from the other – both urgent, both calling her name! Alarmed lest she be caught in such a situation, she began arching her back in an effort to throw the heaving sweating body from her, all the while protesting, 'Let me up! It's the master wanting me!'

Came the reply, '*I* want you! Hold on to me, you wonderful little whore!' And in the grip of a man swept along in spite of himself, her own strength was as nothing. At last, his energy spent and his ardour temporarily subdued, Redford's body lay limp against her. This was her chance. And, with Edward Wyman's voice both increasingly urgent and dangerously closer, she would have lost no time in getting from the bed and, after barely taking time to dress, from that room. But before she could disengage herself from the man's enclosing arms, the door was flung open. And there, his formidable form filling the doorway, was the master of the house.

In a moment he had weighed up the situation. And in another he was across the room and standing by the bed, fury blazing in his eyes which now surveyed the two naked bodies.

It started in the base of his throat, at first a humming sound which quickly grew until it exploded into a roar, which put the fear of God into the woman. 'Tramps! The pair of you – nothing but tramps!' In a swift movement, he had grabbed his son by the hair and hauling him from the bed, he yelled, 'Get yourself *out* of my sight!' To the trembling woman, he instructed, 'Get dressed! Your mistress is in

26

need of you!' When she hesitated, he leaned forward to say in a controlled yet seething voice, '*Now*, I say!' Then, with a brief and cursory glance at his son who, humiliated and enraged, was hurriedly dressing, murmuring the while 'Sanctimonious bastard', he hissed, 'Take yourself where I won't need to look at you!' Then he stormed from the room, slamming the door behind him with such force that it shook a painting from the wall, bringing it crashing to the floor just inches from the bare feet of Redford Wyman.

In the wake of his father's departure, there was a silence, during which Freya Judd got from the bed and in a matter of minutes had dressed and was on her way out of the door, saying, ' 'Appen the mistress has started early with child.' Then, seeing Redford Wyman pulling on the last of his garments, his mouth drawn shut in a tight thin line and his jaws working with temper, she gave a small cruel laugh. 'Aw! Did Daddy come an' spoil your fun?' She was no longer concerned to talk with the respect a man of this house might command, for she had no doubt that the minute her mistress had been made comfortable, she herself would be sent packing and no mistake.

Freya Judd hurried along the broad, galleried landing lined with ancestral portraits which always caused her to shiver, past the array of rooms kept for guests, then on to the west wing and Kathleen Wyman's rooms, where she found her mistress lying atop the frilled and valanced four-poster bed, already in early labour and desperate for her company.

Out in the courtyard, Edward Wyman had summoned the coachman from his room above the stables. On hearing his suspicions confirmed – 'Yes, the mistress *had* paid a visit to Kensington and a Mr Durnley –' he swept off to do as his instincts directed. As he made his way across the courtyard and back to the main house, his son emerged from it, the whip in his hand repeatedly slashing against the leather of his riding boot and his face set in a scowl like granite. As the two men passed within inches of each other, not a glance was exchanged, not a word was spoken. Each was preoccupied with a fury that must break out in its own particular way.

'Whoa there, me beauty! Steady on yer!' Leum Parrish carefully eased back the reins, calming the old cob which was swerving at the unexpected dash of a small furry creature across the path.

Pulling horse and cart to a standstill, Leum looked at his woman, and seeing that she was not far from sleep, he clapped a reassuring hand over her knee, saying in a gentle voice, 'Tired, are yer, flower? Well, we sharn't be too long afore we're 'ome. I'll not be mekkin' this trip to Blackburn too often, I'm thinking! It's a long old trek, an' I don't like keepin' you an' the babby out on these roads after dark.' As he spoke, he surveyed the sparse open scrubland and the shrubby, dangerously steep incline not a man's length from where he stood. With a shrug of his shoulders he draped the long reins twice about the upright brake in front of the driving seat. Then without further ado, he clambered down to the ground, where in a moment he had snatched from the rear of the wagon, two large lanterns, each with glass all round and with a hook projecting from the dome at the top. These he placed at the wagon's edge. Quickly now, he fumbled deep into the pocket of his jacket, from which he presently extracted a box of matches, and opening the box, he took out a match which he struck against the steel rim surrounding the wagon. Twice he tried, growing increasingly impatient as the keen March wind briskly extinguished the small bright flame. Taking out a third, he bent low to protect it and this time when the match was struck, he at once cupped his free hand round the flare which spat and sizzled. 'Open the flap, Rona,' he asked of his bemused wife, who had followed his antics with great interest. Losing no time, she leaned across the seat and reaching down, swung wide the glass panel in the lantern's side, holding it open against the blustering wind as Leum fed the lighted match to the paraffin-soaked wick. In a matter of seconds, the wick began sucking the flame into itself, spluttering and dancing until finally it steadied, to throw out a dull yellow circle of light.

With the match all but burned down, Leum Parrish blew it out, at the same time closing the lantern door. Before starting the same procedure with the remaining lantern he asked, 'Will you take this one to the front, Rona, gel? Hook it onto the for'ard shaft. But mind you secure it well,' he added as she took the lantern by its hook and climbing down to the ground went to the front of the wagon.

At his remark she told him in mock chastisement, 'Go on with you, husband. What? I've *forgotten* the number o' times I've fastened a lantern to this 'ere shaft. I'm not likely to go swinging it fro' the old cob's earhole now, am I, eh?'

At this, the two of them burst out laughing, Leum Parrish loving the woman for her sharp tongue and blessing the day that had brought her to him. A real deep-cultured gypsy girl she'd been, he reminded himself, fetched up and steeped in the tradition of her forefathers. She had often since longed for the gypsy life, loving it with heart and soul. But thank the Lord she had loved him more, and over the years the two of them had come to cherish the same things, each finding a need inside filled by their work with the soil, and taking immense pleasure from God's wild and open countryside, which they had come to know and respect.

As Rona set to with the task of securing the lantern to the forward shaft, Leum made his way towards the rear, his steps cautious because of the failing light and the chasm that yawned not far from where he trod.

It was Rona's heightened sense of hearing that first picked up the sound – a dull rhythmic thumping sound which reverberated along the ground where she stood, its vibrant urgency trembling through her body and raising in her an acute sense of alarm. Closer and closer it came until Rona's fear erupted in a warning cry and taking to her heels she began the seemingly endless journey around the wagon, to where her man was busy at his task.

'Leum!' she cried in a frantic voice. 'Leum!' Her outstretched arms already reached for the small wooden cot which held her child. Then in the space of a single heartbeat, all hell was let loose as Leum turned towards the sound of a fast approaching horse, his arms thrown up in a desperate effort to defend himself, the fear of God alight in his wide-open eyes.

Redford Wyman had left the big house in a fury, the passion of which had not yet abated. So engrossed had he been in his own vengeful thoughts as he turned the stallion loose upon the road, that in the half-light he had not seen the stationary wagon. Even now, he was not aware of its presence until, when it was all too late, he was upon it. With a tremendous roar, he heaved on the reins, driving the steel bit hard into the fleshy sides of the horse's foaming mouth, drawing blood and causing the creature to rear onto its hind legs, its front hoofs crashing down into Leum Parrish's skull.

As his lifeless body slumped, the hoofs came down again and again, beating him into the ground. Pandemonium reigned. Rona's screams startled both horse and rider, and the two surged forward past the wagon. Sheer terror seemed to instil a great strength into the woman. But even as she swung the child from its cot and would have it safe in her arms, the old cob panicked and plunged forward. The violence of the movement threw the woman to the ground and tossed the crying child high into the air, its tiny body helpless. Its pitiful wail stopped abruptly as it thudded back onto the fast-moving wagon.

After her moment of blind panic, during which time Redford Wyman made good his escape, Rona scrambled to her feet and stumbled hysterically after the speeding wagon, then watched in anguish as the terrified old cob galloped away, all the while fighting to throw the shackles from its back until finally in a frenzied fit, it broke apart the shaft tethering it to the cumbersome vehicle. With the cob free and bolting, the wagon spun on its axle and catapulted off the road and down into the valley below.

Rona scrambled to the top of the incline, her tear-blinded eyes peering down into the place below and her loud convulsive sobs pitiful to hear. 'Oh, Leum!' she cried. 'Leum, Leum – see what they've done to our babby!' Losing sight of the falling wagon as it tumbled and crashed against the tree stumps and boulders, she fell to her knees on the stony ground where, burying her head in her hands, she was engulfed by long tearing sobs. If she had thought for one moment she might have saved her child by scrambling down that bottomless pit, nothing this side of Hell would have kept her from doing so. But she had seen the cot, repeatedly clashed against the rocks – its contents tossed and mangled. And every instinct in her body told her that it was done! The child was no more.

On weary feet and in desolation she made a hasty road back to her man, Leum; half-walking, half-running, fearful of what she might find, yet knowing full well what awaited her – for hadn't she still got the violent image etched on her mind, of the horse's flailing hooves tearing into her poor man's flesh time after time?

Now, when she came upon him, his arms were pathetically outstretched – one hand beneath the shattered lantern and the other twisted and broken where he had raised it in self-defence. On his blood-spattered face was a look of surprise, his wide-open eyes set in a glazed expression which seemed to be looking straight at her, tearing the very heart from her breast. For a long full moment she gazed down on him, her vision blurred by the scalding tears which ran unheeded down her face and into the worn crevices of her weathered neck. After the noise and confusion of so short a time ago, the silence all about them was eerie; save for a shrill call of alarm from some disturbed bird, and Rona's murmuring voice which even though little more than a whisper, echoed from every side.

'Oh, Leum! Dear God in Heaven, what's become of us?' Now, she was down beside him, the blue linen square stripped from her head to wipe his face, and his broken, bleeding body clasped tight in her arms and held tenderly against her heart. Closing the lids over his startled eyes, she rocked him to and fro, all the while raining kisses on him and speaking reassuring words in the manner of a lover.

As the night closed in around them, Rona made no move. Here was her man, a *good* man – a man she would love till the end of time. And she would not leave him! No, she would not leave him alone in the wild, in the dark. She would stay with him until help came for them both!

Chapter Three

The next day was Sunday. The wind had fallen to a light breeze. Already the air was impregnated with the scent and promise of a wonderful spring. And on this day, in the small early hours, they brought home the bodies of Leum Parrish and the infant he idolized.

When the poachers came across Rona huddled in the road, they feared they had stumbled on *two* corpses, for the woman was as stiff and cold as the man she held so frantically in her arms! Having been about their successful business in the dark hours, Jack and Abe were wending their way home and, dressed as they were, with strings of rabbits and a fine stout salmon hanging from their belts, their haste along the road was made to compete with the rising of the sun – already pushing its glowing forehead above the rim of the hills. Yet, even in fear of the ever-watchful gamekeepers round these parts, they did not hesitate to throw off the profits of a good night's work to linger at the spot where such a dreadful accident had taken place. All along the road had been evidence of such an accident – splintered pieces of wood and iron, splashes of blood and deep jagged marks made by a horse's iron shoes as it careered dangerously close to the edge of a precipice – at the bottom of which could now be seen the shattered remains of what had been a wagon.

Fearful that there might be others injured, one brave poacher set about comforting the shocked woman, persuading her to give up her burden and wrap herself in the warm tweed jacket he offered, while the other began a descent to where the wagon had come to rest. Using all his hard-earned and dubious skills, he had wended a way on careful feet, using shrub, outcrops and crevices to take him inch by inch down the steep and craggy incline.

Some time later, after he had climbed out of the depths, he came to where the two figures sat on a grassy tuft at the road-side; the third being at their feet and covered over by his own smock. When in all reverence the poacher came to unbutton his jacket and take from it the small bundle nearest his heart, the woman was instantly on her feet. She clutched the child to her breast. Its little head lolled at an angle where, perhaps even before the wagon had gone over, its delicate neck had been snapped. When all at once the enormity of her terrible loss swamped her, Rona buried her dark head in her small daughter's face and cried as though her heart would break. Grown, hardened men though they were, the two poachers cried with her. And these same two thieves of the night saw Rona and her family home – a makeshift litter carrying her husband, her child held tight in her own weary arms.

Word had spread fast of the terrible accident that had taken Rona Parrish's good husband, Leum, and the child not yet two weeks old! And during the long unforgettable Sunday, when neighbours, farmers and traders alike all came to pay their respects, not once did Rona speak of the man on horseback – that fiend from hell which had brought its wrath down on her and her beloved kin. With the darkness creeping in, she had not seen his face, but she knew horses! That magnificent grey stallion would stay forever in her mind's eye, as vivid as the night she had seen it. The day would come when she must see it again. On that day, she would know the man – and may God take care of the consequences.

'You've no family to give you comfort in your time of grief, Rona?' a short stocky woman asked, at the same time coming to seat herself on the wicker chair by the open fire-range. 'Neither you nor Leum?'

'No,' replied Rona, a hardness in her voice that had not been there before. Going now to the window, beneath which the undertakers had placed the coffin, Rona gazed down into it, her eyes washing over the man inside and resting for just a moment longer

33

on the tiny dark-haired child in his arms. As she stood gazing on them both, her heart was first heavy and sorrowful – then hard and bursting with a taste for revenge. Then it was quiet and more painful than she could ever remember. How many times in all that long, long day had she told herself that she must let them go? Her heart was the heart of a gypsy, and it told her that to hold on too long to her darlings would be to keep them from entering the gates of Heaven. She *must* let them go! Oh, but how? How? When they were there, filling every corner of her being and recalling the memories which were now all she had left! Yet she *had* taken that first step, by arranging for them both to be taken from the house that very evening, when the good Reverend in Shillington would pray for their souls before committing them to the earth.

Now, her head still bowed and her eyes downward cast, Rona turned to the woman and in answer to her question, said quietly, 'No, there is no-one. Leum's parents are long gone – there were no brothers or sisters. And *I* have no-one, except my younger brother, Callum, you remember – he last came to see us when I was first pregnant.' Here she paused, glancing towards the window. 'He was talking of making for America to seek his fortune. I don't know if he ever went, but I've heard nothing from him these past seven months.'

'I remember! Yes! Your brother Callum – a dark handsome gypsy boy as I recall?'

Rona gave a small laugh as now she lifted her eyes to the woman's kindly face. 'Not a *boy*, I'm thinking, for Callum is past his twentieth year and should be ready for taking on a wife.' The thought of her wayward younger brother had brought a stab of happiness to Rona's heart. Now, as the kindly woman asked whether Rona thought that Callum *had* gone off across the seas to America, Rona became deep in thought for a moment. So when she gave her answer, it was with studied conviction.

'Yes! And the reason I feel sure of it is because he left his precious wagon in the barn here, for me and Leum to look after till his return. That wagon was his home! He took *nothing* from it – only the strong bay gelding that pulled it here! Yes, I'm sure he's gone across the ocean. Though whether he'll come back rich as a noble, or poor as a beggar, I don't know!'

The woman stayed a while longer, eager to know whether there was anything she could do to help. Did Rona *need* anything? Would she like company till they came to take Leum and the child? Was there anything anyone could do with respect to the tilling of the land, or the making of a new wagon? All of these kind considerations Rona carefully declined, saying that she would prefer to spend these last few hours alone with her family. The woman went shortly afterwards.

In the evening, the hearse came from Shillington, and in slow procession, Rona and the mourners walked behind it, taking some forty minutes to follow the country lanes to the small picturesque church where, in a short ceremony, prayers were offered up. After which, the two loves of Rona Parrish's life were laid in the churchyard beneath the great sycamore tree.

Some short time later, with everyone gone, Rona stayed awhile to say her last goodbyes, for she knew that however long she lived, she would *never* be back. What Leum had given her she would cherish in her heart – there was no need of reminding. He was gone and wherever he was, their child was with him. It was *she* who was alone now. *She* who must go on. And if Rona's instincts told her nothing else, they told her that the strength to do just that lay not in surrounding herself with things from the past, or sweating over the soil which she and Leum had loved and fought these past wonderful years. No! If she was to find the courage and strength she needed, her gypsy heritage urged that she would find it out there in God's own domain – in the trees, the brooks and in the song of a bird. That was where part of her had been all these years. And it was that part which surely must serve her now.

As Rona made her way home, cutting across the fields and lingering to watch the scurryings of little creatures as they went about their daily antics, there came over her a great sense of peace – an inexplicable feeling that Leum and the child were with her. Pressured by this new experience of comfort, she quickened her pace, for there was much to be organized and little daylight left in which to do it.

It was done! Every stitch and personal belonging of both Leum and the infant had been reverently gathered into Rona's arms, then taken into the front yard where it had been piled high and set alight. Rona watched until the last flame had died down, after which she went back into the small stone-walled cottage that had been home – no! more than that, she thought: it had been a love-nest, a place of great hardship, but also of great happiness for her and her lovely man. The like of which she would never know again!

She forced herself to keep moving, for she knew that to stand still and dwell on what had been was to imprison herself here for the rest of her life. Leum would not have wanted that for her, of that much she was certain. Quickly now, she began cleaning the place up, dusting, and polishing until everything in the cottage positively gleamed – the brass ornaments over the mantelpiece, the fender around the open fireplace, and the few items of furniture crafted out of thick weathered oak. That done, she closed every door and window, locking the front door as she left and, hanging the big iron key on a nail in the outer door-frame. This was a sure sign to the farmer that she was gone for good. Aye! The locked door would tell of her departure from this place. As would the barn-doors, which she had also closed and bolted. The farmer would be round for his rent as usual in two days' time – being the last day of March – so fetching out the calfskin purse from the pocket of her long flounced skirt, she withdrew three large silver coins from it and placed them beneath the boot-scraper by the door. He knew the place and would find what was owed to him! If Rona had been so gifted, she would have left him a note. But as a child she had never learned to read and write and then with Leum versed in such matters, there had not been the need. However, the farmer would read the signs, particularly when he saw that her brother's gypsy wagon was gone, together with the dark bay colt Leum had traded for her last birthday, a high-spirited animal which Rona treasured. He would see also that the old cob had gone. The cob had reached home before them on the night of the accident, limping and still frightened. But after more than twenty-four hours with the colt in the field, he was now much calmer and more like his old self.

Rona had taken nothing from the cottage – not a plate or a spoon, not a picture or a rug. Only memories, more precious than material things. One thing, though, she took from the out-house; this being a wind-up gramophone which now and then she and Leum would promise to get some musical records for, but never had. Rona had a passion for music and there might come the opportunity to make the thing sing.

'Come on, me ol' beauty,' she murmured, having fastened the bridle about the old cob's head and now leading him to the large barn, inside which stood her brother's gypsy-wagon. 'You an' me – that's all there is now!' Drawing her lips tight across her teeth, she made the soft clicking noise which was familiar to him and which she hoped might give him confidence, for he might not be too easily persuaded between the shafts again.

With unsure steps, the old cob ventured forward into the barn, his head high and nostrils flaring, his dark eyes big with fear.

'There's a good 'un – c'mon, then, slow as ye like,' persuaded Rona, not forcing his head but letting him set the pace. 'See that?' she said in a soft soothing voice, bringing him to a halt some eight feet from the wagon, 'that there's gonna be our home from now on, d'you see? You an' me – well, we've to mek a new life now.' For a fleeting moment her voice faltered and she lowered her head. Then reminding herself of her resolve to look only to the future, she threw her chin up and set her shoulders with renewed determination, her dark eyes roving over the wagon, its very presence giving her a strange degree of contentment. ''Tis a beauty, wouldn't ye say?' she murmured half to herself, half to the old cob. 'A real beauty!' she said again, taking pleasure from its familiar decorations.

As though seeming to understand what she was saying, the old grey cob dropped his head and together he and the woman walked slowly round the wagon, taking in every glorious detail.

Callum himself had made it out of good strong elm, seasoned well and thick as a man's fist. It had been built in the traditional way: shaped into almost a perfect circle, yet pulled in flat at its base to form the floor. The large and only window was situated at the rear and was a pretty jutting bay design, decorated all round with deeply scalloped carvings and having the centre window fixed, while the two side ones were able to be opened wide. The cherry-red curtains with bulbous silk tassels were of good quality, having been given to Rona's brother by a lady of means. At the front was a door of stable appearance: solid at the bottom, the top half being a windowed section which could be swung out independently of the lower half and latched to the wagon timbers. Here too were the same cherry-red curtains.

The whole thing was painted brown, and festooned over every inch of its body – wheels and shaft alike – were myriads of tiny painted shell-like patterns, all in a light cream colour. All around the rims, back, front and wheels, were red and black flowers, these snaking along the very edges of all jutting and prominent parts, to fetch the whole wonderful wagon alive. The same patterns were all over the inside of the wagon also, although on the larger panels round the bed, cupboards and stove area, could be seen the most vivid and magnificently painted horses' heads – here one done in speckled grey colour, and another in the blackest bay; this one obviously the proud thicker-set head of a stallion! Rona loved it, for it had the same large flashing eyes and straight alert ears as had her own spirited colt, Nero.

Drawing the old cob to a halt, she came to stand before him, her dark eyes looking deep into his. 'I'm glad I've got you an' Nero,' she said quietly, gently moving the flat of her hand up and down his watchful face. 'We can all look after each other, eh?' she finished, at the same time nuzzling her face against his nose and stretching both arms about his great broad neck.

With his trust and confidence now restored, the cob gave no resistance as Rona harnessed him up and strapped him between the shafts. In a matter of minutes, she had drawn horse and wagon from the barn and secured the door. After collecting the colt, which she haltered and roped at a comfortable walking length to the wagon's rear, she brought the small wooden step-ladder from just inside the wagon by the door, loaded the gramophone into it, and after doing the same with some early vegetables and potatoes taken from the field, she secured the wagon door. Now she clipped the small iron driving-seat onto the platform immediately in front; then, hoisting herself up onto it, she gathered the reins in her hands, took one last lingering look around and with a 'Hup! Hup, me beauty!' she was gently away down the lane, the old cob up front, the colt behind. And never a look back!

Chapter Four

'Oh, ma'am! Just think – there'll be a baby soon!' Freya Judd turned away from her mistress, dipped the flannel once more into the bowl, squeezed out the surplus cold water and after flattening it with the palm of her hand, applied the cloth once more to Kathleen Wyman's burning forehead. She thought it odd that with the mistress in so much seemingly unnatural pain, the master of the house had neither attempted to send for help, nor taken steps to attend to her himself.

'Please, Edward,' pleaded Kathleen, 'there must be something you can do!' It was obvious to the man standing at the foot of the bed that his wife was in the grip of an unusually painful and feverish labour. Yet there came no compassion into his heart. He was convinced even now that the child so viciously fighting its way into the world was not his! He had made up his mind on this score – and not a thing on earth would change it. All the same, he thought, the truth would be better coming from her own lips.

With this in mind, he strode round the bed to where Freya Judd was stooping over the groaning woman. 'Out!' he said, briefly touching her shoulder, then, when the young woman straightened to look at him, saying, 'But the mistress . . . ?' his dark scowl deepened. And when he came to repeat his instruction, she thought of an earlier incident – and one which had no doubt assured her dismissal soon. So, with the slightest of curtsies, she hurried from the room. There was no real compassion in her heart for the mistress, for it had been Freya Judd and her instinct for mischief which had fuelled Edward Wyman's jealousy. More than once she had let slip that the mistress had 'gone to London to see Mr Durnley'.

Edward Wyman's features were hard and his voice accusing as he stood over his wife, hands thrust deep into his pockets and her pitiful moans making no visible impression on him.

'There *is* something I can do to ease your labour,' he told her, 'perhaps even give the newcomer a helping hand, so to speak.' Now, he was seated on the bed, his eyes searching Kathleen's sweating face. 'Is that what you'd like?' he asked with a cold smile.

Racked by pain and tortured by that voice she knew only too well, Kathleen dragged herself up on to one elbow; her free hand reaching out would have touched him, had he not instantly gripped her hand in his fist, holding it tight in mid-air. He was smiling as she pleaded, 'What sort of man are you? What kind of *doctor*, to let me suffer so? Help me – oh, please, help me . . .' Her voice trailed off into a scream as she was gripped again by a vicious spasm.

As she lay writhing, he got the flannel from the bowl, squeezed it viciously in his large hand, then taking it to her forehead, he wiped the sweat-laden hair from her face. For one moment he seemed to console her; then he grabbed her shoulders with both hands and lifted her to face him. When he spoke, it was not in the hitherto tightly-controlled manner, but in a scream as violent as her own.

'It's *his*, isn't it? Tell me the truth, woman! It's Durnley's!' With every word he shook her back and forth until her head felt like bursting and her whole body seeming to splinter. 'You want me to deliver it, do you? To see another man's child into the world?' He waited for an answer. But when instead she gave out a long terrifying scream, he recognized the imminence of a troubled birth. Of a sudden, his medical training came to the fore. Going to the door, he summoned back the waiting Freya Judd. Swiftly, he tore away the clothes from his wife, and one look at her heaving body and the pool of blood seeping its bright crimson stain into the whiteness of the sheet, told him that *his* child or another's, it would be born with or without him. The only difference was that his professional help might just save the woman's life.

41

Yet even *that* thought was not paramount in his fevered mind, for his whole being was eaten away with raging jealousy and even as he worked he demanded over and over, 'Whose child? It *is* Durnley's, isn't it? It *is* Durnley's!' Until in the desperation of such terrible pain, and craving only that the raging of his madness be stilled, Kathleen gave him the answer he wanted.

'*Yes!* Think what you must! Dear God! If that's what you want to leave me be, then *yes!* Durnley's!' On such a cry of terrible anguish, Freya Judd and the man paused in their labours, looking at each other in the strangest silence. Then in that moment, the dark elongated head of a child began to emerge from the woman's body. Upon which, and in a voice that frightened her, Freya Judd was instructed, 'Get help!'

'But *who?* The young master hasn't returned! And there's only cook . . .' she protested.

'Then fetch *her!*' came the reply. And as Freya Judd ran from the room she heard, 'This night the devil's being born!'

It was past midnight. The moon was full, as Rona Parrish brought her wagon across the field which ran right up to the back of Bessington Hall. She knew there was likely a brook nearby, and she needed to top up the water-churn. There was no telling when she might again find the opportunity, for she was intending to travel far and wide, in parts unknown to her.

As she drew close, Rona saw the lights of the Hall, and it crossed her mind how these fancy folks liked to stay up all hours. Tethering the old cob to stay by the oak tree, Rona collected the metal churn from its hook in the wagon's side, then on swift silent steps she went down towards the Hall and to the brook which even now she could hear washing over the pebbles and rushing on its way.

It was just as she came up over the bank and was climbing the low skirting wall that the bright moonlight caught the glint of metal in her hand. Then, in a moment, the young woman was on her! Her eyes were wide and frightened as they alighted on Rona.

'Oh, thank God! I could see you in the moonlight!' came Freya Judd's frantic cry, as with her two small hands she clutched at

42

Rona's arm. 'You'll have to come. Please! He's gone mad! *Mad*, I tell you!' And without waiting to reply to Rona's hasty questions, she led the way back to the big house, half-pulling, half-pushing her, but never for an instant letting go.

Once inside the house, Rona was hurried up the wide ornate stairway, along the magnificent galleried landing, all of which took her breath away; and on to the room where a child was finding its way into the world a harsh and difficult one.

As they entered, Edward Wyman swung round, his face empty of expression save for loathing. When his eyes fell on Rona, she felt a fear not experienced before.

'Who's that?' he demanded of Freya Judd. 'What the hell are you doing, bringing a stranger to this room, and a gypsy at that!' he added, taking stock of Rona's swarthy features and the grey fringed shawl tied about her shoulders, together with the blue linen square knotted at the nape of her neck and covering most of her black hair.

'The cook's in a drunken sleep, sir,' protested Freya, 'an', so help me, I couldn't wake her!'

For the briefest moment, he stared at Rona. Then, on a stifled moan from the woman in the bed, he asked quickly, 'You! Do you know anything of delivering a child?'

Rona glanced at the woman in the bed, who looked for all the world as though she'd been in labour far too long already; there seemed little life left in her. And by the look on this man's face, a man she assumed to be either doctor or husband, there was something very wrong.

Without answering, she went to the far side of the bed, where it became obvious that the woman was birthing badly: either she was too small or the baby too large. Keeping her eyes to the bed, she said stoutly, 'I *can* help! Just tell me what to do.' Upon which Freya went to calm her mistress, who was evidently in great distress both physically and mentally, her voice a low whimper and her eyes rolling blindly.

For many years after, when Rona Parrish looked back on that night – as she often did – she could not forget her first sight of the girl-child. Nor could she forget the terrible look on the face of the man she was later told was both doctor *and* husband.

For two hours they worked, two long hours, during which the woman became much weaker. The man worked like a being possessed. He seemed not to care whether child *or* mother lived, but was driven on by his deeper instincts as a doctor. As the minutes ticked away, stretching into hours and seemingly never ending, Rona began to fear that when at last the child left the woman's body, either one or the other – or both! – would be beyond saving. Even the man's obvious skill as a doctor, could not easily persuade the newborn into the world, for although inch by inch, the dark head emerged, it was a slow and painful process. Until in desperation, Edward Wyman was made to resort to surgical means, and in this way released the restrictions which were both holding back the child and causing the mother such great suffering as to rob her of consciousness.

As the knife cut through the confining tissues, there came a long-drawn-out gasp from the mother. At the same instant both head and shoulders of the child slithered into Rona's waiting hands. Then quickly its whole rounded and blood-spattered body was eased out onto the sheets. The sight made Rona cry out.

'Why look! The infant wears a veil! A gift from fortune to keep her ever safe from drowning!' Upon which she tenderly removed from its face the gossamer-fine tissue of skin which was set like a mask across its features. This she reverently laid upon the towel draping the seat of a nearby chair. Then she quickly turned her attention back to the child, whose long sensitive fingers were still stretched open as at the very moment of her birth, and remarked, 'An' born with its hands open too! That's a child who will grow to be giving and beautiful – and of such passionate nature that will bring not only great abiding love . . .' a moment's pause, then, '. . . but also a deal of heart-break – and bad enemies!'

'Gypsy talk!' exploded Edward Wyman. 'The *devil's* tongue! I'll have none of your blasphemy in *this* house!'

But Rona Parrish was not listening to the ravings of a madman, for she had lifted the child, whose abundance of black shining hair was already spiralling into tight little ringlets about her lovely face,

44

and in the gentlest manner was wiping away the mucus from her mouth and eyes – the latter being large and almond-shaped, and of the darkest lustre, the striking beauty of which caused Rona to remark with enthusiasm, 'By! There's a sparkle in them eyes as'd set alight the world! Oh, I'm tellin' you, sir, this girl-child is something very special!'

Now, lifting her smile from the child in her arms to the man who stood against the bed, his form stiff and upright, his eyes narrowed and suspicious, Rona would have continued to sing the lovely child's praises. But her voice was stilled and the smile slipped from her face as she saw the grim set of the man's scowling features. She didn't understand! But then, how could Rona Parrish know of this man's conviction that the child was not his? How could she know that the same exquisite sparkle in the child's eyes, which she herself had enthused would 'set alight the world!' had also set alight something in him. He saw nothing of himself in the dark-eyed infant, noting only two things which taunted him: that the child was of female gender, and that because of her striking dark hair and eyes, his suspicions could only be irrevocably confirmed. The child was not his, but that of the man Durnley. It mattered not that the child's mother was of dark and lovely features, for he chose to believe that a newborn must bear the marks of its father, as did his son, Redford. In his deranged mind he could think of nothing else.

With brooding eyes he watched as Rona bathed the child from the bowl already prepared, after which she carefully wrapped it in a shawl. Inside she placed the facial caul-skin from the towel, where it had been reverently draped, and having given it to the young woman, Freya Judd, who laid the crying child into its cradle, she would have returned her attention to the woman – who all this time had also traced with her half-conscious eyes Rona's every move – but two remarkable things happened in the space of a few moments.

As Rona returned to the bed, her gaze was drawn to the man, whose eyes were alight with the brilliance of a demon as he told her through tight lips, 'Take it! *Take the child*! For it's a bastard who will come to no good here!' His shoulders were stooped and his head hung low on his chest, like a man whose weighty burden had pulled him down. And there was a hardness in his eyes that struck fear into the hearts of both women who now watched him and who heard the words he uttered with such hatred, yet could not bring themselves to believe what he was saying.

Fearing that she had wandered into a situation which took her out of her depth and which truly frightened her, Rona Parrish tore her gaze from the man. Addressing herself to the young woman at the cradle, she said, 'I must take my leave of you. Take care to wash and cleanse the mother properly for fear of infection.' Upon which, she made to turn away from the bed and from the man she was certain was in danger of losing his mind – if he had not already done so. But even as she turned, her eye was caught by a movement – only the smallest, briefest movement. But there was no denying it!

Barely showing itself, yet now visible enough to be recognized, was the head of a *second* infant finding its way into the world, ejected by the reflex spasms of the woman giving birth. At once Rona cried that another child was on its way. Upon which Freya Judd swiftly returned to whisper words of encouragement to her mistress, and, by wetting her face and temples, to cool the fever which still raged within her.

As for Edward, he was visibly shaken when he saw the truth of the gypsy's words; the sight which met his eyes causing him to exclaim in a low trembling voice, 'God help us! Is this the devil's work?' And when in a matter of minutes the child was born, and seen to be a boy of his own colouring, of delicate appearance and of such frailty that even before Rona snatched the child up so as to strike life into it, it was obvious that life was totally extinct in his little form, Edward gave out such a roar as shook the room. In a few strides he was at the girl-child's cradle. He snatched out the now-sleeping bundle. Holding it at arm's length he yelled like a man demented, 'It's punishment! A punishment on her for the sin of adultery. And an injustice to me! What am I to believe? That the boy was *mine?* That she should be carrying the seeds of *two* men?'

He settled his eyes on Rona, 'I tell you, gypsy – *this* one is the bastard! And I swear if you don't take her from my sight I'll *kill* her. *Kill* her, d'you hear?' In an instant he had finger and thumb against the child's throat, poised as though to squeeze the life from it.

As Rona stood transfixed, unable and unwilling to believe that he would do such a thing, the young woman, Freya Judd, rushed to confront her, her eyes large and shocked, her voice a whisper.

'Please! Take the girl, for he's gone mad. And I fear he'll do as he promises! And look! The mistress is beyond saving.' Freya neither believed that Edward *would* murder the child, nor that her mistress had passed from this world. But already her devious mind was calculating how she might gain from all of this.

Rona gave no answer, except to look towards the woman in the bed and to see that she looked as lifeless as the boy-child just come from her. Her eyes were closed, her face like a chalk mask, and her chest unmoving. All manner of things careered through Rona's mind, not the least of which was her own recent loss, and of a bairn not so unlike that lovely little girl being threatened. It came to her that if such a child was so loathed by this man who should be her father – yet who so vehemently denounced her as 'a bastard' – and if this wretched woman was already passed from this world, then was she not justified in taking the girl-child as her own? Emerging from the confusion in her mind, there came the image of a horse and rider, those who had shattered the peace and contentment of her own little world! A dark anger rose up in her as she dwelt on this image, for she knew instinctively that such a magnificent animal as that stallion must come from the stables of gentry. Its breeding dictated so. And that being the way of things, was she not within her rights to take an eye for an eye, a tooth for a tooth as stated in the Holy Bible?

It took only a moment for Rona to decide. Quickly now, she rushed forward before the man should decide to carry out his threat. Then holding out her hands she waited. In a swift movement, Freya Judd thrust the child into the gypsy's arms, saying, 'Go quickly! The child is yours!' This Rona did, not once looking back, for there

47

was hatred enough in that room to follow her for many a lifetime.

With the gypsy gone, Freya Judd made to talk to her master, who stood rock-like against the cradle, his arms by his side and his eyes looking towards the bed, where Freya had laid the dead boy in the arms of his mother and had drawn the blanket over them to reveal only their faces.

'Please, sir,' she ventured, 'I can bring the girl-child back – the gypsy can't be gone far. *Think* on what you've done . . .' Her voice feigned remorse, but her green eyes were most cunning.

Edward Wyman gave no response for a long long while. Then he looked at Freya Judd in silence. Still without speaking, he came to the bed on slow deliberate footsteps, his manner more normal now but an anger still in his eyes.

Then from the bed there came a soft moan, causing both Freya Judd and her master to look up, startled.

He spoke but once before leaving the room. 'It would seem your mistress is not of a mind to leave us . . . just yet! See to her. Wrap the boy in muslin and place him in the cradle. Another doctor must certify him dead.' At the door he turned, his eyes drilling into her, his voice low and intimate. 'The bastard – taken by that gypsy. You will say *nothing* of that!' He flicked his gaze towards the bed where Kathleen was beginning to stir. 'You will say nothing to *her* especially. There was *one* child born in this house! *One* child – a boy, not alive. Do you understand?' Upon the affirmative nod of her head, he added, 'It's Miss Judd isn't it? Freya Judd?' Again she nodded. 'Keep your head – *and* your silence this night. And we'll forget about . . . another matter . . . a rather serious matter, which took place earlier on. You do know to what I'm referring, Freya Judd?'

'Yes, sir,' came the reply.

'Good girl! You have a deal of common-sense, I think – a quality I admire in a woman. You would do well to remember that!'

After his departure, Freya Judd stood looking at the closed door, her mind eagerly turning over the events of this night and a smile creasing the corners of her mouth as she began to realize her own part in them. Going to the bed, she took the child and wrapped it up, before placing it in the cradle. Then she went to the Queen Anne dresser where she sank onto the red velvet-covered stool before it. The smile on her face now spread to light up her eyes, as she looked long and hard at her image in the mirror. Not a great beauty, she thought – her green eyes were too small, too hard. And her hair was neither dark nor fair, but of an insipid colour in between. No, she was not a girl who might trap a fortune on the strength of her looks. Oh, but what now? she mused, what now? There's more than one way to trap a fortune! And with the help of that gypsy, the tide had changed for her – for her and her brother, Lester – who for years now, since being orphaned, had been at the beck and call of their better-offs. Well, now she had been entrusted with a secret. An explosive secret – certainly as far as the young master, Redford, was concerned. For the thought of having to split his inheritance with a newcomer had been like a thorn in his side these past months.

Freya Judd leaned forward so as to see herself more clearly in the light from the lamp. And in a whisper, she said with a smile, 'Oh, Freya Judd! What loyalty you have for the master – to keep such a secret! Such loyalty must be rewarded. Oh, and it shall be! It *shall* be!' For a while she savoured this feeling inside her, a feeling new to her, a feeling of power. She liked it. Oh, yes indeed. Let the gypsy have the Wyman brat – the changeling who came of a high-born lady, and who was rich beyond dreams! Let the brat be brought up a gypsy – never knowing any better. Let the mistress believe there had been only one child born, and that a lifeless boy. And as for the young master? Well now! Wasn't *there* the opportunity, eh? Redford Wyman could go on believing himself to be the one and only heir to the Wyman riches – when *she* knew better.

In all of her life, Freya had never been given such an opportunity as she had been given this night. She felt giddy with the excitement of it. And though as yet she had not decided how best to use the secret with which she had been entrusted, she felt sure that her – and her brother's – future was secured, whichever direction she took. Whether it meant cultivating the old one – who in spite of his

49

pious blusterings was ripe for a woman's arms, a woman without modesty or shame, one who knew how to make a man happy – or whether she concentrated on the young Wyman, already hot for the taste of her: ah, well – she would need to think on it.

Going now from the dresser and crossing to the bed, she stroked Kathleen Wyman's forehead with great tenderness. And as the wretched woman called out in discomfort, she said, 'It's all right, m'lady. It's all right. I'm going to take care of you.' Whereupon her mistress's eyes opened wide, sharpened by a look of fear as she murmured, 'My baby! He'll harm my baby!' 'No, no,' Freya interrupted. 'Nobody can harm your baby now. The master's summoned another doctor. Rest now, just rest. You've to be taken care of.' And so am *I*, she thought wickedly. So am I.

The light of day was fast approaching as Rona Parrish hurried towards her wagon. Only once did she dare to look back towards that big house, her heart fearful that even now someone might be sent to fetch back the tiny bundle warm in her arms. But here she was, standing only feet from the safety of her wagon and as yet no-one had pursued her.

In the light of the fading moon, she turned back one corner of the shawl and peeped inside. What she saw brought a great stabbing pain of joy to her heart and tears sprang to her eyes, for the girl-child was awake and looking straight at her with large black eyes, her little hands open wide as they reached into the air for comfort and a playful gurgle emitting from the sweet heart-shaped mouth.

'Oh, child, child,' cried Rona, her heart aching for her own lost bairn and for the wonderful man with whom she had shared everything.

With a broken cry, she held the child out at arm's length. And with the tears running fast down the coldness of her face, she looked up to the sky, to where the clouds appeared as silver-lined silhouettes against a breathtakingly beautiful canvas, speckled here and there with myriads of tiny flickering stars. And in a firm clear voice she said, 'This *is* my child! You've taken from me – and now you've given back.' There was a small pause, before in a softer voice, the gypsy added, 'This beautiful girl-child shall be named Starlena! A proud old gypsy name.'

Having christened the child by the dictates of her heart, the gypsy, Rona, climbed into the wagon and secured the child in one of the drawers, which she then wedged safely against the roughness of the road ahead. That done, she climbed up to the driving seat, urged the old cob away and made great haste from that place – leaving behind the metal water-churn which had brought her here and which now lay where it had fallen. Some time later, when the morning sun glistened upon it, Freya Judd picked it up. She noted with interest the inscription scraped into its side – the initials C.C. For a moment she was thoughtful, then smiling secretly, she dropped the churn into a deep niche between two sizeable boulders. After which she made her way back to the house, where her mistress was making quiet progress from the trauma of a long and unforgettable night.

Part Three

1901
Starlena the girl

'We two alone will sing like birds i' the cage:
And pray, and sing, and tell old tales, and laugh
At gilded butterflies . . .'

Shakespeare, King Lear

Chapter Five

It had been the most wonderful day! A day when the whole world seemed at harmony – when the flowers showed off their most beautiful colours and sent out a heady perfume which lay across the land like a beguiling mist. It had been a day when the fish took easy bite in the glistening brooks, and the birds sang out their finest songs. But now the day was drawing to an end. And on this evening late in the month of July, 1901, Rona Parrish stretched out her long strong limbs, drew the ankle-length skirt right down to her soft grey boots, whisked the cornflower-blue linen square from her hair, and shaking loose the dark braided lengths to fall about her shoulders, began lazily humming to herself. All the while her watchful dark eyes followed the playful antics of the three-year-old bairn close by.

'Don't you wander away, Starlena me darlin',' she called. 'Stay close to Mammy now!' Then easing her aching back onto the broad trunk of the mighty oak, she let herself relax.

It had been a tiring day – no, not tiring, she corrected herself, it had been an exhausting day. All the same though, it had been profitable and satisfying. She had come across a plentiful supply of willow hereabouts, and from the pegs she'd made and sold to the kindly Lancashire folk down in yon hamlet, there was now money in her pocket and a good meal in the bellies of both herself and the bairn. All the day long, Rona had blessed her old mammy for having taught her the art of peg and basket-making. And if there should come a need, she could also turn out a fine example of lace, the only snag here being the need for bobbins; because, in accordance with the culture of her race, her old mam's bobbins had been burned, together with the rest of her personal belongings, after her death.

For a while her mind was attuned to the past, and Rona indulged in remembrance. She had been only sixteen the day she and Leum had risked the wrath of her people and had run off to get wed. After that, the only one who ever really forgave her was her mam – her father and the men-folk never did. But then there had been Callum – born to her mam soon after, who had grown up with a warm affection for his wayward sister. Then, when an epidemic had taken most of his family, Callum had wandered off on his own, now and then keeping in touch with Rona. Thinking on that great bull of a lad, with his shock of black wavy hair and laughing eyes, Rona chuckled. 'Oh, and where are ye now, me fine fellow?' she murmured. 'Off to America is it? To seek yer bloody fortune?' Well, wherever he was, she hoped he was well and not throwing them sledge-like fists of his about too easily! Yet she suspected he well might be, for Callum Canaar had always been a likely lad for the starting of a fight.

Sitting up straight, she shook her head at her memories. Then after catching her braided hair into the nape of her neck, she knotted the linen square, looped it beneath the braids and pulling it up the back of her head and over to the peak of her forehead, she tucked into it any straying locks. After which, she got to her feet, brushed the clinging bracken from her long dark skirt, and turning to the child, called, 'Come on, bairn! Let's mek tracks afore the night sets in.' Upon which, just as Rona bent to retrieve a tied-up bundle of sticks from the base of the tree, the child came quickly up behind her and in a moment, convulsed by a mischievous fit of laughter, she dived upon the woman, causing her to lose balance and fall in a heap onto the bracken. Then, with the child on top and the woman beneath, the two of them rolled about laughing and screaming in their total delight of each other.

'Ye little vixen!' called the woman, breathless yet exhilarated. 'Ye snuck up on me, so ye did!' Getting to her feet, she caught the child up into the air, making it squeal and laugh even more. 'We'd best be off. It'll be dark shortly, me darlin'.' With the bundle of sticks in one hand and the giggling child in the other, Rona Parrish set off, to trudge the long way back through the spinney, over the open field by way of Craddock Beck, and into the sheltered valley by the running stream, where waited the wagon and two horses.

There were other families camped in the valley: Romany bands of close kin, one of whom had known Rona's own mam some long years back. Now, as she and Starlena approached, the elder was seated on his wicker chair by the front of his wagon, while the women were huddled in a tight busy little group, laughing merrily and peering through the dimming light over the weaving of their baskets. Close by were three children, one a sad-looking boy of tender years who looked on as two others made much fun and noise with the two boisterous lurcher dogs. One of the children Rona recognized as being the grandchild of the elder in the chair – a strikingly vivacious and handsome boy some five years old, by the name of Anselo. Following his every move was the brown-haired girl, Celia, the same age as Starlena and, judging by the hostile manner in which she had witnessed Anselo's open welcome of Starlena on their arrival several days ago, a most sullen and jealous child, to whom Rona had taken an instinctive dislike. This had disturbed her ever since, for as a rule she had nothing but love for the little ones. She had made every effort to excuse the child's unsavoury behaviour, attributing it to the undisputed fact that this child, Celia Devine, was from a long line of true gypsy royalty, this ensuring that she herself would one day be recognized as a gypsy queen.

Having no wish to stop and pass the time of day – being of a hurry to get her tired little bairn to bed – Rona flicked her eyes to where the horses were safely tethered, then hastened up the wooden steps of her wagon, nodding acknowledgement at the women who momentarily lifted their heads to look on her. They too nodded and waved in her direction. But the elder in the chair called out, 'Had a good day, Rona Parrish?' His vacant rubbery mouth stretched into a smile. Upon Rona's assurance that yes she had, thank you, he added, 'We're away first light tomorrow! But ye'll not forget the gatherin' outside o' Blackburn at the end o'season, will ye?'

Rona smiled at the elder. He was very aged – oh, but 'not so aged I still can't sire a good many more strong bairns!' he'd been quick to assure Rona in a proud moment. All the same, though, he was long past his prime. Not so many years ago, he had been a fearless and formidable commander, leading a sizeable gypsy tribe. But time advances on us all, thought Rona sadly. And it brings about many changes – not the least of which is making a young man old, and by necessity scattering hordes of gypsies into small inconspicuous groups. She beamed her friendliness at the elder's eager anticipation, thinking momentarily how like a toothless old bulldog he seemed.

'No, no! I'll not forget,' promised Rona, pausing on the steps, her hand on the brass door-knob ready to let herself quickly inside.

'Aye! Ye'll not forget, I'm sure,' the elder nodded. 'It'll be a grand do, I'm thinkin'!'

To this was added the excited shout of a younger man's voice from inside one of the wagons. 'To be sure! Plenty o' bosh, hotchwitchi an' mullo baulors!' he promised. Rona recognized the voice as belonging to Jemm, father of Anselo and son of the elder. A fine strong figure of a man, who put her in mind of her brother Callum.

At this all four women looked up from their task, to clap their hands and laugh raucously. Rona laughed too, for in spite of the years spent with her gorgio, Leum, she had never forgotten the true gypsy tongue. *'Mullo baulors'*, *'hotchwitchi'* and *'bosh'* meant roasted pig, hedgehog and fiddle-music. It certainly sounded like a real end-of-season do! And yes, she would certainly go, if only that she and the elder could rake over old times during the days when her mam was alive.

Tumbling in at the wagon door, Rona gave silent thanks for the cosy little place that was home for herself and the bairn. But now, wasting no time and aware that with the onset of night would come a chilling air, she lit the wood in the stove, filled the small kettle and removed the iron grid from the stove-top. She placed the kettle over the open mouth, which was already emitting a deal of heat. During the time it took for the water to heat, she stripped the child of its boots, bonnet, little smock dress, and underwear. After which she poured a little of the warmed water into a bowl, then with a wet soapy flannel, she gave the child an all-over wash; this followed by a swift brushing of the hair. That done, she dressed her in the one remaining threadbare nightgown before taking her into a close embrace. After a minute, she disentangled the child's small arms from about her neck, and holding her at arms' length gazed deep into the infant's smiling face – all the while thinking how exceptionally beautiful was her Starlena! The exquisitely-shaped face had about it a wealth of expression – the skin being smooth and of olive hue, the eyes of darkest violet lustre, large yet delicately tapered at both ends. The brows and lashes were of richest black – the latter sweeping over the eyes like a silken fringe. The blue-black hair was of shoulder length and entwined all about in thick shining ringlets.

Beneath Rona's gaze, the child shifted uncomfortably, and raising those huge black eyes to meet the woman's gaze, she murmured, 'Tired, Mammy!' Rona wasn't surprised. The child yawned and, folding her small fists into her now-closed eyes, began rubbing them to and fro.

'Aw, me little bairn!' the woman exclaimed. 'It's been a long wearying day for such a little 'un as you, eh?' Upon which the child nodded and fell against her. Catching the little bundle up into her arms, Rona placed a light gossamer kiss on the sleeping face, lifted her gently into the bed and covered her over, saying, 'I'm sure the good Lord will understand if we're too worn out to say us prayers for once, eh, little one?'

Now, following the same procedure as for the bairn, Rona Parrish got herself ready for bed. But before climbing alongside the little one, she brewed herself a mug of tea, and sitting down to stare lazily in through the open stove-door where the flames had diminished to burning embers, she lapsed into ruminating over a matter long on her mind.

These past three years and more since she had taken to the road, times had been hard, *very* hard. Harder than she had remembered!

So much so that often she had begun to lose heart. And in these low times, only one thing had encouraged her to go on – that one precious gift for which she gave daily thanks – her darling Starlena. Never for a single moment had the bairn given her cause for regret. Not once in these past three years had Rona been subjected to sleepless nights, or temper tantrums the like of which the child Celia seemed to take great delight in. No, there had been nothing like that. Nothing at all which had given her any degree of heartache. For the bairn had brought her only the deepest joy. It was not only Starlena's physical form that was of unique beauty; she had the most passionately loving nature, and a heart strong with compassion. On more than one occasion this had shown itself, sometimes towards the small wounded creatures which they now and then found in the woods, sometimes to Rona herself, on the two occasions when *she* had been accidentally injured. Once, when she twisted her ankle in a rabbit-hole, Starlena, throwing her little arms about Rona's neck, had cried in sympathy. The other time, when the knife with which Rona was stripping green sticks for the making of pegs, had slipped between finger and thumb. The cut had bled profusely. The horrified Starlena had insisted on comforting the injured hand all the way home, in spite of herself being blood-stained in the process.

Yet, though the child's dark eyes seemed made for laughter, they were also often fiery, for she had a fiercely protective instinct where Rona and the two horses were concerned. This was particularly evident on a day in spring the year before, when a poacher came upon the wagon unexpectedly. It had given the man a deal of amusement when, on approaching, he had stopped to stroke the old grey cob – at which moment the colt tethered nearby had kicked out viciously and set up a volley of whinnying enough to wake the dead! At the sound, the toddler Starlena had shown herself at the wagon door. There had come upon her face the darkest scowl. And drawing from her limited vocabulary, she had instructed the intruder in no uncertain terms to 'Go away!'

Thinking on that particular episode now, Rona laughed out loud, in a manner gentle enough so as not to waken the child. That little mite she adored with every fibre of her being! Yet it was Starlena who was at the very core of her troubled thoughts now; for Rona Parrish lived in daily dread of the high-born man who had given the child to her. At every noise – the rustle of leaves in a nearby tree, the sharp crack of a twig or the sound of a galloping horse nearby, she feared herself pursued.

Oh, it had seemed clear enough to Rona that the highborn gent had been of a feverish belief that the child was not his! And such dark suspicions had affected his mind, Rona had been in no doubt that night nor ever since, that he would surely have squeezed the last breath from the new-born girl-child. Yes! She *had* been right to take the young 'un, to take her and keep her! In her heart she knew she had done no wrong. And yet she was afraid and she knew not why. Had the high-born gent bitterly regretted his action once his wife and stillborn son were laid in the ground? Had he seen the enormity of what he had done? And was he even at this moment on her trail? It was a dreadful thought to contemplate. In daylight and darkness alike, it came to haunt her. Always she kept away from main routes and well-used tracks, choosing instead to keep to the back lanes and wooded ways – for fear of being pounced on and having her Starlena snatched away. Oh, that must *never* happen! Not as long as she lived!

All the same, it had always been in Rona's nature to face an enemy square on, to call his bluff. But there was a real danger that in finding the courage to do such a thing, she would end up losing something far more precious. No! Starlena was her life, her whole life. And she would do nothing that might threaten either of them – for there had been such loathing in that high-born gent's eyes on that night! Rona believed that such deep and vicious emotions were not so easily abated. Her instincts had led her away, and the same instincts would *keep* them away. Her mind was made up!

There was yet another matter preying on her mind also. The wandering way of a gypsy was the best in the world during the warmer months, when a body found it easier to keep warm and fed. But Rona had not forgotten the winter just gone, when she and the bairn had huddled together for the heat in their bodies, when her own fingers had stuck hard to the ice on the stalks of the brussel-plant she'd been picking, when on tearing away her fingers she had left behind a layer of frozen skin. And what of the long fearful days when they'd been snowed into the valley this side of Liverpool, when Starlena had taken a chill to the chest which kept her, fevered and fitful, to her bed? These things were not easily forgotten. And more than once it had crossed her mind that mebbe she should be thinkin' o' leavin' the road and somehow aquiring a place more solid. But it would not be an easy thing, she knew. Not easy by half!

Rona Parrish picked a stick from the floor by the stove. With a careful movement, she touched it against the fire-door and closed the heat in. It would keep a glow till morning, she thought. Then replacing the stick on top of the others, she went to draw something out from behind a loose board at the base of a cupboard near the door. It was a richly embroidered and extravagant shawl – the very same in which Starlena had been wrapped on the night of her birth. Pinned to the corner of it was a most expensive brooch engraved with the name of Kathleen Benson. Rona gazed on it for a while before carefully returning it, and climbing in beside the child, where she lay on one elbow, her loving gaze bathing the bairn's sleeping face.

In the smallest whisper, she said, 'Ah, Starlena! I must never tell you of your background, for you're mine now! Mine, who will love and care for you as no other can. Mine, who would gladly die for you, and cherish our every moment. No, I can never tell you of your noble birth, nor of the worldly fortune that might await you. I love you too much, my darlin'. An' I'll show you a world filled with treasures more precious than fine gowns and money! There are jewels in the sky more worthy of you. There are glittering diamonds in the dew of a morning – an' in the setting-sun you'll know a magnificence no high-born lady could ever 'ope to understand! You'll feel the sun and the wind in your face as you ride unfettered across God's free and green lands. Oh, I'll teach you to ride like the very wind itself – an' Nero will be yours to carry you wherever you will. I'll show you the ways an' secrets of a horse until you 'ave the wildest of stallions eating out of your 'ands. Oh, you'll see! You'll see, my bairn.'

Rona's promises were made with passion and came straight from the heart, such was her abiding love for this child. Unaware of the tears spilling down her face, she closed her eyes to sleep. And sleep came – but not before she had prayed that God might bless her with the love of this girl, Starlena, for the rest of her life. And not before she pleaded that he should keep them both from the clutches of danger, or from those who would drive them apart.

The sound of much activity outside woke Rona to the fact that she had slept too long. When, on raising herself to peek through the window above the bed, she saw the wagons alongside, with the horses already to the shaft, she gave a small cry and getting quickly from the bed, she lost no time in putting on her clothes. Starlena, too, awoke with a start and was intrigued to see her mammy rushing about so. Climbing down from the bed, hair tousled and eyes still heavy with sleep, she collected her boots from beneath the stool and put them on.

'Aw, me little bairn!' laughed Rona. 'You're puttin' them on the wrong feet!' And having now done up her own boots, she swung the child up onto the small table where in no time at all she had her dressed and ready for out.

A few moments later, the two of them were in the thick of it, helping to load up the last remaining artefacts into the wagons and saying their farewells.

It was at the very moment before departure when three surprising things happened. The boy, Anselo, ran to where Rona stood, holding Starlena's hand. Without warning, he came to throw his chubby arms about Starlena's neck and with a mischievous laugh kissed her full and loud on the mouth. Then just as quickly he had skipped away, leaving Starlena pink from the intimate contact and looking up at her mammy with a half-shy smile.

As the boy climbed back into the wagon and, much to the great amusement and laughter of the onlooking clan, began waving merrily to Rona and the girl by her side, a second and more sinister incident occurred. The girl-child, Celia, approached from the rear of the wagon to the far side of Starlena. Seeing the size and strength of the lurcher dog attached to the rope the child was holding, it crossed Rona's mind that it was a foolhardy thing for that child's mammy to allow her, for if a lurcher took it into its head to break loose, t'would take a full-sized man to hold it – never mind a bairn not yet four years old.

When it happened, it was so unexpected that Rona was taken unawares. She saw the girl lean to whisper in the dog's pricked-up ear: she saw the wickedness of expression in the girl's eyes. And she felt in her heart that there was an evil at work. But when, of a sudden, the dog was loosed and on swift pads came in a rush towards her and Starlena, she was not prepared. She heard herself screaming, and, blinded by the fear which struck her, she swept the bairn up into her arms. Then, folding her own body around the surprised child, she was herself put at the mercy of the snarling animal. It left the ground at great speed to launch itself upon her. Rona felt the thud of impact against her side and a searing pain as the clothes were shredded from her shoulder. Her screams became hysteria as she clung desperately to the now sobbing Starlena.

'*Down!* Down, you brute! *Away!*' As the harsh instructions were shouted, Rona felt the confusion as man and dog battled for supremacy. Her only thought was for Starlena – that she should not be harmed.

When in a while the dog was led away, still snarling, still hungry, Rona found she could not relax – nor could she loosen the deadly grip with which she held the crying child.

'All right, me beauty! The cur's away now,' came a soft soothing voice in her ear. Gentle hands manoeuvered her to a nearby tree-stump. Only now daring to lift her head, Rona found herself looking into a pair of brown twinkling eyes, eyes which frowned as the man asked, 'Are ye all right, lass?' When she nodded, the eyes relaxed and the face broke into a smile. It was then that Rona saw a man in his mid-forties and she saw the man to be Jemm, father of young Anselo.

'I'm fine,' she assured him, at the same time relaxing her hold on Starlena, who at once stopped crying and threw her arms about Rona's bleeding neck.

'No, no!' said the man gently, easing the child away. 'Yer mam's hurt . . .' At this, Rona looked at her shawl and dress, both in tatters at the shoulder. Her neck was torn and bleeding. 'I'm all right,' she insisted, rising to her feet and drawing the mangled shawl about her. Then, to the other gypsies who had come to her aid and who now stood ashamed and uncertain as to what to do, 'Thank you . . . I *am* fine. A drop o' warm water an' a herb dressing – that's all it needs! As for the shawl, well, I'm known for me darnin'. It'll be good as new!' She even managed a nervous smile.

Satisfied, they nodded their heads and turned away. But the man, Jemm, stayed a while.

'Let me 'elp yer?' he ventured.

'No! Please . . . I can see to mesel',' she retorted, growing impatient for them all to be gone. Her neck and shoulder were throbbing and she was eager to have them bathed quickly, for fear of infection.

With a nod, the man Jemm took his leave, his brown eyes seeming to look right through her as he asked, 'Yer a fine woman, Rona Parrish. Tell me, will we be seein' yer at the end o' season?' Only when she gave an affirmative nod did he turn his back to climb onto the seat of his wagon, his wife quiet by his side and son, Anselo, still gazing at Starlena.

As they pulled away, Rona wondered whether it might be a wise thing to go to the end of season celebration. This man Jemm! There was a look in them eyes that she'd seen before: the man hankered after her. An' him with a wife by his side! By! There was a danger in that. And she had no need of such trouble.

But the danger which Rona sensed regarding the man Jemm was as nothing compared to the deep rush of apprehension which shocked her on glimpsing the girl Celia. She was seated on a flat wagon at the rear of the departing ensemble; pressed close to her doting mam, legs dangling and her two arms wrapped about the lurcher's broad muscular neck. All of this Rona saw – and noted. But the one observation that stayed with her long after they'd gone was the look in the girl's hazel eyes as they fixed themselves onto Starlena.

It was a look of jealousy. A look of hate – and something far worse in Rona's mind; it was the same look she had seen on the high-born gent when he'd threatened to squeeze the life from the newborn.

Of a sudden, there came into Rona's heart a cold fear for her sweet loving bairn. And she wondered how it was that such a lovely innocent as her Starlena could raise up such vicious and deadly enemies.

The elder had asked Rona if she would be going to the end o' season do, and she had said yes – as she had also assured his son, Jemm. But now, after the events of the morning, she dared not! Rona knew from old of endless feuding brought about by the desires of a man such as Jemm – and she would not be the centre of such upset. No, she would *not* make her way to the far side o' Blackburn come October. Instead she would travel in the opposite direction. There was much sane reason in such a decision – not the least being a gypsy queen in the making. A witch by the name of Celia!

Chapter Six

'*No*, I say! . . . and let that be an end to it!' Edward Wyman slammed shut the thick account-ledger and threw down his pencil. Then, without rising from his place before the huge inlaid mahogany desk, and stubbornly keeping his broad back to the woman who lingered in nervous anticipation by the door, he added in a gruff tone, 'So! If that's all? You may go!' On the last word he waved one hand impatiently, while with the other he drew a silver watch from his waistcoat pocket, glanced down at it and snorted, 'And get that damned maid in here to light the lamps!' When the woman made no move, he insisted, 'I said you may go!'

'But, Edward! About the ball. I really *am* unwell – and would not complement the evening . . .'

At this, he sprang from the chair to face her, his eyes small and round as bright glittering marbles and his fists clenching and unclenching by his sides. In a flat controlled voice he told her, 'When my – *our* – guests arrive they will expect to see both Edward Wyman *and* his wife, Kathleen. And come hell or high water, my dear, that is what they will see! Do I make myself clear?' He ventured a step towards her, his features uplifted in a smile. But it was a cold calculating smile, without friendliness or warmth. As he waited for her response his whole manner bristled with impatience, his mind obsessed with the coming event.

In twenty-four hours – on Friday the 31st of December, 1903 – would be held the New Year's Eve Ball, the first in this house for three years. And in spite of his wife's continuing and infuriating malaise he, as master of the house, intended to see that this ball would once more be held in the grand old tradition of Bessington Hall.

'I asked – *do . . . I . . . make . . . myself . . . clear?*' he repeated, the lower half of his uncomely face jutting out and with each deliberately spoken word the thick beard moving in a way which held Kathleen fascinated. When the last word was uttered, she thought how very much she loathed this man, her husband, the fiend who took pleasure in taunting and belittling her! Always, he was at the centre of her nightmare, a nightmare created some five years before and which had haunted her ever since. And which, in spite of Edward Wyman's insistence to the contrary, had told her that she had given birth to not one, but *two* infants. The first had been a girl which she herself had seen carried to the cradle she had so lovingly kept prepared. She *had* seen this! She knew it! Oh, but to get to the truth of it all . . . how could she? When all about her there seemed a conspiracy of deceit and lies! Over and over again she had twisted and turned the matter over in her mind, until at times even *she* suspected that her sanity was in question. There was nothing she could do, nowhere she could go and no-one to whom she could turn. With her parents long gone and no living relatives other than Edward Wyman and his mirror-image son, the only people in whom she had confided were the solicitor, Durnley, and the woman, Freya Judd. But the one, although sympathetic, was reluctant to believe what he called 'her fantasies' – due, he claimed, to the debilitating and prolonged severity of her illness immediately following the fateful night. And the other, the woman Freya Judd, although always of a mind to listen, was never disposed to take the matter seriously. Oh, there was of course the old dowager – a kindly but ancient relative of Edward Wyman's living the privileged life of a recluse in a large country residence out Salmesbury way on the far side of Blackburn. In all the years she had been Edward Wyman's wife, Kathleen had met the old dowager just once, and that was on the actual occasion of their marriage. No, she reminded herself: there was no-one. She felt herself to be utterly helpless. Against this man who stood before her now, threatening, bullying, she could muster no defence.

'Very well, Edward. If you insist,' she reluctantly conceded.

'I do!' he exclaimed. 'I'll see to it that Freya Judd attends you directly. Her help will be invaluable, I'm sure! And as for detailed preparation for the ball, well, you must leave all of that in her hands. In spite of her relatively tender years, the woman is an accomplished organizer!'

Somewhat incensed by having been stripped of all responsibility regarding the running of the house and consequently of a degree of dignity, Kathleen Wyman was made bold enough to utter an observation regarding the woman in question. 'I cannot disagree with you on the merits of Freya Judd's administrative ability,' she told her husband, 'but because of the very matter you have just mentioned – her tender years – the staff appear to have taken a considerable dislike to her, particularly the older and more established members of the household. There has been much envy and speculation concerning her enhanced position here – parlourmaid to housekeeper – and all in a few short years. And even *I* wonder at the wages you must pay her, for I understand she is of a mind to send her brother away for a London education on his eighteenth birthday some two years hence.'

Edward was visibly agitated by his wife's remarks, and upon a matter which was a thorn in his side. 'And if she *has* such intention, my dear,' he said with a look of complacency, 'then I am sure it has nothing to do with us. As I understand, Freya Judd came into a sum of money from an unexpected source – and of course she must please herself how it is to be spent. As for the young man, her brother, he's a very useful pair of hands about the cattle, has a way with them, I'd say. And as far as I'm concerned, there's a place on my land for him for as long as he wants it.' Going now to the door, he opened it and held it wide, saying, 'Has Freya Judd ever served *you* wrong?' To which Kathleen had to answer No, for with reference to herself, the woman was most polite and helpful. 'Good. Then you have no cause for complaint. I take it, then, that you will make it your business to refer to me the discipline of any members of staff who agitate for trouble. And I remind you – yet again – that none of this is your concern. Certainly not regarding what wages I deem fit to pay my staff!'

Now, with the lowering of his eyes to his own brown polished boots, the woman knew she had been dismissed. Whereupon gathering the surplus folds of her long sweeping skirt into her fists, she departed, pausing only when she heard the library door firmly close behind her.

Going now across the spacious hall, her short-heeled boots resounding on the patterned ceramic tiles beneath her feet, Kathleen came to the long casement window which looked out over the front of the house. And there she stood, her dark eyes brooding as they roved the splendid approach to Bessington Hall, where the lawns and drive curved in perfect unison to form a grand sweeping setting for the majestic old trees and stately conifers, whose broad drooping branches were gently bowed by the sprinkling of snow which had fallen since early light. Kathleen had prayed that it would keep on falling, thereby causing difficulty for invited guests and consequently resulting in a cancellation of the planned festivities. Bessington Hall was a good way from most recognized main routes, being situated in the outer parish of Accrington and a long way into deep countryside. But the snowfall had not been a heavy one, had ceased rather abruptly and in the mild December evening had even begun to melt away – taking with it Kathleen's hopes of any reprieve from her painful duties as hostess. Most of the people invited were either old city friends of Edward's or gentleman farmers who had bought up several small farms and, with commercial profit in mind, had merged them into vast money-making enterprises comprising thousands of acres. Edward Wyman, having been one of the very first pioneers, was by far and away the biggest landowner and the most powerful among them.

A number of guests were acquaintances of Redford Wyman: wasters and aimless characters, thought Kathleen bitterly. She had long ago ceased to look upon Redford as any son of hers, for there had developed in him a callousness which at times even surpassed that of his father. What a great pity, she mused, that he could not have been more like Freya Judd's brother, Lester. There was a young man she would have been proud to call son, a young man who knew what hard work was and who had earned a great deal of respect from Edward Wyman's own men. In fact Kathleen had a sneaking suspicion that her husband had come to enjoy having Lester Judd about the place – certainly he placed a deal of responsibility on the young man's shoulders, in spite of his being not yet sixteen years of age. A smile crept into the corners of her mouth as she thought how Redford also off-loaded his own duties onto Lester's young shoulders. And she wondered whether there might come a day when he would regret it. She hoped so, oh how she hoped so!

'Will there be anything else, Ma'am?' The maid appeared from the inner reaches of the drawing-room, a dustpan and brush held discreetly in the folds of her black uniform dress and her pretty brown curls squashed into submission beneath the starched frills of her white cap. 'I've just banked up the fire in the drawin'-room, Ma'am,' she exclaimed in a rather loud nervous voice, her eyes wide and her body half-inclined in the manner of a curtsey.

'Thank you. See if Cook has any further duties . . . Oh! First, though, you had best report to the library. The master is at work in there and the light somewhat dim in the coming evening.' She gave the lately-appointed girl an encouraging smile before watching her hurry away in the direction of the library.

As the girl went away, Kathleen reflected on what a capable young woman she seemed, and regretfully had to concede that Freya Judd did have an uncanny knack of hiring conscientious staff. Yet had she known what was running through the girl's mind at that moment, she would not have been pleased. For the departing maid was wondering what the mistress would say if she was to 'ear the tidbits of gossip below stairs. About 'ow the mistress 'ad not been in 'er right mind since birthin' a stillborn boy some five years back! Oh, an' what might she say if she knew what went on twixt the master an' that fancy piece, Freya Judd! Oho, what indeed, eh? But then, as Cook were so fond o' saying, ''Appen she *does* know. An' thanks the Lord for it!' 'Twere no secret as 'ow the master slept in another room altogether an' the entire 'ouse could 'ear the quarrellin' an' shoutin' as went on! An' as for that *son* o' theirs, well! No good to nobody – an' it were said as the rogue 'ad bedded all the young 'uns in the 'ouse. Well, *she'd* keep well out of 'is way 'an that was fer sure!

For a while, Kathleen stayed by the window, her eyes intent upon the manservant as he went about lighting the tall lamps which lined either side of the drive. It was just as he reached up to the very last one that Kathleen's gaze fell on the two figures approaching from the main gate. One was the unmistakable slim and energetic figure of Freya Judd, well-dressed as usual in brown waist-fitting coat, which reached down to brush against the top of her black button-up boots, her well-groomed upswept brown hair covered by a smart small-brimmed hat tied beneath the chin with a broad expanse of ribbon. One arm was covered in a fur muff. The other was linked with that of the young man by her side, a tall fair-haired fellow with a strong handsome face and impish hazel eyes. The two of them were immersed in much talk and laughter, seeming to derive a great deal of pleasure from each other's company.

Kathleen recognized the young man as Lester, Freya's brother. She thought they must be returning from their usual evening stroll. And while she would gladly have exchanged the time of day with Lester, Kathleen had no inclination towards a conversation with the woman. So she withdrew from the window and made haste up the wide sweeping stairway and along the galleried landing.

Once inside the confines of her room with the door closed against intruders, Kathleen gave a sigh of relief. For a few moments she lingered with her back to the door, her eyes tightly closed, one hand still resting on the brass doorknob and the other stroking itself to and fro across her throbbing forehead. Then, as though settling an argument with herself, she gave a short angry snort and went straightway to the tall cumbersome brown chest-of-drawers where, from the bottom and deepest drawer, she took a bottle of gin and a glass. Then, having poured out a sizeable measure of the liquid, she emptied it down her throat in one go, coughed heartily and proceeded to pour out another. After a while she lost all sense of time.

From outside the door, Freya Judd listened to the familiar

clinking of glass upon glass and the ensuing fit of coughing. Smiling to herself, she moved away, her green eyes hard and satisfied. 'Drink up, mistress!' she murmured with sarcasm. 'The more sozzled your brain becomes, the sharper will mine!'

It was 8pm on New Year's Eve. It had been a hectic day of preparations at Bessington Hall. But now the seeming chaos below stairs had settled to an orderly last-minute routine. Even Cook had recovered enough to sit down with a well-earned glass of milk and brandy – 'in readiness for the evening rush!' she informed all interested parties.

Upstairs there had been much the same hustle and bustle. The great hall and adjoining dining-room were festooned with great spreading plants and fan-shaped ferns, all brought to this area from other rooms about the house, and all attractively displayed in gaily-painted jardinières, each set atop a smart fluted column and strategically placed so as to provide an eye-catching setting for the coming ball.

The whole area was lighted to a dazzling brilliance from the magnificent hanging chandeliers and the many lamps and silver candle-holders which decorated every available surface throughout. Along the far wall of the dining-room the orchestra-players were already setting out their instruments upon the raised dais kept for such occasions. Close by, the long mahogany sideboard was beautifully polished in readiness for the great silver tureens, platters and endless choice of food and drinks which would shortly grace it.

Freya Judd stood in the wide archway between dining-room and great hall, where the double doors were swung back to allow free movement from one area to the other. Having closely inspected everything below stairs, she was now satisfying herself on other matters. And she was pleased! All was as it should be. The first guests were due to arrive in just over an hour, the old dowager herself, together with a young lady by the name of Elizabeth; she was somewhat of a surprise inclusion and one they would no doubt learn more of on introduction.

Turning away now, Freya hurried towards the library, the

flounce of her skirt brushing with a soft swish against her boots and her sharp eyes alert. It was her intention to inform Edward Wyman that all was in readiness. After which she would make haste upstairs to Kathleen's room.

'Enter!' The voice came in answer to Freya's firm tap on the door. On turning to see who wanted him, Edward Wyman's face took on a look of cunning. A half-smile gave his features an air of attractiveness, as he said quietly, 'Oh, it's you, Freya.' As he spoke, he moved forward to meet her. When he had come so close that she stopped before him, his arms went about her and in a moment the two of them were caught up in a savage embrace. The man's hands raked her body, first touching her neck then trembling down to hold her buttocks tight into him. Now his mouth came down on hers in a hard, searing, open kiss, his hands groping at her as though to tear the clothes from her back.

'No! No, Edward!' the woman laughed, pulling herself away, her two hands patting first the dishevelled dress and now the stray wisps of hair back from her face. 'Time enough for that . . . later,' she chided, her smile showing a deal of pleasure.

'Later, then!' came the man's response, his breathing hard and his face flushed with excitement, his calm authoritative manner belying the torrent of greed she had let loose in his loins, 'Perhaps when the guests have gone?'

Freya Judd nodded and, moving towards the door, she added, 'We're ready for the guests. So I'll be away to see to – your wife. She's had nothing to eat all day so I shall take up a morsel or two from the kitchen . . .'

'Yes, yes!' His composure had returned and he was in charge again. 'I don't want anything to spoil this evening. You tell her that!'

Upstairs in her room, Kathleen heard the approaching footsteps and recognized them as being those of Freya Judd. When the polite but insistent knock came on the door, she voiced her feelings by asking the would-be intruder to 'Go away!' She was no more graciously inclined towards the imminent ball than she had been previously, in spite of making every effort to drown her sorrow these past twenty-four hours.

Freya Judd ignored the curt instruction, at once letting herself into the room and straightaway going to put the food tray on the chest of drawers; the scene before her was one of chaos. All about the room was a thick lingering smell of stale alcohol, items of clothing were scattered far and wide. And draped across the bed was Kathleen Wyman, obviously the worse for drink and in a pathetic state of disarray.

At the sight of Freya Judd, looking trim and smart in her grey high-necked dress with frilled collar dressed with a large cameo brooch, the other woman pulled herself to the edge of the bed, her long black hair cascading over her pretty shoulders and her dark eyes wildly accusing.

'Look at you!' she yelled, throwing her arms up above her head and laughing aloud. 'Quite the lady, aren't you?' Suddenly her voice became hard. 'You were here that night, weren't you? You know! You saw my baby girl, didn't you? Tell me! You saw my baby girl!' She was out of the bed and grappling at Freya Judd's brooch, 'She had a brooch too – my mother's brooch! I pinned it to the shawl myself.' Spent of energy, she fell against Freya and began crying. 'Oh, help me – please! What have you done with my daughter?'

'Get up at once!' Freya Judd was not moved by such an exhibition for she had seen it before – seen it and been a little afraid. 'There was no girl-child! Only a boy!' She took the woman by her small shoulders, hoisting her onto the bed with practised ease. In a stern voice she said, 'Only a boy – a *dead* boy! Do you understand what I'm saying, Mrs Wyman? There was only a stillborn boy!'

'Then show me the brooch! And the shawl,' demanded the sorry figure slumped on the edge of the bed.

'I've already told you – the boy was buried in it . . .'

'No! No, he was not! That was not the same shawl – and the brooch was gone!' Kathleen began sobbing, her head bent into her hands and her whole tired body convulsed in grief. 'Oh, why won't you tell me the truth? Where's my baby girl? Where *is* she?'

Moving swiftly and with lips tightened grimly, Freya Judd

swept about the room, clearing the mess and collecting up garments, until once again it appeared orderly. Then, going to the great fireplace, she pulled on the bell-cord to summon help. After which she went to the huge dark-wood wardrobe, from which she withdrew a magnificent silver gown with full skirt and off-the-shoulder puff sleeves. This she draped over the balloon-back chair, before placing beneath it a pair of satin shoes with small square heels, and daintily buttoned overstraps. Then, going to the chest of drawers, she collected items of cream silk underwear and a prettily patterned lace-up bodice; these she laid on the bed.

When the maid arrived, Freya ordered hot water for the bath. Then, when this was brought and the bath water was at the right temperature, the two of them undressed and half-carried Kathleen into the small room where already a cheery fire glowed in the grate. After some difficulty, they lowered the lady into the wood-rimmed metal bath situated in the centre of the floor. All this time, Kathleen made no resistance, having fallen into a sullen and dangerously morose mood.

For the next hour, Freya stayed with the woman in her charge – a woman she tolerated for the sake of Edward Wyman, a woman for whom she had neither liking nor respect. Although there were times in the dark of night when she would think how very much she adored her brother, Lester – at such times, she would feel just a touch of compassion for this woman who craved the love of her lost child. But it was only ever a 'touch' and quickly dismissed, for it played no part in the scheme of things. Over the years since that fateful night, she had acquired a good strong foothold in this grand house – and with the man, Edward Wyman, no longer her master. A good strong foothold, yes indeed! And it was only a matter of time now, before she started that triumphant upward climb – that all important ascent of which for so long now she had dreamed and planned.

It had taken a degree of determination, persuasion and bullying. But at precisely nine-fifteen, Kathleen Wyman swept down the stairs to join her husband in the welcoming of their guests, her whole manner oozing confidence, and any lingering effects from the earlier drinking quite under control. At the moment of his wife's appearance on the stairs, Edward Wyman was crossing the hall below. What he saw when he looked up was a vision of such beauty that it took his breath away! With her rich black hair upswept into coils about her head adorned with glittering diamond pins, her large dark eyes like black jewels in her pale small face and that familiar gently curved figure looking resplendently feminine bedecked in the low-cut silver-grey gown, Kathleen was a woman in her most magnificent prime. And there was awakened in her husband a deep carnal desire for her. Already his passions had been roused this night by that vixen, Freya. And now they were on the rampage, Edward was feverishly impatient to have them satisfied!

At nine twenty-five, the guests began arriving – some in traditional carriages and others of more adventurous nature in the new-fangled horseless carriages which exhaled much smoke and noise. By nine forty-five the guests were all accounted for, and before long they had all danced, eaten and drunk themselves into a merry state.

From a discreet vantage point by the carved wood balustrade, which ran the whole length of the landing above the hall, Freya Judd watched the proceedings. The orchestra was in full swing. Some guests were dancing, some standing around picking morsels of food from their plates and others stood with glasses in their hands, enjoying either argument or conversation.

With the women, the talking-points were mainly to do with fashion and leisure – the one centring round the much admired frivolous and extravagant hat-styles and the other detailed recollections of their most recent reception.

It was with great interest that Freya Judd observed two young people dancing together on the floor. Her brother, Lester Judd, looking tall and handsome in his very first dinner-suit, was partnered by a girl also sixteen years of age, small and pretty in a blue dress which came high up to her slim neck and reached down to the top of her cream shoes. She was light on her feet and dainty to the point of being fragile – this emphasized by her very fair hair and soft blue eyes.

Freya visibly bristled as she watched, noting with annoyance that the girl had eyes for no-one but Lester. Even after the young man had dutifully returned her to the gilded seat beside which sat the aged dowager, Elizabeth Bannion followed his departure with soulful eyes.

Freya made a mental note to keep a very wary eye on that young woman who, according to the dowager's introduction and an explanation to Edward Wyman that 'the child's parents have gone to foreign parts and she is left in my charge', would be around for some time. Too close for comfort! Yes, indeed! She would keep an eye on that one, for she had better things in mind for her own darling brother.

Now, her darting eyes were drawn to where Edward Wyman and his son, Redford, were each breaking away from a small group by the door. Redford at once disappeared into the dining-room, but his father made his way along the outer edge of the dancers to where the white-haired dowager and the girl were seated, each intent on the music and following the dancers as they twirled and bobbed to its pleasant rhythm.

'I trust you are enjoying the evening?' asked Edward, his smile at its best.

'Thank you, Edward,' came the reply. 'I am! We both are, are we not, Elizabeth?' the dowager asked, turning her wrinkled face to the girl, who upon seeing herself the centre of attention, blushed a warm pink and held her head shyly to one side as she gazed up at Edward Wyman, her voice a stammer.

'Why, yes – I am indeed enjoying myself,' she assured them both. At which moment, Lester Judd returned, requested of the dowager that he might once again steal away her charge, and upon an affirmative nod he whisked the blushing girl onto the floor.

'That boy!' exclaimed the dowager. 'Brother of your house-keeper, I understand?' There was a distinct note of disapproval in her voice.

Ignoring this, Edward Wyman confirmed her observation, adding, 'It would come as no surprise to me if one of these days I didn't put that boy in full charge of my livestock. He's a clever and reliable young man. Yes indeed!' He smiled down on her. 'Tonight is a special treat by way of a thank-you for his work in that respect.' Having imparted all the information he intended, Edward changed the subject. 'The young lady in your charge – Elizabeth Bannion – am I to understand that she is staying with you at Whalley Grange?'

'Indeed – and will be for some long time. The poor child does not know it, but her parents have gone their separate ways, he to foreign parts, and she to the devil, I believe! The girl, though, is a well brought-up individual – although too friendly, I think. We have gypsies just outside our grounds, and several times I've had her brought from watching them at play. She appears particularly fascinated by a lone woman and her young daughter – the one apparently teaching the other to ride a horse. A stallion, no less!'

'Gypsies!' Somewhere inside Edward's memory there had been struck an unpleasant chord. As he spoke, his back became stiff and his eyes hostile. 'Tramps!' he said in an explosion of anger. 'Nothing but tramps and vagabonds, who should be sent immediately on their way! Set the dogs on them if you've any sense!'

'They've been gone these four days. A woman and her child, Edward – just a woman, her child, and her two faithful animals.' The dowager smiled, simultaneously bowing her head in acknowledgement of an anxious look from her charge, who nevertheless appeared to be enjoying herself.

At that moment, Edward Wyman's gaze travelled up to where Freya had tucked herself into the shadows to follow the festivities undetected. But she was not so discreet that Edward Wyman's searching gaze could not distinguish her trim shapely form. Then, as his gaze alighted on her cat-like green eyes, his passion was inflamed. In a moment he had excused himself and was wending his way in between moving bodies, to take himself to the foot of the stairs and upwards into the waiting arms of the witch who had entranced him.

Other eyes also followed Edward's movements – other eyes watched and smiled, not without a certain vindictiveness and a little envy. Redford Wyman had long been aware that the fickle Freya had shifted her affection from son to father, and it had done nothing to improve his vanity. Indeed it was very much a sore point which he found difficult to come to terms with. But then he'd always entertained a sneaking suspicion that his father was a hypocritical bastard – spouting damnation from one end and fornication from the other.

Edward's quarters were situated some short way along the landing between the stairway and Kathleen's rooms, and the door to them was easily visible from the hall below. As he mounted the stairs towards her, Freya pressed herself against the wall, awaiting his approach. Then, when the two were little more than an arm's reach one from the other, the woman spoke quietly from the shadows.

'That wretched wife o' yours! She'll be the undoing of us yet, Edward! Ranting and raving about that blessed shawl, and the brooch pinned to it.' Her green eyes glowed in the half-light and in the atmosphere of fear and intimacy, Edward could barely control the urges now raging through him.

Placing one hand on her shoulder and with the other thoughtfully stroking his beard, he murmured, 'That was something I foolishly overlooked.' Now he stepped close enough to touch her body with his own, and bringing up his hands to grip her by the shoulders, his pale eyes bored into hers as with a gentle push, he suggested, 'However, we won't let that spoil the evening, now will we?' Whereupon, he turned her about and propelled her towards his room, she laughing softly and he furtively glancing along the landing. They disappeared inside.

Redford Wyman was not the only witness to their conspiracy, for his mother Kathleen watched also, a look of disgust on her lovely face. Seeing his mother and the loathing so clear in her face, he sidled up to stand alongside her.

In a voice for her ears only he said with a small, wicked smile, 'He doesn't care *how* he humiliates you, does he?' Then, having satisfied himself that he had caused more pain, he returned to his vantage point, his smiling blue eyes trained on the door which led to his father's rooms. In a moment he saw Kathleen stumbling upstairs, her gait unsteady from the numerous drinks she'd consumed. His smile deepened, and it was with positive relish that he snatched a glass of champagne from the tray of a passing waiter. Already somewhat elated by the recent acquisition of a horseless carriage, he raised the glass high in the direction of his mother's angry figure, murmuring, 'Here's to more humiliation, mother dear!'

Without pausing to knock, Kathleen swept into her husband's room. As she flung open the door, she could at first see little. The only light in the room came from the lamps outside and from the flickering firelight emanating from the grate. Now, though, as she stepped deeper into the room and the light cascaded in from the landing, the two figures were easily distinguishable – although so closely entwined that they could have been one! For a moment, neither appeared aware of Kathleen's presence, totally immersed in each other as they were, and the deep throated growls issuing from both having smothered the sound of the door opening.

The woman Freya Judd stood spreadeagled up against the far wall by the window, stripped totally naked with arms stretched out either side of her and fingers excitedly clawing the wall. Her head was flung back, her eyes closed and her loosely-open mouth uttered small painful groans which came in rhythm with the erratic movement of her body. The man's legs were between hers, half-bent, his head lowered to her breast and his whole naked body thrusting into her with a savage urgency.

Only when Kathleen's high-pitched laugh echoed through the room did they look up – the woman shocked, the man's face red and bloated from the climax of his passion. Yet for a moment neither moved, so intricately weaved into each other were they.

'You look like a dog and bitch!' Kathleen Wyman cried out, at the same time flinging the door wide the more to reveal them. 'I've done my duty, *master*!' she sarcastically exclaimed with an artificially subservient sweep on her arm, 'So if you'll excuse me, I'll leave the door open so your guests can see just what kind of low creatures you are!' With her voice raised on the last words, she turned away to flounce out of the room and along the landing towards the privacy of the west wing.

Below, the orchestra had been playing with such verve as to disguise the incident from all but Redford Wyman, who had seen his mother emerge and now saw his father swiftly appear to slam shut the door. Then a few moments later Edward came onto the landing, haphazardly clothed, on his face a look of dark rage. He turned swiftly away in the same direction his wife had taken some short while before, his steps as thunderous as his expression.

Kathleen was pouring yet another drink when her husband burst into the room. Without a word, he snatched both glass and bottle from her hands, then flinging the glass into the wall and after pinning her down against the bed, he forced open her mouth and tipped the bottle into it, emptying the entire contents – some spilling onto the bedcovers, but most of it finding a coughing spluttering way down her throat. After which, he grabbed her up and yelling obscenities while she gasped for breath, he brought his two fists up to the neck of her gown and tore it from her, shouting, 'So you didn't like what you saw, eh? Well now, if you were the wife you *should* be, there'd be no need for me to look elsewhere, would there? You're still my property and don't you forget that!'

Kathleen feared for her life. Breaking from him, she would have run to the door, but he caught hold of her and swung her back towards the chest of drawers. 'I'll teach you a lesson you won't forget!' he threatened.

As the two of them struggled, the woman's hand fell upon the tray brought up earlier and left on the chest of drawers. She felt the fork between her fingers. With a loud scream, she drew it into the air, before slicing it down against the man's face, then again through his shirt and into the soft fleshy folds of his chest. In pain, he released his hold on her, his fingers clutching at the oozing blood which spread into a large crimson stain on his hand. Yet still she swung at him, blinded by fear and incensed by her hatred of him.

Some way down the landing, Freya Judd was warding off the taunts of Redford Wyman. They heard the noise and hysterical voices and made their way towards them at once. As Redford Wyman put his hand on the doorknob, the door was pulled open from the inside, to reveal his father sinking to his knees, the whole of his upper body covered in blood.

There came a soft shocked cry from Freya. But before either she or the man with her could make a move, Kathleen was on them like a crazed thing. There followed a vicious scuffle, during which Freya was pushed aside to fall sobbing against the far wall. From there, she saw Kathleen Wyman plunge the sharp prongs of the fork into her son's unprotected head and face. She heard an awful scream of pain, and saw Redford Wyman's punctured bleeding eye. And she knew he had been blinded!

Suddenly there came the sound of running feet. A confused mass of people, guests and servants appeared. Then the staggering, crying figure of Redford Wyman was led away to be swiftly dispatched to the nearest infirmary. Other helpful hands carried the still form of Edward Wyman along the landing to his own bed. Then, for the sake of all and until they knew what best to do, someone gentled Kathleen back into her room, and locked her in.

For eight weeks and more Kathleen was kept confined to her rooms – Freya Judd being the only one willing to let herself in and out as the woman's keeper. The wretched woman herself never uttered a word, except occasionally to cry for her baby and to sob in her sleep. For most of the time, she sat on her extravagant four-poster bed, sullenly perched high on the feather bolster, with legs tucked up into her arms, and her large dark eyes flickering at every little noise. She followed Freya's every move, sat still and obedient as a child when being bathed or having her long black hair brushed, and said nothing of the night of the ball – when she had seen this green-eyed woman fulfilling the lust that fermented between her and Edward Wyman. Nor did she speak of other matters. And not once did she ask what was to become of her. Although somewhere in the confusion of her mind there was the absolute belief that she would be punished.

It was on a bright spring morning during the first week of March that Edward found the determination to decide, and the strength with which to sit up in his sick-bed and sign the papers which would have his wife committed to an asylum. The term decided was of an 'indefinite' nature. And upon the advice of his medical consultant, Edward dictated that the deranged woman was to receive no privileges or visitors – no well-meaning dignitaries, no priest – and no relatives. The situation was to be reviewed within the year.

The following afternoon, an official-looking carriage drew up at Bessington Hall, drawn by two bay geldings and carrying three men – the driver and two sombre-looking medical officers.

It was on that same afternoon that Redford Wyman was released from the infirmary – strong and virile of body, more vicious of mind, vividly scarred, and blinded in one eye. With the skin puckered and drawn around the sagging cheekbone, his face, although still peculiarly arresting, was not the handsome thing it had been. Instead there was a hideousness about it that seemed to reflect his soul.

Now, as he stepped amidst noise and smoke from the lately acquired motor-car, he saw the carriage that had come for his mother. When, at the same moment, there emerged from the house a group of people, he found it irritatingly necessary to turn his head a number of degrees in order for him to train his one good eye upon them. He saw the struggling protesting figure of Kathleen Wyman encased in a buckled strait-jacket and looking terrified. Crossing the gravelled space which separated him from the little group, he put up a hand to delay the procedures. When the escorting men drew his mother to a halt, he looked down at her with a half-smile, his face turned slightly to one side as had become his habit in order to see better. And in a voice barely above a whisper, he told her, 'So! At last you'll be locked away!' The smile evaporated and in its place there came a look of cold hatred as he promised, 'I'll see to it that you will never again see the light of day!'

His callous statement caused the two officials to look at each other. Kathleen was mortally afraid, for she believed his every word, believed it with all her heart. Yet she gave no response which might satisfy him, no response which might bring back the smile to his features. No, what she did was to spit full in his face and to laugh loudly – an action which unfortunately led the medical escort to believe that she really *must* be the mad creature Edward Wyman claimed, and as such, would need to be watched very closely.

From the long narrow window on the landing, Freya Judd looked down on the incident below. It pleased her to see Redford Wyman stripped of his handsome arrogant looks. It pleased her to see the malignance between mother and son – and it pleased her most of all to see the mistress of the house being led away, perhaps never to return. Certainly – if she had *her* way – never to return to this house! There was room for only one mistress at Bessington Hall. Only one! And she went by the name of Freya Judd.

Chapter Seven

Starlena was so excited she could barely contain herself. It was the occasion of her eighth birthday, and for the first time, she was being allowed to actually mount the stallion without the helping hand of her mammy!

'Like this, Mammy?' she called, reaching up on tip-toes and leaning forward from the tree-trunk which served as a mounting-block, matching her height with the stallion, and serving to give her leverage. Unfortunately, when bringing her weight forward against the horse her foot slipped, banging her against the animal's flank with undue vigour. This startled the creature forward and threw the girl to the ground, where she remained in a heap, to laugh uproariously while the horse indulged in a fit of nervous whinnying, his feet erratically tapping the hard ground and threatening to come too close to the girl, who appeared totally unconcerned about the possible danger.

'No, no child! 'Ave yer forgotten all I've telled yer?' Rona sprang from her seat on the upturned bucket, impatient steps hastening her towards the child, her face a study of frustration. As she came to where Starlena was scrabbling to her feet, she gathered up the loose length of lunging-line, the other end of which was attached to the stallion's halter. It had been a long demanding day, unusually hot for the month of May, and Rona was not inclined to share Starlena's humorous appreciation of the situation. But in the haste of her departure from the galvanized bucket which had admirably served as a seat at the heart of the lunging circle, the long flounced hem of her skirt caught twixt handle and hinge, dragging the whole wretched thing along the hard uneven ground with such gusto that it danced, jumped and clattered in an alarming fashion. The racket gave Rona a dreadful start, and frightened the horse so much that it fought to escape from the restraining lunge-line. Starlena laughed aloud so infectiously that once Rona had disentangled bucket from skirt and calmed the frightened animal, she too could not help but dissolve into a fit of laughter.

When she came back to the task of teaching the girl everything she herself knew about the handling of horses, her manner became altogether more serious. Now, with one hand on Starlena's shoulder and the other stroking the stallion's strong broad neck, she said, 'You see, child, this 'ere's a very special creature, and the first thing yer need to know about 'im is that 'e's a creature o' flight. Tetchy! Allus ready to spring away from yer at the drop of a blossom or the crack of a twig!' Here, her voice fell to an excited whisper and there spread over her kindly weather-worn features a dark intimate expression. 'Oh! But there ain't no creature the world over with such fascination – *none* quite like 'im! 'Orses is proud, child! Magnificent an' noble, servin' you one minute, an' like as not killing you the next! Unpredictable, that's what they are – an it's *that* as meks 'em so wonderfully exciting!' She smiled broadly and began to slide the flat of her hand all about the child's wild black hair, as though unconsciously attempting to bring its natural chaos into some kind of order. 'Ol' Nero 'ere, well, 'e might be comin' up nine year old, but 'e's spirited as a yearling still – an' dangerous! Ah, but that's the way we want it, eh? Don't want no sugar-sweet softie for a gal like yersel', eh? Oh, no! What we want is a creature wi' spunk – one like Nero 'ere, who's just this side of 'aving the *divil* in 'im!'

She looked down at the girl's upturned face, and as always she was struck by Starlena's astonishing beauty and spirit. This child, who made her every day an adventure, who made her existence worthwhile, never failed to amaze Rona – her unique innocence; her extravagantly stunning looks; every wonderful revelation of her warm adoring heart always ready to spill over with affection and laughter. She gazed into those large black eyes glowing from excitement, ran her fingers into the black mass of ringlets which sprang undisciplined across her neat little shoulders before falling almost down to the waist, and she gave thanks to God for his blessing. When she spoke now, her voice was without caution or excitement, softened by a great surge of love. 'D'you understand what I'm saying, child?' she asked.

Starlena looked up at her mammy. Her small heart was proud with love as she answered, 'Yes, I know what you're sayin', Mammy.' And she did! Wasn't her mammy special like no other? One day when she herself was growed, she too would know all about horses, 'cause her mammy would teach her. Then all the folks from far and wide would bring their horses to *her*. So she must listen hard to what her mammy was saying. 'Cause hadn't her mammy already said that she, Starlena, had got the gift?

Now she watched carefully as Rona put both her hands about Nero's head. 'Look, child. It's true a stallion's a law unto 'imself,' she said quietly, 'but there's a way o' fetchin' 'im to yer will. A special way. Watch.' Upon which she took the agitated animal's tossing head between her two hands, then leaning forward she began nuzzling his nose with hers, all the while gazing into his large moist eyes. Of a sudden her voice lowered to a small soft whisper, addressing the animal as one might address a lover.

Now, Rona began gently breathing into the stallion's flared and snorting nostrils, occasionally easing his head back towards her when, uncertain and nervous, he fought to pull away. When Rona at last sensed his calmness, she brought his head down, took the fleshy edge of his ear in her teeth, and into his ear made the smallest whistling sound – hardly audible to anyone but the animal itself.

Then, as Starlena gazed in wonder, both her mammy and the great stallion began slowly sinking to the ground, until Nero was lying on his side as though exhausted of all energy. Entranced, Starlena watched her, not daring to move, hardly daring to breathe in the presence of such magic!

'Oh, Mammy!' Starlena exclaimed incredulously. 'How did yer do that?' At which point, both woman and stallion rose upright. The animal was quiet and pawing the ground, and the woman explained that such a procedure was known as 'brekkin' under' – in the old days often used to show who was master.

'But I ain't seen it done for years! 'Appen folks 'ave forgot the old teachings, child. I'll tell yer one thing, though! Yer must *never* try it on a strange animal – 'specially a strange stallion. 'Cause as easy as they might go down, they can jest as quickly turn on yer with an evil vengence. Aye! It teks 'em both roads, child.'

'Will yer teach *me*, Mammy?' cried Starlena, her eyes still big and wide.

'Aye, lass, I'll teach yer – like me father taught me. Oh, but not till yer growed!' Seeing Starlena's disappointment she added, 'An' I'm thinkin' that'll not be too long, eh?'

Reaching down, she caught the girl up into an embrace, after which she put her down on the tree-trunk beside the stallion. Returning to her place in the circle's centre, she instructed briskly, 'Now! Mount the way I've showed yer!'

Starlena reached both hands up to the stallion's long dark mane, took a deep invigorating breath, and with one determined upward swing of her body, landed herself in the deep of Nero's back. The only obstacle was the fullness of her long cotton skirt. Then, gently touching her heels into him, she clicked him on – first at a walking pace, then into a canter. And as always, when she felt beneath her the muscular power of such a magnificent animal, with the wind whipping into her face and her whole being exhilarated, Starlena wanted more. She wanted to loose him! To give him his head across the open fields and let him take her where he would. As the fever of excitement mounted in her, so the animal sensed it through his every pore. At once he threw back his head, threatening at any moment to break into a full gallop.

'Woa! Woa, me beauty!' called Rona, seeing the bunching of the muscles in Nero's flank, her deeper instincts warning her of the stallion's intention. She was not displeased at Starlena's adventurous and uncautious spirit, but knew only too well how a full-grown and agitated stallion could very quickly get out of hand. Why, hadn't she seen poorer-spirited creatures spike a sizeable man into the ground when he thought himself to be in full charge of them? No!

You didn't give a stallion his head, not without you were twice over in command of it. As for a lass of Starlena's size – well, the very idea of her being let loose with Nero was enough to give Rona goose-pimples.

'That's enough for the day!' she called out, walking the stallion towards her by drawing in the lunge-line. And though she had been given a fright, Rona found herself gently smiling. By God! she thought, that Starlena is enough to strike the fear o' the divil into *anybody!* 'Yer a better jockey by the day, lass,' she told her, having brought both horse and rider to stand before her.

'Aw, Mammy! A little longer, eh? It *is* me birthday an' all.'

'Birthday or no birthday, Starlena Parrish, it's back we're goin'. Both on us fer a bite to eat, then wash an' bed.' Rona was already walking on with the animal alongside her and the girl on top, both more subdued than a few moments before.

Rona's thoughts ran on ahead. She had in her mind's eye the image of the man Jemm, together with his ten-year-old son, Anselo, and the younger girl, Celia. There was bad blood in that one. Bad blood which one day would surely find its outlet, to cause somebody a helpin' o' grief! Aw, there was reason to feel compassion fer the girl to a certain extent, 'cause hadn't her mother died of pneumonia some months back in the bleak winter, and her cowardly father tekken to his heels not long after? If the man Jemm hadn't given the orphaned girl a place to sleep, there's no tellin' *what* might have happened! All the same, thought Rona, that Celia was a bad lot. She'd seen it in the girl the first time she'd clapped eyes on her. And as the girl had grown, then so too had the badness.

It was Rona's intention to keep Starlena well away from her, for it was certain that the girl, Celia, carried a large measure o' hatred in her black heart, most of it unjustly directed towards Starlena. Oh, 't'was plain enough why. Envy! Jealousy! Call it what you will, there was no denying its vehemence and no denying its root! For that girl had cravings and eyes too old for her years, eyes for a boy by the name of Anselo – a boy too good fer the likes o' such a female. A boy who, like her own Starlena, thought nothing of such grown-up passions, but preferred to spend time climbing trees, chasin' the lurchers an' findin' things to laugh at. The girl, Celia, was an old head on young shoulders, grown before her time, egged on by her poor doting mother, who had seen much value in cultivating her daughter in the tradition handed down through ancestry. That same tradition dictated that, one day, Celia would be a gypsy queen!

They had come along the track from the clearing, then along by the wild bramble hedge. And now Rona led the stallion up towards the boundary wall of Whalley Grange. A little further on was an open field, and from there it was a short step to the camp where waited her wagon and that of the man Jemm. Poor fellow, Rona mused, him taking on that evil little creature, Celia, only to lose his own woman in childbirth some three weeks since. Strange how the Lord often repays a good turn with heartache, reflected Rona, shaking her head and mending her step to get them home the faster. With this in mind she set up humming a tune to match the whistling birds, her face lifted to the warm sun and her whole manner jaunty.

Starlena liked to hear her mammy singing. She liked it best of all when she was lying in bed at night and her mammy's singing sent her to sleep. At this very moment, with Nero carrying her home, her mammy up front, an' the sun playing peep-bo through the trees, she was happiest of all. Well – mebbe she was *almost* as happy when she was with that lovely Miss Elizabeth from the big house, 'cause she was so friendly an' dressed in such pretty things. Once, she even gave Starlena a dress – pink an' all frilled, with lots o' bows, an' cut down to fit! It was a real lady's dress, Starlena remembered. But she never did get to wear it, 'cause mammy made her take it straight back, sayin', 'That dress is fer a high-born lady, my gel! An' there's no place in our wagon fer that!' She'd never seen her mammy so angry. An' even though Starlena couldn't understand, Miss Elizabeth did, 'cause when she took the dress back, she just smiled her pretty smile an' said, 'Tell your mother I'm sorry. I should have known better'. All the same, Starlena really *wanted* that dress. An' what was more, she wanted to be one o' them 'high-born' ladies, too! Oh, but only if her mammy could be one as well!

At that same moment, Rona had come to think about what a good spot they'd found to camp these past years – and now through the late spring and summer, they would roam the length and breadth of this country, going across the splendid Yorkshire Dales and the Lancashire valleys looking for work on the land or collecting herbs and wood for selling in the market place. An' there hadn't been a year when the wagon ever failed to rumble across the borders into Cumbria, a place of enchantment with its rugged landscape and contrasting rolling green fields. Oh, aye! The two on 'em were seeing God's green acreage sure enough. But allus the old cob brought the wagon back home to Lancashire at the start o' winter. Back to this particular camp. A place that seemed to ward off the worst weather, being a sheltered hollow bounded on two sides by deep spinnies and having a fast-flowing brook close by as well.

Nearby was the big house known as Whalley Grange, the residence of a kindly-disposed old lady of considerable wealth and noble ancestry. An aged dowager who, far from sending out the gamekeeper with his shotgun as might many a land-owner, had sent out her manservant with food and blankets during the long hard winter just passed. And the young lady, Elizabeth, was a genuine friendly creature also, having taken a particular liking to Starlena. But while Rona was ever grateful, she was also made nervous by the presence of gentry – *any* gentry. It brought things back into her mind, disturbing things that she'd rather forget, which had prompted her to give Starlena a whole new birthday some few weeks past the occasion of her real one.

These past years, she'd mulled a whole heap o' things over in her mind, things to make her uneasy and restless. Such as a grand expensive bairn's shawl and a brooch set with glitterin' stones as fair blinded her! Strange, Rona thought, that even after puzzling her mind for hours there came no exact recollection of the place she'd stumbled on that night eight years ago. She remembered the man's wild and bearded face. She could see the serving-maid's big frightened eyes as she'd come across the brook out of the night. She recalled the long galleried landing with its procession of serious-faced pictures hanging the length of it, and could see, too, the richly-furnished room with its magnificent four-poster bed which held a poor wretched lady. But for all the puzzling she'd done, she knew neither the name nor setting of that grand place. Ah, but 'twasn't to be wondered at, she'd told herself, for the wanderin' an' fearful state she was in so soon after losin' her own man an' bairn! That night her mind weren't her own! Still an' all, it might have been a good thing were she to know of such a place. All the better to be sure and avoid it.

'Are you sulkin', Mammy?' Starlena asked, afraid she might have upset her mammy, who was unusually silent.

'Aw, no lass!' the hearty response was thrown back with a smile. 'Just thinkin', darlin'. Just thinkin'.' Rona's thoughts had made her subdued, but now she clicked the stallion forward at a faster pace, telling Starlena, 'Keep a tight 'old lass,' as Nero kicked out his back legs and threw back his head with a snort.

Holding fast to his mane with both hands, Starlena drew herself up towards the stallion's neck where she settled into a more comfortable and secure position, her little legs tight against his sides and now and then giving him a word of encouragement when he became fidgety.

Starlena had something on her mind, something which had strayed in and out of her thoughts since leaving the lunging-field. She knew how strict her mammy was about getting her washed and into bed as soon as ever it threatened darkness. But there was a good measure of light still left and time enough to do what she had in mind – if only her mammy would agree. Starlena wasn't too hopeful, but she was going to ask all the same!

'Mammy?' she ventured. 'It won't be dark for a while yet, will it?'

'Dark enough atime you've been fed, washed an' put to bed!' came back the answer. 'Why?'

'I've done well today, eh? I've ridden Nero better than ever. An' I've mounted him just like yer told me, haven't I, Mammy?' insisted Starlena.

'That yer 'ave, darlin'!' Rona laughed, turning her head to smile at Starlena. 'That yer 'ave.'

'Well then, I want to go an' tell Elizabeth at the big house. I know she'll be pleased!' There! thought Starlena. It was out!

For a long moment there came no response. And when at last Rona spoke, it was after all the answer Starlena had expected. 'You will not go to the big 'ouse, my gal! There'll be time enough fer that, tomorrow! An' it seems to me yer gettin' far too pally wi' that one!' Rona went on, a degree of impatience showing in spite of herself. Starlena was none too pleased yet none too surprised. Her mammy did sometimes get tetchy where Elizabeth was concerned. So she gave up the idea of arguing further, instead shrugging her shoulders in reluctant agreement. She knew only too well not to question her mammy too much. It was a pure waste of time.

When, some ten minutes later, Rona led the stallion into the camp, she was not surprised to see the elder seated as usual on his old wicker chair outside Jemm's wagon, his nutbrown weathered face closed in sleep and the familiar clay pipe clutched tight in the fist against his knee. Poor ol' soul! thought Rona, a pleasant smile wreathing her features as her gaze fell to where the two lurcher dogs flanked his spreadeagled feet. Some fifty yards or more away, the burly figure of his son, Jemm, could be seen bent over his wood-chopping, his deep voice lifted in a gypsy song. His handsome ten-year-old son, Anselo, was busy stacking the chopped sticks into a round wicker basket, he too raising his voice in accompaniment to his father. So immersed in song and work were they, that neither saw Rona's approach. And as Rona's gaze was directed towards them, she did not notice the quick movement at the door of her own wagon.

But from her high vantage point, Starlena saw it. And she saw the girl, Celia, closing the wagon door behind her, and on careful feet beginning to slink away down the steps, her arms jealously clutching an uneven and ragged bundle.

With a cry of 'Mammy! She's been in the wagon!' Starlena slid from the stallion's back and raced towards the foot of the wagon steps, where Celia stood seemingly frozen in her tracks, her eyes starting, not in fear, but in fury at having been discovered.

94

Suddenly chaos was let loose as Starlena threw herself at the girl and the two of them fought furiously. At the same time, both lurchers bounded forward and ran in a feverish circle round the struggling girls, yapping ferociously and intending to attack at any moment. But Jemm and Anselo ran to catch them by their collars. While Anselo held both animals his father grabbed each girl apart by the scruff of her neck.

Taken by surprise at the incident, Rona lost no time in tethering the stallion alongside the old cob, then straightway hurrying to where Jemm still had a secure hold on the girls to keep them apart, as they each still had a mind to flay the other alive.

'Wildcats!' declared Jemm to Rona. 'Bloody wildcats, set to tear out each other's throats!'

Starlena was the first to move. She took from the ground the bundle with which Celia had been intent on making away.

'Look, Mammy!' She ran to where Rona stood, her eyes already taking in the significance of the ragged bundle. 'She was stealin' from our wagon! She had this!' She held up the shawl, its delicate silk embroidery dirtied in the struggle, but its beauty and quality nevertheless unmistakable. As Starlena raised it to her mammy's outstretched arms, the setting sunlight played upon it, searching out the brooch pinned carefully to one corner and drawing out the colour of the stones, to dance and glitter and to light up the eyes of those watching.

'By! How in the name o' Jesus did yer come across such a thing?' Jemm spoke in awe, bringing himself to touch the brooch with reverent fingers. 'That's *real*. That ain't no trinket. Anybody can see that!'

Rona saw the look in his dark eye, and she was afraid. Snatching both shawl and brooch into her arms, she deliberately forced his attention back to Celia, saying sharply, 'That girl's got no right in my wagon! You know that, Jemm! An' it meks no difference *what* she took. The fact is she's been rummaging through somebody else's belongings. Broken a strict rule o' trust! She's a thief! A *thief*, Jemm!' One wrong word and Rona would have taken it on herself to punish the girl, for if gypsies didn't have much, they had

95

a strong code of honour, and in doing what she had, the girl had committed a sin. It pleased Rona to see the watching elder furtively nodding his head in full agreement with her angry words. And as she had suspected, Jemm also began to appreciate the seriousness of the situation.

Turning his attention from Rona and her precious bundle, he strode with some determination to where Celia stood, her stance proud and her hazel eyes sparkling defiance in the dying sun's rays. It was obvious to all that she felt no repentance or shame for what she had done.

'Did you go into Rona's wagon?' he demanded.

'Yes!' was the defiant answer.

'And you stole … you took things from the wagon?' When there was no response he became angry. 'Answer me!'

'Yes, I did!' came the retort. 'And I'm not sorry!' Tossing her head towards Rona and Starlena, she added vehemently, 'Who are they to have such special things?'

Jemm gave no answer. Instead, with a look of dark anger on his face, he gripped his hand about the girl's shoulder and pushing her forward, he made towards the area where only minutes ago he had been contented to sing and chop wood with his son. As he passed Rona he muttered in a low tone, 'And her of "Kaulo Ratti".'

This caused Starlena to ask in a whisper, 'What's "Kaulo Ratti", Mammy?'

Rona replied softly, 'It's the gypsy mother-tongue for "dark blood". An' it means she's the true descendant of a noble and royal tribe – over whom one day she'll be queen.'

This at first filled Starlena with awe. Until, of a sudden, she recalled the sneaky thieving nature of the girl, Celia. Whereupon, in a tone of disgust, she told Rona, 'That don't mean *nothing*, Mammy! 'Cause she's still a thief!'

Anselo, being close by and overhearing Starlena's comment, caught her eye. Then, coming close, he said 'I'm sorry Celia's tekken things from yer wagon, Starlena. She'll be punished. An' I'm sure when she's had time to think on it, she'll tell yer how sorry *she* is too!' He looked deep into Starlena's shining eyes, his own glittering with threatened tears. And of a sudden, it came to Starlena just how fond Anselo was of that awful girl, who to her was a thief, but to this kind dark-eyed boy was like his own sister, of whom he was so obviously fond.

'It's not *your* fault, Anselo,' she said in as gentle and reassuring tone as she knew how. She liked Anselo – liked him a lot. And she knew that he liked *her* also.

The boy said nothing in reply, but appeared pleased at her response. And with a nod of his dark curly head he turned away, to stride in the opposite direction to where his father was at that very moment meting out punishment to Celia, by means of a flat sharp willow twig brought down time and time again on the back of her bare legs.

The evening was uncomfortably humid. And in the stifling hours of dark, sleep seemed elusive to both Starlena and Rona; the two of them fidgeting and turning in the narrow confined bed, until in the small hours when it seemed that, finally, Starlena had fallen asleep, Rona eased herself from the bed. Then, after wrapping the long knitted day-shawl about her shoulders, she went stealthily out of the wagon and across the open space immediately before it. Coming to rest at the mouth of the spinney, she leaned wearily against the broad trunk of an oak tree, her brown eyes looking back at the wagon, and her restless mind thinking on the events of the day.

There was a churning uneasiness inside her – about the girl – about the beating Jemm had given her. And most of all, Rona was deeply concerned at the discovery of brooch and shawl. This very night, Starlena had been full of questions concerning it! Questions to which Rona had no suitable answers – not yet. But she would need to find some, and quick. For Starlena was a persistent little creature and would not now let the matter go easily. That brooch and shawl spelled trouble, as Rona had suspected they might. But she could not let them be sold, for her instincts told her they would be safer in her own keeping. And their value might also one day prove to be a life-saver when she was too aged to provide for herself and the bairn.

'You can't sleep either, eh?' The low voice startled Rona, until in the moonlight she saw it was Jemm.

'No,' she replied, pulling the shawl tight about her.

He held up his arm, to display two plump rabbits dangling from the string between his fingers. 'I couldn't sleep neither, so thought I'd track down tomorrow's dinner.' He searched Rona's thoughtful face and said in a subdued voice, 'She should never a' gone in yer wagon, Rona. All the same, I took no pleasure in leatherin' the girl.'

'It gave me none either!' said Rona, although she knew it had been the right thing to do. She smiled up at him, saw a certain measure of kindness in his dark eyes and admired the cut of his strong craggy features. She felt a little comforted.

Jemm was also taking stock. He saw before him a woman of good able character who, in spite of being alone save for a small daughter, wanted for nothing, for she worked hard and provided well. He saw a woman of some forty years, a little worn and past her best, but a darkly handsome woman all the same. And whether it was because of these things, or whether it was the effect of the moonlight – or indeed perhaps because of a certain expensive and jewelled brooch – he was moved to ask more closely, 'Rona Parrish, would you ever consider tekkin' me fer yer 'usband?'

Rona thought it strange that she wasn't surprised by such a proposal. But then, hadn't she felt it in her bones for a long time now? Hadn't his wagon always seemed to follow hers? Yet she couldn't say yes, and she couldn't say no. Dropping her gaze she would have excused herself and made haste back to the wagon. But Jemm touched her hand and said, 'There's time enough! Yer needn't tell me yer answer 'ere an' now.' After which, he abandoned the subject and went on to discuss the merits of poaching, an' the problems of being a poor man who'd tekken on the role of a certain girl's father.

The same girl was now looking from the wagon window, her hazel eyes afire with a burning emotion. She loathed Rona and her girl, Starlena – loathed them with such ferocity that it hurt! And it would be a long long time before she ever forgave Jemm! He'd shamed her in front of Anselo and the others. He'd thrashed her like she was a common diddicoi – and she of a *royal* tribe! Oh, she wouldn't forget in a hurry, that was fer sure. In her vindictive thoughts, the germ of an idea took root. In her fevered mind it grew and opened until she could see nothing else. And uppermost in it was the girl, Starlena – whose very name caused her to tremble with hatred.

Starlena woke to find her mammy gone. In a rush of anxiety, she lifted herself out of the bed and went to the door. Easing back the threadbare cherry-red curtains, she peeked out of the window. What she saw was her mammy deep in conversation with Jemm, and she was alarmed. Like her mammy said though, he had 'seen a deal o' grief lately' and he seemed a good man. Starlena heard the two of them gently laughing, and contented in herself, she went quickly back to bed, soon after to be joined by her mammy who, until the two of them got to snuggling close, had brought the chill of the night air in as well.

Sinking into deeper sleep, neither Rona nor Starlena were aware of the small figure which silently emerged from the nearby wagon, a dark evil look on her face, in her hand a stout spiteful-looking whip.

It was some short time later, in the darkest hour before dawn, when the whole camp was abruptly awakened by high-pitched screams intermingled with the frantic whinnying of a frightened and furious horse. The sight which greeted her on scrabbling from her bed recalled a nightmare to Rona, of the time she had lost her man, Leum. Yelling for Starlena to 'stay put', she ran outside to where the stallion was feverishly pitching himself again and again at the nearby wagon, his flailing hoofs cut and bleeding as he relentlessly thumped them into the wood which now began to splinter beneath the onslaught, sending all occupants running from inside. All save one! For the girl, Celia, was already outside, crouched beneath the wagon, her eyes filled with terror as the horse tried desperately to seek her out and to treat her to the same pain that she had inflicted on him.

Seeing that it was Nero who seemed to have gone mad, Starlena ran from the wagon. Amidst all the confusion and noise and in her eagerness to quieten the animal she might herself have tumbled beneath the stallion's hooves, had it not been for Rona catching and restraining her, saying in a firm voice, 'Back inside the wagon, Starlena! And stay there!' At the same time she thrust the girl from her and watched as she ran up the steps into the wagon, from where she could look out at the beloved Nero, who was in such frenzy that he would not be easily calmed. She saw Rona attempting to calm him, and she saw Anselo take the elder to a safe place. She watched as Jemm ran back into the shaking wagon, shouting to the crouching Celia to 'keep back'. On his swift return Starlena watched as he raised the shot-gun high to the stallion's head. On the resounding shot that followed, the proud horse fell to the ground, where he lay mortally wounded, his magnificent body shivering in nervous spasms, until another shot rang out and he was still.

There followed an eerie silence, tempered only by the breeze murmuring through the branches overhead, which dipped and danced in a curious slow motion, their spreading fingers silhouetted by the moon's yellow glow and soon rendered motionless with the dying of the breeze.

Running out to the felled stallion, Starlena brushed past Rona's restraining hand. Seeing Nero's wide eyes dark and empty, she fell on his neck and burying her face into his, she sobbed as though her heart would break. 'Nero, Nero,' she murmured through her tears, as though in calling his name she would call him back to life.

Rona had not moved. Her eyes were heavy with grief as she gazed from the shocked Anselo and the silent elder, to Jemm, still charged with emotion as with shot-gun by his side he went to draw out Celia from beneath the wagon. What Rona saw on the girl's face was unmistakable. There was a look of pleasure, a badly-disguised smile of satisfaction. And as she witnessed Starlena's pitiful grief, her expression turned to a deep gloating. Rona took note of all this. She looked again at Jemm, in whose home this evil child was rooted and she knew without a shadow of doubt that never could she give herself in wedlock to him. Never!

On weary feet, Rona went to where Starlena in anguish was

wrapped about the stallion's neck. Stooping, she gently withdrew the small clinging figure. Then, with Starlena safe in her arms, she stumbled back to the wagon. In a hard voice she said to Jemm, 'Don't touch him! Leave him be!'

The man resented Rona's accusing glare. He glanced helplessly at the sobbing child in her arms. In his mind's eye he saw the fancy shawl and the valuable brooch, whose precious stones spelled out the name Kathleen – Kathleen and the beginning of another which he could not fully distinguish, but which began with 'B'. As he mulled the whole thing over in his mind, two things emerged. One was that he had now lost any chance of taking the woman as his wife. The other was a feeling of curiosity and greed for he knew the brooch did not rightly belong to Rona Parrish. How could it, being precious as it was, and bearing another woman's initials?

He now ushered everyone before him into the wagon, and as he climbed the steps, he wondered what to do and how best to benefit himself from what he considered to be a little touch of luck! Did he know enough of Rona Parrish's background to follow a discreet but particular line of enquiry? It was a thought, but not one to rob him of any sleep.

Strange how though filled with anxiety and uncomfortable from grief, a body must finally succumb to the balming influence of sleep. But even in the cradle of sleep, Starlena could see over and over the stallion sinking to the ground, the life swiftly ebbing from him. She sensed his anguish and felt his pain. More than that, she felt a part of herself dying with him! Images of his sleek black body played in her fitful mind; of the proud way he had held his magnificent head, of how he had moved, whether at full gallop or whether at a slow deliberate walk. Starlena had known that beautiful stallion all of her life. She had walked beside him, had been allowed to sit on his warm rough back, and had felt the heat of his blood and sensed the beating of his heart against her skin. And oh, how she had admired him! How she loved him! Now he was no more and Starlena thought her heart would burst inside her.

For what seemed like hours, Rona had lain awake, comforting

as best she could the girl who clung fearfully to her, and who went on sobbing long after she'd fallen asleep. Until at last she, too, gave herself up to the night and uneasy slumber.

When Starlena awoke, her first thought was for Nero. Carefully now, she eased herself from the bed so as not to wake her mammy. Then, without waiting to dress, she silently opened the wagon door and crept away. The sharp morning air was not yet warmed by the sun and struck chilly through her nightgown.

As she approached the stallion's body, Starlena was overcome by sensations both alien and hurtful. Falling to her knees before him, she gazed on his poor wretched form, wondering how it was that something which had been so vibrantly alive could of a sudden be so very silent and still. Reaching out a small tender hand, she stroked his neck, the hard coldness sending a shock right through her. 'Oh, Nero!' she said, not in the wild grief of the night before, but in a quiet sadness which left the tears silently falling, wrenching from her an overwhelming feeling of loneliness. The new emotions within her stole forever that special innocence which spans that time between child and woman. There came into her heart a new awareness which puzzled and frightened her, bringing with it a fierce protective instinct towards the only other who lived in her heart – her precious mammy.

Bowed in remembrance and with eyes only for the fallen stallion, Starlena didn't hear her mammy come up behind her. Only when the shawl was slid about her shoulders did she sense her comforting presence. Then, as she continued gently to stroke Nero's neck, she sensed that something was not right. She had stroked his neck so many times before and knew every inch of it. Now, her sensitive fingers alerted Starlena to something different – something not natural to him.

Leaning forward to examine the area as she again ran her fingers over it, Starlena perceived a long ridge of raised and broken skin, edging a deep ugly gash which ran the whole length of Nero's neck. At once she was on her feet, pulling at her mammy's hand. 'Whipmarks! They're *whipmarks*, Mammy! On his neck!' she cried. Rona went to her knees and saw they were indeed marks made by the forceful lash of a whip. Now she examined the stallion more closely, and found more of the very same marks across his chest and flanks. Then, incensed by the implications, she looked about and sure enough, there in the undergrowth was the vicious whip which had evidently been used against the stallion.

It was only now when they turned with the intention of confronting the culprit that both Starlena and Rona realized that Jemm's wagon was gone!

'Like thieves in the night!' exclaimed Rona, her grief at Nero's death replaced now by a surge of fury.

'We'll see them again, won't we, Mammy?' asked Starlena in a strange voice.

The sound alerted Rona to the danger of emotions which, if allowed to grow, could be overpowering and destructive. With Starlena's well-being in mind, she answered carefully, 'What's done is done, child. We'll not chase the country after that little vixen. Nor will we let our every day be marred by a desire to come upon that particular wagon. Instead, we'll learn from this day. But now it's over, we'll forget it as best we can.' Then seeing the surprise on Starlena's face, she insisted, 'I want yer to promise me, child. Yer'll not let this eat away at yer? Put it out of yer mind. Promise me!'

'She *did* it, Mammy! She thrashed Nero, an' that's why he attacked the wagon.'

'I know – at least we *think* that's what 'appened. But we can't be sure, can we, eh?'

'We can ask her! Make her tell the truth!' protested Starlena, who couldn't understand why her mammy didn't go after them this very minute!

'Did yer 'ear what I said, Starlena? I want yer to put it out o' yer mind. We can't accuse if we're not sure, yer must understand!' Rona was fearful of the consequences should this turn into some kind of vendetta. Starlena must be kept from thoughts of vengeance!

'Yer *will* put it out o' yer mind, won't yer, child?' she asked anxiously. Then, when Starlena gave a reluctant nod, she clasped the girl to her. 'That's a good lass,' she said. 'Yer mammy would never ask yer to do the wrong thing, would she, eh?'

'No, Mammy.' Starlena wasn't fully convinced. But she must trust her mammy an' go by what she said.

As for Rona, her thoughts dwelt on two things. One, she would keep as much of God's country between Starlena and that divil's daughter, Celia, as was humanly possible. And secondly, should there ever come the opportunity to repay her for the bad deed she'd done, then she, Rona, would take it up whole-heartedly!

Clasped in each other's arms, it was a while before either Starlena or Rona realized that there was a third person present. When that person stepped forward, it was Miss Elizabeth, the girl from the big house, looking, Starlena thought, like an angel, with her long bright fair hair and big sad blue eyes. Now, pulling her flowing grey cloak tight about her, she brought those kindly eyes to gaze on the stallion, saying quietly, 'Some of the household said the shots were coming from the woods to the west . . . poachers, they thought. But I had a feeling they were much closer. What happened?' she asked.

'An accident!' came Rona's immediate response. 'An accident, best forgotten.' She loosed Starlena from her and, addressing herself politely to the visitor, she said, 'I'll away an' get a shovel – 'e needs burying proper.' She turned away towards the wagon, leaving Starlena to rush into Elizabeth's comforting arms. Yet she too would not answer any questions, mindful of her mammy's instructions. All she would tell her friend was there had been an accident, and now, sadly, poor Nero was dead. In the act of saying it, she began crying, whereupon Miss Elizabeth told her, 'Take heart. And see what surprises might follow!'

By the time Rona returned, having unstrapped a spade from beneath the wagon, Starlena was alone, her unhappiness somewhat tempered by the visit of her friend, who had left abruptly.

'Give *me* the spade, Mammy!' she said, holding out her hands, with a look of determination on her face.

Rona looked at the small sturdy figure before her, at the little hands, then at the great cumbersome spade. She marked the fiery determination in those coal-black eyes, still wet with tears. And her heart swelled with love.

'Aw, child,' she said in a hoarse voice, 'you'd best leave this to me, eh?'

Then, fearful of the choking emotion which threatened to spill out in tears, she strode to a small clearing nearby, where with a swift slicing movement she thrust the spade deep into the turf. 'We'll put Nero 'ere,' she told Starlena, who had followed and was standing by her side, intent on helping.

Later, when Rona looked back on it, she thought that it was the hardest thing she'd ever done; not only because of the pain it caused her to put such a proud creature beneath the ground before his time, but also because of the sheer physical effort of first making a hole big and deep enough, then of actually dragging the stallion across the ground the short way to his last resting place. For the latter, she'd had to employ the great strength of the old cob. But for the digging of the hole, it was pure grit and perseverance. And what Rona would not forget for as long as she lived, was her child, Starlena. For, against her mammy's protests, and seeing how drained the woman was, the child had taken the spade, climbed down into that deep dark hole where, with the sweat dripping from her and the blisters rising on her hands, she had given of her little best. Until, between these two determined and devoted friends of that faithful stallion, the job was done – with even a little prayer murmured over him. After which Rona observed, ''E might 'a fotched a few bob at the knacker's yard, but Nero's been like a friend to me, lass. An' I'll not do that to 'im!'

By late afternoon, when woman and child had eaten a light meal consisting mostly of fruit and cheese, the two of them stripped off in the warm sun and, confident of their privacy, they had taken themselves down to where the brook became a pond, and there they lazed and swam about beneath the weeping-willow, whose branches draped like a giant umbrella.

It was some three hours later that Rona found Starlena seated on a boulder some way from camp. The spot was a particular favourite of both Rona and Starlena, so whenever the one went missing, the other would always know where to look. The area was one of outstanding beauty. From this one vantage point could be seen for miles and miles the valleys and hamlets across an expanse of Lancashire. From the top of the high hill, the green fields fell away in a gently rolling undulation until some four miles in the distance they merged with a small wood. Then they appeared again beyond, and from there they stretched away as far as the eye could see. The whole magnificent panorama was breathtaking, awing the onlooker into a profound silence.

'Dreaming, are ye, me darlin'?' Rona came up to seat herself on the boulder beside the child. The two of them gazed out across the world's expanse and lost themselves in the trembling wonder of it all.

'What's the name o' this place, Mammy?' asked Starlena at last. She had been there many times with her mammy, and had always delighted in its awesome beauty. But she wondered now whether such loveliness had a name. It *ought* to have a name, she thought.

'It's called Whistledown Valley.'

'Whistledown Valley?' Starlena murmured the name as though savouring it. It gave her a warm contented feeling. 'Oh, Mammy!' she breathed. 'That's a lovely, lovely name!'

Rona smiled and, taking the girl under the arm, she said, ' 'Twas given the name, oh, many years afore you or I were born, lass. 'Tis said that on a certain day in a certain month, the whole valley comes alive – moanin' and singin' like the wind were suddenly let loose from the top o' this place, to dance an' whistle all the way down!'

Starlena was entranced. 'Is that *true*, Mammy?' she asked.

'Well, I don't know, lass. 'Tis sortah o' legend.'

Starlena fell silent, mulling over what her mammy had just told her. And yes! It *was* true – she *knew* it! This place was magic, she could feel it all over her. She belonged here – wanted to belong. She remembered something her mammy had told her a while back: that she'd been birthed special. That one day her mammy would tell her about the fine gossamer that had covered her skin and would help keep her safe.

Suddenly, oh, so many questions pushed themselves into

Starlena's mind that it threatened to burst open if they were not asked right away.

'Was I born here, Mammy?' she asked, hoping desperately for the right answer. 'Here, in Whistledown Valley?'

Rona gave a small laugh. Whatever gave the child *that* idea, she wondered, seeing at the same time the merits of encouraging such an idea. The child would want to know the place and manner of her birth, as a body had a right to! The truth could not be told, oh no! So what was she to say to this delightful and sensitive girl? Would she confess that for eight years and more, from that fateful night in 1898, right up to this day in the month of May, 1906, she, Rona Parrish – the woman Starlena called Mammy and who for all that child's life had *been* her mammy – was *not*? Could she tell her how on the night of Starlena's birth, her own wretched mammy had left this world? And how, in the most terrible fit, her blood-father had threatened to squeeze the life from his newborn daughter? Could she then relate how Starlena was not a true Romany destined forever to wander God's free and open sky, but was instead a real high-born creature, more high-born even than Elizabeth? Would Rona ever find it in her heart to tell her only child that she came of aristocratic breeding and great fortune? No! No, she never would. Because above and beyond her own heartbreak should she ever be called on to give the child back, there remained in Rona a deep-seated instinct that in that grand house there was evil! Evil that night! And evil still! Every bone in her body told her that there was mortal danger for her darling Starlena. And she was never to go back! Never. *Never!*

'Was I, Mammy?' Starlena sensed her mammy slipping into one of those strange silent moods which took her such a long way away. And shaking her mammy's arm she insisted, 'Was I born in this place?' Then when the answer was given that, 'Yes darlin', you were born 'ere in Whistledown Valley', her small heart soared and clapping her hands together, she laughed. 'I knew it! Oh, Mammy, I *knew* I belonged to this place!'

For a moment, Rona stayed silent, her own heart happy on behalf of the child. It struck her also that she herself must have been blind all this time; for she ought to have known that a body by its very nature must have some sort of roots. She herself had been given a measure of belonging by her own mam very many years ago. In fact, Rona's mother had birthed her in a spot not far from this very place, alongside Billinge Gate near Blackburn. All the details had been told her, how it had been a freezing cold day in the darkest of winter, the snow two feet thick, and her mam had started labour three weeks before her time. Rona recalled the pleasure she had felt when all of this was told her.

Now drawing the girl against her, she placed a hand either side of that wide-awake and strikingly beautiful little face. Smiling into it, she said, 'Aye, lass! Yer *do* belong 'ere. My little whistledown woman! That's what ye are!' Then, when Starlena fell against her with a giggle and a hug, Rona squeezed her tight, saying, 'Shall I tell yer 'ow it was, the night ye were birthed, lass?' On Starlena's eager nod, Rona began to tell how her child had come into the world. It hurt her to look into Starlena's shining eyes and know how she must deceive her. Yet the story Rona told was no lie – for it was a poignant recollection concerning the birthing of the baby girl long lost to her and now in Leum's keeping. And as she remembered, so did the image grow strong of the horse and rider who took them away from her. She had not forgotten, and she never would.

'So there ye are, lass,' she concluded. 'That's 'ow yer come into the world, easy an' beautiful! In yon very wagon, parked atop o' Whistledown Valley, with yer poor daddy so thrilled 'e were runnin' about like a dog wi' two tails!'

Starlena had paid great attention to all of this. But now, at the mention of her daddy, she asked, 'What was he like, my daddy!'

The question caught Rona unawares. When she gave her carefully-considered answer, it was in a broken voice and with a great hard lump blocking her throat. 'Leum was a good man. One o' the very best!' she murmured half to herself and half to the attentive child.

'No bairn ever had a better father, and no woman ever a better 'usband.'

108

'An' tell me again of the accident that took him from us, Mammy,' urged Starlena, her whole manner bristling in an attitude of defence. 'About that wicked man who ran his horse into the cart.'

Rona had related the truth of that particular incident to Starlena, to explain the absence of a daddy, but had left out the tragic death of her little bairn. For to all accounts and purposes Starlena had been that bairn, and like her mammy had survived the ordeal.

Suddenly Rona felt again the acute loss of that night. She resisted any further discussion of it just now. 'Look, I've some'at to show yer,' she told Starlena, changing the subject and directing the girl's interest in another direction.

Starlena had noticed the ploy, but said nothing. Instead, she watched with great interest as her mammy dipped a hand inside her loose green blouse, slowly drawing from within it what Starlena took to be a piece of patterned print, small and misshapen. Then, as her mammy carefully unfolded it, she saw too that it was not without shape altogether. For it became a tiny pouch, delicately stitched and embroidered, the whole miniature creation drawn up into a pretty frilled rouche at the mouth – by means of a long and attractive attachment made of the finest stripped lace, which was beautifully plaited into an exquisite necklace. 'Oh, Mammy!' Starlena had never seen the like. 'Did you mek it?' she questioned.

'Aye. 'Twas med fer a particular precious thing, Starlena. Inside o' this tiny pouch is a gift, a special gift from God to you,' explained Rona, handling the pouch reverently, as now she reached two fingers inside it, and drew out a small rolled-up piece of white silk. Then, laying the pouch into the deep safe folds of her skirt, she proceeded carefully to undo the roll to expose what Starlena imagined might be some sort of spider's web, so delicate and intricately woven it was – yet of the strangest intriguing colours, which might be described as the subdued red of a newly hatched bird, or the crimson-purple of a magic sky, and marbled into the whole was a rich velvet-blackness.

'What *is* it, Mammy?' Starlena asked incredulously.

Quietly now, and at the same time folding it back into the pouch, Rona told her. 'This is a "caul" – the gossamer skin which covered yer little face the night ye were birthed. Oh, it's something to be cherished, me darlin', 'cause very few people are given such a gift.' She went on to explain how such a thing would keep Starlena safe, and how she must always keep the pouch about her person. Now she put it round Starlena's neck, tucking it close to her skin and out of sight. After which, Starlena hugged her mammy extra hard, wondering how it was that she had been so blessed.

The next day was Saturday. Because both Starlena and Rona were still deeply mindful of what had happened to their beautiful and sorely-missed stallion, Rona suggested that the two of them should trek the long and pleasant way into Manchester. This suggestion was enthusiastically received by Starlena, who quickly set about getting the cob ready, just in case her mammy had a sudden change of heart.

Rona thought she might go a-duckerin', which she explained to Starlena was the gypsy word for fortune-telling, a skill she had been taught by her old mammy. 'An' we'll tek two o' them rush-mats I've not long finished, lass,' she instructed, amused when besides the two, Starlena brought out the one she herself had been practising on, and which was neither finished nor pretty.

'Shall us tek *this* one, too?' she asked, her little face alight with pride. Seeing how eager she was, Rona had to think of a way to let her down lightly, for to show that one in such a sorry state might cost the sale of the others. So, taking the mat in her hands, she pretended to look it over with pride saying, 'Aw, child, this is such a clever piece o' work, an' yer very first effort. I think we'll keep it fer us own little fireside, eh?'

Starlena swelled with pride. She gave her mammy a hug, and ran back up the steps into the wagon, where with great deliberation and much fussing, she positioned the sorry little mat in front of the stove.

Not long after, it being still only seven o'clock on a morning which held all the promise of a glorious day to follow, Starlena climbed up behind her mammy, and together atop the old grey cob, they set off towards the brook, from there to the locks, and after to follow the long winding canal all the way into Manchester.

It being a Saturday, the streets about the market-place were unusually busy with people thronging to purchase the goods sold from the many stalls. Ladies dressed in long flounced frocks and pretty crocheted shawls, were already swarming the flagged pavements, all heading for an early bargain with their wicker baskets hooked over their arms and a look of bargaining power about their determined expressions.

Children bowled their hoops along the cobble-stones, laughing and dodging as the wandering mongrels seemed set to dive in and join the fun. And all about the market-place itself there was an air of festivity and great excitement. This affected Starlena to such a degree that it was a hard thing for her even to sit still on the old cob's back, as she pointed out this and that, her dark eyes merry and her feet impatient to get down.

Even the old cob seemed to get caught up in all the excitement, for when at last a suitable pitch was found he took great delight in snorting and nuzzling with a piebald shire who, according to Rona, was 'a right flighty piece!'

The two rush mats were sold, one to a stooped elderly man with a ducks-head walking-stick, the other to a thin nervous girl who shyly told Rona that she'd not long been married, and hoped her husband would appreciate her considered purchase. Rona replied that the mat would serve them well for years to come.

Starlena was curious to see how the bonneted and beshawled ladies queued up boldly to have their fortunes told, placing a silver coin in her mammy's outstretched and wrinkled hand before being told all manner of secrets in a hushed and mysterious voice. After which they came away all pleased and with their faces a bright shade of pink. Starlena made her mammy promise to teach her the duckerin' gift when she was growed.

When the hubbub of the market began to die down and the people started to go home, Rona counted the cache of silver coins, gave a satisfied grunt and untethering the old cob, she quickly swung herself up on his back. Then she gripped Starlena's hand and swung her up too.

'A good day, lass!' smiled Rona as they set off by way of the back streets, 'an' I think we'll treat us-selves afore we mek tracks back 'ome, eh?'

So, squashed up to her mammy and content to enjoy the cornet-shaped bag of pink fleshy shrimps bought for a few coppers from the white-pinnied shrimp-ladies round the market, Starlena sat swaying to the rhythmic ambling of the old cob, as all three tired but happy creatures made a leisurely path into the darker back-streets, Rona being intent on her destination, which was Queen Victoria Street and a quaint old second-hand shop situated some half way down.

Once there, the two riders alighted. Then the cob's leather reins were wrapped securely round a fluted iron lamp-post, while Starlena ran ahead to gaze through the bulbous dimpled window-panes, behind which were piled artefact upon artefact, each different in shape, size, colour and function from the other.

Upon the clattering of the great brass bell, which hung silently above the door until provoked into thumping echoes by the entrance of customers, there emerged a little crooked man by the name of Tolly Shuttleworth, the same kindly human who, during the recent bad weather, had paid Rona a whole shilling over the value of a load of firewood. Now, she intended to buy from *him* – that was, if he might have such a thing as a musical-record for playing on a wind-up grammy-phone.

'I have!' he told her, his shiny bald pate bobbing with such zeal that Starlena felt his small egg-shaped head was set to tumble right off its skinny mounting.

There followed a most delightful hour of hustle and bustle, with Rona searching through a wooden crate for a big black musical-record, while Starlena rummaged in every cobwebbed corner of that magic place, trying on a handsome shawl, or a big straw hat with long curling feathers which dangled down to tickle her nose and tease her neck, lifting the heavy lid of a black tin chest to reveal such a fright that she cried out, only to collapse in a fit of laughter when she realized that the fox was no longer alive and those sharp piercing eyes could not really see her. Taking it gingerly from the chest, she draped it loosely about her neck, and stroked the red

112

silken fur with great reverence, at one point even daring to place her finger between those razor-sharp and evil-looking teeth. Then, with the grand shawl about her shoulders, reaching right down to the floorboards, the fox-fur elegant around her neck, and on top of her head a fancy wide-brimmed straw hat with admirable feathers, Starlena strutted about the shop, spending much time preening herself before a full-length mirror on a swivel frame, which tried her temper when it insisted on swinging into a horizontal position just as she had herself nicely framed like a picture! All of this was much to the amusement of her mammy and the crooked little man. All the same, such mischief did not dampen her absolute delight at the image she presented in that disobedient mirror. For she looked every inch a lady, almost as fine as Miss Elizabeth, she thought.

And when they finally departed the shop for the homeward journey, Rona with a musical-record and Starlena with a feathery hat some three sizes too big for her, it was 'Miss Elizabeth' who was waiting with a surprise to make this adventurous day even more wonderful. Dressed in a pretty blue frock with tight ruffed collar and pleated ankle-length skirt, Miss Elizabeth looked lovely, although it crossed Rona's mind on seeing that pale narrow face and the eyes of such a soft delicate blue that this young lady was not of strong constitution, and was likely to depart this world before making old bones.

Starlena quickly alighted from the old cob and ran to meet her friend. Miss Elizabeth told her, 'I've brought you something.' Then glancing at Rona, who was tethering the old cob to a luscious patch of green grass, she went on, 'That is, providing your mammy doesn't mind.'

'Well now, that'll depend,' replied Rona, coming to stand aside Starlena. 'What is it you've brought the lass?' She looked Miss Elizabeth up and down, then looked about and could see nothing by way of a 'present'. The only thing evident besides the young visitor was the bay mare which had accompanied her, and which now stood with some impatience, eager to loose her head from the restraining bridle, constantly tugging at the reins in the girl's hands and chomping at the bit in her mouth.

Now Miss Elizabeth inclined her head towards the animal, at the same time asking Rona, 'What do you think of her?'

At once Rona became all horsewoman, stroking her face and regarding the mare first this way then that. 'Hmm – nice animal,' she said, running her sensitive fingers down its four legs in turn, then over its flanks, after which she prised open its mouth with her two hands, peered inside with great deliberation, and having done so, stepped back to take a more general view.

All this time, Starlena watched her mammy's every move, now and then exchanging a secretive smile with Miss Elizabeth. Both waited for the gypsy-woman's verdict.

'That's a quality animal,' came Rona's considered opinion. 'Good temperament an' clean lines. Top breeding, that's fer sure!'

'The best!' remarked Miss Elizabeth. 'I've got all her papers, showing that she comes from a line of champion stock. Have you noticed anything else about her?'

'D'yer mean that she's in foal these, what – seven, eight weeks?'

'You certainly know your horses! Yes, she *is* in foal – and by one of the best stallions in the country. You've no doubt heard of the Wyman strain?'

'I have! A racin' line bred specially fer that purpose. Aye! They're known well.' Rona loved to talk about horses and as she'd pointed out, the strain cultivated and bred by the Wyman family, wealthy aristocrats who owned more property and land that anyone on God's earth had a right to, were among the finest horses ever. Oh, not that the likes of her sort would ever be fortunate enough to own one. But on the few occasions when her Leum had taken her to the races, she'd seen these magnificent animals, watched them take every honour available, leaving all contenders many trailing lengths behind. Oh, yes, she'd heard of the Wyman horses well enough! She doubted there was a gorgio or gypsy anywhere who hadn't.

Now Miss Elizabeth held out the reins of the mare, saying to Starlena, 'Please take her, Starlena.' Then, seeing the incredulity on the faces of both the girl and her mammy, she added, 'I know how much you loved Nero. And I know a mare could never be the same, however well bred she is. Oh, but listen! This mare has been serviced by one of the Wyman's most prized stallions, a racehorse unbeaten anywhere.' She smiled and stroked the mare's neck. 'And Misty Morning – that's her name – she has a reputation for producing colts. In five confinements out of six, she's born a colt every time.'

'Oh, but Miss Elizabeth!' Starlena was astounded at the offer. As was Rona, who even now was torn between being grateful that the young lady thought so much of her lass that she wanted to ease the heartbreak over Nero, and an impulse to thank her, but add a curt refusal.

'*Please* take her. And who knows, she might well give you a champion, to leave all the others standing. Look, I've got her papers!' She produced a leather wallet, which she put into Rona's hand.

Then there followed a brisk three-way conversation: Rona pointing out the obvious value of such an animal; Miss Elizabeth assuring her that such consideration must not come into it, for in a way it was the only gift she was able to give Starlena in view of the loss of Nero; and Starlena herself adding a persuasive voice, pleading that she be allowed to accept Miss Elizabeth's wonderful gift. In the end, the papers and relevant background information were passed over to Rona, and the spirited dark-bay mare to the excited and grateful Starlena.

Long after Miss Elizabeth had gone and Rona had retired to her bed, Starlena sat under the stars with Misty Morning, handling her, making friends and outlining to her the merits of having a colt rather than a filly.

It must have been 3 a.m. when Rona woke to find Starlena's half of the bed still empty. Going to the wagon door, she swung it open and peered out into the half-light. There she saw the mare lying on the thick grass, with Starlena's sturdy little body pressed up close to its head, her arms about its neck and both of them fast asleep.

Smiling, Rona went back into the wagon, where she collected a long dark shawl. Then, her heart warm and aching with love, she went to where horse and child lay and gently draping the garment over them, she murmured, 'Aw, child! Yer'll never know the many times a day I thank the Lord for the gift 'e's given me! An' though 'twas against me better instinct, 'ow could I deny Miss Elizabeth's gift to you?' Then as she turned away, she again shook her dark head, saying with uplifted eyes, 'I only 'ope there'll not come a day when I live to regret it!'

Now, as she stood atop the wagon steps, Rona looked down once more on the small figure, her arms still secure about the animal's head, lovingly nuzzling the creature's face, her wild black curls lost in the darkness of the horse's mane. Smiling, she would have turned away to close the wagon door behind her most quietly, so as not to disturb such a peaceful union. But as she half-turned, a small sleepy voice murmured, 'G'night, Mammy.'

Rona's smile broadened. Quietly she replied, 'Night, me darlin'. Sleep tight.' And she went off to her own bed where, shortly, she too was deep in contented slumber.

Chapter Eight

'Quickly, Mammy. There's a carriage coming!' Starlena hurried forward towards the bent, shawled figure some few steps ahead of her. Wrapping her long slim fingers about Rona's arm, she urged her mammy across the gravelled driveway, over the jutting triangle of closely-mown grass, then on to where the path would take them round to the tradesman's entrance. Only very briefly did Starlena glance backwards, and this at the rear of the carriage as the big chestnut geldings swept it close to the huge red building, their great iron-clad hooves scrunching the gravel in a rhythmic but muted clippety-clop. Then the carriage-wheels ground to a halt as the cry of the coachman steadied the whole team, in preparation for the disembarking of his passengers. Starlena caught only a glimpse of the occupants of the private black carriage – three of them: a lady and two gentlemen. Their flamboyant entrance, the elegant cut of their clothes and the unmistakable arrogance in the gentlemen's posture suggesting great wealth and some kind of authority.

Her curiosity aroused, Starlena would have liked to linger for a moment. But if she and her mammy were seen loitering here, they'd swiftly be sent on their way, and that would be the end of their work in this place, work that was dirty and hard, but which had kept them fed and warm these last few weeks, and had given them a shilling or two to put by for possible hard times through the coming winter. In a way, Starlena was looking forward to the winter months, for she would see Miss Elizabeth again, a prospect which always gave her a deal of pleasure. But equally she looked forward to returning to Whistledown Valley, for she had come to think of that beautiful place as her very own. No matter how full of delights might be the long lazy summertime, Whistledown Valley was ever in Starlena's thoughts, giving her a sense of belonging, and warming her heart with cherished memories, which always grew the more poignant at this time of year. For it was now the beginning of October, in the year of Our Lord, 1910. And in a few days' time, she and her mammy would be making their way back once again to camp the winter at Whistledown Valley.

It had been a wicked summer! It had been mercilessly hot for months on end and Starlena had bitterly resented the drought which had withered the crops in the field, dried up the brooks and caused anguish to many helpless little creatures. It had been nigh on impossible to keep the three horses fed and watered, for there had been little grass of any goodness, and water had been jealously guarded. In the end, the mare had been lent to a farmer, in exchange for the well-being of the old cob and the magnificent colt, the eventual produce of Miss Elizabeth's gift. The mare had brought forth a colt of supreme thoroughbred lines, just as Miss Elizabeth had promised. And from the instant of its birth, the colt had been Starlena's pride and joy.

The work which Starlena and her mammy had come to rely on through the summer had also greatly diminished, for there were few crops to harvest and the supply of sticks for peg-making and basket-weaving had dwindled badly. Because of the constant hot weather, very few folks were tempted into buying bundles of fire-wood. Oh yes, it had been a long and wearying summer! So when the old cob had pulled their wagon hereabouts, Starlena and her mammy were glad to take on laundering and floor-scrubbing in this God-forsaken institution some few miles out of Liverpool.

Quickly now, Starlena knocked on the great wooden door which led straight into the kitchen. In a moment it was flung open, to reveal a misshapen lump of a woman with dark overall and, beneath the grubby mop-cap, an even darker scowl. On seeing who it was that had so rudely interrupted her daily tipple, the lump emitted a bad-tempered grunt, grudgingly stepped aside and impatiently beckoned them to enter.

118

As these two poorly dressed and shivering creatures were unceremoniously ushered in through the back door, three elegantly-attired persons had stepped down from the carriage and approached the great arched doors, over which were chiselled into a stone-slab the words:

KINGSTON ASYLUM
May all who enter
here be God-fearing

With much bowing and scraping the trim white-pinnied girl who answered their summons politely requested them to enter. Quickly, the great ornate door was closed behind them, and without delay they were taken to the man of the house – a portly, self-satisfied and obnoxious personage by the name of Oliver Drew, a man without compassion, without mercy and, save for a sacred reverence for money and self-gratification, without love! When the three visitors were brought to his study, he leapt at once to his feet and extended a greeting, first to a young lady of timid disposition, who was at that very moment regarding him with alarmed blue eyes. 'Miss Elizabeth Doughty, I understand?' he quizzed, smiling and nodding on her reassurance.

The second visitor thrust out his hand impatiently. 'How do you do? I'm Redford Wyman,' he offered, his voice brisk and authoritative. As he returned an equally impatient handshake, the appointed officer of this wretched house discreetly observed Redford Wyman from beneath wild grey eyebrows. He took note of the crimson-velvet eye-patch, the fierce unsmiling features and that one dark-blue eye which pierced like a knife, and he formed two swift conclusions: one, that here was a dangerous animal; and two, that in spite of the young man being of wealth and high birth, he was possibly even more of a villain than himself.

The third visitor, a dark-haired man who seemed to be in his mid-forties, of rather effeminate speech and manner, although authoritative enough, was already known to him through several communications and a recent visit to this institution, in pursuit of what was a most delicate line of legal inquiry.

'Good morning, Mr Durnley. I received your letter – everything is ready.' Here Drew paused, his bloated features arranging themselves in a repugnant apologetic expression. 'Of course, as you must understand, we have a dire shortage of room here. I have moved the woman in question away from the main body. But one cannot escape the necessity of having to go through that particular area in order to reach the small back room, which will afford privacy for the woman in question, and for this young lady.' He did not look at Elizabeth as he spoke, but continued to address himself to her legal representative, Mr Durnley. 'I hope it won't be too much of an ordeal for Miss Doughty here?'

'Please do not concern yourself on my account, Mr Drew,' interrupted Elizabeth. 'We're ready now, if you please.'

At this, the portly officer gave a sickly smile and gestured with a stocky fist in the direction of three upright chairs, all of comfortable proportions with wide wooden arms and padded amber-coloured leather seats, and all neatly arranged about his desk. 'Oh! Of course, of course, my dear! Please be seated,' he spluttered, again displaying the most repugnant of mock servile expressions, this made all the more abominable by his forced laugh as he said, 'You women! Not the meek and mild little creatures *I* grew up with!' In a tone of strong disapproval, he launched into an energetic account of how the very evening previous, 'them blessed suffragettes' had set fire to an empty building, causing much expense and great annoyance to others. 'Don't these poor misguided women realize they'll get no sympathy from Parliament? Not with *that* kind of behaviour, they won't! No, indeed!' So agitated had he made himself that for a moment he seemed to have quite forgotten the presence of company. Then taking from his top waistcoat pocket a small round silver tin, he opened it, dipped finger and thumb into it and lifted them to his nostrils where, with a great intake of air, he sucked up the snuff into his head, promptly coughing and spluttering and leaving the airways to his nose stained and smudged brown.

'Can we get on, Mr Drew?' insisted Durnley. 'Miss Doughty has made a long journey and is anxious to satisfy herself of its outcome!'

120

There was no doubt that Elizabeth Doughty *was* impatient to discover whether the poor woman incarcerated in this wretched place was in fact her own estranged mother. Should this prove to be the case then she wanted to lose no time in securing her release, and a course of more caring treatment in much more humane and pleasant surroundings, before hopefully mother and daughter might at long last be reunited. It was a possibility which Elizabeth had long cherished in her heart. Yet she was not the only member of this sorry little party to be extremely impatient about the outcome of their journey. Redford Wyman was also anxious as to the indentity of the woman in question, as anxious as Elizabeth Doughty herself, but for a very different reason. His concern was born of greed and cunning. Indeed being the grasping fellow that he was, Redford Wyman was hoping against all contradictory evidence that this creature they had come to see was *not* Elizabeth Doughty's mother. His most fervent hope was that the woman who had deserted her daughter all those years back should be found dead and buried, rather than alive and as such constituting yet a further delay to the acquisition of a fortune. His motive stemmed from a revelation some six weeks before, on 24 August in this year of 1910, when the young lady, whom for ulterior motives he had since secretly cultivated a desire to wed, had received from the solicitor, Durnley, a communication recalling the death of her father, who had separated this world a very wealthy man, leaving all his worldly goods to his neglected daughter, Elizabeth. The sizeable legacy, however, had proved to be a mixed blessing. For, as Mr Durnley had been at great pains to point out, the inheritance could not be forthcoming until a thorough search for Elizabeth's wayward mother had been undertaken. If she was found to be still alive, then the greater proportion of the inheritance would be hers. If, on the other hand, a time lapse of three months had not produced her whereabouts, or she was found *not* to be alive, then the entire estate, including sizeable holdings of property, and lucrative boot, shoe and trading companies in Fall River near Boston, America, would revert to his daughter Elizabeth. So far, Durnley's enquiries had turned up no useful information; with the dubious exception that a vagrant of similar age and description admitted to this asylum by a local magistrate some months back, might possibly be the woman in question.

Now, as a concerned member of the party assembled here, Redford Wyman felt compelled to display such sympathy and affection as was required by the quietly developing understanding between himself and a young lady naïve enough to entertain his attentions. Such fawning upon a woman – any woman – was against his nature, yet he deemed it necessary, as part of his broader plan, that the young lady should see a pleasing facet to his nature. The rift between himself and his own father seemed wider than ever, with Lester Judd taking up the position he appeared to have lost. There was much at stake here, notwithstanding his own rightful inheritance. For it was plain as a pike-staff that Freya Judd's brother had not only wormed his way into Edward Wyman's affection, but also entertained notions of his own with regard to Elizabeth Doughty, who seemed not impervious to the young man's irritating charm. Redford had never been more grateful for the possessive streak in Freya Judd where her brother was concerned. For she alone had been a most willing and welcome ally when Redford Wyman set about attracting the innocent Miss Doughty towards himself. The promise of a fortune had not swayed Freya, for she had greater things in mind for her brother than mere money. It was said by some that she secretly cultivated the notion of launching Lester as a politician, and by others, that she idolized him in an intimate way that no sister should, or that she saw him as ousting Redford Wyman as future master of Bessington Hall and all its land and glory. Concerning the latter, Redford Wyman chose to conceal the bitter opposition she would encounter on *that* score, and his fervent intention that she and her brother would end the losers! At this time he needed her on his side, and to that end he would play her little game – until the moment came for revenge. As it surely would.

For now, however, Redford Wyman was employing his wiles to the matter in hand, beseeching Oliver Drew to 'Get on with it, man – have some consideration for Miss Doughty!'

'Oh! Dear me, yes, yes!' blustered the portly officer, seeing all three visitors seated in the chairs and awaiting his attention. 'Now, then, let me see,' he started, his voice assuming an air of authority, as he quickly returned the snuff-box to its pocket, clapping his chunky hands together to release a powdery shower of brown residue. In a moment he was seated behind his desk, gathering up a sheaf of official-looking documents. 'I think the very first thing is for you to go over certain information we have, regarding the woman in question! Yes, indeed! Close inspection might reveal details which could save you a most unpleasant task.'

Both Mr Durnley and Redford Wyman fervently agreed. As for the young woman, she spoke to all present when, touching her heart, she said quietly, 'I carry my mother's image here. If this woman is she, I will know.'

As the four of them began to pore over the documents with much intensity, none was aware of the wide-eyed white-pinnied girl outside the door, her ear pressed closely to it so as not to miss a single word.

In the great kitchen another discussion was taking place, but on a very different and less urgent level. Once inside, with the door slammed shut to keep out the weather, Rona had loosened the fringed shawl from her head and dropped it to her shoulders before blowing out her lips in an exaggerated shiver and exclaiming, 'By! There's a wind out there to cut the 'eart from yer!' Turning to the girl by her side, she added, 'Unbutton thi' jacket, lass. Let the warm in, eh? Then 'appen this good lady 'ere can find us a drop to warm us frozen bones.'

Starlena did as she was bid, all the while aware of the suspicious glares being levelled at her by the woman who had let them in from the cold, the same one who for these past weeks had given neither her nor her mammy any peace. She was a slave-driver, who at every turn demanded her pound of flesh in exchange for the measly wages they were given. Oh, how glad I shall be when we're gone from this awful place, Starlena thought. For she had taken an instant dislike to this place the very first day they'd set foot in it. She liked it even less after these past weeks. There was misery here, evil and suffering which gave her nightmares. People crying out and moaning like lost souls who'd lost their way. And such screams as made her blood chill! Day and night they went on, never ceasing, those woeful sounds that had the power to hurt her, and even when deeply involved in her work, she found herself praying and crying for the poor miserable bodies who cried out so. She'd become deeply angered, and wondered at the folk who could allow their loved ones to abide in a place such as this.

Starlena had said as much to her mammy, who had quietly assured her that it was a pitiful thing, and that no gypsy would ever allow one of theirs into such a place. Starlena had sensed how disturbed her mammy was, and she loved her all the more for it. But none of it had any effect on that rasp-voiced woman who seemed not to hear the chilling sounds emanating from the end of that long dark corridor.

Starlena felt the woman's eyes still on her as, having unbuttoned her jacket as her mammy had told her, she took the deep cowl from about her head and face, at once revealing the dark vivacious beauty which gave her a womanly charisma far beyond her twelve years. The long black skirt which fell to the top of her dark leather boots, the brown three-quarter jacket, which had been cadged along the way and served as a shield against the biting wind: all of these things – together with the superb darkness of her eyes and hair – gave the impression that Starlena was a true Romany. Yet there was something else! For in the way she stood and moved, in the classic and exquisite structure of her lovely face, and in those magnificent eyes, so black they reflected a breathtaking and liquid brilliance, there was a striking air of pride and aristocratic bearing, which set Starlena apart from others.

Deliberately ignoring the woman's narrowed eyes, Starlena enjoyed that moment before she and her mammy would be given their work-instructions and savoured the warmth here in this room. She looked around her, taking in the awesome character of the kitchen, a place of monstrous proportions, bedecked with pots, pans and paraphernalia of all descriptions. The ceiling was curved high, the walls distempered in a distasteful brown colour, and the floor a sea of grey stone slabs which, were it not for the roaring coal fire in the open range, would throw off an atmosphere more chilling than the promise of winter outside.

With their outer garments stripped off and flung over the peg behind the door, Starlena and her mammy stepped further into the room, Rona hoping for that 'drop o' warm for their frozen bones' and Starlena, having read the misshapen lump's character these past weeks, expecting nothing more than swift and hard instructions regarding their workload.

'If yer bones is frozen, gypsy-woman,' came the retort, 'I've got the very answer to it, not two steps fro' where I'm standing!' She gave a quick crooked smile as full of venom as Starlena had ever seen. Stooping, she thrust her arms into the space beneath the big pot sink, dragging out a pair of great galvanized buckets, two handy-sized scrubbing brushes, a bag of foul-smelling carbolic soap and two thick coarse drying cloths.

'There!' she said triumphantly, clutching her square fists against her deformed thighs. She set apart her squat linen-draped legs, dipped her head at a peculiar angle, and, gathering together that vixen of a smile, she laid out her orders. 'The main corridor and big ward. Don't miss the corners nor the bed-legs!' Cause I'll check, I'm tellin' yer! An' if the job's not to my likin', yer'll do the bugger agin! Understand, do yer?'

She fixed Rona with her eyes, and waited until she received the desired nod. Then, darting her head about, she cast a glare at Starlena that might have shrivelled a lesser mortal. In that same rasping voice she demanded, 'An' you, yer young whipper-snapper – d' *you* understand?'

Beneath the misshapen lump's hard spiteful eyes, Starlena stood tall and proud, her own dark gaze unflinching beneath such hostility. In a voice calm and clear she replied, 'I understand.' Then she stepped forward to collect first one bucket then the other, filling each in turn with equal measures from the cold-water tap and from the great black iron pan which sat on the trestle by the fire, contentedly bubbling with hot water. The lifting of such a burden sorely tested Starlena's youthful muscles, but to the misshapen

125

lump looking on and to Rona; who busied herself dropping scrubbing-brushes and cleaning materials into the buckets, there was no outward sign of strain, neither sound nor grimace.

'Hmph!' The lump moved itself towards a door alongside the great fireplace. 'I'll tell Barker yer 'ere.' Pausing at the door she threw a cursory glance at Starlena, an angry shake of the head accompanying each departing word and skewing the mob-cap precariously perched atop the iron-grey tangle of hair about her head. 'I want them floors scrubbed proper! *Proper*, I say! No missin' out the corners or leavin' soapy puddles aback o' doors!'

At this, Starlena straightened her back and said, 'You've had no complaint before. Our work is always done "proper". It'll be no different this time.'

Somewhat taken aback by this retort, the lump seemed just for a moment to be lost for words. Then, flaring her nostrils and tossing her head, she flounced out of the door, calling behind her, 'Bear in mind, I'll check! An' touch nothing in my kitchen save yer work-tools. I'll be back afore yer draw yer next breath!'

'By! That one's a mean ol' sod, an' no mistake, eh, lass?' Rona stretched her back up straight. She rolled up the shirt cuff which had escaped down to her fingers, and wondered how she'd see the day out scrubbing, when for some irritating reason the small of her back was already in revolt.

'Come on, lass, we'd best get down the corridor wi' these 'ere buckets afore that Barker woman gets to 'ollerin' an' shouting!' The last word escaped on a shiver, which spread the length of Rona's body, leaving her trembling.

'Cold, are you, Mammy?' Starlena was at once alert to the fact that even in spite of the rosy glow emanating from the big fireplace, her mammy was still fighting off the effect of that bitter driving wind outside. At once her arm was about the woman's waist, drawing her into the warmth of her own slim body. 'Take a minute by the fire, Mammy,' she urged, looking anxiously around the room. Suddenly she saw a huge elm dresser, resplendent with plates of blue willow pattern of all shapes and sizes. Along the top stood an army of brown stone jars and bottles, each labelled with a pretty name. All but one! This was a tall narrow-necked jug cunningly secreted behind another, but not so hidden that it escaped the quick eye of Starlena.

With a cry of triumph, Starlena pounced on a stool, elevated herself to within reaching position of the dresser-top, and with the deftness of a thief in the night recovered the jug from its hiding-place, to transport it to the shivering Rona. 'Here ye are, Mammy!' she urged, taking out the cork and holding the rim to Rona's mouth. 'Take a good strong gulp. There's more than enough here for the sharing!'

'Oh ho, ye little darlin'! Yer found it, eh!' Rona chuckled, at the same time clasping her two cold hands about the jar's body in a bid to hold it steady while she partook of its liquid warmth. After which she smacked her lips and licked them with some satisfaction, her eyes that much brighter and her smile a deal bolder. 'By! That's the stuff!' she whispered, somewhat afeared that any minute they'd be interrupted, and the wrath of authority would fall on their sorry heads. 'Now, lass! Put it back. Put it back, I say, afore we're caught in the act.'

At which point there came the sound of hurrying footsteps echoing towards them along the corridor. 'Quick, lass! Lord 'elp us – quick as yer can!' Rona told Starlena, who had to smile as she saw her mammy's stricken face and watched her cross herself.

'Ssh, Mammy. Don't alarm yerself!' she chided. With the stealth of a gazelle, she mounted the stool, replaced the jug in its exact position, and when the misshapen lump flung open the door, she had returned to her mammy's side. The two of them gathered up their work-tools, came towards the lump and declared themselves ready to make their way down the corridor, to where Barker no doubt at this very moment was waiting to allow them access into the big ward.

'Away with yer, then!' the lump exclaimed. 'An' think on what I've said!' The last word died away as she caught sight of Rona's rosy cheeks and twinkling eyes as they departed the room. At once the sharp eyes switched to the dresser-top. Then, having satisfied herself of the jug's position, the lump visibly relaxed, swung itself about and slammed shut the door after the gypsy woman and her offspring. After which she made haste towards the jug, which for the next hour or so she greedily anticipated would keep her good company. In her haste, however, she neglected to take into account the precariousness of a tall slim-legged stool combined with the short clumsiness of her own grasping arms.

A short way up the corridor, Starlena and her mammy paused in their hurried flight from the kitchen and 'that one'. 'Hark, Mammy!' Starlena gasped, protectively grabbing Rona's arm as they heard the sounds of breaking coming from behind the kitchen door, followed by a volley of abuse and wailful lamenting.

Watching her mammy's surprised expression, Starlena began to giggle as her vivid imagination conjured up images of the misshapen lump spreadeagled over the stone slabs, pinned by the stool and splattered head to toe in rich red wine. It gave a warm glow to her heart as she saw her mammy respond to her giggling with a furtive smile or two.

'Oh, Mammy!' she said, in mock anxiety. 'I do believe the poor darlin's fell from top to bottom o' that dresser! An' I'm thinkin' she'll not miss the drop o' warm we took the liberty to borrow!' At which both she and her mammy fell against each other in a fit of laughter before, at the impatient sound of Barker's voice calling, they quickly set off again up the corridor, their chuckles of delight going before them.

Barker was the chief warden. And the biggest, most fearsome female Starlena had ever clapped eyes on. Some six feet tall and broad as the girth of an old oak tree, she stood erect and unsmiling, her straight brown hair scraped back from the homely features into an ungainly bun. Every inch of her was covered in blackness, save for the great bulk of shining brass keys at her waist. She made a truly formidable sight.

'Quick! Quick as yer can, you two!' she urged in an authoritative voice. 'There'll be no dawdling today. We've got visitors – *important* visitors! Gentry, no less!' In a moment she had lifted the cumbersome bunch of keys and having selected one, she lost no time in unlocking the door and ushering Starlena and her mammy inside. Then, on the sharp utterance of the word 'Davis!', there appeared a second version of herself – lesser in stature, more subservient, but nevertheless set in the same mould as her senior. 'Davis, watch that they're in and out of here with some speed today. The work's to be done smartish, for inside the hour we'll have Mr Drew's visitors on our necks.'

Turning to address Starlena, who found her a source of unbounded fascination, Barker instructed, 'I don't want you taking up unnecessary time in talking to these wretches, as you've done on other occasions. Besides which, they've all been suitably sedated so as not to cause embarrassment to the visitors. Now – get on with it! And out in record time, I say!' At this she physically manhandled the dithering Davis into position by the door, saying, 'Keep a sharp eye out, Davis! You've got your whistle if you need me?' Here she waited to be shown the long silver whistle encased in the folds of Davis's skirt before, with an exaggerated nod of the head, she marched out of the door, locking herself out and everyone else in.

It amused Starlena to see how, on her senior's departure, the woman Davis slipped easily and quickly into the role of stern-faced sentry, back stiff against the door, legs apart, watchful eyes following Starlena and her mammy's every move.

Rona's cynical comment of 'Hmph! "Gentry" indeed!' echoed Starlena's own sentiments exactly – with the exception, of course, of her friend, Miss Elizabeth.

Looking first at the guard by the door and then down the ward at the 'suitably sedated' inmates, Starlena felt shame for her own species. Not for the first time, her large dark eyes misted over and in her heart there was a particular heaviness which seemed especially reserved for this God-forsaken place.

The room itself was never pleasant, but today it took on an even less cheerful and more desolate air. This was accentuated by the siting of narrow lightless windows high up in the walls and smothered on the outside by countless decades of rampant ivy and other creepers. From the centre of the grimy ceiling there hung one solitary bulb, suspended by a thick brown flex and bearing no shade. As always, when Starlena and her mammy were admitted here for the scrubbing of floor and bed-legs, the bulb was lit. Yet the light it shed gave little relief to the dusky atmosphere, and even smaller comfort to the occupants of the room.

Always aware of Starlena's compassionate spirit and impatience for the day when they could leave behind this place for Whistledown Valley, Rona smiled into the girl's sad eyes. 'Come on, me darlin',' she said, 'let's get it done an' away, eh?' She put her bucket on the floor and drew up the corners of her skirt to tuck into her waistband – there was nothing so cumbersome as the full swing of a skirt about your knees when scrubbing the floor.

Starlena also followed this now familiar pattern, yet her thoughts and gaze were elsewhere. Both were travelling along the rows of narrow iron-framed beds which lined either side of the oblong room. As always, Starlena was engrossed in the occupants of these beds – women of poor circumstances, women of every age and appearance – wretched creatures with only two things in common: the fearful desolation in their eyes; and the low-pitched moaning which filled the clinging atmosphere like the weirdest humming song.

Here, one aged being tore at the air with clawing fingers as though to tear out for herself a way of escape. There in the far corner a younger creature grasped a grey pillow to her face, forcing herself to gasp for breath, staring out over it with empty eyes. Starlena watched as the appointed keeper left her post by the door to race down the room to this one. With a vicious sweep of her arm, she snatched the pillow away, fetching it back to the top of the room, where it was flung to the floor and caught hard beneath one of her booted feet.

Now, Starlena's undivided attention was given to one woman, a woman different from the others, with grace in her movements and beauty in her dark tragic eyes. This woman was of special consequence to Starlena, for between the two of them there had developed a kind of comradeship: the one seeking only to touch and embrace; the other to offer a degree of comfort and solace by way of story and song.

Starlena had heeded her mammy's warning not to let the poor creature come to rely on her too much, for soon they would be gone

130

from here. And what a wrench that would be if the poor thing had come to depend on the snatched moments in the young gypsy girl's company. It would not do for such a spiteful thing to come about. And so Starlena had learned of late to keep her distance. Yet it was all a source of dreadful anguish to her, so much so that she wanted to tear this place down brick by brick, so that those incarcerated here could flee to find peace for their haunted souls. Yet even in the thinking of it, Starlena was all too aware of the utter hopelessness of such a plan. How many times had she come across a small feeble creature set upon and cruelly discarded in the woods, victim of an adversary stronger and more vicious? 'Twas a savage thing! Recently her mammy had used such an example to explain what would befall these unfortunate weak-minded beings here, were they ever set loose to fend for themselves.

All the same, Starlena believed that their lives were most miserable in this institution, and that they should be made easier by the powers that be. It was a pain to her, an anxiety which filled her waking hours and prompted many an anxious barrage of questions to which Rona herself could provide no answers.

'Aw, child!' she would cry. 'Will ye not let the matter be? Sure, 'tis a cryin' shame! But there's nowt us two can do to change it.'

But to Starlena it remained a dilemma, in turn creating a deeper dilemma for Rona, whose heart ached more for her own child's well-being than for that of a poor stranger's. To this end, she had lately contemplated cutting her losses and taking to the high road. Now, seeing Starlena's gentle and concerned expression as she looked down the room towards the dark-haired one with the tragic eyes, her decision was prompt and irrevocable. This very day would be their last at this work; on the morrow they would up sticks and be off.

Starlena was startled by the sharpness in her mammy's voice as it chided, 'Bide what you were told, lass! Pay less attention to the women, and more to yer work. Let's get it done and tek us leave!'

Then, as Starlena carried her bucket without a word, to the back wall where part-hidden behind a partition she fell to her knees and began her scrubbing, Rona felt a deep pang of regret for the quickness of her tongue. Yet there was something here which frightened her, some odd thing which roused her instincts and made her deeply uneasy. At first she had thought it a reaction to the unnatural character of this awful place; but 'twas something else also. A jealousy perhaps, of the affection Starlena shared with others so easily, and with one in particular? But no! That was a foolish notion, and one she must discard in a hurry. All the same, Rona felt a deal easier at the prospect of returning to Whistledown Valley, even if it was some weeks afore the time. The two o' them would manage well enough, what with the few shillings put by, and the pile of unsold kindling-wood which should carry them through a greater part of the winter. Oh aye! 'Twas away they'd be on the morrow, rising with the first songbird. And glad to do so!

In the next few moments there was a flurry of activity by the door. The ungainly figure of Oliver Drew swept in, pompously leading an entourage consisting of the man Durnley, his client Elizabeth Doughty and the obnoxious Redford Wyman. Smartly bringing up the rear was the military figure of Barker. Locking the door behind her, she addressed the one of lower rank who was subdued by the overpowering presence of a party of gentry, and both her superiors.

'Davis! I must accompany our visitors into the far quarters. You keep a sharp look-out for any mischief. Be on your toes, woman!' Having spat out the instructions with due sternness, she swung away, key at the ready for the unlocking of the far door and eyes swivelling side to side watching for signs of misbehaviour. Then, satisfied that the sedation administered that morning had secured the desired effect, she left the inmates to their humming and proceeded to overtake the group ahead. Her sharp eyes had not missed the frantic expression of the female in the group, nor her sympathetic though nervous glances as her bright blue eyes took in the scenes about her. For a young woman of her obvious breeding, 't'would be all quite a shock. Which was why Barker carried out her duties at the double, for the sooner the woman in the far quarters was identified, the better. And the sooner these gentry were out of here and on their way, the better still!

Starlena emerged from behind the partition, having scrubbed that part of the floor with the help of her mammy. Her curiosity was aroused by the comings and goings down the ward. Both women still on their knees, they exchanged quizzical glances as they watched the entry of the visitors into the small room at the far end of the ward. Starlena was particularly drawn to the fancy black bonnet worn by the lady, whose profile was swallowed beneath a swathing of finest cornflower-blue ribbon. And Rona was intrigued by the mystery of it all.

In a moment, the door was closed and whatever mystery was going on behind it would not influence the scrubbing of the floors. Nor would curiosity pay their wages. So, with a shrug of her shoulders, Rona again bent her back into her work and, impatient to scrub her way along the wooden floorboards to where the dark-eyed creature lay abed, Starlena attacked her own labours with increased vigour.

Having made her way there with some speed, but without neglecting the demands of her work, Starlena stole a moment to straighten her aching back and to speak in a whisper to the figure in the bed, which by now was buried beneath the coarse grey blanket. 'Are ye awake?' she asked. When there came no reply nor movement, she coaxed again, this time gently prodding with the flat of her hand, always conscious of watchful eyes from the main door and fearful of rising from the floor. 'Kathleen! It's Starlena. Are ye awake?'

For the most poignant of moments, Starlena waited, holding her breath and stretching herself away from the probing fingers of the curious bedmate next door, a wrinkled hag who had demonstrated on previous days a most undesirable and peevish disposition.

Now, as the bedclothes were inched back to reveal the thin emaciated face, Starlena gazed gently upon it, her heart curiously moved and a warm smile lighting up her lovely face. The features she saw held only a semblance of what Starlena suspected must have been a great beauty. The mouth, though not as full as beauty demanded, was evidently shaped for smiling, although on this occasion it was sulkily turned down at the corners. The nose was small and straight, the forehead rendered higher and more prominent by the hair which should have fallen softly about it, but which was harshly short, matted together and drawn back from the face by means of thick clumsy slides. The real essence of loveliness lay in her eyes. Dark they were, and softly shaped, yet they were shadowed in a way that Starlena often likened to a window obscured by rain. In Kathleen's eyes though, the haze came from within, giving them an expression of tragedy which was fascinating.

Those eyes seemed to come alive a little now, though, as they focused on Starlena's small friendly face. In a trice the woman had wrenched herself further out of the blanket and in a furtive movement she reached out her long slim hand, the colour of parchment, to fold it over Starlena's own. She said not a word and in a small way Starlena was glad of that, for had she spoken she would have said over and over again, as though in a desperate attempt to convince not only those who would listen but also herself, 'My name is Kathleen. I am not insane. I am *not*!'

Starlena squeezed the hand which had found hers, saddened by the poor creature's pained silence. Oh, what dreadful thoughts were even now assailing that tortured mind. What dreadful sequence of events could have brought such a delicate, graceful woman to such a miserable end? Starlena thought about this for as long as ever she dared, for there came a point when to think on them further might keep *her* imprisoned forever in this place. There was a grain of comfort in what the misshapen lump had told her once, in a rare unguarded moment when the wine had loosened her tongue. 'Yer don't want to bother yer 'ead over that one! Money arrives 'ere reg'lar as clockwork to see to its needs. Oh, yes indeed – better off than most is that one! Even though it's got a black murderous 'eart by all accounts on what it's done!' Beyond that, the lump would not say or perhaps did not know. Indeed, the following day it had denied all knowledge of ever saying any such thing.

It was evident even to Starlena's untrained eye that the woman, Kathleen, was heavily drugged. It seemed a great effort for her to keep her eyes open and once open, an even greater determination to keep them trained on Starlena's anxious face.

'Tired, are yer?' asked Starlena, stealing closer to lower her voice the more. 'Well, you sleep to yer heart's content, me darlin'. There's visitors here today, posh visitors on some important errand!'

No sooner had the words left Starlena's lips than the door to the far quarter opened. Emerging from it came two men – the woman, Oliver Drew and Barker were apparently left inside, as the murmur of voices confirmed.

Being no more than ten feet away from the men, Starlena could hear their every word. Worse, she was easily in their line of vision, as they were in hers, and this was most unpleasant, if only because of the offensive appearance of one of them, the one wearing a remarkably handsome eye-patch over what must be a remarkably grotesque and empty eye-socket, judging by the scarring which showed about the sunken cheek-bone. But worse in Starlena's opinion, was the one good eye, as it swivelled and darted about until it alighted upon her. At once she fell away from the bed, stooped to the floor, and with great gusto began slapping down cloths full of soapy suds, which she then ferociously and single-mindedly attacked with her scrubbing-brush.

There was little warning of what was about to happen next, for it took shape in the matter of a mere heartbeat. And then all hell was loose!

Pleased that the wretch within had turned out not to be Elizabeth Doughty's mother, thereby bringing a fortune that much closer, Redford Wyman's thoughts had taken on a pleasanter aspect. The sight of a slight but immensely attractive girl stooped over a bed had caused a stirring in his loins, increased by the apprehension in her large black eyes as they had met his gaze. In his arrogance, he swept forward to where Starlena was now intent upon her work. His purpose was unmistakable: he had stooped to pluck her up, the easier to gratify his curiosity, and perhaps, at a point in the near future, his lust.

At this moment, the woman lying prostrate in the bed thought the intruder to be coming for *her*, whereupon she sat up startled and through the layer of numbness put upon her by the use of strong sedatives, she saw the man: saw him – *recognized* him! And the doing of it struck the fear of God into her deranged senses.

All at once she was screaming and thrashing, in a frenzy which even the terrified Starlena was helpless to stem. With her arms about the sobbing woman, Starlena told the man in no uncertain terms to 'Go away – you've frightened her!' To the terrified woman she said in a soft voice, 'Ssh now, Kathleen. Yer safe enough. Shh.' But her voice was not so soft that Redford Wyman had not recognized the name by which she addressed the cringing woman in the bed. Assailed by nightmarish memories, he leaned forward to examine the woman's features with terrifying intensity. Even with only one good eye and some twelve years since he had seen her, it was enough to tell him that here, thin and almost unrecognizable as the proud, exquisite lady she once had been, was without doubt his mother, Kathleen Wyman, the target of his deepest loathing, someone he had hoped never again to encounter. How much more fiendish would his reaction have been if it had been known to him that the young gypsy girl comforting his mother was his blood kin also.

Seething, and yet showing no more sign of it than the tightness of his mouth and the agitation of his fingers as they caressed the destruction of his face, Redford Wyman took a pace back. Then, while Starlena stared at him indignantly, his arrogant expression altered to an evil smile. He made no attempt to recognize his mother publicly. Instead, he bade the unsuspecting Durnley to follow him and the two smartly departed the scene in the direction whence they had come. There they and the rest of the group could huddle for the few moments of ensuing uproar! With the exception, however, of Barker, who marauded into the main ward with all the grace of a bull elephant and a rage to match.

Just as swiftly as the whole sorry incident had erupted, so it was contained. The two keepers successfully cowed into submission the greatly agitated patients, restoring order and directing both Rona and Starlena out onto the streets – with nothing in the way of financial compensation for their hard work. They blamed the entire pandemonium on Starlena's mischief.

Only one voice was raised in contradiction. This was Redford Wyman who, sweeping past the bed whose occupant was even now trembling beneath the blankets, pointed to the quivering object and said maliciously, '*There's* your culprit, Drew! A bad example to the rest, and should be suitably punished!' Gratefully trusting the word of a gentleman, the shaken proprietor instructed his chief keeper to 'See to it, Barker! Make sure it's done, and with no quarter, I say!' After all, he could not have his authority undermined in such a way. No, indeed. It was bad enough that the patient within had turned out not to be the personage they sought, for he had greedily envisaged a reward, had these 'ere gentry made a profitable journey. But 'twas not the case. And his temper was not improved by it!

Chapter Nine

'Get the hell out of here!' Edward Wyman sprang from his chair, lifted an arm, and with one vicious swipe sent every object flying from the desk-top. 'How many times do I need to tell you, woman? Stop hovering about like a bloody vulture!' He fixed the indignant Freya Judd with furious eyes, defying her to stay in the room a moment longer. As she met his wild stare with her own steely gaze, it came to her with wicked satisfaction that Edward Wyman had grown old: old, weary and desperately dissatisfied with his enviable lot. She looked at his face, at the puffy eyes and drooping jowls, the deterioration of which was highlighted by the straggling iron-grey beard and receding hair, which had left an unattractive purple patch of skin stretching above his wrinkled brow like another forehead. When he stood to full height, as he did now, the grotesquely huge stomach strained at his silk-figured waistcoat, giving him both a repugnant and a comic appearance, which effectively rendered ridiculous any show of bad temper.

'Are you deaf, woman? I said out! *Out! Out!* OUT!' With every word his face grew redder and more bulbous, until it seemed it would burst open. Then, as though his rage was spent, he sighed deeply and fell back into the deep leather chair with a groan, burying his face in one hand while with the other he gestured to the door, saying in a more subdued voice, 'Leave me be. I must be on my own for a while.'

'But of course,' came the crisp reply. And turning stiffly away, Freya Judd added, 'Don't forget you have a meeting with Lester in an hour. There's business to be discussed.'

'Yes, yes!' Again he gestured, but with more agitation. At which point, smiling with satisfaction, Freya left the room.

Once outside, with the door closed behind her, Freya leaned back against it, a look of bitterness in her small green eyes. These past fourteen years had not been easy and certain plans had not yet fully materialized. Edward Wyman had grown increasingly difficult: always griping and complaining, finding fault with this and that, and filling the house with an atmosphere of depression and fear. This morning had been particularly bad! Oh, but the whole thing had been building up for some months. What with Redford's preoccupation with Elizabeth Doughty and certain business matters left to fall on Lester's shoulders . . . Here Freya smiled. She wasn't complaining on that score, because Redford's greedy attentions to the Doughty creature would keep her away from Lester, who all in all was too fond of the woman for his own good! Whatever business matters fell on Lester's shoulders could only enhance his capabilities and edge him nearer yet to the old man's will. If Redford was too busy to see the error of his ways, then who was she to point them out? Oh yes! Redford Wyman's blatant neglect of his father's affairs was to her mind a very foolish thing. But all the more advantageous for Lester, for whom she sought status as well as wealth.

Feeling pleased with herself, Freya Judd went to summon a maid from the kitchen. 'Give the master a good half-hour, then go in and clear up the mess he's made,' she curtly instructed. Then she hurried along to the drawing-room, where she might sit awhile before Lester arrived for the meeting with Edward Wyman. Oh, how she had come to resent that man! His tantrums these past weeks had been hard to bear. If it wasn't the constant neglect of his duties by Redford, it was Lloyd George's new National Insurance Act, by which every employer was obliged to pay to the government 2½d per week for every man in his employ. Being the stout capitalist he was, Edward Wyman was incensed that he should be made to contribute to the workers' welfare, 'As if I wasn't already paying them exceptionally good wages at two pounds, four and sixpence a working week!' had been his loud lament. Then there had been the poorest grain harvest for many years, for in this autumn of 1911, the ground was still bogged by the incessant rain which had relentlessly besieged the crops.

To Freya's keen eye, however, there was another reason for Edward's darkening moods. This gave her real cause for concern and took her mind back some thirteen years to a night when there had been two brats born into this household: one a boy, already lifeless; the other a dark hauntingly beautiful girl-child. From that night when the newborn was given away to a gypsy woman, there had evolved a sequence of events, not the least of which had been the confinement in some asylum of Edward's wife, Kathleen. The closely-kept secret of that newborn girl-child had presented many possibilities to Freya. And she had used them well! Hence her elevated position here, together with a handsome sum of money put safely by, and Lester rising faster in the old man's esteem with every trick she could muster.

Freya crossed the drawing-room with slow deliberate steps to the long casement window. She gazed dreamily out over the well-manicured lawns, absent-mindedly reaching to return a straying brown lock to its rightful place in the nape of her neck. Yes! She had employed every trick and art of blackmail at her disposal. The devilish deed committed by Edward Wyman in giving away his child and to a gypsy-woman, no less, would be considered by all to be a heinous thing. Were it ever to be known amongst his own kind that the same diabolical act had been the root cause of his wife's 'insanity', then ostracism could only follow. And for a man like Edward Wyman, to be ostracized by his own kind would be an unbearable thing! Oh yes indeed! In retrospect, Freya Judd could see that the entire happening had served her well.

At this point and in a fit of pique, Freya punched her clenched fist into the softness of a chair-back. 'It's not *enough!*' she muttered through clenched teeth. 'Not enough to show for all these years!' She had been bedded many times over by both the Wyman scoundrels. She had given herself gratefully, in the hope that she might at last wed into the wealth and tradition of this prestigious family. But she had deluded herself after all. For all the while

140

she had thought to be using them, they had been using her.

Still she had yet one almighty powerful card with which to play. Redford Wyman might not be so casual about his father's vast holdings were he to discover that he was not the only heir. For years he had played fast and loose with the legacy he took for granted, convinced that however much he neglected his duties, there was no question his father could do any other than to honour the family name and that of his only son, by ensuring that the Wyman fortune was duly passed on to a Wyman! Freya Judd was convinced that Redford's attentions to Elizabeth Doughty were prompted only by greed. By marrying the woman, and so perhaps producing another Wyman to perpetuate the line, he would not only win his father's enthusiastic approval, but at the same time he would secure the Doughty woman's reputed fortune to swell his own.

Here, Freya chuckled aloud. Wouldn't the fine gentleman's feathers be ruffled if he was to discover that he had a sister? Another Wyman, who could so easily lay claim to half his fortune? This, the knowledge she had concealed all these years, this was her best card. Every selfish instinct in her body now warned Freya Judd that the time to play this mischievous card had come.

Edward Wyman's deep brooding of late put Freya in mind of a man plagued by an attack of repentance. Often, when dozing in the library and unaware of her entry, he had murmured certain things which had left Freya in no doubt that Edward Wyman's conscience was beginning to haunt his old age. She suspected that it would not be too long before he made some move towards releasing Kathleen from the hellish prison he'd put her in. And if that was the case, Freya Judd thought with alarm, then how long might it be before the memory of the girl-child lay equally heavy on his mind? Oh, there was a rot setting in, enough to eat away at the very roots of her hard-earned life-style. And she did not take kindly to that.

With her lips pursed tight and her pinched features a study in treachery, Freya Judd sank into the nearest chair. The daughter of Kathleen Wyman must never be found. Never. Or at least, not alive! A plan began to take shape in her fevered mind. Alive, that girl represented a very real threat, and not to her alone. Oh no! The threat to Redford Wyman was far and away the greater, and as such he must be just as eager as she to have the creature out of the way once and for all. For if Wyman Senior was to take it into his head to find the child he had given away almost before it was warm with life, then how much better that she be found dead and, as such, a threat to no-one.

With every devious thought, Freya Judd became more convinced that she must approach Redford Wyman as an ally, and soon! So engrossed was she in deciding when and how she would confide in him the delicious secret which had kept her nest feathered these many years, that she did not hear her brother's approach. When suddenly he came upon her, so still and deep in thought, she started with fright.

'Ah ha! Caught you napping – now *there's* a rare experience!' he said crisply. Then, as guilt wrote itself plain across her narrow features, Freya's brother bent to kiss her, saying with a laugh and a wag of the finger, 'Well now, if I didn't know better, I'd say I'd caught you in the middle of planning a murder! Or at *least* six of the best across Cook's backside!'

With practised finesse, Freya Judd regained her composure. She rose smartly from the chair, brushed out the creases of her long black skirt, patted the coiling hair in the nape of her neck, fidgeted with the neat black ribbon at the collar of her crisp white blouse, and without further ado, smiled nervously and said, 'Don't be silly, Lester. I was *not* napping, and well you know it!' As always when Freya looked at her brother, a picture of youth and health with his boyish lean figure dressed in brown serge trousers, dark pullover and mottled tweed jacket, a great surge of pleasure came over her.

'Go on, Freya,' he joked, fondly trying her patience. 'Admit it. I'll not tell anybody.' He leaned back against the wall by the great fireplace, one elbow crooked on the corner of the wooden mantelpiece, one foot leisurely resting on the black iron fender, his light brown eyes twinkling and the strands of his fair hair still wayward from the breeze outside.

Freya's hard green eyes softened as she returned his smile.

And as always, her every nerve bristled at the thought that any other woman should ever lay hands on him. Such a prospect stabbed at her heart, filling her with such venom that she could almost taste it.

When she spoke, it was in words that wiped away his smile. 'You've not been to see that Doughty woman, have you?' she asked harshly.

When he was slow to answer, she insisted, 'Lester! I said . . .'

'I know what you said!' His mood was cruelly changed, and with quick angry strides he moved towards the door, unwilling to take up a conversation that could only end as it always did: with him arguing that it was his own business; and his sister flouncing about in a fit of temper which might last for days.

'Don't fob me off, Lester! I know she's back this very day. She's tired of business, and she's left Redford Wyman in London to deal with her affairs.'

'If you know all that, then you have no need to question me.' He paused, and with his back still to her, he said in a softer voice, 'Just now, Elizabeth is haunted by the task of locating her mother and having her father's affairs put to rights. When all that is put behind her, I intend to ask her to marry me – and the sooner you accept that, the better.'

'Ha! If Redford doesn't beat you to it!' The moment the words were out of her mouth, Freya Judd could have chopped out her tongue. The last thing she wanted was to alert her brother to the growing intimacy between those two. But Lester was no fool. When he turned to face her, Freya saw the spark of jealousy and suspicion in his sad brown eyes.

But all he said was, 'Redford Wyman is Elizabeth's business adviser. Nothing more. Good God! The man's in his mid-thirties, a good ten years her senior!'

'Of course! Of course! Take no notice of me, Lester, you know well enough how my tongue can run away with me.' Gathering the fullness of her skirt into her fists, she went quickly out of the door and started towards Edward Wyman's study, smiling secretly when it was evident by his footsteps that Lester was following her, and congratulating herself on having brought the conversation to so swift an end.

Half turning her head, she called a warning over her shoulder. 'You'd best choose your words carefully in here, my darling. He's in a foul mood.' With that she would have cautiously opened the study door to admit him. But at that precise moment, the same young maid summoned earlier by Freya Judd to clear up the master's study came bursting out. She was in tears, stemmed only momentarily by the look of stark fear that came to her eyes as she became sharply aware of Freya Judd's icy stare. Even as the terrified girl was about to receive a tongue-lashing there came from within a great bellow. 'To hell with *all* of you!' Then she began to sob and ran headlong across the great hall before disappearing down the side stairs which led to the pantries below.

'I see what you mean.' There was a half-smile on Lester Judd's face, although this was tempered by some concern for the fleeing girl. 'Don't concern yourself, sister dear. I've learned how to read his moods.' Then, with a thoughtful grimace he added, 'Which I must admit have got worse of late.'

'Hmh! Well – if anybody can handle him, you can!' retorted Freya, at the same time inching open the heavy door which had swung to on the maid's speedy retreat. Then with a curt nod of her head she ushered him inside, saying in a whisper, 'Go on and soften the old bastard's heart, my darling – for one day I mean for all of this to be yours.'

A moment later Lester Judd stood before the huge polished wood desk, behind which was slumped the large ungainly figure of Edward Wyman, his arms folded over the desk and his grey balding head laid at a crooked angle upon them. For a long moment there was no sound from either man, no greeting, no acknowledgement from the one of the other's presence. Outside, the watery sun played behind the gathering clouds, its weak light casting a dim illumination through the small window panes and coming to rest on the objects scattered about the floor.

Not far from where he stood, the heavy ornate brass ink-stand lay on its side, its dark-blue contents having flowed in a meandering path across the deep red carpet, coming to rest at the foot of the bulbous carved desk-leg. Over by the walnut glass-fronted bookcase, the large leather blotting pad had landed in a comical position, with one point as an unsteady pivot and another balancing cleverly against the wall.

Bending to retrieve the open cigar-box, its expensive contents littered all around, Lester replaced it on the desk and requested quietly, 'Would you rather I came back later, sir?'

With surprising speed, Edward Wyman pushed himself up into a smartly attentive position and fixing his watering eyes on the young man, he said, 'Ah! Lester. It's good you're here. And no, I would not prefer you to come back later. Good God, man! You're the only one I can get any real sense out of!' Here he drew in a great chestful of air. Then, clamping shut his mouth and noisily releasing the air through flared nostrils, he gestured for Lester to be seated on the upright green chair in front of the desk. Then, when the two of them were facing each other, he went on in a saddened tone, 'Lester. I've a great deal to thank you for. You know that, don't you?'

'Not at all, sir. I just do my job, a job I am most grateful for, and one which I enjoy very much.'

'That may be so! But I'm not blind to who's really held this place together of late. Lord knows *I* haven't done my share . . .'

'Only because you've been ill.'

'Stuff and nonsense! I've been molly-coddling myself, that's all – things playing on my mind that won't let me be, don't you know.' Here he paused, got to his feet and crossed to the window where for a long uncomfortable span, he stood, his hands stroking the iron-grey beard over and over as though caressing it. Then he came back to the desk, snapped open the cigar-box and, seeing it empty, rounded the chair where Lester sat and with a groan bent to collect one of the cigars from the carpet. Tearing the slim gold-band from around its fat form, he bit off the end which he spat onto the floor, and reached inside his waistcoat pocket. He hissed out an expletive when he found it empty and when Lester offered him a lighted match, he smiled, showing his teeth, before the cigar clamped firmly between them, he leant towards the flame and after sucking life into the cigar, gave a satisfied grunt. Then he took to pacing up and down the room, puffing his cigar and patting his waistcoat pocket with some agitation.

'Y'know, Lester, I had a mind to put you in my will . . .' he began.

'But sir . . .'

'Don't call me "sir", blast you! I said I *had* a mind to put you in my will.' He began chewing hard on the cigar, his ruddy features puckered as though in deep thought. Then, 'I *would*, too! Only I'm in a dilemma. It may well be that leaving you part of this land – and my God, I *should* do that, if only to show that no-good son of mine that he doesn't have all the say – well, it just may be that I'll be robbing another of her rightful inheritance.' As though relieved that the idea was out in the open, he marched in quick steps to the desk, stubbed the cigar out on its corner and threw the concertinaed remains into the box.

'Mr Wyman, I have never expected at any time to be included in your will. Indeed, I would certainly rather you had never even considered such a thing!' Lester Judd was naive in his honesty, an honesty which, together with his hard work, had endeared him to the old man in the first place.

'You're a decent lad, Lester Judd. And like it or not, there'll be a little something for you when I'm gone, all the same.' Letting out a deep-throated chuckle, he leaned back in his chair. 'But I'm not ready to go yet, young man, for I have some deep thinking to do and perhaps some wrongs to put right. We shall see. We shall see.'

Although Freya would have known exactly what Edward was intimating, her brother had no inkling. So, feeling somewhat embarrassed by the turn of the conversation, he hurriedly launched into the business which had summoned him here. For the next half-hour he explained how there was a sickness affecting two of the prize Hereford breeding bulls, the latest additions to the Wyman stock, magnificent beasts especially brought over from Wales and highly valued.

'You've had the veterinary out?'

'Soon as I suspected it.'

'And the dairy stock?'

'They're fine – I've had them checked and the affected bulls have been placed in isolation.'

'Good lad!' In two strides Edward was at the door. 'Before I take a look, is there anything else on your mind?'

'There is, but I'll tell you as we go along.'

'Give me a minute to get some boots and outdoor clothes on.' Suddenly he was excited at the prospect of going outside. But to the groom who came scurrying across the courtyard at his loud impatient summons, the master was still the cantankerous, bullying fellow he'd always been.

On the way to the barns in which the Herefords were enclosed, Lester Judd discussed the current prices of milk and beef, always markets to watch. He went into a detailed account of the labour force and how he'd reluctantly given one of the men notice, following an attack on another with a pitchfork. All in all, though, things were running smoothly.

'And how often have you seen that philandering bloody son of mine? No disrespect to you, young Judd, because I know I can rely on you to do a good job. But it's he who should be looking after things. Lazy bastard!'

'Your son is here when he's needed,' lied Lester, anxious to see father and son on good terms. But his noble attempt was quickly dismissed with a grunt.

Eager to change the subject, Lester voiced his considered opinion that one of the old hunters was past its prime and had earned an easy retirement.

'Have it slaughtered, man! If it's of no further use, at least it'll give the hounds a good feed!' Chuckling at the thought, Edward turned to the horrified young man at his side. 'Unless *you* want it?' Lester quickly agreed, if only to save a loyal friend from a sorry end.

'Very well! Is the Master agreed that the animal is past hunting?'

Lester confirmed that he was. And besides that, he had strongly advised a trip to Appleby Fair in Cumbria, which would secure a magnificent creature and introduce fresh blood to the stable.

'Appleby Fair, eh? That's the gypsy horse sale, isn't it? So he thinks we need to take a look at what they've got, does he? Huh! Can't say I'm altogether convinced . . .' Suddenly he was struck silent at the thought of what might be found at a gypsy sale, and with the image of a certain gypsy woman persisting in his mind, he said no more. That is, until after he and Lester had inspected the Herefords and been satisfied that they were on the mend.

At the entrance to the house as he removed his boots to replace them with finer footwear, Edward Wyman gave an answer that surprised even himself. 'Tell the Master I'll take him up on his suggestion, providing he accompanies me. Appleby Fair it will be, in the summer of next year.' Then, in a quieter tone, 'It'll get me away from that sister of yours, give me time to think.'

The two men parted: the young one to report to the Master with Edward's unexpected response to his suggestion; and the old one to his study, where, in a matter of moments he was using the telephone, which since its instalment, frequently went wrong and which he regularly referred to as 'more damned trouble than justifies its bloody existence!'

'Hello! Hello, Trask! Is that you, man?' A small pause as the private investigator confirmed that yes, it was he on the other end of the telephone. 'Good! Now then, why haven't you got back to me on the matter of two weeks ago? Have you dug up any information on that fellow Durnley? . . . No! No, you useless bloody idiot! I'm not interested in his financial status! I told you the sort of thing, dammit! Is he married? Does he have children, responsibilities of any kind? His moral character. Is he a bloody womanizer? That's what I need to know. Damn it, Trask! I told you to get your best man on it!' Here he let poor Trask get a word or two in, and their impact on Edward was staggering. The whole of his face lit with astonishment, with the exception of his bottom lip which fell trembling into a loosely shaped half-circle. 'The devil you say! Is that so?' He grew excited, his voice falling to an intimate whisper and a satisfied smile curving his mouth. 'There's no way your information could be wrong, is there, Trask?' He listened intently. Then, 'It won't do! Be quite sure of your facts, man! There's a lot hanging on the truth of it all. No! I won't be patient. I'm getting older by the bloody minute, damn you! Find out, I say – come up with real facts, and real evidence to support it . . . Don't worry about the cost. It's vital that I know this fellow and his habits inside out. Get to it right away!'

The unpleasant smile returned to his face, and he hung up the telephone receiver with exaggerated tenderness. Then, leaning back in his chair, he rested his elbows on its leather-padded arms and put his large hands together, the fingers steepled. After a moment's thought, he addressed himself in a sober tone. 'If what Trask suspects about Durnley is true, then it's been a very cleverly concealed secret these past years. Yes, most discreetly kept altogether. Hmh! Could it be, after all, that that dark-eyed child was my own flesh and blood? Hmh! Hmh!' Growing too agitated to remain seated, he rose to his feet and paced the carpet, the rhythmic thud of his footsteps interspersed now and then by a pondering 'Hmh! Hmh!' Then he halted, thrust one hand deep into his jacket pocket and with the other stroked his beard in feverish fashion, his head high, lips pursed tight and eyes closed, the better to marshal his churning thoughts – thoughts which both aggravated and disturbed him. Was it possible that he had given away his own flesh and blood? That tiny dark-eyed girl-child who, even through his hatred, he'd thought exquisitely beautiful, charged with an enchantment that he in his fury had seen as 'witchlike'. Had he been the grossest fool? Had he wronged his own daughter and condemned his own wife to hell because of his blind jealousy? Oh, God! He had loved that woman – *his* woman, Kathleen! Loved her still! Loved her all these years, but been too proud, too bloody stiff-necked to climb down. Yet now, if what Trask had come across was the truth, then he *would* climb down. He *must*! All these years. Such bitterness! Such destruction! But if she had deceived him, as he must believe until evidence to the contrary was put before him, then both she and the girl could rot in hell. And his conscience would not suffer because of it.

With renewed vigour he increased his pace, his chin stiff and straight and both fists flung into one behind his back. He was growing a little soft in his old age. He must watch that! It was a weakness, a weakness which might attract all kinds of predators to tear him to shreds. Two in particular: Freya Judd, and his own obnoxious son.

With this sobering thought in mind, Edward Wyman returned to his desk, and in a sudden frenzy he flung himself into his work.

From a vantage point just outside the door, where she had been feigning the removal of a stain on the brass doorknob, Freya Judd had eavesdropped on Edward Wyman's telephone conversation with the person called Trask. Then she had angrily swept away up the wide galleried stairway to Kathleen Wyman's old quarters, which were now hers, lavishly furnished with the best that money could buy and all looking splendidly arranged with highly-polished sideboard, circular single-pedestal table and a scattering of deep-backed chairs upholstered in a comfortable shade of claret to match the long heavy curtains at the windows. The bedroom was exactly as it had been on the day of Kathleen's removal from the house, although the rest of her quarters had been redecorated in a pleasing cream.

However, just at the moment nothing was pleasing to Freya Judd. She had deliberately heard what was not meant for her ears, and was suffering because of it! It was obvious to her, that Edward's thoughts were, as she had suspected, veering towards the incident which had taken place here in this house some thirteen years before. Else why would he be pursuing some sort of inquiry about the man Durnley? The very fellow whom Edward Wyman had abused to his wife, even as she was in the deepest and most dangerous throes of labour?

Oh, she did not like the way of things and it was plain to Freya that certain developments augured ill. Ill indeed! Worse than she had imagined. So, the child – and perhaps the mother also – *was* on his conscience. Now was no time for dithering. Not now! She must confide in Redford Wyman the moment he returned from London. The two of them would have to trace that dark-eyed girl before Edward did and, having found her, *deal* with her immediately.

Freya took a moment to calm down. The finding of the gypsy woman and her brat would not be easy. So many years had passed, with the trail long grown cold. No, it would not be an easy thing at all. Freya could only console herself with two facts: the trail had grown just as cold for Edward; and somewhere in the back of her mind was an image, a bright image in the shape of a brooch pinned to a shawl. Both were very valuable and no doubt the gypsy woman had sold them long ago. Such items were most eye-catching, and better still, easier to trace than a wandering gypsy woman and a dark-eyed girl!

With that thought, Freya Judd's smile deepened into true malevolence.

Chapter Ten

'Meks a body glad ter be alive, don't it?' The ditch-digger paused in the glory of his work, lifting his nut-brown weathered face towards the wagon as it clip-clopped along the country lane. Greeting the two handsome gypsies up front, the one a stripling girl of a presence that could steal a man's senses, and the other older, though still good to look on, he threw down his heavy shovel, tilted the cap back on his head, wiped the sweat from his brow, and squinting against the sun grinned them a broad toothless welcome.

'Aye! That it does,' agreed Rona, smiling down into the ditch as they ambled by. 'On a day like this, we're all glad ter be alive, old man.'

As the old cob drew the wagon away, Starlena dipped into the wicker basket of large rosy apples beneath the seat, withdrew the best, then skilfully and with true aim sent it sailing through the air, and into the ditch-digger's ready hands, calling back, 'Make sure and don't work too hard in this June heat!' Whereupon the old nut-brown face buried itself into the apple, as he nodded his head and waved a free hand in acknowledgement.

'Oh, Mammy. It's a glorious day!' breathed Starlena, settling back to dream while Rona smiled at her for an instant, before returning her full attention to the winding tree-lined lane ahead.

Of all the seasons, the summer was the time Starlena loved most, when the sun was at its highest in a sky of brilliant blue and everything below was warmed and lazy in contentment, when the wild flowers along the hedges seemed to blossom in their most vivid colours and nature altogether threw off restraint to display

152

such life and beauty as was breathtaking. This spring and early summer of 1912 seemed to Starlena the most wonderful of all. There was something magical about it, something ecstatically promising. She thought she could never be happier than she was right now. Starlena wasn't able to say just why she felt the way she did, but wondered whether it was because of her approaching birthday, when she would be *fourteen!* Or was it perhaps because her mammy had at long last agreed that in the coming autumn the colt could be broken and backed? Then again the reason for her unbounded exuberance might be because on this very day, and for the first time in her life, she was going to Appleby Fair. And oh, how Starlena had dreamed of that wonderful day when her mammy would take her to Appleby Fair in Cumbria where, in the tradition of hundreds of years, gypsies from all over the country, and even from abroad, would gather for dancing, bartering, ceremony and the highly charged buying and selling of some of the fastest and finest horses in the land. So gradely and handsome were these creatures that even wealthy gentry were attracted to wheeling and dealing for them.

Yes! Starlena was, as the old ditch-digger had put it, 'glad ter be alive!' And over these past eighteen months since the October when they had been so unceremoniously ejected from Kingston Asylum, so much had happened. Her mammy had never taken the road in that particular direction again, yet Starlena suspected that the entire incident had plagued her mammy's mind, as it had done hers. How she wished she was able to read and write, for it had crossed her mind many times that it would have been a pleasant thing to send the woman, Kathleen, a kindly letter. But it was not to be. Nor would she probably ever again see that poor creature, not in the whole of her life. Yet in her prayers, Starlena remembered Kathleen, and all unfortunate wretches like her, requesting most humbly that they come to know peace of heart.

With this particular train of thought, there came to her the image of Miss Elizabeth who, on the less frequent occasions when she had not been 'away on matters of family business', appeared to be deeply troubled and most unsettled. Starlena had remarked as much to her mammy whose swift retort had been, 'No doubt it's one o' two things as plagues 'er! Love or money! 'Tis usually one or the other.' And with that, Starlena had to be satisfied.

All the same, she hoped that when they made for home this winter, Miss Elizabeth would be less agitated. And maybe her mammy was right in the matter of it being 'love', because hadn't Starlena herself witnessed a most hesitant and tender kiss between the shy Miss Elizabeth and that good young man known as Lester? Oh, but there was another suitor also, one that Starlena had seen from a distance holding hands and walking with Miss Elizabeth. 'Twasn't difficult to see that with two gentlemen after her favours, she was faced with a dilemma! Starlena sensed the winds of change blowing through Miss Elizabeth's life, for there had been so many comings and goings this past year at Whalley Grange, with Miss Elizabeth absent more than Starlena cared for. And even when that kind lady was at home, there were so many strangers visiting, it was no wonder there was little time for the comfortable chats and quiet moments she and Starlena had shared. 'Twas a pity, because Starlena sorely missed that special intimacy, and she was impatient for things to return to normal at the big house; although these were not her mammy's sentiments for, as was her way and for reasons unbeknown to Starlena, Rona Parrish strongly objected to 'gentry mixing wi' the likes of us!'

All in all, these 'gentry' fascinated Starlena, who took great delight in observing their antics from her own special hidey-hole up in the aged branches of the grand old oak whose roots and trunk straddled the hedge which bordered the grounds of the big house. She had watched the big black carriages arrive and even on one occasion a snorting smoke-consumed monstrosity which her mammy had indignantly referred to as 'one of them God-frightening motor-vehicles'. And out of the grand carriages and the offensive 'motor-vehicle' had stepped all manner of gentry – ladies with long flounced dresses and feathery frilly hats, gentlemen with smart black toppers to match their dark formal suits.

Starlena had been wondering at the number of visitors, when, on a bright morning in the spring just gone, the head gardener had spied her up the tree. After spouting suitable words of chastisement as to the dangers of such foolhardiness, he had given out the information which had explained all the comings and goings. The aged dowager had been taken seriously ill: 'close to her Maker', they said. As for the ward, Elizabeth Doughty – well, that dear lady, already concerned for the dowager's health, had received a second blow. After months of intensive investigations with regard to her mother, the news had been brought back of her mother's untimely demise in some foreign land. ''Tis a crying shame, for we all have a fondness of Miss Doughty, that we do,' had been the head gardener's lament. Then, with a sharp and noticeable change of mood, he commented on another source of anxiety to his old mistress's ward. 'It's young Lester Judd's sister, Freya. Oh, now there's a divil in skirts if ever I saw one! Gives that fine brother of hers no peace – no, nor Miss Doughty, whom he would take for his wife given the chance. And better him than that brute Redford Wyman! 'Tis unnatural, the way them two young 'uns is tormented by that one and Freya Judd. What! 'Tis unnatural the way she fawns over her brother. Unnatural, I tell yer!' Whereupon he had shaken his head and hurried away, leaving Starlena to think about all he'd told her. Oh, poor Miss Elizabeth, she had thought at the time, and she thought it now on recollection. Yet, though they saddened her, try as they might these unpleasant observations could not quell the excitement of the ever closer Appleby Fair. Oh, what a time that was to look forward to! What adventures indeed, thought Starlena who, in the face of her mammy's outward indifference to it all, could hardly contain herself.

When Rona drew the wagon to a halt, the day was already beginning to fade, the sun was slipping away and all about them dusk painted its own unique pattern upon the landscape.

'It's tekken us longer than I'd thought,' observed Rona, flipping the flat of her hand to swat a persistent insect, one of many, attracted to them by the musky staleness of the old cob's coat, warmed and dried by the long day's heat. 'Let's set awhile, eh? Give the horses a well-earned breather,' she added, looking out over the valley below and falling into a quietness which drew Starlena's attention.

'What is it, Mammy?' she asked, peering at Rona with some curiosity.

It was a moment before there came an answer, then, 'Look yonder, child! Feast yer eyes on God's workings,' she told Starlena in an awed murmur.

This Starlena did, she too being deeply moved by it all. It struck her at once that this place was as lovely as any she'd seen – with the exception of Whistledown Valley, she promptly reminded herself.

They were stopped on the main entry into Appleby itself, having come upon it with little warning, in spite of the ancient castle which now loomed out of the trees behind them, to tower in magnificence over the village below.

Enjoying the same position of vantage and commanding glorious views all about, Rona and Starlena were able to see right down the cobbled road, past the tiny quaint cottages on either side, and into the picturesque market square below. Then beyond, to where stood a grand old church of remarkable beauty, with its tall iron and brass entrance, thick moss-covered walls and heavenward-reaching graceful spire into which was embedded an exquisite clock with figured hands and gilt frame. To the right of the church wound away a narrow lane, which after a while opened out to form a bridge flanked by aged stone walls interspersed here and there with little round, open turrets, into which a body might run and be safe from marauding horses or wide, clumsy flat-wagons. The bridge spanned a fast-moving river which even now was churning and rushing, occasionally fretting at the banks with white frothy fury.

The wider and more frequently-used road from the far side of the bridge meandered between the broad sloping banks of lush green grass on the riverside and the narrow flagged pavement on the other. From here, it began to rise away from the village, past the thatched and rambling inns where the wealthy gentry lodged while the Fair was on, up to the brow where straddled a pretty curved viaduct at the road's fork – the left of which ran away across the moors never to end and to the right to where the road aspired to the top of a green and velvet hill.

Starlena gazed at all of this wondrous architecture, man's and God's, merging in such perfect unison. She looked beyond the houses and the hand of man, to where the moors stretched away to the farthest horizon in a sea of blues, greens and heather purples, with here and there a scurry of woodland or an open lake, all rising and dipping like the waves of an ocean, playing peek-a-boo with the onlooker and never giving away its secrets all at once.

'Look over yon, Starlena!' Rona's arm was outstretched and leading Starlena's gaze to the hills on the far right, the most prominent being clustered about by hedges and trees, and dotted thereon with numerous shapes, white, grey and dark in colour and close enough to look like a settlement. 'That's Gypsy Hill, my gel! They're all 'ere afore us an' waitin' fer the start o' festivities.' At last! There was excitement in Rona's voice, and Starlena was greatly affected by it.

'Oh, come on! Come on, Mammy!' she cried, her heart soaring, 'Let's hurry. It'll be dark soon!'

Rona collected up the reins, slapped them against the old cob's neck, and clicked him on, saying, with a crafty peek at Starlena's face which was deep-flushed with excitement, 'Aye, it'll be dark afore we get there right enough, child. But not so dark we won't find a square o' land to set us-selves on. An' not so dark you'll miss anything, I'll be bound.' Then, chuckling to herself, she gentled the cob away down the road and on over the bridge towards Gypsy Hill.

As they approached the hill-side, by now speckled with myriads of lights, the dark was closing in about them and the sound of fiddle-music was emanating from one big camp-fire around which were gathered gypsies, from a bairn in arms to the most aged of all tribes. A fit of exhilaration seized hold of Starlena's merry heart. Without even thinking, out blurted the words, 'Oh, Mammy! Do you think Anselo's here? Will we see Anselo? Will we, Mammy?'

Rona gave no answer. The same thought had crossed her own mind, and it was not a pleasing one. For if the young man, Anselo, was here, then so too would be the one destined for gypsy queen: the witch-child, Celia.

'*Maduveleste! Maduveleste!*' called the gypsy women from their doors as Rona painstakingly inched the wagon up the steep, bumpy incline. It was hard work, what with the jutting stones which every now and then threw the wagon wheel up in the air before crashing to the ground, and every minute the night grew thicker, its blackness punctuated only by the lighted wagon windows and the glow in the sky which emanated from the gypsies' communal camp-fire some way in front. With her hands and full attention thus employed, Rona could give small response to the women's welcome, merely inclining her head in a curt but polite nod.

Starlena, on the other hand, was far too excited by it all to curb her enthusiasm. There was magic in the air tonight, she could tell! The warm aroma of roasting potatoes and barbecued rabbit twitched tantalizingly at her nostrils. Somewhere away to the left of them, a babby began crying lustily; above its wails came the lilting soothing tones of its mammy easing into a soft lullaby. Soon the babby gave up its loud protest and fell quiet beneath the persuasion of its mammy's loving song. All about was the sound of hustle and bustle, doors opening and closing, lights going on and off, and smiling happy faces emerging from the wagons. All were touched by the magic of Appleby Fair and all were making their way to the top of Gypsy Hill, and the camp-fire.

'Oh, Mammy! Look yon. Listen to the music!' breathed Starlena, her eyes glowing in the moonlight and her straight white teeth revealed in the most bewitching smile. Pressing close to her mammy, she put an arm about the dear woman's narrow shoulders, and lovingly touched the weathered face with her full soft lips. And in the lowest of whispers, she asked, 'Will we go to the camp-fire, Mammy? Please?' Her heart stood still while she waited for her mammy's response, for she would just *die* if the answer was no!

Turning her head at just enough of an angle to place a swift warm kiss on Starlena's cheek, Rona said kindly, 'Sit still, child! Fidgeting and fussin'! Keep yer eyes for'ard an' watch fer the stones. Else we'll be arse over tip an' going nowhere at all!'

Starlena did as she was told, her heart heavy at her mammy's mood, but her love for the darling woman was so deep that she made no complaint. Instead, she concentrated all her attention on the path they must negotiate, her spirits lifted somewhat by the great bright flare which rose from the camp-fire to light up the sky. Now ever nearer came the laughter of revellers and the jolly sound of fiddle-music accompanied by voices uplifted in song and merriment.

Soaking up all of these sights and sounds, and lost in the wonder of it all, Starlena was not prepared when suddenly her mammy laughed aloud, saying with mock impatience, 'I suppose if you've set yer 'eart on it, we'd best show us-selves at yon camp-fire.'

Starlena couldn't help herself. The bubble of happiness which had carried her all the way here exploded in a shower of ecstasy, as in a rush she flung her arms about her mammy, laughing and crying all at once, and kissing the darling face enough to raise a bruise. 'Oh, Mammy! Mammy Parrish! I love you!' she cried, her exuberance threatening to unbalance not only the two of them, but cob, wagon, trailing colt and all.

'Hey! Get yer eyes back on that road, young 'un! Keep 'em sharp fer a place to set down!' protested Rona, fighting with the reins and skinning her eyes for the first opportunity to come off the path where too many wagon wheels had etched deep ruts into the earth, making the way much more difficult.

Suddenly a jolly shawled gypsy woman called out '*Maludeveste!*', stepping aside so they could pass and raising a hand in welcome. Starlena knew the meaning of '*Maludeveste*' very well, for hadn't her mammy murmured it to her many times since as far back as she could remember? It was 'God bless' the gypsy woman had called out to them. And the wish was warmly returned by Starlena, whose heart was brimming with joy. She was *here*, at Appleby Fair, *here* on Gypsy Hill, and soon she and her mammy would be round the camp-fire and in the middle of all the festivities.

It was some twenty minutes later, after Rona and Starlena had settled the wagon onto a good flat site and were tethering both cob and colt over a patch of green grass, when the sound of approaching footsteps caused them to look up.

The figure emerging was silhouetted in the light of the moon, a young man of slim build, but with strong broad shoulders and an easy way of walking that was most attractive. As he drew closer and at last was recognizable, Starlena saw that it was Anselo, the boy she had never forgotten and who had a special place in her heart. But he was no longer a boy! Gone were the roundness of face and the soulful expression in the brown eyes. In their place were the strong dark features of a young man, proud and confident. And when at last as he stood before her, he spoke softly saying, 'Starlena. I knew you'd come to Appleby this year. I just knew!' his deep brown eyes were the eyes of a man, handsome and full of that certain suggestion of passion which no woman could mistake.

The effect of his lingering gaze on Starlena was startling. Somewhere deep inside her a trembling was awakened and beneath the smouldering intensity of his gaze, she suddenly felt afraid and insecure. Yet in the midst of it all, there was an inexplicable sense of wonder, a longing to stay held in the spell of those brown eyes that suggested so much and gave away so little.

'Anselo, is it?' Rona's call interrupted the spell. 'I'd 'a thought you'd been looking to yer *own* kith an' kin!' In a surly manner, she grabbed the water-jack from its hook beneath the wagon, swinging it in her hand and adding sharply, 'It's nice ter see yer, lad! But we've no time fer gabbin'.' Then to Starlena, 'C'mon, lass. We'll fotch us water afore we do owt else.'

Starlena knew her mammy's moods well. It was plain she was not enjoying Anselo's presence. 'All right, Mammy,' she assured Rona, 'I'll be along.' Then returning her gaze to Anselo, she said quietly, 'Oh, Anselo, I'm so glad you're here. I was hoping you would be.'

For a moment there was no response as, caught in the pleasure of her nearness, Anselo continued to gaze down on Starlena's beauty. He was acutely aware of her pretty slight figure and the two gently thrusting points beneath her blouse, which suggested approaching womanhood and which stirred him deeply. He admired the exquisite structure of her face with its high cheek-bones and full rich mouth. The eyes enchanted him, so large and striking, their moist blackness marbled in the moonlight with tinges of violet. And all about her head and shoulders a wealth of wavy black hair. He thought her the most ravishingly beautiful creature he had ever seen, so devastatingly magnificent that it almost took his breath away.

In a whisper he told her, 'Do you believe me when I say you're always on my mind?' He would have said more, but Rona's impatient voice cut across his own.

'Starlena! Yer mammy's waitin' on yer!'

Starlena quickly smiled an apology to Anselo and collected the second water-jack from beneath the wagon, then together with her mammy she hurried away to find the brook which Rona remembered ran along the other side of Gypsy Hill.

For a long while, Anselo stayed on the spot where Starlena had left him, her face alive in his mind, in his heart the affection he'd always felt for her painfully growing into love. In that moment, Anselo dared to think that she might feel something of the same.

Following her mammy over the hill, their way lighted by the moon. Starlena was for a time quietened by her meeting with Anselo. There were strange emotions stirring inside her, that were both frightening and exciting. She couldn't recognize them, for they were new to her and, in a way, pleasing. Only one thing emerged with certainty from the trembling awareness in her heart, and that was the desire to be close to Anselo again. Such a strong desire that she could not deny it. So intense a longing that against all her instincts she might even be tempted to go against her mammy's will!

Some two hours later, Starlena sank to the warm rough earth. Exhausted but deliriously happy, she sat cross-legged next to her mammy.

'There, me darlin',' Rona laughed, shaking the slim wooden flute into the air. Though silent now, it had come alive beneath Rona's persuasion, playing its pretty musical notes while Starlena's dainty feet had carried her wholeheartedly into a dance all about the camp-fire. 'It's been a while since I played Callum's penny whistle, but y'see I've not lost me touch, eh?' She was evidently pleased to have given Starlena so much delight and in the process had thoroughly entertained all present.

'Oh, Mammy, 'tis beautiful. You will teach me to play, won't you?' coaxed Starlena, still flushed and breathless from her dancing.

'There's time enough, child,' cautioned her mammy. 'Yer 'ave a colt to back and school, remember. That'll see enough o' yer time away, I'm thinkin'.' Rona put away the flute into her skirt pocket, at the same time bringing out the little clay pipe which Starlena had found beside a brook some time back and from which her mammy had derived a deal of pleasure ever since. Now, she packed it tight with a fat strand of baccy taken from the string purse about her neck, then reaching forward she cadged a light from an elderly gypsy man close by. After which she settled back against the tree-trunk, a contented smile on her face, the puffs of smoke from the pipe causing her to screw up her eyes into little narrow slits. All the while she was humming along with the music of fiddle and accordion now played with great enthusiasm by a couple of gypsies, accompanied by much foot-tapping and hand-clapping from all around.

Such a time Starlena could never remember! She had danced to the tune her mammy played on the penny whistle which had belonged to her brother, now gone to America. She had watched mesmerized while the gypsy women flung themselves with abandonment into the excitement of the fandango, quickly joined by the dark-eyed men who twirled their partners with ease and snapped their fingers to the rhythm of fast exciting music. She had eaten succulent fruits; laughed at her mammy's teasing antics while under the influence of a glass of red wine; happily chased the little children who ran about – brown, wild and naked as fox-cubs. Now her quieter thoughts embraced the memory of Anselo, for whom she had kept constant watch since the incident at the wagon, and whom she had not once caught sight of since.

Somewhere in the distance a clock chimed, each stroke reverberating in the sultry night air until, on the twelfth tone, there fell over the camp-fire such a silence that Starlena was suddenly afraid. Every man, woman and child had ceased their revelry and were now moving towards the clearing on the far side of the camp-fire; in their eyes was a look of pride and expectancy, and in the soft tread of their steps, a great degree of respect.

Intrigued and a little disturbed by such unusual behaviour, Starlena gripped her mammy's hand, looking up at her with big wondering eyes, and asked quietly, 'What is it, Mammy? What's wrong?'

But Rona spoke as if to herself when she murmured, 'So! 'Tis tonight, eh? The night a gypsy queen is made!' Then, in spite of all misgivings, which were somewhat dulled by her rare indulgence in a drop of wine, and driven by the gypsy blood which ran strong in her veins, Rona stood up.

In a moment, Starlena found herself taken firmly by the hand in the same direction that drew all others. When she came to rest at the clearing, she was to see so beautiful and heart-stirring a sight that it would never leave her.

Emerging from a wagon situated some way from the clearing, came a procession of three people: the man Jemm, his son Anselo, and between the two of them, the girl, Celia. They walked close together, covering the ground in slow reverent steps, heads high, eyes intently forward.

Starlena allowed her gaze first to dwell for some time on the upright figure of Anselo. Handsomely dressed in blood-red cords topped by a stark-white full-sleeved shirt and vivid red waistcoat, he struck a particular chord in her heart. He wore no hat, and his thick black hair fell from a centre parting to cover his ears and touch the collar of his shirt. In the moonlight it shone magnificently, accentuating the darkness of his skin and eyes.

His father Jemm also looked handsome, in spite of his more mature years, although he was not so splendidly attired, having chosen less colourful garb in the form of black trousers and waistcoat, with a plum-red shirt done up tight at the neck.

The figure of Celia, protectively placed between adoptive father and son, seemed to Starlena a vision of absolute loveliness. Her long dark brown hair hung loose down her back, and was interwoven

163

with the most scented and delicate of flowers, which shone like so many stars in her hair. Her head was held proudly high and in her eyes there shone a glow to put the moon to shame. She had on a long cream dress with scooped neckline which laid bare her slim shoulders, and in her hands, which were held before her, she carried a small spray of purple ragged robin, snow-in-the-summer and other pretty wild flowers.

One of the elders stepped out to meet the one who would be queen. Taking her hand, he led her towards the people where, with quiet and well-rehearsed words, he proclaimed her right to the title. Then there was much cheering, drinking and making merry, with Celia receiving all manner of gifts and congratulations.

Once, in the full glow of triumph, she stole a glance at Starlena. And even though Starlena was filled with wonder at such pomp and ceremony, she could not mistake the blatant hatred which was alive in the gypsy queen's gaze as it enveloped her.

Throughout the occasion, both Anselo and his father were required to attend at Celia's side, receiving offerings on her behalf and making polite thanks. Yet Anselo was not too occupied to smile on Starlena from time to time, his warm eyes telling her what she wanted to know.

'C'mon, child! We've seen enough fer one night. It's away to us beds we're going,' Rona said. Without further ado, she propelled Starlena to the wagon, and once inside, she secured the door and hurried the two of them into bed. For a while, Starlena lay awake, her mind made too restless for sleep. Her heart was too excited by the intimate looks which had been for her and Anselo alone!

The next day, Starlena rose bright and early, still full of excitement over the occasion and wondering what treats still lay in store. Yet never in her wildest dreams could she have envisaged the outcome of it all.

'What's going on down there, Mammy?' she asked, peering out of the doorway, her black eyes alight.

'Where, child?' Rona put down her mending, came to the door and looked out towards the foot of the hill where some sort of meeting appeared to be taking place. 'Hmp! I'm sure I don't know what it is,' she replied, going back in to resume work on the tear of her shawl.

Starlena's curiosity was aroused. 'It's all right if I go and see, isn't it, Mammy?' she asked.

It was a question which Rona had anticipated. After thinking for a moment she could find no objection. 'Go on then,' she nodded. 'But mind you stay well away from that gypsy queen – and that brother of hers!'

'Anselo's not her brother!'

''Appen not. But I'd not mind betting it won't be long afore he's her husband.' The thought gave Rona a deal of satisfaction, which revealed itself in her little snort and in the crafty smile which played about her lips.

As a rule, when leaving the wagon even for a short while, Starlena would hug and kiss her mammy. But she had been deeply disturbed by Rona's prediction on Anselo's future, so with only a slight backward glance, she went out of the door, down the steps and away towards where the disturbance was growing bigger and noisier by the minute! Rona gazed after her, the torn shawl abandoned on her lap, and a look of sadness in her eyes. 'Sorry, me darlin',' she murmured after Starlena, 'but that one ain't fer you. And never will be.'

As Starlena skipped down the hill with the birds singing high in the trees and the hot sun bathing her face, she felt exhilarated. Today was all a new experience for her and one which she meant to savour to the full. However, when she came upon the cause of all the noise and uproar at the foot of the hill, her heart sank to her boots and the joy which had lightened her step became a knot of fear deep down inside her. For there, in the middle of all the excitement, was Anselo; Anselo, as she had never seen him!

She had pushed her way through the gypsies' yelling surging bodies and, without warning, had come to an inner ring of men, all intent on what was taking place at the very heart of the meeting and upon which, according to conversations Starlena overheard, rested many a fortune. As she broke through, Starlena found herself before a crudely erected boxing-ring, constructed in a series of stout rough timbers, each linked to the other by means of thick plaited rope, creating an enclosed square. The ground within it was beaten earth liberally sprinkled with sweet-smelling sawdust.

The hub of activity emanating from the corner to her left drew Starlena's attention. Here a rough-looking fellow, with thick stubbly chin and flat cap tilted forward almost to cover his eyes, was loudly proclaiming that a fist-fight between two men was no place for women! 'Let them be removed,' he finished, nodding his head in grateful acknowledgement as a cry of encouragement arose from every man present.

'Fie on yer!' screamed an old hag not far from Starlena who, judging by her villainous expression and by the way she had settled herself in front complete with an old arm-chair and a basket of food, had probably enjoyed more gypsy fist-fights than every man-jack there. 'Stop wastin' time, yer old bugger! Gerron wi' it!' she yelled, her gnarled old fist waving in the air. By now she had the crowd on her side, all adding their own impatient voices to the suggestion that it was time to see some action.

Suddenly everything was quiet. Then a handbell was rung, and as Starlena watched horrified, there came a flurry of activity from opposite corners. Without further warning, the two men lunged into action and within seconds were drawing blood from each other, to the glee and encouragement of the crowd, and in particular from the old hag, who was cackling one minute and ramming food into her mouth the next.

Every instinct in Starlena's body urged her to flee from such a bloody scene, but she could not. Something held her rooted to the spot. It was hard to tell whether it was the exhilarating atmosphere which held her gripped, or whether it was the sight of Anselo. Certainly to see him this way was deeply exciting for stripped to the waist as he now was, and though still not yet seventeen, Anselo had the strong muscular physique of a man in his prime. It was clear that the heavy labours of life against the hardships of nature – wood-chopping, demanding work in the fields and the basic necessity of keeping horse and wagon in prime condition – all went to make a boy a man that much quicker.

Of the two men, Anselo proved to have the greatest stamina, the hardest fist and the swiftest feet. As in all gypsy fights, there were no Queensberry rules observed. It was no holds barred and may the best man win! There was no doubt that Anselo was the better man and, in spite of her fear for his safety, Starlena was proud of him. A film of sweat had covered his broad tanned body and, as the two men launched into each other with unbridled viciousness, the sweat erupted in glistening rivulets tumbling down every inch of his naked torso.

Starlena winced as the other man landed a crunching blow to Anselo's cheekbone, ripping it open to a bloody mess. Anselo was reeling with pain. Encouraged by his success, the other fighter came in even faster and more furiously, obviously thinking to move in for the kill.

But he had not reckoned on his opponent's determined disregard for what was evidently a bad injury. Anselo lashed out time and time again, hitting home with bone-breaking savagery, until his opponent was forced to abandon his own attack and go on the defensive. In a matter of minutes both men were bleeding. Anselo's cheekbone had swollen to block his vision and the torrent of blood still flowing from it fell to his shoulder and chest, mingling with the sweat and creating a macabre pattern. This excited the old hag to such an extent that she was on her feet screaming that the other fighter should 'finish 'im off!' This in turn brought Starlena to Anselo's defence and, caught up in the atmosphere of it all, she too began shouting. 'Go on, Anselo!' she cried. 'Put him on his back! You can do it!' Anselo looked round seemingly startled at her presence. Just for a fleeting second he was caught off guard. It was enough! The other man seized his chance. His clenched fist tore into the side of Anselo's head and a great cheer went up from that section of the onlookers who had put money on Anselo to lose.

Starlena's hand flew to her mouth. But when Anselo faltered and fell against the ropes, she mustered all her energy to run to where he could see her and tears filling her eyes at the sight of him bruised and bleeding, she told him, 'Show him, Anselo! Show him you're the better man!'

The smile he gave her was distorted by the lumps and tears on his face. But the brief intimacy of her encouragement was enough to send him roaring back to where his opponent was even now preparing to raise his arms in triumph, a triumph which swiftly turned to bitter disappointment as he felt the sickening thud of Anselo's cruel right hand.

Now Starlena was joyfully jumping up and down, and she would have stayed to the bitter end, had it not been for the burning curiosity of her mammy who had determined to find what had become of her child and who at this very moment burst through the wall of bodies to grab Starlena by the arm, and in no uncertain manner to march her smartly away. 'Yer want yer arse tanned, my girl! Did yer mammy give her permission fer you to witness such a spectacle? *Did she?* No, she did not!' she scolded. The old hag nearby was amused, and along with the others burst out laughing, to which Rona responded, 'An' you lot ought to be ashamed! *Ashamed*, I say!'

But Starlena felt only regret as her mammy dragged her away, all the while cursing and grumbling. From behind her, Starlena could hear the crowd baying for the blood of the young man not much older than herself; the same young man who had long been a dear friend, but who so recently had become very much more. Anselo had stirred something deep within her, a sensation which filled the whole of her being, and which she liked. Liked a great deal!

It was some two hours later when Starlena stepped out to follow the path down the hill which led to the village below where the grooming, buying and selling of the best horses was already under way.

Behind her, Starlena could hear her mammy's boot-heels chinking against the fine stones underfoot. She called out a word of encouragement. Back came the response, 'I may be gettin' old in the tooth, cheeky arse! But I'm still as sure-footed as you'll ever be!' Starlena smiled to herself. The business of the fist-fight this morning had certainly upset her mammy, that was for sure. At one moment, she'd been saying yes, they would stay till the week's end when the Fair was finished for another year, and in the next she'd been threatening to pack up there and then and to be 'off down the road and away'. It was only Starlena's pleading, together with a promise never to watch such a thing again, that had persuaded her mammy to stay.

As it was, the dear woman had been so upset by it all and by Starlena's complete lack of respect for the gypsy queen that for more than a full hour she had sat on the three-legged stool, lecturing Starlena on the dangers inherent in being born a gypsy. Then she had mended first the tear in her shawl and after, every little rip in every garment there was; and had gone on to mount a vigorous and devastating attack with rag and elbow-grease on every piece of crockery and each brass object throughout the wagon. That done, and her piece to Starlena said, she had sat perfectly still, arms folded and her little clay pipe gripped fast between her teeth, emitting great angry puffs of smoke. Starlena had been wise enough to set quietly by the window while all this was going on, making no comment and offering little resistance. It was a good ploy, because here they were, the two of them, washed, changed, mutually forgiven and, at long last, on the way to the village.

Skipping down the hill, Starlena drew many admiring glances and even a flurry of wolf-whistles, which in turn drew a number of black looks and a few choice words from her mammy a few steps behind. Yet there were still men bold enough to loudly appreciate this dark vision of beauty which had arrived with the glory of a wonderful June day, when the heat made a man both lazy and amorous.

Starlena was magnificent. She was enchanting, exciting and most desirable to all whose covetous eyes followed her on the downhill journey. A proud graceful figure she was, dressed in white sleeveless blouse and frilled skirt of black and yellow, her lovely dark eyes glowing, her waist-length black hair lifted and tumbled by the warm breeze which teased the hillside in playful gusts.

From the open door of her adoptive father's wagon, Celia also looked on. Her face was a study of malice and in her black jealous heart wrestled a hatred of Starlena. It was a sore point with the new gypsy queen that Anselo still looked on her as a sister, even though she had exploited almost every means at her disposal to persuade him otherwise. But her time would come! Anselo would be her man in the true sense, she knew. For there would be no let-up on her part until the two of them were merged as one. And the only real obstacle she saw to the fruition of her dream was Starlena. Even the name seared across her mind like a white-hot branding-iron.

Some way up the hill, hurrying after Starlena, Rona's quick eyes caught sight of the brooding Celia, and her old heart was troubled. That one had spelt mischief over the years and she spelt mischief now! Yet there was little to be done to pacify the creature, except maybe to keep Starlena well away and to discourage any deepening friendship with Anselo, whom it was painfully clear was considered by the gypsy queen to be her own property. That being the case, Starlena was the greatest threat, and as such was in real danger. Oh, how Rona wished she had never brought Starlena here, for with the dear girl so enthralled by it all and with the hub-bub of mounting excitement all about her, Starlena would resist any attempt to take her away from it so soon. And in all truth, Rona wanted her girl to enjoy the gypsies' heritage, even if only because for too many years they had skulked along back lanes and in out-of-the-way places because of Rona's constant nightmare that the light of her life might suddenly be snatched from her by those who were by birth her rightful people. Nothing of Rona's innermost fears, however, was ever suspected by Starlena, who found blissful happiness in just being close to nature, as free as any bird and spending both day and night in her beloved mammy's company.

Rona watched Starlena now, thinking how near the brink of womanhood she was, how strikingly lovely – running and laughing without a care in the world and, though her deeper instincts remained troubled, she prayed with all her heart that it might remain so.

Throughout the day, Starlena was in a state of enchantment. Hand in hand, she and her mammy wandered about, taking in all the sights and revelling in all that made the annual Appleby Fair the magical adventure that it was. The sprawling colourful market square came alive with the vendors, who competed against each other, each trying to out-shout the others. In a row of wooden pens situated by the harness-stall there were goats, of long- and short-haired variety, chickens which screeched and flapped their wings if anyone approached, geese that loudly hissed, brown dewy-eyed calves, fat pink pigs, and hung in cages above these, row upon row of bright colourful singing-birds, the delight of every gypsy with a song in his heart.

When the ponies and traps were sent racing up and down the road so that each driver could display the prowess, speed and proud carriage of his particular outfit, Starlena cried out in excitement. Three times Rona found reason to caution her not to wander so near to where their flailing hooves might catch her. Each time she was exasperated when Starlena, laughing, caught her mammy in a warm embrace and said, 'Oh, will you look at them, Mammy? Aren't they beautiful?' Her complete trust in the drivers' expertise gave Rona no opportunity to relax until after a while she took Starlena by the hand and led her to the river-bank. There, gathered at the water's edge, were numerous horses, each held by its owner and each waiting its turn to be soaped and bathed in the fast-flowing waters. Wetted blocks of green soap were vigorously rubbed all over an animal's body, after which fistfuls of water were splashed on. A frothy lather was worked into the horse's hide and then, with the rider on its bare back, the horse would be encouraged first into the shallower part and then on into the deep. After a step or two the river would completely engulf both horse and rider. Then they would come out – horse washed clean and shining, and the rider with his soaking clothes clinging to his breathless frame.

Interested onlookers from far and wide lined the banks below and hung over the bridge above to witness this often spectacular event, after which the horses were paraded before prospective buyers. These included gypsy and gentry alike, all keen to own the best. To them all, money was no object.

Certainly it was not to Edward Wyman, that bitter-faced man of advancing years whose narrow eyes relentlessly scanned the scene before him, as though searching hard for something. At this very moment he stood no more than five feet from where Starlena herself sat upon the grass, her eyes alight, totally transfixed by the proceedings.

Rona never strayed too far away and was presently resting against the wooden spokes of the wheel of a handsome trap which was parked by the bank while both driver and pony enjoyed a well-earned break. These past few minutes she had been preparing to fetch Starlena away, but each time she'd started forward, some new horse was brought to the river's edge and as the previous one was driven out of the swirling river, Starlena had been so filled with the excitement of it that Rona hadn't the heart to draw her away just yet.

'If you don't mind me saying so, Edward,' ventured the Master of Foxhounds, a droll-looking fellow with serious face and nervous manner, 'you've let a few choice beasts slip through your fingers.'

'No matter! No doubt there's as many to come as have gone before,' returned Edward Wyman with obvious impatience, his scowl deepening as he continued to look on. 'If I'm taking a beast back, then it'll need to be worth the trouble.' He wasn't pleased to be here amongst this chaos, nor in such close vicinity to so many gypsies. He was impatient: impatient with what life had offered him so far and despairing of what it seemed to see fit to offer him in the future; impatient with his no-good son who, after that Doughty woman had spurned him and chosen Lester Judd as husband, had become even more impossible than before. Of course the Doughty woman had chosen the better of the two; there was no doubt about that in Edward Wyman's mind. And he was convinced that the old dowager had had a hand in that before she had died. Freya Judd, however, had not taken kindly to the whole thing, for since her brother had wed and moved out of Bessington Hall she had been like a thing demented. She had chosen to disregard her brother's new bride and by so doing, had alienated Lester·so much that his visits to Bessington Hall had grown much less frequent. Bloody shame, that! fumed Edward Wyman, for he himself put great store on the young man, hoping he might have continued to manage the Bessington Hall acreage. Instead of which, Lester had his hands full at Whalley Grange and also spent a deal of time organizing his wife's extensive business holdings in America. While he himself was left to contend with his useless bloody son and that scheming viper, Freya Judd!

Here a wicked little smile crept over his face, as he thought of the nasty surprise the two might receive in the future – in the very *near* future if all went according to plan. Only a week ago there had come a telephone call from London and with it a communication calculated to turn the Wyman household upside-down. Hopefully it would shake out the vermin such as the drink-sodden Redford and the devious woman who for too many years had taken much pleasure in blackmail – all because of the shameful thing he had done under the influence of jealousy and desire for revenge. And to think everything now pointed to the possibility that his wife Kathleen had not played him false – certainly not with the man Durnley, who by all accounts had been deeply immersed in a love affair of his own at that time and for many years before. It had been kept very quiet because his lover was a *man*. Such a thing was deplorable. There was not the slightest doubt that Durnley's career would come to an untimely end were it ever to become publicly known. Trask had done a good job, yes indeed. Now all that was required was that he should come up with equally satisfying and startling results concerning the finding of that newborn child he had given away, now almost a young woman, lovely no doubt, and his daughter. The heiress to Bessington Hall and a fortune, which, when the land, livestock, and inherited treasures were taken into account, would amount to something in the region of one million pounds, with on top of that, a further half a million invested in long-term securities.

Edward Wyman took particular delight in his thoughts, for he had already decided on two courses of action. The minute his daughter was found, Redford's inheritance would be reduced. And at the earliest opportunity he planned that Kathleen be brought home and reunited with the daughter who had been most cruelly snatched from her. If that happened – and once his wife was in full possession of all the facts, armed with his own most sincere apology and reinstated as mistress of Bessington Hall – there would be no room beneath his roof for either Redford Wyman or Freya Judd. To hell and damnation with them both! However, his son was a Wyman and he would not shame the family name by paupering him. All the same Edward had it in mind to place him in a most frustrating and impossible position when he himself was gone.

At a sudden exclamation from his colleague, Edward was made to bring his full attention back to the matter of horses. 'Now, *there's* a handsome beast, Edward!' The Master stepped forward a pace, the better to examine the bay stallion being brought up to the river's edge. 'A real hunter – look at the front on it, man! And spirited by the look of it!' He was clearly excited.

So too was Starlena who, apologizing most profusely as she pushed by the large portly figure of Edward Wyman, took herself to within a few feet of the animal in question. He was magnificent. As she gazed at him, her eyes wide and admiring, there came into her mind the gentle image of another, a horse she had idolized and whose life had been so violently ended. Remembering, her heart grew cold and were it not for the words her mammy had impressed on her, she would have torn herself away this minute, rooted out a particular girl and thrashed her within an inch of her life. But her mammy's wishes went deep, and the offender was like a sister to Anselo, whom she wouldn't wish to hurt and whom she had looked for all the while since coming down to the river – in vain, for there was no sight of him. She hoped he had not been too badly beaten up in the fight.

'He is a beauty!' The voice could have been summoned up by the intensity of Starlena's thoughts. Turning quickly, she found herself looking straight into the laughing brown eyes of Anselo, who seeing her surprise, came up to her and draping an arm about her shoulders in a casual manner, smiled down into the great black eyes which softened beneath his tender gaze. Strange, thought Starlena, how he could have such an effect on her, causing her heart to catch in her throat, his very nearness setting up a wonderful trembling down inside where she was helpless to control it.

Instinctively, Starlena brought the tips of her long slender fingers to his face. She stroked the swollen flesh and the raw gashes which, despite treatment, still lay open and vulnerable.

'Will your face be left scarred?' she asked, acutely aware of the severe beating he had taken.

Anselo laughed aloud. 'No, my angel. I've had worse these past twelve months. Funny, y'know, but after a while your skin likens to leather. Also, it hurts less when you win!'

At this point Rona stepped forward to make her presence known. Anselo, seeing her disapproval, withdrew his arm and directed Starlena's attention to the bay stallion who seemed dead set against taking a bath of any kind, particularly in that raging river! Already soaped down, he was objecting to being handled in such a way and making life difficult for the rough-looking gypsy who grimly held on to him.

Starlena thought the animal the finest she had seen, with many characteristics of her own stallion, which she was greatly looking forward to backing for the first time this coming autumn. This one, though, while of the same dark bay colouring, had a white blaze running from brow to nostril and was of more mature years, judging by the deep strong chest and the broad muscular neck. He was certainly a spirited creature, Starlena mused, restless and angry, occasionally showing his temper by throwing up his head and to the apprehension of nearby spectators, setting back on his hind legs with the intention of rearing his front hooves high into the air.

When his fidgeting and nervous tap-dancing caused the portly well-dressed gentleman and his solemn-faced friend to step quickly backwards, Starlena smiled in amusement, thinking it would take a gypsy to handle such a beast and that if the fancy gentlemen saw themselves as possible purchasers, then they'd better think again!

'Woa, yer bugger! Woa!' Even his owner, who by now had mounted him, found the stallion as much of a handful as he could master. When the time came to ride him into the swirling river, he would have none of it! Bucking and snorting, he would *not* be forced away from the security of firm ground. In a rage, the gypsy dismounted and set about thrashing him with unbridled vigour. 'I'll show yer who's boss 'ere! Skin the bloody back off yer, I will,' he yelled, with each word laying the crop deep into the terrified animal's flanks.

Thinking about it later, Starlena couldn't remember making up her mind. But when she saw that magnificent beast taking such a thrashing, his great bright eyes fearful and his mouth white with foam, something snapped inside her. In a moment, she had bounded forward and in the next she was on the stallion's back, her body lying flat across him and her arms wrapped about his neck, while her voice soothed, caressed and coaxed him out of his terror. While his gypsy owner stood open-mouthed, crop raised and eyes startled, Starlena gently coaxed the big animal towards the water's edge.

Both Rona and Anselo had lunged forward, fearful for the girl they loved. But they dared not make any sudden move for fear of panicking the stallion into a run or a bucking fit. Instead, they quietly prayed.

Silent also was every man, woman and child who watched and found it difficult to believe what was before their eyes. Gorgio and gypsy alike were held entranced as Starlena took the mighty stallion into the water, first to cover his ankles, then, oh, so gradually, deeper and deeper until the lapping water wrapped itself over his legs, splashed beneath his belly and finally covered his shoulders. All the while he was dancing and snorting, his nostrils flared and his eyes flashing. And always Starlena's gentle whisper was soothing the terror in his breast.

Now they were out in the middle of the river, the spectators still not daring to move a muscle or mouth a whisper. The water crept up and up about Starlena and her mount until all that could be seen were the upper flanks and head of the stallion and, lying closely along his back, Starlena's small slim body. Suddenly they had reached the plateau beyond which ran the deepest part of the river. In a moment they were gone, completely submerged beneath the foaming water. The silence grew thicker as all who watched feared the worst.

Then, with a shout of, 'She's up! Christ Almighty, she's up!' Starlena's dark wet head burst through in the calmer water, quickly followed by the horse's pricked-up ears and large surprised eyes. Hurriedly now, the horse surged forward, strong and sure in his swimming, until, exhausted but victorious, both horse and rider emerged to reach the patch of firm ground where waited the gypsy owner, mouth still open in astonishment.

For a moment, no-one moved. It was as though they were paralysed with shock. Starlena sat bolt upright on the stallion's back, her hair hanging past her waist, lank and shining blue-black, her clothes clinging to every curve of her slim body, a look of great joy on her face.

It was only when she patted the stallion's neck, saying, 'You *did*, it, you beauty!' and he began to shake himself and whinny, that the crowd began roaring, cheering and clapping all at once. At the same moment, Rona and Anselo surged forward, together with others who wanted to touch this slip of a girl who had mesmerized a stallion.

Edward and the Master came forward also, caught up in the wave of jubilation.

As so many enthusiastic hands reached out to grab Starlena from the stallion's back, Rona was quick to intervene, catching Starlena firmly by the hand and in a voice still thick with fear, telling her, 'Aw, child! Yer could'a been killed! *Killed*, I tell yer!' After which she pulled her into a tight embrace, rocking her back and forth as one might a babe. 'Yer never to do owt like that agin, d'yer 'ear me, child? Yer frightened yer ol' mammy, that yer did!'

Too breathless and shivering wet to answer, Starlena clung to her mammy, smiling over her shoulder at Anselo, who returned her warm smile in a most intimate manner, his love and admiration for Starlena growing by the minute until he thought he would burst with pride.

As her mammy flung off her shawl to wrap around Starlena, Edward Wyman looked long and hard at both the old gypsy and the girl who now intrigued and disturbed him. Glancing back as she led her child away, Rona's eyes met his. It was as though a great cold hand had clasped her heart and in an instant she was almost running, for she had recognized the portly gentleman. Oh, somewhat broader, greyer and more advanced in years, but 'twas he, she knew. That man was Starlena's real father!

Greatly disturbed by what she had seen, and still trembling from the fright Starlena had given her, she neither saw nor heard the fast-moving pony and trap until, with a sickening thud, it struck her hard in the side, sending both her and Starlena reeling.

For some time after Rona had hurried away with Starlena, as he brooded deep into the evening over his jug of ale at the inn, Edward Wyman could not get either of them out of his mind. It was as though a fever had gripped him. He could see in his mind's eye the frightened look on the old gypsy's face, and he wasn't fully convinced that it was brought on solely by the girl's hair-raising escapade. Also, that girl, that beautiful creature: too exquisite, surely, to be a gypsy? There was something about her, something about the both of them. God! If only he could be sure.

Edward decided there and then. He must go after them, he *must* be sure!

Part Four

1912
Starlena awakened

Who can say when child becomes woman,
When day becomes night,
When bud becomes blossom,
When wrong becomes right?

J.C.

Chapter Eleven

'You're a natural scholar, Starlena – so quick to learn. Why, in just four weeks you've virtually mastered the art of reading and writing.' Elizabeth Doughty, now Judd, came across the room, her small dainty feet making no noise on the thick red carpet.

At her approach Starlena looked up from the polished desk-top where rested her labours of the day, a book of lined pages upon which over and over again were written in large copperplate letters the words 'Starlena Parrish', 'Rona Parrish' and others of common usage and everyday necessity, words such as 'Thank you', 'Please', and 'Good day', with the entire alphabet most beautifully and painstakingly copied out beneath.

'Oh, Miss Elizabeth!' Starlena had never in her life known such a wonderful friend as Elizabeth Judd, and she had come to love her like a sister. Holding up the exercise book for Miss Elizabeth to scrutinize, Starlena took one delicate hand in both her own, her face aglow with pleasure. She was hardly able to contain herself when at last the book was placed back on the desk and Miss Elizabeth clasped Starlena's entwining fingers, her warm gentle smile assuring Starlena that she had done well.

'Is it all right, Miss Elizabeth? Is it getting better? Is it?'

'All the time,' Miss Elizabeth promised, adding with a wistful expression, 'What with your mother getting stronger each day and there being little else for me to teach you, well, I don't suppose it will be too long before you're looking to leave me, will it?' Then, before Starlena could answer, she freed her hand from Starlena's grasp, stroked a stray dark lock of hair away from Starlena's uplifted eyes and, as though afraid that her suspicion might be confirmed, she turned smartly about and went towards the door. Just before she disappeared through it, she called back, 'You carry on, Starlena. I'll arrange for some refreshment for the two of us.'

Left alone, Starlena thought about what Miss Elizabeth had said. 'Twas true! She couldn't stay here in this grand house forever, although, if she was honest, Starlena had to admit to herself that she had been very happy here in these magnificent surroundings, with Miss Elizabeth the best of company and her mammy getting attention from that fancy doctor.

Her mammy had put the fear of God into her on that day in Appleby and for some time after. When the pony and trap had sent the two of them flying down the hill, she herself had scrambled to her feet only to see with a rush of horror that her mammy had cracked her head on a boulder and was lying apparently lifeless against it. Yet even as Anselo had carried Rona back to the wagon, her head bleeding profusely and her senses befuddled, she had pleaded with Starlena to go 'home to Whistledown, lass!' Again and again she had whispered from her sick bed until Starlena could pacify her no other way.

The two weeks it had taken to cover the seventy miles or more to Whistledown Valley had been to Starlena like the worst nightmare she could remember. The journey was tortuously slow because every few miles she must stop to tend to Rona. All along the way she scoured the banks of the road for medicinal herbs: tansy, known for its benefits to kidney and liver, hore-hound and others whose healing secrets her mammy had taught her long ago. But none of them seemed to help at all. Starlena even kept a pot of raspberry jam suspended for days from beneath the wagon, until the mould had grown thick and ripe on the top, and as she had seen Rona do with other cuts and wounds, she had used it to treat the festering gash on the sick woman's temple. For a while she began to think it was working. Then Rona had sunk deeper into unconsciousness, feverish and fretful one minute and deathly still the next.

At this point in her memories, Starlena was so affected by the fear which had consumed her then and which at times still came back to haunt her, that she began to pace restlessly up and down the room, her thoughts too agitated to allow her to appreciate the beautiful things all about her – the extravagant floral tapestry curtains hanging to the floor, the enormous fireplace with its exquisitely carved surround and gold-framed painting of a hunting scene above it, and all about her the choicest furniture, resplendent in its heavy ornateness, its surfaces polished to a mirror finish. None of these things mattered beside the well-being of her mammy who, thank God, had been taken in by Miss Elizabeth on the very night of their arrival in Whistledown Valley, when in sheer desperation Starlena had sought help from the only person she could think of.

Not only had Miss Elizabeth brought Rona right into the house and straightway summoned the doctor, but she had ordered that the wagon, cob and colt be well cared for also. On top of that, she had afforded Starlena the run of the house, given her some exquisite dresses and among other things, had taught her to read and write. Nothing was too good for Starlena! So much so that in spite of herself, Starlena had begun to compare this rich pampered life with the hard demanding gypsy existence which exposed a body to the mercy of all weathers and, like her mammy, made a girl old before her time. 'Appen even left to die for lack of medicine!

Here, Starlena paused before the huge sideboard. For a long moment she gazed deep into the mirror above it, trying to reject the thoughts which were a betrayal of her gypsy heritage by taking stock of her reflection almost in the detached way one might regard a stranger.

Starlena had asked if Miss Elizabeth would put up her hair in the same fashion as her own, but the answer had been a firm, 'No. You have that most wonderful hair, Starlena, thick and wavy, with a sheen to shame a raven's wing. Hair like yours cries out to fall loose, framing your face and shoulders. No! I won't tuck it away out of sight, and neither must you.' She had been adamant and in the face of her opposition, Starlena had not dared to ask again. It hung loose now, jet black as her eyes and springing about her oval face in a cluster of natural curls before the deeper waves fell over her shoulders and down to the small of her back. Against the stark whiteness of the frilled high-necked blouse, it looked like a black shimmering mantle, mingling at last with the dark full skirt which finished at the hem in a little frill. Skirt and blouse were set off to perfection by three small silk-covered buttons at the tiny waist. On her feet Starlena wore the daintiest of shoes, done up by means of a slim bar reaching across her ankle to fasten onto the button at the side.

'I know you'd be cross if you knew, Mammy,' Starlena spoke to her reflection, 'but oh, I do so love these pretty things.' She excused her self-indulgence by reminding herself that the clothes she had had on when tumbling down that hill were no more than torn rags afterwards, too far gone for mending, and with her decent garments used for dressing Rona's wounds, there was nothing left but to accept Miss Elizabeth's kindly offer. 'And you yourself have on one of her nighties, Mammy!' she added, consternation clouding her lovely features. She knew well enough what her mammy would have to say about *that*. Yet Starlena didn't care, for when that familiar voice spoke at last, it wouldn't matter what was said.

With this thought in mind, Starlena felt a flood of gratitude to Miss Elizabeth and the gentle doctor, for hadn't they said only this very morning that her mammy was fit to fight her way back any minute? And less than half an hour ago, when Starlena had paid one of her frequent visits to the quiet bedroom where Rona had lain these past weeks, the signs were already there, in the calm contented expression and in the constant flickering of her eyelids. Oh, it was wonderful to know that Rona would soon be her old self again! Excited by this prospect, Starlena hoped Miss Elizabeth would realize where she'd gone, for she felt she must go now and sit beside her mammy, hold her hand and talk softly to her.

It was nine o'clock when Starlena was called from the bedroom. The maid seemed a little surly as she delivered her mistress's message that dinner was about to be served and 'would Miss Parrish be so kind as to make her way down to the dining-room?'

Starlena thanked the girl, not minding her brusque manner for she understood how demeaning it must seem to the maid, being

184

used to genteel folk about the place suddenly to have two lowly gypsy women of the road thrust upon her. 'Thank you. I'll be down straight away,' she smiled, feeling daunted by the grudging nod and fierce scowl that was the reply, before the neat little capped figure went off sulkily to report to her mistress.

'There you are, Mammy. We're not made welcome here by *all*, are we, eh?' She gave a little laugh, bending to kiss the quiet face whose cheeks had lately resumed something of their weather-worn ruddiness. At the touch of her lips there was a moan and flurry of movement from the bed. Starlena lifted her head to see the extent of it. As she watched, Rona's eyes opened just slightly, rested on her for a moment and then closed again. Yet Starlena was pleased, for that was the third time in as many days that her mammy had wakened to look at her. Each time she had seemed reassured before sliding off into a contented sleep again. 'Rest easy, Mammy,' Starlena whispered now, pulling the silken bed cover to a more comfortable level. 'I'll be in to see you before I go to me bed.'

Downstairs in the wood-panelled dining-room, Starlena found Miss Elizabeth already seated at the table. In her extravagantly-embroidered cream silk gown, with her fair hair pinned up with a ribbon as blue as her eyes, she put Starlena in mind of a little china doll.

'Ah! At last, Starlena. I was just about to come for you myself.' Miss Elizabeth gestured to a chair opposite her. 'You know how I hate to eat alone.' A nod of her head sent the maid scurrying to collect the soup tureen from the sideboard. 'You must be hungry, Starlena, seeing that you missed your tea?'

Starlena, however, was not hungry, and when some twenty minutes later she rose from the table, Miss Elizabeth expressed her concern. 'But you've eaten nothing!'

'I know, and I'm sorry. I'm really not hungry.'

'You know, Starlena, you mustn't fret over your mother. She's going to be just fine. Really!' Her smile was bright with concern and Starlena thought how very kind she was. What a great pity her husband, Lester, had been so long in America. Miss Elizabeth did seem to love and miss him so, and with the old dowager gone now, life must be very lonely for her.

Starlena remembered her own dreadful fear when she thought Rona would be taken from her. It was something she would not easily forget, and her heart warm with compassion for Miss Elizabeth, she came round the table to hug her. 'I'll always remember what a friend you've been to me,' she said. 'Always!' Then straightening up, she added, 'I'll just look in on Mammy, then I think I'll walk beyond the spinney to the lake.'

'How lovely. Yes! It's a lovely evening, with the night air cooled by a breeze. You do that, Starlena. As for me, I'm ready for an early night.' Her blue eyes lit up. 'My Lester's coming home tomorrow. I must look my best.'

'Goodnight then, Miss Elizabeth.'

'Goodnight. Now don't be wandering about too late. It can turn chilly.'

'I won't,' promised Starlena as she left the room.

It was the most wonderful evening. The silver August sky covered the land in the soft afterglow of day. Somewhere deep in the spinney the sound of scurrying creatures filtered through the trees, and as the sky grew ever richer in colour, the light played on the tree tops in brilliant hues of red and purple, as darkness began to fall. The air was scented by the abundant blossoms which decorated the lake's edge, colourful shrubs of massive proportions whose now sleeping blossoms weighed so heavy on the bough that they dipped their sweet heads gently into the water.

The sultry night air closed in about Starlena as she made her way down the bank towards the water. There, seating herself on the grassy edge, she slipped off her shoes and stockings and in a moment had slid her bare feet into the cool wetness below.

Leaning backwards onto her outstretched hands, she threw back her head and sighed from the sheer pleasure of it. Staying like this for a while, Starlena closed her eyes, letting the coolness enter her whole body while all her senses lazily tuned in to the sounds of nature all about her. Not far away, a lone bird of the night gave out a single cry; small creatures carried on about their nocturnal activities; and in soft musical tones, the water agitated by her toes sent out a series of ripples across the lake.

It was in moments like this that Starlena felt at one with God's universe. There were things back there in that lovely house which had pleased her other senses, material things like silk against your skin, water in a jug that you didn't have to walk miles for and a bed so large and luxurious that you might never want to leave it. Oh, but on a night like this when the air cloaked itself about a body in a warm caress and the sky above seemed almost to come down and touch you, there was never any comparison! Starlena wondered how she had ever thought to put such value on those material things, for should she ever be asked to choose one life over the other, how could she deny that her heart was like a wild thing, out here in the free open fields with the creatures of nature? The open road and the gypsy way of life: that was her passion. It could never be any other way, of that she was certain.

Suddenly, as though to purge herself of all those material longings which had threatened to rob her of all that was in her blood, there came upon Starlena the urge to strip off all her clothes and swim in the lake. Once the thought had occurred, together with memories of other warm sunny days when she and her mammy would swim in the brooks, there was no going back. The urge became too demanding. Unaware that she was not alone, Starlena took only a moment to discard all her finery. Then she stood for a moment in the light of the rising moon, naked as on the day of her birth, feeling the night's embrace upon her skin and steeling herself for the dive which would thrust her into the cool, still lake.

From his place a few yards away, camouflaged by the trees and shrubs which formed part of the spinney, Anselo would have stepped forward moments before, when he had first come across Starlena. But now he was held spellbound by the sight of her nakedness. Never before had he seen such beauty. Starlena! With a figure perfect in every youthful curve, her luxurious black hair cloaked about her and those magnificent eyes alive with quiet passion. She touched him deep within himself, awakening every male instinct in him, and even in the uncomfortable heat of evening, sending an icy chill up his spine. If ever he had wanted anything with a fever that frightened him, it was she, Starlena, no longer a child but a woman of great beauty and charm, a woman not yet fully awakened, but ready to be so. A woman he must have!

With admirable grace and strength Starlena launched herself through the air and into the water, sleek and silent as an otter. Anselo stripped off his clothes and prepared to follow. For a moment, though, he took pleasure in just watching her. Now she would disappear beneath the surface, her long hair floating until that too went under, then after what seemed a dangerously long time, she would reappear some way out across the lake, her slim shapely form moving through the water like a nymph of the deep.

Starlena's sharp eyes saw the dark bobbing head of the swimmer coming towards her and, instinctively afraid, she would have made haste out of the water, grabbed her clothes about her and fled to the safety of the big house. Already she had turned towards the shallows where she might clamber out and be quickly away. But Anselo was an accomplished swimmer, as were all gypsies, and seeing her panic, he pursued her, calling out her name in as loud a whisper as he dared, for fear of alerting any other.

Hearing her name and seeing that it was Anselo, Starlena's fears were allayed but suddenly conscious of her nakedness, she drew herself into the shelter of a large shrub which was rooted on the grassy verge and hung over the water.

'Anselo! Why are you here? How long have you been here?' she demanded.

It took only a moment for Anselo to explain that her sudden departure from Appleby had greatly concerned him, especially with her mammy so ill. 'The very next morning there was a gentleman along Gypsy Hill asking after you and your mammy.'

'Asking after us? A gentleman?' For some reason she couldn't explain, the news had frightened Starlena. 'What did he want, Anselo? Who was he?' she asked, beginning to shiver and not knowing whether it was the night air playing on her bare shoulders, the news that some strange man – a *gentleman* – was looking for them, or the surprise appearance of Anselo and his nearness to her at this moment – and both of them stark naked! Starlena was not unaware of the desire she was provoking in Anselo. In such matters she was no longer a child, and not altogether innocent.

Anselo made no reply to her questions, being too overwhelmed by such beauty little more than an arm's reach away. Instead, he levelled his brown gaze deep into her eyes, the passion and longing in him no less naked than were their bodies. 'I love you,' he murmured. 'I think I've always loved you.'

Held by the intensity of his gaze, Starlena made no move, not even when he came deliberately closer, his hand reaching out to touch her face and to trace the fullness of her mouth. When, wrapping his other hand about a branch he drew himself close to her wet trembling body, she could not resist. There was something about Anselo which gave her a warm feeling inside. It had been like that since the first day of their meeting, when they were little more than babes. Her tongue seemed tied so she could not speak and her arms strengthless, leaving her at his mercy. Yet her need of him was as compelling as was his for her!

Now one strong muscular arm went about Starlena's tiny waist, the other reached down into the water to crook beneath her legs. Then, with effortless ease, Anselo lifted her clear of the lake. All manner of emotions surged through Starlena as she felt herself swept up into Anselo's arms, and when he drew her close to his chest, his gaze still locked fast on hers, there came over her the strangest feeling – a sense of fear and soaring exhilaration. When his mouth opened over hers, his kiss was at first tender then increasingly demanding and finally so fierce it frightened her. She made no resistance, however. Instead, she responded with equal demand, her arms twining round his neck to draw him ever closer. His fevered murmurs and gasps of delight raised in Starlena a great longing, the like of which she had never known. She was trembling violently, yet she was hot beneath his touch and loath to let him go.

When at last he drew his head back to gaze with unbridled passion into those eyes that glowed so fiercely and which he likened to midnight itself, Starlena could no more have refused him than she could have refused herself. 'Oh, Anselo, what we're doing is wrong,' she moaned. In the softness of her gaze there shone the threat of tears and the innocence of a child. Yet in her heart there were no tears, no regrets, for she knew that on this night, beneath such a quiet moon and for the first time, she would give herself to this man. To *this* man, so young and so cherished in her heart. If she must lie in the arms of a man, then let it be Anselo, who had stirred and awakened the woman in her. Tonight would be theirs – tomorrow she would count the consequences.

Starlena had no sensation of being carried to the bank, but when she was laid down on the grass and she saw Anselo kneeling before her, a thrill shivered right through her body. Her gaze lingered on his magnificence, moving slowly from the dark shoulder-length hair, to his brown eyes, narrowed and sleepy in his passion. She saw the strength of his masculinity in the broad shoulders and the thick squareness of his chest. If Starlena had remembered him in her thoughts as the boy he had been, there was no doubt now that he had matured into a man. His desire was not that of a boy, nor was his readiness. And when in the gentlest manner he covered her body with his, the sudden warmth of his wet skin striking against her sent a delicious shock through her heart and on down to that most private and intimate of places, triggering every nerve and sense within her.

Now his mouth was whispering softly against her temple, on her ear, down the crevice of her neck, until, moist and tantalizing, it played upon the nipple of her breast, setting up in her a rhythm which left her trembling and still a little afraid. Now the tips of his fingers were creeping lightly over her nakedness, touching her breasts, her thighs, stimulating exquisite sensations which pulsated through her until she thought she must cry out. At the very height of her excitement, Starlena sensed that the moment was near. In heart and soul she prepared herself for it, but when Anselo closed his arms tightly about her and with a shivery cry took her to himself, there exploded in her such an exquisite pain that it made her call out his name while he, ever gentle, whispered words of endearment, all the while loving her, all the while replacing her fear with sensations of deeper pleasure.

Long moments later, after the rush of passion was spent and the two of them lay still enclosed in fond embrace, Starlena was stricken by the enormity of what they had done, and her fear returned: fear of the unknown; fear of the future; and fear of what her mammy would say were she ever to find out. Rising quickly, she exclaimed, 'We were wrong, Anselo! Wrong!' Then she ran to her clothes and began dressing. 'I must go. Please don't ever look for me again.'

Anselo was devastated. Undeterred, though, he rushed forward to grab her by the shoulders. 'We were *not* wrong, Starlena! I *love* you, don't you understand that? Don't you?' His anger was vivid in his voice and flashed in the darkness of his eyes.

'I'm afraid, Anselo. Celia is your intended . . .'

'No! She is *not*,' he protested, now shaking her in his desperation. 'I'll see your mammy. It's you I want – no other.'

In his bid to calm her fears, Anselo had only fired them. Now, as she looked up at him, tears first trembled on her long dark lashes then spilled out to move his heart. He knew then he had lost her, at least for now.

'You *won't* see my mammy! You *mustn't*! She's been so very poorly. Please, Anselo, please. Just go.'

Starlena felt his hands caressing her shoulders. She felt the anger leave him and when he lifted her head to place the sweetest kiss on her mouth, she felt only deep emotion for him, which she supposed was love. So when he asked gently, 'Do you love me? An answer, Starlena, then I *will* go,' how could she but answer the truth? 'Yes,' she whispered, her eyes shining up at him. 'I do love you so.'

'Then I'll keep my word. I'll leave you here, on this the most wonderful night of my life. But I will be back for you. I will have you for my own.'

As she hurried away towards the big house, there was a painful fluttering in Starlena's heart. She could not shake off the feeling that this night would have terrible consequences, even though with every vital instinct in her, she could never wish that it had not happened. She did love Anselo and would go on loving him. If love was this all-consuming emotion which even now raked through her at the memory of what had taken place back there, with her wrapped in his arms and he a part of her, then yes, she was indeed in love! It seemed to Starlena, who had fallen asleep filled with guilt, that the awful nightmares which had troubled her sleep had suddenly taken shape in the light of day.

When the piercing screams woke her, she rushed from her bed into the room next door where, hands to her face, eyes wide and terrified, her mammy stood by the window, looking out over the lawns to the hedge beyond.

''Tis *him*!' she cried, as Starlena ran to take her in her arms. 'That's him. That's the one, I *know* it!' She pointed a shaking finger out of the window, and bade Starlena look at the man on horseback, a man with a particular proud and angry way of sitting a horse, a man who had long haunted her: the same upright figure she had seen on a night many years ago, on the night her darling Leum had been dashed to his death. 'Look! '*Tis* he! 'Ow could I ever forget! Every man sets astride a beast in 'is own special way. Look! Look, child!' she insisted.

When, to pacify her, Starlena did look, she saw nothing but the lawn and the hedge which formed the boundary between Whalley Grange and the public bridleway. She did not see the man on horseback nor the grim face of Redford Wyman as he paused in his gallop to gaze across at the big house, fuming inside himself at the thought of what should have been his. If only he hadn't got stupidly drunk and forced his attentions on the frightened Doughty creature. But he'd been damned if he'd let anything else of his be snatched away. On Freya Judd's revelation that he had a sister, he had moved heaven and earth to trace her, all to no avail. When he did, neither she nor the one who took her would live to tell the tale. That brooch Freya had spoken of, it must have been sold, for gypsies sold all that was valuable, he was certain. Every second-hand shop, pawnbroker and even shady dealer was alerted. When that brooch turned up, he would have them at last.

'Come, Mammy, back to your bed,' coaxed Starlena, delighted that Rona was well and truly awake, but anxious that she should not undo the good work with such imaginings.

'No! I tell you, it *was* he . . .' Only now did Rona stop to look about her. 'What place is this?' she demanded. Standing fast against Starlena's coaxing, she plucked agitatedly at the cream silk nightgown draping her body. 'What's this? Where's me own clothes?' Then, her darting eyes alighting on the finery of Starlena's own exquisitely embroidered nightwear, 'Answer me, child! What place is this? I must know at once!' All signs of past illness had gone as, her voice rising, she demanded all manner of answers to her questions.

'Mammy, you mustn't take on so,' urged Starlena, afraid that any minute the uproar would bring the house down about their heads. She wasn't surprised when the door burst open and, in a flurry of concern, two figures rushed in, Miss Elizabeth and the same young maid whose expression and manner had shown her disapproval of the situation many times before, a situation which, had the dowager been alive still, would never have been allowed. Gypsies in the house! Whatever next? The mistress was too soft.

'Goodness! Mrs Parrish, whatever is it?' Miss Elizabeth's face creased with alarm, her blue eyes growing wider and wider and her pretty little mouth falling open. Not to be pacified, Rona Parrish insisted that the likes of her and her child had 'no rights to set foot inside a place like this'. Even when assured that it had been necessary to save her life, she would not be pacified. Although, learning the reason for her being there, Rona Parrish expressed her deepest gratitude, 'We must be away this very minute!' she entreated, her mind carrying her back to a house very like this one on the night of Starlena's birthing, a bedroom almost identical, and a gentleman who would have strangled the life out of his newborn. That same gentleman whose eyes had locked onto hers that day in Appleby. Oh God! Even now, at this very minute, he could come upon them. The thought was too much for Rona Parrish. Shaking Starlena from her, she instructed, 'I want me own clothes brought to me this minute! An' *you* – tek them fancy garments off, child. We must be ready to go. D'yer 'ear me, Starlena? *Now*, I say!'

Starlena was taken completely aback by her mammy's seizure. There appeared to be no consoling her – no way of reasoning with her. What *was* it that terrified her mammy so? Was it the same thing which had driven them from Appleby? And who was this 'gentleman' who'd wandered Gypsy Hill looking for them? Oh, she *should* tell her mammy about that, yes indeed. But then how could she answer the questions which would surely follow? Starlena blushed deeply at the thought of having to explain how she had only learned of it the very evening before from Anselo – whose very name raised such anguish in her mammy's heart and who had no right to be pursuing them as he so obviously had done. Certainly he had no right at all to be making love to *her*!

'Mrs Parrish, your own clothes were little more than rags after your accident – there was nothing to be done with them. I'm sorry.' Miss Elizabeth looked extremely uncomfortable beneath Rona's harsh accusing stare.

'You mean yer *burnt* 'em?' As a nod confirmed it, Rona added smartly, 'Yer 'ad no right ter do such a thing! No right at all!'

At this, the young maid stepped forward to address her mistress. 'Beg your pardon, Ma'am. I'm sure Cook can find some "suitable" togs to satisfy Mrs Parrish.' The smile on her face did nothing to conceal the look of contempt she directed at Starlena and her mammy.

So it was settled. The maid was sent forthwith to fetch some decent hard-wearing and practical clothes from downstairs. 'Oh, but I do wish you would accept the garments set aside in my own wardrobe for you,' protested Miss Elizabeth.

Starlena answered for both her mammy and herself. 'You've been so kind to us both, Miss Elizabeth. But y'see, the way of the gypsy won't allow for the garments of a lady, so fine and delicate.'

'We'd end up sellin' 'em!' snorted Rona, hoping that would be an end to the matter.

'Then take them, and sell them, if it will help,' insisted Miss Elizabeth.

At that, Starlena said, 'No. You've done enough. We'll be on our way and I'll be able to write to you now.' The thought gave her a great deal of pleasure and drew a most odd glance from Rona who, Starlena was sure, would question her later.

At that moment, the maid came back with an armful of clothes: tweeds and dark woollen things which, although well-worn and unattractive, were practical and inconspicuous.

Some time later, Starlena helped Rona down the great winding stairway to where Miss Elizabeth waited, her manner full of consternation.

'Please, Mrs Parrish, will you let me give you some money to help you on your way?' she pleaded.

'Thank you, but no!' In the brusque manner in which she was refused, Miss Elizabeth recalled the time, when it had been an arduous task to persuade the old gypsy to allow Starlena the present of that mare from these stables. She had shown her fierce independence then. She showed it now, with ever more stubbornness. Yet tempering Miss Elizabeth's concern was her satisfaction on recalling the valuable brooch she had accidentally discovered when, in her natural curiosity, she had given a hand to securing the gypsy wagon for a long stay. It mattered not how such a piece of jewellery had come into Rona Parrish's possession, only that she and Starlena were not entirely destitute.

Starlena came forward to hug the young woman who had been such a friend and whom she at least was loath to leave. 'I will keep in touch, Miss Elizabeth,' she said quietly. 'I promise.'

'Mek no promises, my gel!' Rona interrupted. 'Folks such as us don't mix well with gentry!' Feeling weak, she gestured for Starlena to help her across the wide expanse towards the door. 'I sharn't rest till I'm in me wagon wi' me own things about me, child!' she remarked. When Starlena gave her the support of her arm, she thought how light and frail the woman seemed.

All the while Starlena helped her outside to where the wagon had been prepared, cob harnessed in front and colt impatiently fidgeting at the back, Rona Parrish spoke not a word. Her mind was too busy with other more pressing matters, as it had been that day at Appleby Fair, when that figure from the past had set up the fear of the divil in her. Her mind was made up and there would be no changing it. Not now, not ever! She and Starlena would escape the past and those who threatened to haunt her, and there was only one sure way to do that, Rona had decided. They would sell the wagon and horses, every single thing they owned, including that fancy shawl and the studded brooch. Then, with the money fotched, she and her girl would sail away to 'Merica! Oh, aye! They'd not find 'em there, that was fer sure. Her brother, Callum, shouldn't be too 'ard to locate – 'e were a good lad an' 'e'd look after 'em both, that 'e would. The prospect thrilled Rona and suddenly she blurted out her intention to Starlena, who was about to climb up beside her. 'Child! It's settled – we're goin' to 'Merica!'

'*America!*' Starlena was shocked rigid. 'Across the great ocean?'

'That's right. We're goin' ter find me brother, Callum.'

Starlena was struck speechless, her mind a whirl of images: Anselo, Whistledown Valley and Miss Elizabeth, whom she might never see again. Suddenly she ran back to the house, to the figure waiting to wave to them. Flinging herself into Miss Elizabeth's arms, she cried, 'I don't know if I'll be able to keep in touch with you. Mammy intends to take us to *America!*' The word conjured up both fear and excitement. It was an adventure to look forward to, after all. 'I might never see you again – not in the whole of my life!'

Elizabeth Judd at first was amazed, but quickly composing herself, she laughed good-naturedly, saying, 'Oh, Starlena! America isn't the end of the world, you know. Why, Lester constantly pesters me to accompany him on his visits there. Look! Come with me.' She took Starlena by the hand and rushed her up the steps and into the hallway. 'Quickly now – your mother looks set to have my blood,' she laughed.

In the hall, Starlena waited impatiently while Miss Elizabeth collected a piece of notepaper, on which she wrote an introduction to the manager of the textile company near Boston, Massachusetts which had been her father's and was now hers. Giving Starlena no time to read it, she thrust it into her hand, saying, 'Just keep it safe. There might come a time when you'll need it.' Starlena didn't imagine there ever would, but to please Miss Elizabeth, she carefully folded the paper and thanked her profusely.

'Where are yer, child? I'm impatient ter be off!' Rona's voice invaded the hall and separated the two young women from their last friendly embrace. Then, stuffing the paper into her skirt pocket, Starlena skipped down the steps, clambered up onto the wagon and with a little hug to pacify Rona, she set the old cob in motion.

'Y'know, Mammy,' she said with a smile, 'I think I'd like to see America.' In fact, the more she thought about it, the greater an adventure it seemed, particularly now that Miss Elizabeth had pointed out so lightly that 'it isn't the end of the world'.

As the wagon rumbled away, Rona's thoughts flew ahead to how a body went about securing a passage on a packet to 'Merica. She was in deathly fear of pursuit. She hoped against hope that where they were going would indeed be 'the end of the world', and above all, *safe*.

Chapter Twelve

'Sold for passage to America, you say?' Freya Judd could not disguise her jubilation. At last, she had the Wyman brooch in the palm of her hand, brought to her by the grubbiest, most foul-smelling fellow in the world, but who became an angel as far as she was concerned when he produced the contents of his pocket after she had waylaid him on his way to find 'the younger Mr Wyman'.

''Tain't meant fer *you*, missus!' protested the fellow after being bullied to 'state your business, ruffian!'

'I 'as the very divil for me master, missus,' pleaded the poor creature, 'an' if I don't deliver that there bauble to the gent intended fer it, well, then I'll be beaten black an' blue an' no mistake!' So agitated was he that in his fright he would have grabbed it back had not Freya swiftly dipped into the pocket of her skirt, from which to draw two silver coins. With the same deftness she dropped them into the flat cap which he had previously whipped from his head and which was now trembling in his hand.

'You go quickly back to your "divil of a master", my man, and you tell him that the bauble was delivered to the younger Mr Wyman. I myself shall see to it, you need have no fear.' When, still trembling, he made no move, she stepped so close that her nose was no more than a whisker away from his face and in a voice to frighten the dead, she hissed, 'You heard what I said?' He nodded, in fear for his life. '*Then do as I say!*'

It was enough. The sorry fellow could take no more. With a strange little cry, he plucked the coins from his cap and rammed the limp ragged thing over his head and down to his ears. Then, with never a backward glance, he took to his heels and away through the spinney, leaving Freya chortling, surreptitiously examining the exquisite brooch grasped so firmly in her hand.

The brooch was worth a pretty penny to be sure. Several hundred guineas? A thousand? Easily that! Ah, but the same amount several times over to a certain party, a party who was moving heaven and earth to find the one who threatened his rightful inheritance.

Smiling in the devious fashion that only she could, Freya Judd shivered violently in the sudden surprising chill of a September evening. Then, with smart purposeful strides, she made her way back to the house. Yes, she would do as she had told that unfortunate messenger. Redford Wyman would have the brooch, together with the accompanying information. Yes indeed! Both were his rightful property and he must have them. And so he would. But on her terms!

The grandfather clock in the great hall was striking four in the morning when Redford Wyman arrived home from an evening of gambling in the nearby town of Blackburn. Much the worse for drink and mumbling curses at yet another bout of ill-luck and heavy losses, he stumbled up the staircase to his rooms.

Throughout the house, all were deeply asleep. All save one. Freya Judd had waited patiently for Redford's return and though it had been the longest night of her life, she had far too much on her mind to give in to sleep.

'What the hell are you doing in here?' The shock of seeing Freya sitting bolt upright in his bed without a stich on had a sobering effect on Redford Wyman. 'Out! Get out!' he yelled, staggering across the room and preparing to wrench her from the bed. But he stopped short when with the most cunning smile, she held out her hand to show him the jewel nestled there.

'Not so fast!' she warned in a calculating voice. 'D'you see what I have here?' Now, she lowered her voice to a whisper, the smile slipping from her face leaving in its place an expression of deviousness to match his own. 'Worth more than a mere fortune, don't you think?'

'What's that you say? Hold it up, woman!' He made a snatch at it, but was not quick enough. 'What bloody games are you playing, witch!' he snarled, cocking his head to one side and peering down with his one good eye, as she revealed the brooch to him once more.

'This is your grandmother's brooch, Redford Wyman,' she told him with relish. 'The very piece pinned to the shawl in which your sister was carried away the night of her birth.'

'Ah! Is that so?' His voice was both a laugh and a whisper as he crumpled gently to one knee, his body leaning over the bed. He kept his head ever cocked and his blue eye riveted to the brooch, even as though in slow motion he sidled his hand towards the softness of Freya's breast, which he proceeded to fondle most affectionately, drawing a small gasp of delight from her.

'So! This is the brooch? Tell me more. Where did you find it? Will it lead me to her?' He began softly, but on his last words he turned his gaze upon her, and suddenly it was most unpleasant, although his mouth, still oddly attractive, shaped itself into a smile. 'You *do* have such information, Freya Judd?'

'Hmh! Yes, I have the information you want. I have it all!' She was greatly affected by the touch of his fingers on her breast. It was so very long since a man – any man – had caressed her so and that old appetite which she had thought to master cried out for satisfaction. Remembering was a pleasant thing. Remembering how it had been with the younger and more virile of the two Wyman men was even more of a thrill.

In a moment, she had secreted away the brooch and had flung back the bedclothes to reveal her nakedness. To the waiting man, whose own lustful cravings were sharpened by the sight of her still-shapely figure, she presented a temptation he was unable to resist. Affected by the quantities of drink he had earlier consumed, yet somewhat sobered by the sight of that dazzling brooch, he fumbled his way out of his clothes and clambered onto the bed where, his face uncomfortably pink from the effort, he straddled himself across her, saying in a voice as rough as was his handling of her, 'You bloody vixen! Make me wait for one thing, would you, and hand me another without a second thought, eh?' He laughed aloud, his concentration for a moment lapsing.

'You shall have all the news that goes with the brooch,' Freya whispered from beneath him. 'In the morning, for a handsome sum of money.'

For a while he was still, his head pulled up sharply, his eye devouring her. Then he made a strange sound which could have been a snigger or a grunt, and grabbed her to him. She responded with equal vigour.

'There's five thousand in there, as agreed!' snarled Redford Wyman, flinging the bulky package across the dining-room table. 'And another thousand to see you gone from this house, for good! Do I make myself clear?'

'Dear, dear! What a man of moods you are, making passionate love to a woman one minute and throwing her out on her ear the next,' goaded Freya Judd, to infuriate the man even further. Snatching up the package, she feverishly opened one end and peered inside. Then, with the tips of her fingers, she flicked the notes over with some deliberation before saying in more serious tones, 'You could have saved yourself the extra thousand. I always intended to leave this place forthwith – there's little to keep me here any longer!'

Regarding her with some contempt, he demanded, 'Quickly! What news were you given with this?' He turned the brooch over and over in his hand, as though the very touch of it seared into his flesh.

'It was placed with a pawnbroker in Liverpool, down by the docks. There were two who brought it. Gypsies, so the fellow said. A woman and a girl. It was given to understand that the money changing hands would secure passage to America for the both of them.'

'America, eh?' He was quiet for a moment as though considering. Then, 'It changes nothing!' Nor did it, for he had it in mind to stop them, either on the docks before they set sail, or if needs be, to have a man board with them. It made no difference where the deed was done. For if he had entertained any doubts before about his inheritance being threatened, they had disappeared after the raging row he and his father had had that very morning, when, in a fit of fury, Edward Wyman had let slip that his son must not be too surprised to find his inheritance sliced to the bone!

A few moments later, having returned to her rooms where she had packed only the very basic necessities, Freya Judd was startled by a sudden burst of noise. Coming into the hall she found the groom searching about in a panic, shouting for help and telling all who could hear, 'The master's done for! 'E's done for, I tell yer!'

When she and Redford, with the parlour maid and a greatly harassed cook, found Edward, Freya thought at first he was indeed lifeless. He was lying still and twisted on the gravel where he had fallen from his mount. In a moment, though, his face began twitching and he emitted a deep throat-rumbling groan.

'Lord, 'elp us, 'e's alive!' exclaimed the groom, launching at once into a long garbled account of how the master was intending to ride down to the far pastures where the men had been busy erecting new fencing, 'when all of a minute, he grabbed at the back of 'is 'ead an' just fell off the 'orse like a dead 'un. Like a dead 'un, I tell yer!'

'Well, 'e ain't dead, yer blatherin' fool!' snorted Cook. 'But 'e soon will be if'n somebody don't gerra doctor!'

Everyone's eyes turned to Redford Wyman, whose features were set like stone and who had made no move to assist his father. He summoned up interest, however, on Freya Judd's mocking words as she brushed grandly past him.

'You surely wouldn't leave him to depart this world? Not yet? Not when you can't be sure what nasty surprises he might have written into his will, eh?' Upon which, taking satisfaction in the look of apprehension on his face, she swept away from the little group, heading for the gates and beyond them, a new challenge!

'Thrown out? For what reason?' Lester Judd put down the communication he had just received from America, in which the financial adviser to his wife's inherited business properties there was requesting a meeting to discuss the usual annual review, investments, productivity and so on. Lester had proved to be a most able and conscientious businessman since taking on a deal of responsibility in this particular area, and Elizabeth was both proud of and confident in her husband's acumen. As she herself was not too fond of travelling abroad, these matters fell under his jurisdiction. Now he made a mental note to reply urgently to the letter, and to book a berth in the immediate future.

He was most surprised at his sister's sudden appearance at Whalley Grange, for since he had taken Elizabeth as his wife, Freya had made her vehement disapproval very clear; painfully so! Not once since the wedding had she condescended to set foot across this threshold. Now here she was, bag in hand, and in a most tearful condition.

'Redford gave no reason,' she told him. 'He's a law unto himself.' The last words were delivered in pitiful voice, while she dabbed at her eyes with a white, daintily-embroidered handkerchief, and occasionally let out the most woeful sigh.

'Oh, really, Lester!' chided Elizabeth, at once stepping forward and assuring her sister-in-law, 'You must stay here with us.' Without further ado, she collected the bag from Freya's trembling hands, then, gently propelling the near-distraught figure to the comfort of one of the very best rooms in the house, she called back over her shoulder, 'Lester, be so kind as to have some sandwiches and a hot drink sent up.'

For some minutes, Lester made no move, his gentle brown eyes troubled and his mind going over what his sister had told him. If indeed it was true that Redford Wyman had thrown Freya out onto the streets, then what could be the reason after all this time? Why hadn't Edward, his father, intervened? If he thought for one minute that his sister had been the butt of Redford's foul temper and that there really had been no justification for turning her out, there would be no alternative but for Lester to go straight over there and demand an explanation. Yet something told Lester Judd that there was more to this than met the eye. He knew his sister well enough to realize that she could take care of herself, was a past master at it. He suspected, also, that there was a lot she had not confided in him. Until she did, he must leave matters as they were. Freya was welcome under his roof and in a way, it did his heart good to see her and Elizabeth being friendly to each other. It certainly wasn't before time, for he loved them both.

Upstairs, Freya watched while Elizabeth fussed about the room, plumping up the cushions, pouring out the tea and, in her own gentle kind manner, telling her sister-in-law, 'You don't know how pleased I am to have you here, as I know Lester is also. Of course I'm sorry about the circumstances which brought you here, but you must look on Whalley Grange as your home.'

Freya, still feigning a fit of sobbing, made no reply. Instead she looked up, her grateful smile giving away nothing of her thoughts – devious, scheming thoughts which spoke in silence of her contempt for this foolish young woman! A woman of immense riches, a woman who had driven a wedge between brother and sister, a woman who thought her little nest safe and secure. Yet that same woman had been naive enough to let in a cuckoo to ravage the nest. Such women deserved no pity.

Chapter Thirteen

'Wohey.'

'Yahoo.'

'C'mon, me darlin', dance yer little 'eart out!'

The cries echoed down the street, to the tune of excited hand-clapping and the merry music of Rona's wooden flute.

Starlena was in her element as she skipped and danced across the cobbles, twirling this way and that, a happy smile on her lovely face bright enough to light up the whole alley. Oh, how she loved to hear the folk clapping to the rhythm of her dancing feet; how she adored it when in their excitement, the onlookers would shout and cheer, urging her on faster and faster until her mammy grew breathless from playing her flute. Then, when the excitement became too much for them, everyone present would join in, throwing themselves wholeheartedly into the fun and frolics, warmed by the glow from the brazier and caught up by the magic of Starlena, under whose enchanting spell they had all fallen.

For over two weeks now, the entire community of these dark and dingy little alleys had waited patiently for the arrival of a ship which would carry them from the rat-infested streets of Liverpool docks to the promise of a new and wonderful life in America. In the waiting they had suffered cold and hunger and had been at the mercy of racketeers, rogue-landlords and rival companies fighting for the price of a passage ticket – that much at least, all would-be emigrants possessed.

So when Starlena and her mammy came amongst them, every man, woman and child had been uplifted by the friendly nature of

.

the girl and, to a lesser extent, by the old gypsy, whose tongue could be a bit cutting yet whose flute-playing and presence added a colourful note to the gatherings which took place most evenings, usually after the closing of the pubs, when everybody was that much jollier.

Tonight, there was great excitement in the air, for it was rumoured that not one but two ships would be berthed in the harbour on the morrow and, with that in mind, the dancing and singing went on a bit longer. It was gone midnight when Starlena bade goodnight to the folks who had gathered around to tell her how much they loved to see her dance. After much chatter and laughter, they quickly went on their way after a wonderful evening and the prospect that the next time they saw the young gypsy girl dancing, it would be on the deck of a ship. At long last they would be on their way!

Only one of them looked forward to the voyage for a very different and more sinister reason. A furtive-looking creature, always capped and muffled, he had watched Starlena more closely than the rest, but had missed his opportunity to carry out the deed for which he was being suitably rewarded by a man with money to burn. But there was no rush. His instructions were to do the job properly and, always a careful fellow, he would do just that – never in haste, but always thorough.

Starlena felt invigorated by the evening – such an evening, the sky overhead black as velvet, pitted here and there with small perfectly shaped stars which dazzled and winked like so many precious jewels. Now she went to where Rona sat on an old fruit-box, thoughtfully tapping the little flute against the back of her hand, her attention greatly preoccupied by some inner matter which was evidently troubling her.

'What is it, Mammy?' Starlena had knelt to place both her hands on Rona's lap. Looking her straight in the eyes, she waited for an answer – as she had yesterday, and the day before, indeed, ever since that day when they had gone into the pawnbroker's not two streets from where they were at this very moment.

Starlena had felt a pang of guilt ever since, for when she had excitedly blurted out to the obnoxious character behind the counter that 'we're going to board a ship for America!' her mammy had snapped, 'Be quiet, child!' After which Rona had swiftly completed her bargaining and hurried the two of them out. Starlena had been convinced that Rona could have made a better deal with the man if only she'd held on a few minutes longer.

'It's my fault, isn't it?' Starlena now insisted. 'For telling that pawnbroker we were going on a ship to America!' She knew that was the truth. Confirmation or denial would make no difference. Her mammy was greatly afeared of something. Either that, or she thought to fulfil two wishes at one go: to put a great ocean and many thousands of miles between Starlena and Anselo, and now she was getting older, to find her brother Callum and be reunited with him at last. The former saddened Starlena, but the latter gave her comfort. Such a thing would do her mammy a power of good, she was sure, and she herself had begun to look forward to meeting her Uncle Callum. That would be grand indeed!

'Look, child. I've told yer afore. Yer did no 'arm tellin' the pawnbroker, although yer ought not to give away yer business so easily. And there's nowt wrong wi' me that can't be cured by us being put on us way aboard a ship. Now then, will yer stop yer worryin'?' Though she did her best to sound convincing, Rona had not really fooled Starlena, who thought it best just now not to push the matter.

'An' are you feelin' better, me darlin'?' concluded Rona, her sharp eyes searching Starlena's features, which had lately become thinner and somewhat pale.

So her mammy knew! Starlena smiled inwardly. In spite of her trying to hide the fact that on two occasions she had been very sick and as a result was feeling less healthy than usual, her mammy had missed nothing!

''Twas something I ate, I'm sure,' she replied, making light of it, but convinced all the same that she hadn't heard the last on the subject.

'Hmh!' snorted Rona. Slipping the flute into her pocket and drawing her shawl tight about her, she rose to her feet, saying, 'As you say – as you say!' in a peculiar fashion. Then she took Starlena's arm in her own and the two went down the alley in the direction of a seedy boarding-house where they were presently lodging. There were better lodgings to be had where a body might be protected from the scum who roamed the streets looking to make a guinea or two from unsuspecting would-be emigrants, but those lodgings were too public, and too revealing into what might otherwise be kept private.

Starlena thought there'd be precious little sleep along the docks that night. What with folks excited by the thought of the steamship leaving on the morrow and now her mammy deciding, 'We'd best be up wi' the larks, my gel. We'll not want ter be left be'ind, will we, eh?' the idea of sleep was farthest from her mind.

Some two hours later, after she had helped Rona tumble into the ramshackle bed fully dressed, and soon after, watched her fall into a deep sleep, Starlena was still wide awake. A whole mountain of things kept her from sleeping. First there was her excitement at the adventure they were about to embark on, even though she felt deeply concerned for Rona on what she had heard from others would be a long and uncomfortable voyage. Then there was Anselo: the memory of that beautiful night when he had made love to her; then afterwards her feelings of remorse at what they had done. Now there was the awful possibility that she might never see him again. Yet she knew that if it was so then it would surely be for the best. Other matters niggled at her, too, concerning a certain gentleman who, Anselo had said, had spent a deal of time combing Gypsy Hill for her and Rona. Then there was the brooch which, ever since she could remember, had always been hidden, and her mammy so secretive about it. The very sight of it had lit up the pawnbroker's eyes and for it he had parted with a handsome sum, enough for two tickets and even a little left over!

Sneaking a look at Rona now, Starlena thought she began to understand.

'You *stole* it, didn't you, Mammy?' she whispered into the gloom. 'You took it, and that's why we're being chased.' Of course! That must be the answer. There could be no other.

It seemed as though a weight had been lifted from Starlena's heart. There was no mystery about it. The truth was that Rona was a thief. But that didn't matter so much: how often had she herself taken fresh warm eggs from beneath a hen, so she and her mammy could greet the day with a hearty breakfast? And how many times had all gypsies been robbed of a day's pay in the fields, on the testimony of some 'gent' that they had not earned it? 'Twas true! In the very art of survival, animal stole from animal, man from man – and there was nothing in the world to change it.

In looking for every justification for her mammy's act of theft, Starlena, however, found little comfort. She would not reproach her on the matter, for it was not a daughter's place to rebuke a parent. All the same, Starlena wished it had not happened and she was very glad that on the morrow they would hopefully be gone. Especially now, since she realized the possibility that her mammy could so easily be caught and thrown into prison. The thought horrified her and as though to protect her, Starlena went and hunched up on the floor by Rona's bed, wrapped in a moth-eaten blanket which reeked of tobacco, and so positioned that if anyone got into the room after her mammy, they would need to get by *her* first!

When morning came, it was heralded by the hustle and bustle of a busy dockside area. Outside the grimy small-paned window, the cries of a paperboy entreated all to 'Read all about it! Women on the rampage for the vote! Windows smashed – many arrests. Hunger-strikes!'

Startled, Starlena scrambled up, stiff and painful from her night on the hard floor. Going quickly to open the window, she looked out to see people already milling around: barrow-boys, flower-sellers, men with flat caps, hungry faces and signs of the dire necessity that took them day after day to the docks where, with desperation or resignation, they would line up to be chosen as the fortunate recipient of a day's pay. Dock-workers all of them, good men who laboured hard when given the chance; but who all too often were turned away.

But on this particular morning, there was something else: an air of great jubilation, as folks below scurried away in the direction of the docks, some struggling with bulging bags and cumbersome boxes, others moving faster because of the lightness of their luggage, every face aglow with enthusiasm.

'Mammy! Mammy, wake up. They're away to the docks!' Starlena cried, all stiffness and discomfort forgotten as she rushed from the window. In a minute she had gathered together all of their scant belongings into the cavernous tapestry bag, and hustling the still-sleepy Rona from her bed, urged her, 'Quickly, Mammy. 'Tis time! The ships are getting ready to leave, I know it!'

And so they were. The chaos down at the front was feverish. Runners were darting this way and that, fighting off the opposition who might get to the emigrants' bags and baggage before *they* did! These ruthless touts scurried about like so many rats, pushing, shoving and urgently propelling the poor victims this way and that, parting them from their belongings and even their precious money should they be foolish enough to fall for such roguish tongues. Unfortunately, many were, for these runners were skilled at fleecing the unsuspecting traveller. They were physically strong and given to such cunning wiles as took a body by surprise.

All the same, when one of them came bounding towards Starlena intending to snatch the bag from her hands, saying, 'I'll tek yer bag, Miss,' she fetched the weighty article up in a full swing, bringing it down aside his ear and telling him in no uncertain terms, 'Clear off! We'll do our own carrying!' Somewhat taken aback, he clutched his aching ear and sidled away to search out some less aggressive unfortunate. As he did so, Rona added her own weight to the argument. 'Piss off!' she yelled. 'Yer bloody thief!'

Squeezed in now by the ever-surging bodies, Starlena guided her mammy with great care, her fist gripped tight to the bag. The precious beautifully-embroidered shawl was knotted tight about her shoulders in case anyone should take a fancy to it. It had taken a great deal of persuasion from Starlena to prevent the shawl being deposited in the pawnbroker's along with the brooch. 'Very well,' her mammy had at last agreed, 'but you're not to wear it till we're on us way to the ship.' It was a lovely thing, and though its original creamy colour had faded to an off-white, with tiny little holes beginning to appear here and there, Starlena felt proud and privileged to have it about her person. It was a thing she would never part with!

Suddenly the throbbing wave of humanity burst out into a wide area cobbled underfoot and flanked on two sides by awesome, official-looking buildings. To the front, stretching out like some mighty canvas framed in barriers to keep the emigrants back, was the River Mersey.

'Oh, do look!' exclaimed Starlena, her concentration on the official matter in hand being momentarily diverted by the fascination of such a scene.

It seemed as though every boat, every tug and every vessel that ever sailed was congregated here in Liverpool docks. Little boats with dark or plum-coloured sails scooted proudly about, yachts and pleasure-boats showed off their perfect dimensions, larger ships pulled and tugged at their moorings as though impatient to scour the seven seas, and all along the shore, masts, sails and funnels created an intricate jungle whose skyline stood out stark against the dazzling morning sky like a great forest of trees. Small steamers plied up and down the river, lending an air of industry to the scene, while in the foreground, towering above them, rose the great cylindrical funnels of a mighty steamship, whose tall graceful masts fore and aft rose higher than all around.

'Is that the one we're going on?' Starlena asked, her face alight, unable to tear her eyes away.

'Aye! I've no doubt that's the one!' returned Rona, adding sarcastically, 'If we ever get to it, that is!' She smiled when her comment caused Starlena to grab her tighter and to shuffle forward amongst the crowd with greater determination and, most surprising for so slight a figure, such a vigorous pushing that she cleared an easier path.

It was over an hour later, after having gone through the gauntlet of the 'Doctor's Shop' where they were required to 'show your tongue' and answer various questions which would satisfy the examiner that they were 'quite well' and where an eagle-eyed matron systematically weeded out any women whom she suspected might be pregnant; the inspection and stamping of tickets; and thereafter the push onto the docks that Starlena, with a sigh of relief, bundled Rona safely towards the area to which they were unceremoniously directed. Here they sat for another two hours amidst dozens of confused, excited emigrants of all nationalities, class and mood. Here sat a woman, ravaged by poverty, her face lined with the worries of a lifetime, cuddling to her breast a great grubby bundle of rags and worldly goods. Beyond was another woman, younger but no less harassed, who clutched tightly to her breast an infant who suckled with a mighty noisy appetite. All about were families, distraught and restless, poor and not so poor, some suitably dressed, some in rags, and others so drained of strength and purpose that they fell against the nearest upright in a stupor.

At two p.m., amidst great confusion, Starlena helped her mammy onto the deck of the great steamer. The immediate area was thronged by passengers, some so excited they ran about not knowing quite what to do, others quietly crying as though lost, and some, like Rona, who sat down where they were out of sheer exhaustion. At one point, Rona had taken out her clay-pipe to smoke in an effort to calm her nerves but had been promptly instructed to 'put that away!' by some over-zealous safety officer.

As the afternoon wore on, with little organization from any quarter, Starlena too, began to grow tired and impatient, her sense of adventure and feeling of excitement becoming replaced by a mood which swung between irritation and compassion for those who were burdened with small crying children, themselves impatient to be under way.

Suddenly everyone was bustled about, tickets were reproduced and folks were consequently dispatched this way and that, some to the better accommodation, some to moderately-priced cabins and some – those of Starlena and Rona's restricted means – directed towards the lower and more crowded berths in the darkest bowels of the ship.

'Y'mean we've to spend weeks down here?' Starlena was mortified. The quarters to which they had been shown were little more than dormitories, with hardly enough headroom in which to stand upright and no privacy whatsoever! The berths were like rows of coffins and, save for the long rectangular tables and little square lockers here and there, with no partitioning between them.

Hearing Starlena's remarks, another of the passengers, a tall lumbering fellow with a dark ruddy countenance, laughed aloud. 'Yer think yersel' fortunate,' he said. 'At least it's more civilized than 'twere some ten years back when a brother o' mine went out. 'Tween't a berth to yersel' – oh dear me, no! There'd be up to four folks sharin' it wi' yer!' That said, he threw his sack up to a bunk and following it, was quickly stretched out and asleep. Soon there were others piling in, too exhausted to stay on deck and all too ready to claim the better berths, climb into them and lay themselves out with a groan of satisfaction.

Rona too, followed suit, telling Starlena, 'You go up top if yer've a mind, lass. I must rest me weary bones, else I'll be fit fer nowt.'

'How long will it be, do you think, afore we're away?' Starlena bent over the berth, fussing about to make Rona comfortable and surreptitiously slipping the tapestry bag beneath the blanket with her.

'Don't ask me, me darlin'!' came the reply. 'But at least we've come this far, eh?' she chuckled. Then, as Starlena smiled at her, Rona's thoughts became more serious. She looked at this young, lovely girl who meant the world to her, and noted with a pang of sorrow the rough tweed-like garments that hung baggily from her slim shoulders like so much sack-cloth. She did not like what they had come to and already she missed the cosy bow-fronted wagon which had been their home. She longed for the sting of a fresh heather-laden breeze against her face and wondered, not for the first time, whether she was being outright selfish in denying Starlena her rightful heritage. She made as if to say something, but then, recalling incidents and harsh loathsome faces, she thought better of it. Starlena was hers! There was nothing – nothing in this world – which would induce her to give up this delightful, affectionate little creature who asked very little out of life, yet gave so very much!

Gently easing herself up onto one elbow, Rona gazed deep into

213

those fathomless dark eyes so filled with love and concern and absent-mindedly stroked the wild mass of hair that waved about Starlena's exquisite features. 'Yer ol' mammy'll be all right,' she assured her. 'Go on, away wi' yer. Up top an' see the sight o' land afore we sail long away from it.'

Starlena laughed, kissed Rona softly and in a moment was on her way back to the upper deck, where the air was a deal fresher than the putrid atmosphere which filled every crevice in the confined space below.

A few minutes later she was entranced by all the activity and confusion which seemed to be part of preparing for a big handsome steamship to set out on a journey across the ocean. Crew-hands yelled at each other, when not abusing passengers who were careless enough to get in their way. Folks were making tearful farewells to their loved ones. Latecomers scrambled aboard in such a hurry that many a bag and bundle fell into the Mersey, never to be seen again.

Starlena, like her mammy too, she didn't wonder, felt home-sick for the little wagon which had been swapped, with all in it save for a few particulars, for a sum of money still carefully stitched into Rona's shift. The mare was sold to the farmer who'd kept her these past months. The old cob was sold with her, and the magnificent colt which Starlena had so longed to back this very autumn, he too was gone for a guinea or two. It was the selling of the cherished colt that had struck so hard at Starlena for the mare had been a gift from Miss Elizabeth and so, in a way, was he.

No matter, Starlena chided herself at once. 'Twas small sacrifice, and if necessary she would have sacrificed much more in order to save her mammy from the confines of a prison cell. A frown creased her brow as she thought how tired and old-looking Rona had seemed just now.

'Oh, but she'll be just *fine* when we get to America,' Starlena said aloud. On impulse, she jumped up onto the railings, and, swinging merrily from a stanchion she yelled above the din, 'My mammy and me, we're going to *America!*' There was a burst of laughter from all about and somewhere away to the stern arose a rousing song in the broadest Irish tones. It was plain that America was for all of them, the land of opportunity and promise, the reason for so many souls having uprooted themselves in search of a better life.

Yet not all sailed to America for the same reason, for there lurked on board a certain emissary who was dedicated to one mission only: the prevention of a certain gypsy woman, and the girl with her, from ever reaching the shores of the 'promised land'!

The ship was not long out of Liverpool and still within sight of the estuary, when the tragedy occurred.

In the pitch black, fetid atmosphere below, Starlena had lain awake, too tired for sleep and disturbed by memories of Anselo and the trembling nearness of him on that beautiful star-studded night just a few short weeks ago. With her eyes open in the darkness and her ears assailed by loud snores, occasionally interspersed with the cries of a child lost in the depths of a nightmare, she wondered whether she would ever again set eyes on him. Then, as though afraid Rona might hear her thoughts, she deliberately thrust his dark laughing image from her mind, concentrating on her tiredness, relaxing to the gentle rolling of the ship and forcing herself to sleep. But it was the hardest thing, for like her mammy, who had instructed her, 'I'll not 'ave yer tekkin' off yer clothes afront o' so many pryin' eyes,' she had clambered into the berth fully clothed. With so many bodies lying so close to one another, it was unpleasantly hot in so confined a space.

Then there had come the sound of running feet from somewhere above, swiftly followed by several people all shouting at once. Just as Starlena was shaking Rona awake, there came a cry, 'The ship's lost! Lord 'elp us, she's lost!' And with the cry came the warm dry stench of burning – and pandemonium broke out!

Someone called 'Show us a light!' but none was shown. Another pleaded for help, but none was forthcoming. Amidst the screaming and the panic, Starlena threw both arms around Rona, while scrambling, surging bodies trampled over them, caring for nothing but that they must escape! All the time the smell of burning

215

increased, and a thick choking wall of smoke arose, from which the bodies stampeded, still screaming, leaving in their wake the weak crushed underfoot.

'Hold on to me!' Starlena yelled. By dint of sheer determination and a strength she didn't even know she had, she pulled the two of them to their feet and fought their way forward.

'No, child! We'll burn to death!' Rona had never in all of her life been so terrified.

'Just hold on, Mammy. *Hold on to me*!' Starlena kept going, her hand aching from its grip on the figure beside her, her heart bursting, her eyes stinging, her lungs choked by the thick black smoke. In a moment, she had whipped the shawl from her back and thrusting it towards Rona, she shouted above the confusion, 'Wrap it round your face. Cover your mouth!'

After what seemed an age, the mass of bodies erupted onto the deck. Even here, the air was not much better. To Starlena's horror, the whole ship seemed afire from stem to stern. People sped this way and that, falling over in their panic; some were shouting out a prayer to heaven before pitching themselves over the side and into the sea below. She could feel Rona's trembling running up her hand and right through her own body. She could hear her begin to cry, then to pray. And she was astounded for there were none braver or stronger than Rona Parrish.

'You stop that!' Starlena told her, shaking her hard and marching forward to take her quickly to a place of safety, where the seamen had lowered boats and were frantically loading people into them.

'Take my mammy,' she said, thrusting Rona forward. Then a renewed burst of panic forced a wall of bodies between her and Rona. At which point, Rona was snatched up and manhandled into a lifeboat.

'Starlena! God above, don't leave me, child! Don't leave me!' she screamed. Her sobs were loud and pitiful.

Starlena was pushed back further and further until she was hopelessly hemmed in by the weight of the rampaging mob. She suspected she might never again see Rona this side of heaven, but she thanked God that at least her mammy was safe.

From above there came the most awful sound, as though the ship was wrenching itself in two. Then with a deafening crash the whole mast came down. The screaming of the fugitives intensified, while for those poor wretches pinned beneath the wreckage, there was only silence.

Staring about her at the shattered ship, littered from end to end with debris, ravaged by fire and swarming with panic-stricken passengers fleeing in fear of their lives, many limping, some already ablaze like human torches, Starlena thought that hell must be like this. Even as she looked on, not certain whether to dart towards the rail and launch herself from it into God knew what, or to thrust forward with the main body, a searing sensation of heat ran from her shoulder to the tips of her fingers. She was on fire! Quickly, she tore the burning garments off over her head, frantically clawing at her hair when it too began to smoulder!

She *must* make a move – but which way? Every avenue was a trap! She began to inch forward, picking her way over the bodies and obstacles at her feet. As she did so, she heard a sound, a whimper close by. There! There it was again! Pausing for as long as she dared, Starlena listened intently. 'Help me.' There was no mistaking it: the weak cry of an injured soul coming from beneath the bulk of the fallen mast.

Quickly Starlena began to seek out the noise, ever more desperate in its plea. 'Please, help me!' Under there! It was a man, pinned fast by the chest, his neck twisted in a curious angle by the long dark muffler about his neck. At once Starlena knew the face – narrow, peaked, with pencil-thin moustache and small expressionless eyes which had a most unnerving stare – the same stare she had seen levelled at her and Rona on at least two occasions since boarding this God-forsaken vessel. Idly she had thought that perhaps the man was lonely – certainly he was always on his own.

Being slight of build and already exhausted, Starlena pleaded with passing passengers to give a hand, but none would. So, mustering all that was left of her strength, she began tugging and pulling at the block which held him fast, encouraged all the while by his pitiful cries of pain and entreaties: 'Please save me! I'm not ready to meet my maker.' And nor am I, thought Starlena, nor are *any* of us!

Looking back later, Starlena never knew how she *did* save the man but somehow she found the strength to deliver him from that ship, to get him over the side and into the water. Then she kept him and herself afloat with the aid of a piece of wreckage, which saved them both till help came at last. And while she did so, the scribbled note which Miss Elizabeth had given her was forever lost and with it the chance to make life in America less of a hardship.

'Oh, child! Child!' cried Rona, the tears streaming down her face. 'The Lord knew if He gave me back my life He must also give me you, for what good is one without the other?'

Starlena clung to Rona for a long time, afraid to let her go, calming her as she exorcized the horror and fear of those last terrible hours. The nightmare had been brought on by the careless act of a stowaway, or so it was said by the few seamen who survived. ''Appen a thrown away match, or a hot wedge o' pipe-tobacco, knocked out and still alight.' But nobody knew for sure and maybe nobody ever would. All that was certain on this black hellish night was that when the ship went down, some four hundred souls and more went with her!

The captain of the steam frigate who had by some miraculous turn of fortune been lying not too far away when the disaster occurred was swift to assure one and all that, 'Had I not been able to play a part in taking off the strongest and in fishing the ocean for straggling survivors, then every last one would have been swallowed up.' The survivors were taken to Regent Street, in the north end of Liverpool. The majority were men: most of the women and children perished in the flames, or had been sucked down into the deep.

Starlena and Rona's reunion was a most emotional one. Rona muttered over and over in her state of shock that, 'I saw this night as my last on earth. Oh, child! Thank the Good Lord 'e's brought us together! Thank the Good Lord!' she kept saying. Then she would look around at the injured, the bewildered and the bereaved and she would send up a heartfelt prayer for one and all.

'Easy darling . . . calm yourself,' coaxed Starlena, her every bone aching, a sick feeling in the pit of her stomach. She too was devastated by the pitiful moans of pain and grief that arose from every corner and in their presence the burns on her own shoulder seemed of little consequence. Her mammy, thank goodness, was unmarked, save by the horror which she had witnessed and which she must carry forever in her mind!

'There you are, miss!' The kindly medical assistant finished treating her shoulder, after which he handed her a package containing fresh dressing. 'It's not too bad,' he admitted. 'You're a very lucky young lady. I've heard how you saved at least one life at the risk of your own. Yes! Very lucky and very brave. You must have a special guardian angel watching over you.' As he moved away, still smiling, a middle-aged woman dressed in the uniform of a Salvation Army officer came forward. Handing Starlena a thick, warm skirt and sensible button-through top, she told her gently, 'Here. Put these on, child.' Starlena did so and thanked both the woman and Rona for the shawl she had parted with on their escape from the bowels of that ill-fated ship was once again about her shoulders. Her mammy had somehow kept it safe.

When, some time later, she and Rona were given brandy and generously fed, then made more comfortable before being bedded down for the night, neither resisted, for the experience had been a harrowing one, not to be erased by a night's sleep, nor even by a thousand nights' sleep. Yet within minutes of being put to bed, they were both quickly slumbering and, for a while at least, blissfully unconscious.

In the morning, after enjoying a surprisingly hearty breakfast of steaming hot porridge and warm buttered rolls, finished off by a piping-hot jug of tea, Starlena and Rona were both terrified and relieved when, in answer to their anxious enquiries, they were told by an official, 'Soon as ever you're ready, we're preparing to put you aboard another ship, which is waiting this very minute to take you on your journey!'

'Must we go, Mammy?' Starlena's experiences were too recent, too vivid. Yet even as she asked, she remembered that Rona had stolen the brooch, a crime for which the penalty didn't bear thinking about. So when the answer came back, she was not surprised.

'O' course we must! We've got no other choice now, child.' All the same, Rona's recollections of recent events preyed heavily on her mind, and as she answered, her voice was trembling.

Before the two were put on board another ship, Starlena and Rona were hurriedly summoned to the infirmary where, slowly recovering but in need of major surgery on his chest, lay the man whose life Starlena had saved. When a somewhat nervous Starlena was ushered closer to him, he grasped her hand and into it he thrust a wallet. 'There's money in there,' he said, 'enough to give you a little start in America.' Then, after a short spasm of coughing, he went on in a whisper, 'I've been a rum 'un in my time, I can tell you! I was on that ship for one thing – to do away wi' you an' the old 'un.' Here he nodded towards the watching Rona. 'I can't say no more. Except to tell you that you needn't go in fear of your lives any longer. Oh no! The person who hired me will be told that the both of you went down with that ship. It'll be enough! The fiend will be satisfied, I promise you.'

'Who is it, this – "fiend"?' Starlena was very much afraid. Surely nobody could wish her and her mammy dead! Not for stealing a brooch?

She said as much to the injured man, who quickly replied, 'That's it, d'you see? A person of consequence don't like to be robbed by somebody of *no* consequence. Oh, but don't worry none now, 'cause that person won't pursue you no more. You have my word that a very detailed account of your fatal accident will be delivered forthwith.' With that, he fell back exhausted, but satisfied that he had paid his debt. It mattered not about the brooch of which the girl spoke. He knew nothing of that, nor wanted to. But as far as Redford Wyman was concerned, the gypsy woman and the girl were done for!

'C'mon child. Let's away from here!' Rona had heard and she knew why their lives had been threatened. It had nothing to do with any brooch, no, indeed. It had to do with something far more sinister and as she took Starlena by the hand to hurry her away,

220

back into her mind came the face of a 'fiend', the fiend who had once before threatened to take his daughter's life and who no doubt still had his own reasons for wanting her dead.

'It's all right, Mammy! It's all right!' Starlena couldn't shake off Rona's grip and the look on the dear woman's face was awful to see. It was a look of terror, the same dreadful expression Starlena had seen once before, on the face of a deer which had been cruelly snared and left to die in agony. 'We're not pursued any more. That's what the man promised,' she assured her mammy.

Rona began at last to take heart but only a little. Of course, the man who had followed them was back there in the infirmary. She had believed in his promise. The truth of it was in his eyes. All the same, she would only truly relax when she and Starlena were safe in America. The Land of Opportunity, it was said. Well, she hoped so. She certainly hoped so, for all their sakes.

As she hurried along, grabbing frantically at the shawl which kept slithering from her shoulders and clutching in one free hand the wallet given her by that man, Starlena's thoughts were much the same. A new life and the opportunity to live it in peace; that's what her mammy needed. If it lay in her power to make it happen, then Starlena would work her fingers to the very bone. For she adored her mammy and she owed her *everything*!

Chapter Fourteen

At all hours of day and night, New York teemed with people. Starlena thought the whole world must have spilled out its inhabitants, to land them here in this one spot. All along the lower East Side of this sprawling exciting whirlpool of humanity, people lined the sidewalks, clustered about in small excited groups, yelled one to the other, sold their wares, fought their neighbours and generally kept alive the throbbing pulse of a city swarming with every nationality under the sun.

During the first week after landing, Starlena had been fascinated by all about her, from the moment she and Rona had emerged from the trauma of what was described as 'landing procedure'. This could really only be described as utter bedlam. They had been subjected to a battery of tests, both verbal, written and medical. Their hearts had almost stopped when a young woman directly before them, who looked as strappingly healthy as anyone Starlena had seen, was pounced on by the doctor, who wrote in chalk upon her back the letter 'H' – which signified to one and all that she was suspected of suffering heart-disease and as such was to be detained for possible deportation. What a fright that had given Starlena! She suspected that not a single soul in that nightmarish line-up was more glad than she when finally she came to the door marked 'Push to New York'. She had rushed both herself and her exhausted mammy through it, as though the very devil himself was on their heels!

Behind them were weeks of deprivation on a wild and spiteful ocean which tossed them about at every turn. Behind, too, was

Starlena's unforgettable distress when that monthly body clock, which only a woman is cursed with, first failed to function, then, with the most frightening fury, burst on her with a vengeance. Starlena was not naive where such matters were concerned. She had suspected that the consequences of her and Anselo making love by the lake had already begun to take shape inside her. But now the sheer physical effort of saving the life of one soul on board that doomed ship, had probably lost the life of the unborn.

For a long time afterwards, Starlena was deeply upset by the possibility that she might have been a mother, had not fate intervened to dictate otherwise. Yet, in the wisdom so long instilled in her by Rona, she accepted things for what they were and, after much agonizing, decided it must all be for the best, after all. A body must always be prepared to face the consequences of a deed done, be it good or bad.

Now, after all that, actually to set foot on the streets of New York, which were said to be paved with gold. Oh, what a feeling of accomplishment! What a daring, dandy, darling place to be! Starlena wanted to touch everything, to see all there was to see, to satisfy her curiosity down every alley and every street where certain nationalities had congregated and which were given the identities of 'Little Italy', 'Little Russia' and so on. To Starlena, it was like a different world altogether.

To Rona, it was all a heartache. 'We'll never find 'im, will we, lass?' she murmured as though to herself but, tuned in to Rona's needs as she always was, Starlena heard her and her heart was moved.

'Aw, c'mon, Mammy darling. It ain't all that bad! We've already had one or two promising leads . . .'

'Aye! Which all came to nothin',' interrupted Rona, trudging along reluctantly and thinking how very much she had come to rely on Starlena. 'Twas as though the lass had suddenly become the more decisive and stronger of the two, she the weaker and more disheartened. Rona blamed that terrible ship-wreck, when she'd thought she'd lost Starlena to the deep. Oh, what horrors they had seen that night. And now there was this place called New York, with all its trickery and sharp-tongued villains just waiting to fleece a poor unsuspecting body. It was all too much for Rona. 'After all,' she told herself by way of justifying her lack of enthusiasm, 'I'm getting longer in the tooth and fainter of 'eart by the day.' She didn't even understand the money. Why couldn't it be in coinage she knew, like pennies and guineas, not fancy pieces called dimes and cents and the dollars which folk seemed 'allus ready to part yer from'?

Yet for all that, Rona never forgot their reason for coming to America, and so long as she had her darling Starlena by her side, that was all she really cared about. But to find Callum – now that would be a cause for celebration!

The same idea was in Starlena's mind. Where to look next? That was the question. Maybe the errand they were on now might give them the very lead, straight to Callum Canaar and a deal more security than they'd had up to now. These past four months had been hard, harder than she had ever dreamed. What with their scant savings all gone and no prospects of regular decent work, they had been forced on the streets like so many more, to earn what they could. But folks had taken delight in seeing Starlena kick up her heels and dance to the melody of Rona's little wooden flute, and the handful of coins thrown down to the pavement was just enough to keep body and soul together and to pay the rent for one room in a seedy basement. There were others in that dingy room also: long grey rats and little scurrying mice who came and went as they pleased. Even the hardest winter Starlena could remember in their gypsy wagon could not compare to the bitter cold and clinging damp in the winter in that room, when the walls ran wet and the wind whistled in through every crack and crevice. So much so that Rona had developed an irritating cough which, when it caught her unawares, rendered her weak and exhausted. The evening ritual did nothing to improve it. Starlena would take off her own cherished shawl and lay it over the cold pavement. Rona would then settle herself on it cross-legged and would blow with all her strength into the flute. Starlena would be tapping her dainty feet, swirling her skirt and attracting the appreciative eye of all who passed. But though Starlena loved to dance and the tune from the flute was a merry one, she longed with all her heart for Whistledown Valley and the open rolling countryside of a land she would probably never see again.

It was no shame to be poor. Starlena had known poverty often. But to be poor and alone in a foreign land was not something she enjoyed. However, always the optimist, Starlena kept up her mammy's flagging spirits and her own, by promising that come what might, they would find Callum Canaar, who no doubt must by now have made the fortune he came for. On that day there would be much cause for celebration! And even if they found he had not made a fortune, well, no matter – for her mammy would have her much-loved brother, she would have an uncle at last and they would be a family. That was fortune enough to start with! Then they could make plans for building a future here in this promised land. For they must not risk ever returning to England, for in spite of what that man said, Rona could still be in danger of imprisonment. Oh no! However much she longed for home, Starlena knew that it was up to her to make a life for them *here*. And she would!

'Fer the life on me, lass, I can't understand what's tekkin' so long to find 'im. 'Tis as though 'e's disappeared fro' the face o' God's earth.' With a skip which belied her approaching fiftieth year, Rona stepped smartly aside when two mangy mongrels took a fancy to each other and began zealously mating there and then, much to the delight of an appreciative audience of ragged, snotty-nosed kids and to the quiet amusement of Starlena, who noted that this activity had drawn at least as much attention as she and her mammy ever did with their musical renderings.

'Look, Mammy, you mustn't take on so about your brother. We shall find him, I'm sure.' Starlena's voice was confident, but deep inside, she too had begun to wonder what might have happened to the man. These past weeks they'd searched high and low, been sent this way then that, by well-meaning folk, and every time their hopes were raised they were cruelly dashed again. The last lead had taken them to a man down by the docks, a somewhat dubious-looking character, who'd spent more time leering at and ogling Starlena than he had in paying attention to Rona's insistent questions. The eventual outcome had been that yes, he knew of the big man called Callum Canaar, 'a bruiser who knew how to use his fists. The type you didn't mess with!' The last he had heard, the fella had made his way to Boston, where there was better work to be had. But there were others, men who had overheard the conversation, and whose knowledge of Callum Canaar was somewhat different. 'Naw, he never went to Boston,' one of them offered. 'Didn't you know he was laid low in a street fight and died soon after?'

There then followed a chorus of voices from all sides supporting this latter statement; even, from one fellow, a vivid eye-witness account of how this same gypsy 'slung his sledge-hammer fists about like dynamite, until he was overpowered by sheer numbers'! When questioned further by Rona, he could not remember the exact place, 'being meself the worse for drink,' he told her with a proud shake of the head. But, on his description of the gypsy, Rona's heart sank, for it was so like that of her wayward and hot-tempered brother.

Rona knew then that her search for Callum was over. He had met the very end she had always feared for him, she was certain. On seeing Rona's crestfallen expression, Starlena made every effort to cheer her, in spite of her own belief that Callum Canaar had indeed met a sorry end. 'We'll go to Boston!' she declared with an encouraging smile, weaving a way through the chattering groups who, encouraged by an unusually bright and warm February evening, had spilled out of their miserable little homes and onto the sidewalks. Here the men settled to their card-playing, while the women busied themselves darning, mending and feeding their babes at milk-laden breasts. All around them, children ran and screeched joyfully, bare-footed and ragged, yet happy in their play.

Boston! Rona knew it was a ploy by Starlena to give her hope, and though her search for Callum was no more, she would play along with Starlena in her decision to go to Boston. It was as good a place as any, she supposed, to make a living.

'But that's two hundred mile away, child! It'd tek us a month to collect the rail-fare,' she pointed out. The plain truth was that Rona was bone-tired. Bone-tired and despairing of their awful situation. By now, she had little strength left, and to Starlena who constantly encouraged her it was a great worry.

It was eight o'clock, just coming twilight, when Starlena settled her mammy on the shawl and began to dance. They had found what seemed a good place, not far from a club where the better-off spent a fortune and, where well-dressed 'proper' Americans sauntered by on the broad uncluttered sidewalk.

Some two hours later there came tumbling out of the club doorway, a trio of men, full of liquid merriment and making their presence known in a loud and hearty fashion. Concerned at their rowdiness, Rona took the flute from her mouth, urging Starlena, 'Let's away from 'ere, lass.' But it was the sudden stopping of the music which attracted the men who, shouting and laughing, quickly approached. One leaned over Rona, urging her to 'play the flute. Me and my buddies here, we like your music. Don't we?' he asked the others, one of whom had grabbed Starlena by the shoulder and was attempting to twirl her about. The third man was a mountainous fellow who, both hands in his pockets and trying desperately to steady himself, was eyeing Starlena in a way that made her blood run cold. It was he who said, in a gruff throaty voice, 'Sure! we all like your music, old woman.' Then, to Starlena, 'Now, you'll dance, won't you? Y'see,' he threw a fistful of coins into Rona's lap, 'we're paying good money here, just to see the little lady dance.' Suddenly his voice seemed to Starlena more sober than drunk and darkly menacing.

Snatching herself away from the one who would have her twirl about, Starlena dashed to Rona. 'C'mon, Mammy – quickly,' she urged, helping Rona to her feet and stooping to collect the shawl. But it was plucked from her grasp as the mountainous fellow pushed his way forward. Throwing the shawl to one of the other men, both of whom were grinning, and thrusting Rona out of his way, he grabbed Starlena's shoulders, lifted her high into the air and with a roar of triumph, plunged his bloated face towards hers and covered her mouth with his own, spurred on by her frantic struggles.

'Let' er be, ye bloody animal!' shouted Rona, throwing herself at him and punching at his back. When the other men, excited by the turn of events, flung themselves at her to drag her away, Rona launched into them, her efforts pitiful against their strength. Throwing her bodily against the wall, they each restrained one thrashing arm and, when she began yelling for help, one cruelly stuffed a corner of the shawl into her mouth.

Starlena had seen all of this and fought with the fury of a tiger, using her fists and her feet and biting the attacker's face as time and time again his wide-open dribbling mouth sought hers. When, in a frantic effort to attract help, she began screaming, he relaxed his grip on one shoulder and brought his hand back to smash it hard against her mouth, warning her with a frightening little laugh, 'You may well have something to scream about, but not yet, little lady. Not till you've danced in private for me and my buddies!'

Still reeling from the blow, Starlena didn't hear the stranger's voice say, 'Is that so, friend? Then, as you're so fond of dancing, how about *you* dancing for *me*?' Nor did she realize what was happening when the big man was viciously yanked from her and smacked hard in the mouth, much as she herself had been.

Free of the big man's hold and her first thoughts being for Rona, Starlena rushed to her side and grasped her in a close embrace. 'Are you all right?' she asked, still trembling and ready to flee. But when Rona answered, 'I'm all right, child, thanks to him!' Starlena was alerted to the fracas taking place. One of the two who had pinned Rona against the wall was lying in a dead faint on the road. The other two men were laying into the stranger who had appeared in answer to Starlena's screams.

Suddenly it seemed that the stranger had them at his mercy. His fists were like lightning, striking out again and again to send both men reeling from him! As the one on the road came to and charged once more into the fight, both he and his partner were seen off with sledge-hammer blows to their already bleeding faces and, for good measure, a kick up the rear end as they swiftly retreated up the road, now surprisingly sober and calling for the big man to do the same. Encouraged by the stranger's skilful handling of his fists, the prospect of a possible broken nose and the certainty of humiliation in front of friends and women, it was only a matter of moments before he took their advice.

At the sight of such a large man escaping at a clumsy run down the road, his pals going even faster, Starlena couldn't help but smile.

'Thank you.' Starlena thought the word inadequate but didn't know what else to say. She was still holding on to Rona, who had begun one of those exhausting coughing spasms which prevented her for the moment from moving away. Starlena looked up at the stranger and, for the first time, she could see he was not very tall, though of above average height, lean and hungry in build, his whole appearance one of strength and aggression. Even now, with her assailants gone, his manner seemed threatening. In the half-light of the street-lamp, Starlena thought him a commanding and intriguing figure, some nine or ten years older than she – twenty-five or twenty-six, maybe. His hair, the colour of rugged brown earth, fell attractively from a high side-parting, to tumble in unruly strands over his ears and down to the collar of his shirt. His face was lean and handsome, the square strong chin deeply cleft, the eyes compelling as a cat's – dark green, fathomless and very beautiful.

'All right, are you?' he asked, with a small kindly smile which showed his white even teeth. Then, as Starlena nodded, grateful that Rona's cough had eased and they could quickly go, the smile disappeared from his face. 'Have you no more sense?' he demanded. 'Dancing in the streets, at the mercy of', he flicked a thumb in the direction the assailants had fled, 'trash like that!' The anger had not yet left Jackson Grand. It wasn't often that he came to New York, and he hated the occasions when, on business, he was forced to! Some of the worst slime in humanity was to be found here, if the right stone was overturned. A gypsy woman and a dancing girl provided just such a stone to bring out the worst in a good many. Yet, he could not help but be moved by the sorry pair, the old one bent double in a coughing fit and the girl with her ravishing dark eyes, unruly spill of jet-black hair and, easily visible when she danced, as he had witnessed earlier, the figure of a fresh and desirable woman. Jackson shook such thoughts from his mind. After what he'd been through, he had no time for women, women of any description. And the farther away they were from him, the better!

'Get off the streets,' he told them now, addressing himself to Starlena for in spite of her youth, she seemed the stronger of the two. 'Hell! There's been gypsies hanged for causing less trouble than you two.'

'And hang *you*!' Starlena burst out, infuriated both by the original attack and by this man's attitude. Who did he think he was? 'We're very grateful for your help, sir, me and my mammy both. But it ain't for you to tell us what to do. We earn our living the only way we know how!' Her eyes blazed into his and as he stood there, Jackson felt a wave of emotion strike right through him. He could never remember seeing anyone or anything as magnificent as this lovely creature. And she was gutsy. He liked that. Looking at the pair of them more closely, he noted the rags they wore and the poor state of the older one, who had a particular sadness in her eyes which touched him deeply.

Stepping forward, he reached out to wipe away the trickle of blood from Starlena's lips. Then, dipping his hand into his pocket, he withdrew a small roll of dollar bills which he pushed into Rona's hand, saying, 'I'm telling you, lady. Don't let this girl dance in the streets.' Then, gazing into her eyes, he added quietly, 'You do know what I'm saying?' Rona knew, and she nodded gratefully. 'Okay, ma'am,' he drawled. Then, to Starlena, 'What else can you do, besides dance?'

Starlena found herself deeply disturbed by this handsome man, and as now, his gaze was locked on hers and he was speaking in that slow deliberate way she suddenly felt conscious of the way she looked and wished it could be otherwise.

In her pride, she would have made no answer. But Rona was quick to sing Starlena's praises, declaring with a sly smile, 'Starlena can break a horse better than any man!'

'You don't say!'

'I'm tellin' yer, yer've never seen a horse handled proper till yer've seen my lass wi' it!' Rona's pride in Starlena had brought the shine back to her eyes.

For a long moment, Jackson Grand took careful stock of these two. His first instinct was to turn his back and leave them with the dollars he'd given, for it was well known that gypsies could be trouble, being a law unto themselves. But his deeper feelings saw in them kindred spirits who had been kicked in the teeth by adversity and led along by false hopes. Deandra, the woman he'd adored, was gone for good; he had lost her forever through his own foolishness. The experience had been painful, leaving him bitter. Never again would he trust another woman, he reminded himself. *Never*! Not as long as he lived!

Starlena began to feel uncomfortable as the stranger continued to stare at her. Then just as she prepared to take Rona away, he asked, 'That's true? You're good around horses?'

'So they say,' she answered cautiously.

Another moment, as though he was considering her answer, then, 'If you want work and a place to stay, I can offer you both. Hard work, though. And only a shack in the outfields.'

'What sort of "work"?' Starlena was hesitant.

'With horses. I have a farm outside Boston.'

Whether it was the mention of Boston, where Callum was reputed by one to have gone; or whether it was the idea of working with horses again; or even the vision of green fields and open countryside summoned up by the mention of 'farm', Starlena didn't know, but, all three seemed heaven-sent.

'Thank you. We accept, Mr . . . ?'

'Mr Grand is all you need to know.' He was on the defensive and already beginning to question the wisdom of his offer. Now he began to walk away, saying, 'There's enough money there for the rail tickets. Make for Boston, then Dorchester, just outside. Ask for Grand Farm – everybody knows it.' And with that, he was gone.

'Do you think he means it, Mammy?' Starlena wasn't too sure. Mr Grand was not the friendliest of folk, in spite of having helped them. There was something in his manner which resisted being drawn to people. She had sensed it right away. Yet, it was strange how she had been drawn to him! A feeling of panic took hold of her. 'Maybe we shouldn't go, anyway,' she said, her anxious thoughts forced into the open.

'O' course we'll go, child!' retorted Rona. 'O' course we will. Why, it's the good Lord shinin' 'is favours on us after all!' Rona felt better than she had for some long time. Things were lookin' up. Yes, indeed!

Starlena's heart was gladdened by Rona's sudden change of mood; her brown eyes seemed more full of life than they'd been for many a day. So! They would deliver themselves to Mr Grand's farm, in Dorchester, outside Boston. And if he was in any doubt about her ability to handle horses, well, she'd soon put him right.

For a minute Starlena was surprised at herself. There was excitement in her heart again and a real sense of purpose in her thinking. Like Rona, she was actually looking forward to it, though in truth they should both be apprehensive. After all, Starlena reminded herself, what did they know of this man, apart from the fact that he was brave enough to fight off three men with his bare fists and generous enough to give them a few much-needed dollars? Here, Starlena's pride was aroused. It wasn't charity, either! He would get his money's worth for she would work out every last dollar, till her back broke, if needs be!

As they walked away to get a night's sleep before boarding a train for Boston on the morrow, Rona was happy at the thought of the little shack which she would make into a cosy home and, who knew, they might find Callum after all! Starlena's thoughts were similarly occupied. But they were interspersed with persistent images of a bad-tempered man named Mr Grand, with unruly hair the colour of earth, eyes of green, deeper and more magnificent than the ocean they'd crossed, and a way of speaking that made a body hang on to his every word.

Suddenly life seemed a great deal rosier and when Rona took out her flute to play a merry tune, Starlena danced a few steps along the sidewalk. After which, they fiercely hugged each other and broke into laughter. It felt good. It felt wonderful!

'Oh, Mammy,' breathed Starlena, lifting her face up to where the towering buildings scraped the star-studded sky, 'do you think the sun's beginning to shine on us at last?'

'Aye, lass, I do!' declared Rona, with such emphasis that Starlena was prompted to hug her again.

'Oh, I do hope so,' she said. Then, a feeling of apprehension tempering her enthusiasm, she repeated in much quieter voice, 'I do hope so, Mammy darling.'

Part Five

1919
Starlena's American Dream

'Pity . . . we who thus together roam
In a strange land and far from home'
                                    Wordsworth

Chapter Fifteen

Redford Wyman was pleased with himself! Standing on the steps of his mansion, he presented a picture of undisguised arrogance. He stood motionless for a moment, the wintry sun glistening on the blood-red eye-patch and sharpening the features which had shaped themselves into a cunning expression. It could be either a smile or a sneer. With Redford it was always hard to tell. Then, rhythmically slapping the horse-whip against the rich leather of his riding-boot, he cocked his head to one side in that comical and sinister fashion he had adopted and with the piercing stare of his one seeing eye, he surveyed the scene before him.

It was early on a day in January 1919. The snow lay thick all around and, impatient to be away, the horses pawed the ground, churning up the snow and exciting the hounds. These were foaming with excitement and straining to break free across the fields, in pursuit of a creature far more cunning then they.

'Here's yer flask, sir.' The maid was a pretty young thing whose dark hair was suitably complemented by the dark uniform with its white scalloped pinafore and high lacy collar. With a look and a smile, both of which were too intimate for an exchange between maid and master, she handed Redford a small silver hip-flask filled with a good measure of best brandy.

'Good girl!' he exclaimed, taking the flask in one hand, and with the other, smacking at her buttocks as she turned away. When this brought a fit of giggling from her, he threw back his head and roared with laughter.

These past years had brought him much to be pleased about.

First there was the pleasant knowledge that the gypsy woman, and the sister who could have taken all this from him, were food for the fishes. Then his father had been permanently paralysed by a brain-seizure, and his mother was more deeply incarcerated than ever in some obscure asylum. Now there was a plentiful supply of young virgin maids to whet his lusty appetite. It was all most gratifying!

'We can't hold them much longer, squire!' The whippers-in, impatient and finding the dogs a real handful, were appealing in desperation for Redford to make a move.

'Come on, Wyman!' called a rather important-looking gentleman from the back of his fidgeting mount. 'We're all bloody impatient, man!'

Redford Wyman resented being spoken to in such a manner, and deliberately kept the pack waiting. Then the noise of dogs baying, of horses whinnying and snorting, and of several riders calling, 'Dammit man, what ails you?' 'Let's be off!' 'They've got the scent of blood', finally persuaded him to make a move.

With practised horsemanship, he swung himself into the saddle, buttoned up his black swallow-tail coat, adjusted his topper and with a cry of 'Let them go!' he surged forward with the body of riders, in full pursuit of the fleeing hounds.

The hunt was on! Away they went, the whole colourful ensemble of black tops and white breeches, some riders in bowlers, others brightening up the scene with coats of scarlet. All dressed to kill!

It was some eight miles on, as the pack raced towards the boundaries of Whalley Grange, that the accident occurred. With the Master in front, the whippers-in riding too close and the remainder pushing forward at tremendous speed, hounds with the scent strong in their nostrils, the ensuing catastrophe seemed inevitable.

Hounds dashed beneath a thick, towering hedge. There was a warning cry that came too late, as horses and riders threw themselves into the air. Some effortlessly cleared both the hedge and the deep ditch beyond, but others, incapable of such a feat, were going too fast, and were forced to make the attempt. The result was complete and utter chaos! All hell was let loose. Too many riders found themselves unable to cope. One man's back was suspected to be snapped; a woman's leg was so obviously broken; and a great number were left with scored, bleeding limbs, their only thought now to get help immediately.

Redford Wyman, being one of the most accomplished horsemen and possessor of the best mount, had easily cleared the hedge. But in the confusion, the pack was lost to sight and he, along with several others, was obliged to return to the scene. What he saw sickened him. He had no stomach for such things so, reining his mount away, he called out to one of the hunt servants, 'I'll ride back to Bessington Hall for help. You make your way over the brow of the hill to Whalley Grange. Quick, man! Do as I say!' He waited until the man galloped off to Whalley Grange. Then, 'Good,' he told himself. 'Let them dirty their hands. I've got better things to do!' and set off at full gallop. Once out of sight, his gallop was no longer so furious. All the same, it was fast enough when he cleared a fence which divided the land of Whalley Grange from Whistledown Valley and frightening enough to send the gypsy, Anselo, scurrying from beneath the hooves of the horse as they thudded into the ground not two feet from where he was boiling water over the camp-fire, in so doing, burning his arm with the spilled liquid.

'Yer a madman who shouldn't be let loose on a horse!' he shouted after the disappearing pair. 'Come back an I'll teach you a lesson or two.' He shook the fist which so easily could have delivered that 'lesson'. But Redford Wyman was away and, having no reason to like gypsies, he laughed aloud, well pleased by the upset. Anselo was left to dress his arm, tidy up the mess and settle into a black mood.

Since that unforgettable night at the lake, Anselo had hunted the land far and wide in search of Starlena, even deserting his father and Celia, who would both have sought to keep him from finding her. But she was gone. Just as surely as each day the sun disappeared, taking with it its warmth and light, so too had Starlena. Anselo was devastated.

Several times in these past years he had approached the big house where he suspected Starlena and her mammy had been staying. He had heard Starlena talk often of the woman who had befriended her. Yet whenever he went to the house, whether back or front, there was only a sour-faced creature to greet him, a surly woman, armed with a shotgun, who, he felt quite sure, would not hesitate to blow him and his kind to Kingdom Come. Ah, but he was not a man to give up. He would bide here in Whistledown Valley, until late spring, waiting an opportunity to spy this young woman Starlena had mentioned, for he was convinced it could not be the sour-faced one. All other avenues had been exhausted and, if Starlena was planning to camp anywhere this winter, it would surely be in Whistledown Valley. All the same, Anselo was not confident because, in these past five winters, there had been no sign of her and he suspected both she and her mammy were staying well away from him.

Redford Wyman was in no mood for games. 'State your business,' he told the bedraggled fellow, 'then be on your way!'

'Surely you must recognize me, Squire?' asked the man. 'It'd be in your interest if yer did!' He stepped forward a pace and smiled a beguiling smile, as though that might do the trick.

Suddenly Redford Wyman's deepest memory was stirred. Intrigued, he cocked his head and pinned the creature with his one eye. There *was* something! He glared at the man from the top of his scruffy head to the tips of his shoes which, judging by the parting of the upper from the sole, had seen better days. Still, he wasn't sure of the man's identity until, his unfriendly gaze taking in the signs of hunger, he was arrested by the moustache on the upper lip. Suddenly he had the fellow to rights!

'Why, you're the man I put on board the steamship bound for America!' he declared, somewhat taken aback that this emaciated creature and the well-heeled fellow he had employed could be one and the same. 'You saw the job done well, I must say.' Here, he gave a short laugh. Even his sound of mirth had a bitter impatience about it. 'Though it was the hand of fate and not yours that dispatched the wretched creatures to the deep!'

'Ah, well – now, that's the very matter I've – er – I've come

240

about,' spluttered the man who was feeling increasingly uncomfortable beneath that one-eyed gaze.

'What are you getting at, man? Come on! Out with it. I haven't got all day, damn you!' Then, before the fellow could continue, 'If it's *money* you're after, you can go to hell. You've been well paid once. And that's enough!'

'If yer'll just let me explain. Y'see . . .'

'Go on! Go on!'

Clearing his throat with a nervous little cough, the man went on, 'Y'see guv, I've come on 'ard times – else, so 'elp me God, I'd never a' found mesel' 'ere afront o' you! Oh, no! As a rule, I'm a man o' me word. But . . . y'see . . . the gypsy woman an' 'er girl . . .' He felt the need to bow his head in shame, as he recalled how that gallant little girl had risked her own life to save his. Oh, but life had been very hard on him this past year and, well, he could see no option but to go back on the word he'd given, for if he didn't soon make a bob or two, he'd surely not live to tell the tale anyway.

'What about the gypsy woman and the girl?' Redford Wyman had begun to feel apprehensive. Now in a fever of agitation he shouted, 'Out with it, you bloody fool!'

Faced with such fury and trembling uncontrollably, the man's response was almost as loud. 'They're *not* gone ter the deep!' He trembled the more as that eye struck right through him.

'Did I hear right? Are you telling me they're still alive?' The voice was low and chilling.

In a hurry, the whole story was poured out: of how they were saved and he was saved, and how, as far as he knew, the gypsy woman and the girl were put on another steamer to finish their journey to America.

'Don't yer see, guv, I lied ter yer 'cause that girl dragged me fro' a terrible finish on a burning ship!' He felt a sorry mess as he twisted his cap round and round in his grubby fingers and his eyes grew bright with tears of self-pity. 'You'd a' done the very same, I'm sure. But I've told yer the story now, an' all I'm askin' is a guinea ter set me on me feet.' With Redford's silence he began to grow bold. 'Make it worth me while, an' I'll find the pair of 'em – finish the job proper . . .'

The news had stunned Redford, who took a moment to recover. When he did, it was with the blackest rage and with a compulsion to take the fellow by the neck and squeeze out this life that he valued so highly! Instead he thrust his fist hard into the man's bony chest, causing him momentarily to lose his balance. 'You had better take to your heels!' he demanded. Then, clicking his fingers to raise the two black hungry-looking dogs from their place at the hearth, 'Unless you want to make a meal for these two!' Here, he made an angry clicking sound again. The dogs placed themselves between their master and his quivering victim, their eyes intent and their lips drawn back over most fearful sets of fangs, through which came a low throaty growl.

The fellow needed no more encouragement! He was away at speed and in a moment was completely out of sight, leaving Redford seething with rage and unsure of what to do next. That his inheritance could still be threatened, was more than he could bear. Where to turn? Who might know of their whereabouts now? He must get someone reliable to track them down – yes, and he would! But after all this time, they could be anywhere.

With his head bowed, eyes closed and finger and thumb tightly pinching the bridge of his nose as though to concentrate the harder, Redford began to pace the carpet at a furious pace, back and forth, back and forth, still trying to absorb the enormity of what that creature had told him. Could he trust him? Was he telling the truth? Or could it just have been a ploy to draw money from him? No, he didn't think so for there were ways of checking. Here Redford cursed himself for not having checked more thoroughly in the first place when the fellow had reported before.

Suddenly, the name of Freya Judd crept into his mind. She too was a devious creature. Was there something she knew about that night when Edward Wyman had given the brat away? A lead, even the slightest, that might suggest why the gypsy woman had gone to America? Did she have somebody there? Did she make any mention of it on that night? What did she say that could betray her? If anybody remembered, it would be Freya Judd. She forgot nothing, ever. He *had* to see her! But first he would contact a firm of investigators, and this time there would be no slip-ups.

Freya Judd watched from the window of Whalley Grange, her mouth taut and her green eyes glittering with jealousy as they followed every move of Elizabeth Judd and her brother, Lester. She couldn't hear what they were saying, but suspected it would be the kind of romantic nonsense they whispered to each other when they believed themselves unobserved.

All the same, she had little to complain about, for since being accepted into this household, she had succeeded in getting her feet under the table, as she knew she would, of course. And during the time in the latter years of the war when, despite her pleading with him not to, her brother had been away fighting for his country, she had been able to twist that weak trusting wife of his round her little finger. Yes, indeed, Freya enjoyed her place in this house and, what with one thing and another, she could easily settle the rest of her life here, near the brother she adored.

'You'll be all right, Lester darling?' Elizabeth Judd couldn't help fussing over her husband, who effortlessly swung himself up onto his horse's back.

'Of course I'll be all right,' he replied with a warm smile. 'Why shouldn't I be?'

In spite of her anxiety when Lester had gone to fight in the Great War, which had not yet been over a year, Elizabeth had been proud of her husband and still was. On the ground, his shattered knee dictated an ungainly limp. But astride his mount the affliction was undetectable, and with his fine tall figure, soft laughing hazel eyes and the sandy-coloured hair which had a mind of its own, he was everything a man should be.

As she waved him away on his morning ride, only two things marred Elizabeth's happiness. The first was Freya, who at every turn undermined her authority at Whalley Grange and constantly strove to come between her and Lester, although Elizabeth would never compromise Lester by pointing certain things out to him, with regard to his sister. After all, it was she who had admitted Freya Judd to their home and told her to consider it her own. So it was her problem, and as such she must deal with it.

The other matter constantly on Elizabeth's mind was the fact that in four years and more she had heard nothing from Starlena. Several times she had communicated with the managing director of the Textile United company in Boston. It was to him that she had addressed the letter of introduction she had given to Starlena. But neither Starlena nor Rona Parrish had presented themselves for work.

It was all a mystery to Elizabeth, who had been so sure that she would have had a letter by now. Often she wondered whether in fact they might have changed their minds, and not gone to America at all. But if that were the case, then what could have happened that would keep Starlena from getting in touch? It was a sad thing, because Elizabeth had grown very fond of the gypsy girl – a delightful creature, with the grace and inborn charm which one might associate with a high-born lady. Oh, she did wish she could see her again!

It was with this in mind that Elizabeth made her way back to the rear of the house, not wanting by any chance to be confronted by the overpowering Freya. However, as she came into the hall via the great kitchen, where for a brief moment she had discussed the evening meal with Cook and found that Freya had already issued the order, she was brought up sharp by the sound of raised voices coming from the drawing-room. One of the voices was Freya's and the other was a man's.

Not wishing to pry, and feeling embarrassed that there was obviously a heated argument taking place between Freya and her visitor, Elizabeth had every intention of making her way to the library, where she might sit and browse amongst the books and journals before lunch. When, however, she heard the man's voice say quite clearly, 'That bloody girl and the gypsy woman with her will haunt me to my grave! I thought when we had the brooch, we had *them*!' it gave her pause.

Intrigued, and with Starlena still on her mind, Elizabeth came closer to the drawing-room. Then she heard Freya. 'Ssh! Ye damn fool! There's ears to every wall.' After which the conversation continued in lower, more cautious tones.

Some ten minutes later Elizabeth crept away, her ears burning and her fears aroused for Starlena and Rona Parrish.

The story had come to her via waves of argument, growing louder and quieter with shifting emotions. The whole of it was not easily decipherable but, it was plain enough that for some reason, Redford Wyman sought to be rid of this certain gypsy girl and the old one with her. The two of them, he had discovered, had travelled to America. On the offer of making it well worth her while, Freya Judd had agreed to assist him. To this end, she had agreed to take him to a place where, on a night some twenty years ago, a certain gypsy had left a water-jack in her desperation to get away. This water-jack, Freya recalled, was inscribed with a set of initials which might lead them to the present whereabouts of its owner, if shown about in the gypsy community. 'I understand they keep close tabs on one another,' she had told the delighted Redford. To which, even more intriguing to the listening Elizabeth, he had grimly replied, 'There's no-one alive going to take away what's mine.'

Then Freya with a laugh, had said, 'Then they mustn't *be* alive, must they?' adding quickly, 'Just so long as I'm well rewarded for *my* part in it.' They had both laughed softly, before preparing to leave in order to retrieve the water-jack and, in Freya's words, 'Hope it's been protected from the weather, in the small crevice where it was dropped.' She made a parting observation, 'Strange how I'd completely forgotten about that water-jack. But then, it was a night of confusion, and, of course, the memory will bring to light certain things – if tempted enough.' There was a smile in her voice.

Elizabeth had it in mind to follow them, but decided against it, because it would not help what she must do. If there had been any doubt in her mind that the two gypsies they spoke of were Starlena and Rona Parrish, that doubt had vanished when Redford Wyman went into a rage regarding a certain brooch. She recalled a brooch of considerable value which she had inadvertently come across in

245

the gypsy wagon. She wondered whether the jewellery had belonged to Redford and been stolen from him by either Starlena or her mother. But surely the theft of a brooch did not warrant him wanting the thieves *dead*! No, she had a feeling there was more to it than that, and that same feeling warned her against confronting either Freya or Redford. But what about Lester? Would she confide in him that his own sister was conspiring to murder? How could she? In all truth, she herself could not be completely sure. Not so sure she could disturb Lester's peace of mind with it all.

Yet she did see the need for confiding in him to a certain extent, with a view to him taking her to America on the next available passage. After all, he enjoyed her company and he had expressed concern that she seemed not to be in the best of health lately. Yes, she would agree to such a trip, and once in America, would use every means at her disposal to find Starlena. After which, God willing, she would hope that Lester would help her in getting to the root of this business with Redford Wyman and his own loathsome sister. For the moment, however, the very first and most important thing was to get Sarlena and her mammy to safety.

A few moments later, as Elizabeth watched the two conspirators leave the house, she wished fervently that Starlena had written to her. Such a letter would have made her task that much easier.

Freya, as she walked from the house, was also thinking of letters. Four, to be precise. All from the rightful heir to the Wyman fortune and, all addressed in the most elaborately-practised handwriting to:

> Miss Elizabeth,
> Whalley Grange,
> Whistledown Valley,
> Lancashire,
> ENGLAND

And all four at this very moment tucked very safely away in her desk. Freya knew exactly where Edward Wyman's daughter was. The choice the knowledge presented was delightful. For some time now she had been taking great pleasure in the prospect of approaching Edward Wyman with the information. Something told her the time was ripe and he might well be pleased to pay for such information. But the dire state of his health might well require that she act through a third party – probably a lawyer. She was hesitant to risk that because what she proposed might well be viewed by less enterprising people as a form of blackmail. The second alternative was to squeeze a great deal more out of Redford. She wouldn't pass up an offer of marriage, but she doubted whether he was ready to make such a sacrifice. Yet another alternative was much more ambitious, but a prospect she was coming to like more and more. No doubt the rightful co-heiress to the great Wyman fortune would not in the least mind signing over a large part of it to the one who restored her to her inherited birthright.

Freya Judd smiled secretly as she explained where the waterjack might be found. Let the fool hawk that about, she thought cruelly, and while he wastes time, I will have better things to plan. But not so fast, not so fast she cautioned herself. There were all manner of things to be considered carefully before she showed her hand.

Chapter Sixteen

'Jesus, Mary an' Joseph! Away outta me kitchen, woman, sure yer a blatherin' nuisance, wi' yer pokin' an' pryin', pokin' an' pryin'!' The accent was broader Irish when raised in temper. The short round figure of a man who chased Rona and the child from the kitchen, with his wild shock of snow white hair, an uplifted saucepan in his hand and a face which was bright red – partly from frustration and mostly from testing his taste-buds with 'a drop o' the ol' stuff' – was quite rightly defending his bit of Ireland from would-be invaders.

Rona took hold of the small boy's hand, then with a cheeky grin on her wrinkled old face and with as much speed as her old legs could muster, she grabbed up the cumbersome folds of her skirt and fled to a safer spot, some twenty feet away. 'Yer just an ol' bag o' wind, Paddy Riley!' she laughed, as with an aggressive shake of the saucepan, the little pot-bellied figure went back inside. Promptly fishing two warm muffins from her pinnie pocket, Rona gave one to the small fair-haired boy, saying, 'There y'are, Danny, get that down yer!' Biting deep into the other, she added with a grunt of satisfaction, 'That crazy fella might be drunk as a coot when 'e mixes these 'ere muffins, but I 'ave to admit they're the best I've ever tasted!'

To Starlena, who by now, had grown used to seeing the old Irish cook and her mammy at loggerheads, the scene was an absolute tonic. To see Rona with a new lease of life, and at fifty-six, finding delight in childish pranks, did her heart a world of good. She watched as, chuckling, and with Jackson Grand's boy, Danny, trailing alongside, Rona went off in the direction of the little shack which, during these past easy years, had been the cosy home she had promised.

When the two of them were out of sight, Starlena smiled contentedly and returned her attention to the matter in hand. 'To have your loved ones well and happy is a good feeling, wouldn't you say?' she asked the horse who, with a soulful look, pushed his nostrils hard into the palm of her hand, where was hidden a little mound of oats. 'Does that mean you agree?' she murmured with a gentle laugh, 'Or are you putting food before conversation?' Opening the five-barred gate which led into the paddock, she turned the mare loose, her heart flooded with a gypsy's pleasure when, after being confined to a stable for many weeks following a fetlock injury, the animal enjoyed its freedom at last.

The sky was blue, the birds were singing, the horses, in their delight in spring, kicked up their hoofs, shivered their manes and, in a fit of sheer ecstasy, raced each other about the field at bursting speed, their magnificent feathery tails aloft. Glad to be part of it on this glorious day in February 1919, Starlena thought she would never be happier.

The terrible war which had raged throughout Europe for four long and bloody years had finally drawn to a close. The last shot was fired in the month of November 1918, just three short months ago. It had been a war which had inflicted a devastating impact on mankind. Many millions of gallant men on both sides had been slaughtered.

Starlena had followed the progress of America's involvement through newspaper reports, her heart saddened by the atrocities which war must, by its very nature, entail. Yet she was proud to be staying in a country which had extended the hand of friendship to her own mother-land. Because of it, America had gained a very special place in her heart.

She had been present when, on a particular day in the final months of the war, Jackson had received a telegram telling him that his younger brother, David, had been reported missing. Later, it was confirmed that he had been killed, and Jackson had been devastated. For two days and nights, he never left the house. During this time, old Paddy had told Rona and Starlena how Jackson had so much wanted to volunteer for active duty, but was prevented on three counts: first, the needs of his own son, only a baby; then the fact that he was the sole means of keeping the farm going; and finally, sadly, the frail health of his mother, who had passed away only days before news had come of the death of her youngest son, David.

To Starlena, it seemed especially cruel that Jackson should suffer two such losses one after the other, although she herself had never become acquainted with Mrs Grand, for that quiet delicate woman had rarely left the house.

America had turned out to be everything Starlena had prayed for. Yet dear old England was ever in her heart and would always be home. There was no changing that. And there were other things also, which often carried her in her dreams the many miles across the ocean: Anselo, whose image and whose gentle love lay curled in her heart, like a cherished surprise, to warm and thrill her again and again on the darkest night, in her quietest most secret thoughts; the memory of Whistledown Valley, with all its breath-taking beauty, under that particular part of God's sky where she knew He had built His heaven; and Miss Elizabeth, that dear gentle lady, who had been a real friend when she had desperately needed one.

Here, Starlena paused in her reflections. Why hadn't Miss Elizabeth replied to the letters she had so carefully written? In those letters, Starlena had poured out her heart, telling Miss Elizabeth how she and her mammy had been saved from a gang of ruffians by a wonderfully kind and handsome man called Jackson Grand. She explained also why sometimes he could be bad-tempered and impatient, and how he was a lonely sad man since his wife, Deandra, had run off with another man, leaving Jackson with their child, Danny, not even a year old at the time. Starlena had also written again and again, 'I can't understand, Miss Elizabeth, how any woman could ever leave a man like Jackson.' It was only on reading over her finished letters that Starlena realized Miss Elizabeth was sure to guess what she had tried to keep secret – that she loved Jackson Grand.

Starlena didn't know how or when it had happened. It was just that one day, she knew. It had crept up on her over these past wonderful years, working here on his farm. Starlena tried now to pinpoint the exact day, the precise moment, when it had happened. She wondered, was it when she'd been thrown off that spirited stallion and had lain twisted on the ground till, in the gentlest manner, he had collected her into his arms? Could it have been when, soon after they had come to live in the shack, her mammy, still weak from that exhausting cough, had taken a turn for the worse and he had sat with them through the long fearful night, helping Starlena and occasionally embracing her in a bid to bring her comfort while she tended Rona? Then there was the time when a mare was suffering a particularly difficult birth and both she and Jackson had gone without sleep for two days and two nights, at the end of which she had collapsed, exhausted, into his arms. Though physically drained himself, he had carried her to the shack and laid her on the bed. Still in his arms, Starlena had felt the soft warm passion of his mouth on hers – just a fleeting gesture, but one she had never forgotten. She never would, for it had moved the heart within her. The following morning, though, he had made no mention of it and, if anything, was more aloof and short-tempered than before!

Oh, there were so many moments – moments of tenderness and even moments of anger, when they would rage at each other in a passionate clash of wills. There was no telling just when he had captured her heart so completely. Starlena only knew that he had. She only knew that her every day began when she saw him and ended when he was gone.

Many times she had compared this feeling with the emotion she had felt for Anselo at the lake, when he had made love to her and for the first time had awakened the woman within the child. But somehow the feelings she felt for both men were as different as were the men themselves. Anselo was a passion within her, a stirring and wonderful memory which she clung to and, yes, there

251

remained deep inside her a longing to see him again, even for him to love her as he had done on that wonderful night. In her heart there was a great deal of love for him still.

With Jackson, it was not the child who loved him, it was the woman. She had blossomed just being in his presence. She knew his every mood. She admired him, adored him, challenged him, loathed him – made him the butt of both her successes and her failures. She taunted and praised him, watched over and coveted him. And, in all of her dreams, she desired him in the way only a woman could!

Starlena looked about her, at the green rolling paddock, at the houses which lay beyond the stretch of those acres which belonged to Grand Farm. Then she turned to the farmhouse itself, a white-painted strong wooden-clad house, with shuttered windows and expansive verandah, an attractive single-storey dwelling of rambling proportions and homely atmosphere. Oh, she loved it here and, so did her mammy, for many a time lately, that darling woman had told Starlena, 'Oh, lass! God's been good to us. We've found our paradise on earth!' Looking across the land, on a day like today, Starlena had to agree. It was very beautiful, and peaceful to the soul. Yet by the same token, there was an air of hustle, bustle and great urgency about this America which was a contrast to her memories of England.

From where he stood by the big barn, Jackson Grand also thought that what he was looking at was very beautiful. No, more than that, for Starlena's loveliness outshone all about her. Being American through and through, he had a fierce pride in his homeland and a deep love for this homestead which had cost him blood, toil and sweat. Yet it was all as nothing, compared to the deep emotions he suffered for this gypsy girl who had come into his life. 'Suffered', because he had not intended to love her. Suffered, because he had no *right* to love her. Suffered, because however hard he tried to suppress that love, it only grew stronger, until night and day, she was the very pivot of his existence.

He was a man torn asunder! The only other woman he had ever trusted his heart to had caused him so much pain and anguish that he had vowed never to give his heart again, to fill it only with the needs and love of the child he adored, his son, Danny, who also had suffered because of a woman, a woman who had deserted him with less thought than a mare would leave its foal. But this gypsy girl, even without knowing it, had won his bruised and lonely heart with her gentleness, her goodness, her gift of compassion and her caring, delightful nature. In spite of himself, he was drawn to her like a magnet and just the glimpse of her made him feel more of a man than he had felt for years. Yet for all that, he could not reveal his love to Starlena, for two very good reasons. He did not know how she felt – and he was more than nine years her senior. Also, more important, and however much it rankled, he was still a married man!

For a few moments, Jackson made no move, content to gaze on Starlena from a distance. Her beauty never failed to astonish him. She had been little more than a child when she and the old one had come to Grand Farm and, even now she was barely twenty. Yet in a strange way, she had never been any less than a woman. Maybe because of the responsibility she had carried for the old one, he thought, looking at her with longing. Someone should paint the picture she made at this moment, he mused, against the backdrop of the fields and the prancing horses. Starlena, dressed in brown leather boots, black calf-length skirt, white blouse billowing in the gentle breeze, her figure slim and perfect as a goddess, her wealth of long black hair lifted and teased by the wind, and those magnificent raven-coloured eyes gazing into the distance.

The longer he looked at her, the deeper his love became. So, stretching his shoulders and setting his features into the hard indifferent expression he wore like a mask to hide his true feelings, Jackson braced himself and strode across the yard to where she stood leaning against the fence, her arms crooked on top of it and her chin resting on the pillow they made.

'I guess the mare was glad to be out, eh?' Jackson had come up behind her and, as usual whenever he was near or whenever he spoke to her in that slow, deliberate way he had, Starlena's heart gave a series of little skips.

'Oh! Jackson,' she exclaimed trying desperately to hide the deep spreading blush which coloured her face. Smiling at him quickly, before turning her attention back to the mare who was now quietly grazing on the new grass, she replied, 'You could say that. She went across that field at such a speed, I thought she'd damage herself for sure.' Her heart was beating fast and it took a determined effort for her to keep her voice steady.

'No doubt you wouldn't have let her out unless she were as good as new,' Jackson declared in a detached voice. All the while he wished he could take her in his arms and hold her so tight she couldn't escape. But he could not and her nearness to him, the fresh scent of her hair and his overpowering need for her made him all the more frustrated.

As always when he found himself losing the fight, he used the only defence he had. 'You've done a good job!' he said abruptly. After which he nodded as though in approval or dismissal, quickly striding away and making for the stables, where he would saddle up the most evil-tempered mount he could find. A mile or two of hard galloping should calm the both of them.

It was gone midnight when Starlena saw him again, under circumstances that were neither anticipated nor pleasant.

'Are ye never goin' to bed, lass?' Rona had waited till the last stroke of midnight before putting the question which had been on her lips these past two hours. Although she herself was forcing her own eyelids open against the persuasion of sleep, there were other things more pressing, which kept her awake. Starlena was in a strange sort of mood, the sort of mood which puts up barriers and says, 'Keep back! I've secrets to keep.' Rona didn't like it. She did not like it at all.

With some agitation, she plonked her darning on the floor and rose from her chair with that particular groan that comes when a body's poor aching bones make a protest. Then, ambling towards the dresser, she wound up the cumbersome wooden-cased clock, which had bided here in the shack much longer than she, replaced it on its little lace doily and ambled back across the bare polished floorboards to her big wooden rocking-chair, all the while eyeing Starlena.

Once settled back in the chair, she collected her darning, resumed her work and rocked back and forth in the chair at a furious pace, waiting with increasing impatience for an answer to her question. When, after some minutes, none was forthcoming, Rona brought her rocking to a halt, sighed a deliberately loud sigh, drew her shawl tighter about her, and in firmer voice than before, demanded, 'What in the world's ailin' yer, child? Yer've been moonin' about ever sin' yer come in fro' them blessed stables!'

Starlena looked up from her favourite corner by the wood-stove where, seated cross-legged on a rag rug made by Rona, she had stayed this past hour, arms cosily wrapped round her legs, knees bent to her chin and her dark head resting on them in thoughtful fashion. At Rona's last words, a smile crept to her lips. It had been a long time since her mammy had called her 'child'; she resorted to it only in frustration or chastisement and of late there had been little cause for either. She wondered now, what Rona would say if she was to confess her abiding love for Jackson Grand. For some reason she couldn't rightly put her finger on, the thought disturbed Starlena. But then, to Rona's way of thinking, the whole thing would be a cardinal sin, what with Jackson being a married man and all. And of course what she was feeling towards him was a sin! Harder by the day to keep under control. More than once, of late, she had toyed with the idea of leaving, but where could she go? What work would she find that gave her such pleasure? And, with Rona to care for, Starlena dared not take the risk of them finding neither home nor work.

'Aw! Away with you, Mammy!' she said at last, a loving smile lighting up her lovely face and disguising the anguish beneath. 'Stop your scowling and give us a kiss!' She was on her feet in a moment. Crossing to where Rona sat stern-faced and attacking the darning with a vengeance, she threw both her arms about the stooped shawled figure and planted a smacking kiss on top of that familiar, dearly-loved grey head.

'Huh! Don't think yer can get round me easy as all that, my gel!

I might be old an' grey, but I'm not blind! An' I've still got me wits about me. Now then, there's some'at yer not tellin' me. Deny it if yer dare!' Rona challenged, turning her head to fix Starlena's smiling black eyes with a direct and determined stare. To Starlena who knew well enough when her mammy would not be easily pacified, that look spelt trouble for sure.

The ensuing silence – Rona bristling for an answer and Starlena frantically searching for a way to avoid giving one – was abruptly shattered by the unmistakable Irish tones of Paddy Riley, who also sounded unmistakably drunk!

'Fer the luv o' Mary!' he yelled, shaking the door on its hinges with a great volley of banging and crashing of his fists against it, 'Will ye open the bloody door? 'Tis a matter o' life an' death, I'm tellin' ye! Open up! Open up!'

'Hold your horses, Paddy Riley!' Starlena pleaded over the din, both curious and alarmed at an interruption at such an ungodly hour. 'I'm unbolting the door just as fast as ever I can!' Was there ever a body more excitable than a drunken Irishman? she mused wryly, convinced that the entire pandemonium was created by nothing more than Rona and young Danny having pinched a handful of muffins.

When, in a rush, she threw open the door, the sight of the Irishman, his snow-white hair in utter chaos about his purple face, his bloodshot eyes wide and fearful, put the fear of God into her. Dressed only in long-johns, over which was hastily flung his greatcoat, and displaying a mountainous area of flabby bare belly, old Paddy was in floods of tears and urging Starlena, 'Come quick as ye can!'

'What *is* it, Paddy? What's wrong?' Starlena was already throwing on her shawl.

Agitatedly dancing on the spot, the Irishman began making an exaggerated sign of the cross on himself, at the same time bursting into a fresh fit of sobbing. 'Sure 'e'll not last till mornin' I'm thinkin'. Oh! Jesus, Mary an' Joseph an' all the saints bless us!' he exclaimed over and over.

'Shut yer silly blatherin', yer ol' fool! Why, yer drunk as a bowlegged coot!' scolded Rona, who had pushed her way to the door. Starlena grabbed the two ends of her shawl across her full flowing nightie and without another word, sped away towards the house, leaving Rona to deal with the Irishman. As she ran, all manner of terrible thoughts careered through her mind. Drunk he may be, she thought in a panic, but the old Paddy had been well and truly frightened by *something*!

Starlena hadn't waited to hear who it was that wouldn't 'last till mornin'.' She only knew that it was Jackson who had leapt into her mind, Jackson lying even now at death's door! Her fleeting steps may have numbered fifty in that endless period before she reached the house, but when, breathless and frightened, Starlena hurried in through the wide-open door, her frantic prayers had numbered more. The knot inside her, which had wound itself tighter than a coiled spring, collapsed with relief when Jackson's tall reassuring figure appeared in the doorway from the small back bedroom.

'Starlena!' he called, his taut features visibly relaxing at the welcome sight of the woman he secretly adored. Rushing forward he grabbed her by the shoulders with both hands. 'Thank God! I'm at my wits' end!' he groaned, his deep green eyes sorely troubled as they searched her face for comfort. In a helpless gesture he ran his hands through his hair and said in a broken voice, 'It's Danny!'

'Danny?' Starlena darted past him and into the bedroom, where the doctor was already tending the boy, whose eyes were closed and whose breathing was distressingly laboured, and who was intermittently affected by spasmodic coughing.

'I didn't want to worry you with this.' Jackson was right behind Starlena, his voice little more than a whisper, as the two of them watched while the serious-faced doctor pulled the bedcovers up to the boy's neck, before snapping shut his little black bag. 'I came in to make sure Danny was comfortable, as I do every night before turning in. I could see straight away there was something wrong: his breathing was so heavy and he was lying so still.' He stepped forward as the doctor approached. 'He'll be all right, won't he, doc?' Then, as the doctor turned to look again at the boy, 'He *will* be all right? He *will*, won't he?'

Starlena, too, waited for the answer. Her heart was pained to see how frantic Jackson had become, his eyes *pleading* with the doctor, whose thin jutting features and sour expression gave nothing away. After what seemed an age, during which he hummed and hawed, did up his jacket-buttons and straightened his battered trilby, there came the doctor's answer, which struck fear into the hearts of Jackson and Starlena both. 'It's my considered opinion, Mr Grand, that your son is suffering from broncho-pneumonia.'

Starlena was horrified. There had been two children of Danny's years struck down on the steamship when she and Rona had first come to America. They had not survived, for pneumonia had no compassion when it came to children. It took them just as surely as it did any other unfortunate soul.

'Pneumonia, you say? My boy has *pneumonia*?' Jackson stared first at his son, then at the doctor, as though there had been some dreadful mistake.

'I've done all I can for now. Keep him covered, let him sweat and should he fight and struggle, you must hold him down.' The doctor's expression remained stiff, as he looked about the room. His eyes alighted on the wood-stove in the far corner. 'This room must be kept hot, like an oven, you understand? Pile up the fire. Stay with him. I'll be back first thing.'

Before he left, the doctor gave Starlena a curious look and a piece of advice. 'You'd better pray,' he said. 'Pray real hard!'

And she did. That night and the next three days and nights that followed, Starlena prayed as she had never done before. She and Jackson took it in turns to nurse young Danny, one snatching a few hours sleep in the chair while the other watched over the child, bathing his brow, murmuring words of encouragement. When, in the stifling heat from the constantly banked-up stove, he threw off his blankets, they were gently put back on again, while both Starlena and Jackson wilted in the same clinging exhausting heat. There was no let up, day or night.

Rona and Irish Paddy also were run off their feet, bringing in soup and liquids for the boy, food and drink for Starlena and his daddy, washing and supplying clean dry sheets and between all that, seeing to the horses and the general running of the stud farm. As Rona told the Irishman more than once, 'It's a good thing yer've no time for dippin' into the ol' stuff, yer bugger!' He had to agree that it was the first time in many a year that, 'I've been able to set one foot afront o' t'other, an' know where they both were, to be sure an' all!'

At which point both he and Rona had a good chuckle, for this was the fourth night since young Danny had been at his worst, and Lord help them, the fever had raged itself out at long last.

'An' I'll not be sayin' no, should ye give me back the bottle ye' hid away!' laughed old Paddy.

'On one condition,' agreed Rona.

'That being?'

'That yer man enough ter offer a tired ol' lady a drop an' all!'

'Well now, sure aren't I just the very man?' he laughed. His laugh became a chuckle of glee as Rona produced the said bottle from deep within the folds of her skirt.

Inside the house, Starlena kept her last vigil. Danny was sleeping more peacefully than he had for many a long fretful night, his colour healthy and his fever under control. Unlike her, he was at last contented. Getting up from the chair, she peeked a look at him, glanced briefly to where his father, Jackson, was sleeping in the wooden-framed chair not far away and on quiet feet, went to the window, where for a long time she stared out into the darkness.

There was such a tiredness in her, a weariness of spirit and soul which brought with it a mood of discontent and deep-felt unhappiness. There were emotions too, far beyond the conscious ones which had begun to plague her from day to day: writhing, troublesome emotions which swept her spirit from the heights of joy when in Jackson's company, to the very depths of misery when in his absence. Yet of late, and particularly during these last days and nights when they had been so close yet so far apart, even his nearness could not bring that same happiness, for it told her more surely that Jackson Grand was *not* hers, had never been hers and, never could be! She knew it, had always known it. And that knowledge had become harder and harder to bear. So, too, had her

259

very presence here, on his farm, within touching distance of him yet forbidden ever to do so. She had been so very happy here, yet she knew without doubt that it was a cruel sort of happiness and one which was destined not to last. But oh! how she wanted to be near him always, even though in being so she was punishing herself mercilessly.

'Mommy.' The soft cry shook Starlena from her melancholy. Rushing quietly to the child, she placed an arm under his head, gently raising him to her breast and laying her face into the dark ruffles of his hair.

'It's all right, darlin',' she reassured him, rocking his exhausted little body back and forth and crooning softly to him, a gentle lullaby crooned to her as a babe.

'When the stars are peeping bright
In the glory of the night
With the birds in Slumberland
Let the angels hold your hand.'

So engrossed was Starlena in her singing and in the little boy whom she had grown to love, that she was not aware of Jackson, who had awakened and was quietly watching her. It was a scene he was to hold close in his heart and to cherish during the hard and bitter times which were to follow.

Long after the child was again resting peacefully and Jackson had once more closed his eyes in much-needed sleep, Starlena sat curled in the chair, still restless, still caught up in a whirlpool of emotion and filled with a sense of impending catastrophe, though she knew not why.

It was in the small hours when, after a cat-nap, Starlena woke up to feel the cold. The fire had burned low and after the raging heat of this room since Danny's illness, there was a sharp chill in the air which caused her to shiver. Going to the bed, she drew the floral eiderdown up to the child's neck and went immediately to where the basket of wood rested beside the stove. She placed two sizeable logs on the low-burning embers before going to where Jackson was sprawled in the chair, his long lean body looking decidedly uncomfortable.

For a long poignant moment, Starlena gazed down on his sleeping face. The dark circles vividly etched beneath his eyes, and the look of anxiety that troubled his lean handsome face, reflected serious lack of sleep and the torment he had endured. Suddenly, there came into Starlena's heart a wave of compassion and love so overpowering that it made her want to cry somewhere deep inside.

'Oh, Jackson! Jackson!' she murmured, stooping to rearrange the blanket over him which had, sometime in the night, slithered to the floor. Having done so, she would have silently resumed her place on the far side of the room. Then, safe in the knowledge that the child's recovery was assured, she would have gone with the first light of morning. But as she began to straighten up from her task, she felt her hand enclosed in Jackson's strong fingers. Astonished, she raised her eyes to his face and what she saw there sent her heart soaring.

In the half-darkness, relieved only by the flickering light from the wood-stove, she found herself looking straight into his green, dark eyes and with a shock which set her trembling, Starlena thought them incredibly beautiful. During that surprising and tender moment, when his gaze stayed locked in the velvet darkness of her own, Starlena felt sure that he must hear her every fluttering heartbeat. She would have spoken his name, whispered some small remark to relieve this unbearable intensity. But, fascinated, she could not. It was as though in the whole world there was only her and this wonderful man whom she loved and desired so much that in such a moment she would have given anything just to know that she really was his and that he was hers.

Slowly and with great tenderness, Jackson brought his hand up to her face, touching it with the tips of his fingers, tracing the full richness of her mouth and stroking her wild flowing hair, without a word. His dark green gaze sapped her of every ounce of strength and will. When his hand spread itself out on the back of her head, Starlena felt herself being drawn forward. She saw him rise towards her and she waited for that kiss which her every heightened nerve

261

told her must happen. When it did, when in the space of a heartbeat his mouth found hers, Starlena melted beneath the warmth and passion of it.

All the pent-up emotion and longing for him came flooding into her heart, releasing itself in that wonderful ecstatic moment which she had so long dreamed of and had dared not believe would ever really happen. 'Oh, Starlena!' he was murmuring into her mouth, caressing her hair and pressing her against his taut hard body. 'Forgive me. You're so lovely – so good.' His voice was trembling. His kisses grew bolder. Like Starlena, he was losing control.

It took the voice of a sick child to tear them apart, the sob of a child for its mother. When Danny's cry pierced the warm dark room, Jackson was the first on his feet.

'Mommy! Mommy!' the child was quickly grabbed up into his daddy's arms and pacified with words of love. But even as Jackson held him, he wondered two things: why was it that Danny had called out for his mommy, whom he had not seen since taking his very first baby-steps? And what in the name of God had come over him, to take advantage of Starlena in that way? With the child now quiet in his embrace, Jackson lifted his eyes and would have asked Starlena's forgiveness. But she was gone.

'Goddamn you, Deandra!' he hissed between his teeth, before lapsing into a black and angry mood. He was only a man, after all, a man deeply in love, and though he felt he should be ashamed of it he was not. Yet, for all that, Jackson was filled with a driving remorse. He longed to have things returned to their right and proper perspective. He was a man of great loyalty. But not even he could realize how his very virtues, though admirable every one, would bring down on his head a deal of heartbreak, the like of which he had never known before.

It was Thursday following one of the most difficult weeks in her life when, at six o'clock on a bright shining morning, Starlena emerged from the shack, leaving Rona still fast asleep.

Since that night when Jackson had first kissed her in that special way a man might kiss a woman, only to turn his back on her immediately afterwards and ever since to deliberately avoid her, Starlena had at last begun to know her place. Oh, she was hurt and, to a certain extent angry, at having put herself in so impossible a situation, which had allowed Jackson Grand to draw out her deeper feelings, only to spurn them and to humiliate her. Because of it, she had thrown herself into work with a vengeance, the sense of utter desolation which had settled on her being relieved only by the fact of Danny's improving health, as he grew stronger by the day. Whether by accident or design, Starlena couldn't rightly say, but whenever she went to see the boy, his father had either just left, or was in the process of doing so. Yet, strangely enough, each time their paths crossed, however briefly, she got the distinct impression that Jackson would have much preferred to linger a while, in order to tell her what was so obviously preying on his mind. But he never did, and in a way, Starlena was glad of it.

'Top o' the mornin' to ye!' called Paddy Riley from the kitchen garden, his pride and joy. 'Yer mammy still abed, I dare say?' he asked, yanking out from the hard ground a sad-looking cabbage, which he promptly thrust into his wicker basket.

The curious scene brought a smile to Starlena's face: Paddy Riley in a pinnie and carrying a wicker basket over his arm. Was this the man who would fight to the death anybody who had the gall to question his manhood? It was all Starlena could do to hide her amusement at the picture he made.

'Morning, Paddy,' she called back with a friendly wave of her arm. 'Mammy'll be over within the hour, to see to young Danny.'

''Tis all right. The lad's sleeping still,' came his reply. 'Is it the stallion yer after tamin' on this lovely mornin'?' When she nodded, he shook his white head, warning, 'Oh, sure that one's an evil bugger! Take care now.' Clutching his basket, he waddled off towards the house, his voice raised in a dreadful rendering of an old Irish drinking song.

Still giggling, Starlena watched as he disappeared into the house. But the smile slipped from her face when, in the far paddock, she caught a glimpse of Jackson walking the recently injured mare in a tight circle, the better to strengthen her fetlock. With renewed determination, Starlena made for the stables and the big grey stallion which Paddy had described as 'an evil bugger!' Starlena would have described him as 'misused' rather than evil. Stormer was not yet three years old, and as his name suggested, he was mottled grey, big and handsome, but with a most unpredictable and tempestuous nature. There was a wild rebellious streak in him which had terrified grown men. But not Starlena. She meant to bring this exquisite but unruly animal to heel.

Yet such a task would take time – and time was the one thing she did not have. Stormer had been bought by Jackson some six months back, at an auction the other side of Charlestown. He had seen at the time that the stallion was touchy, throwing up his head and snorting nervously whenever anyone went near him. Yet Jackson had believed that he was capable of breaking him in, saying, 'He's such a magnificent animal that he'll be worth the effort.' He envisaged making a handsome profit on the stallion at the next auctions, where he would be catalogued as 'Broken and trained to racing standard. Also, easy to handle and having excellent breeding pedigree.' He had told Starlena that he'd come across animals before, who, because their previous owners had ill-treated them as colts, were defiant and dangerous. With the asking price being so low and the horse having such an excellent pedigree, he'd be a fool not to 'give it a go'.

In the four months following his acquisition of the stallion, Jackson had worked more hours on him than he had ever allowed for such an animal before. He had ceaselessly cajoled, threatened, persuaded, talked to and fought that creature for hour after hour. During which, he'd been kicked, bitten and dragged round the paddock more times than he cared to count, on one occasion being so badly bruised that he could hardly walk for two days!

Finally, in exasperation, he decided to call the meat-wagon, telling the horrified Starlena, 'He's a bad son of a bitch! He's given me no choice. I want him off this place before he kills somebody!' Then, in answer to Starlena's protests, 'I hate to admit it, but there's only one thing he's good for, and that's dog-meat!' All the same, there was still a residue of respect and admiration in him for that glorious devil, for when Starlena pleaded to be given her chance with him, and in spite of the fact that Jackson was at first adamant that the stallion was untameable, he finally gave in. 'What in hell makes you think you can succeed where I failed?' he asked her. 'One month! If you've got nowhere in that time, the meat-wagon can have him!'

In the time Jackson had given her, Starlena began the most intensive and delicate love-affair imaginable between animal and human. For a whole week she had made no attempt to enter his stable – not to muck out his bed, nor to feed or groom him. Instead, she had swung open the top half of the door and with gentle slow movements, had reached inside to lay his food by the door. Mostly it was good wholesome hay, with the occasional titbit of a large juicy carrot. But no oats, not in that first week, for Starlena knew of old that too many oats would fire up his blood and fuel that black temper of his.

At the end of the first week, Stormer was ankle deep in his own droppings and the stench when Starlena swung open the top door was breathtaking. But still she made no move to go in, and still she was not made welcome by him. Whenever she opened the door, he would either threaten her by throwing himself towards the door, head up and whinnying ferociously, or he would remain in the far corner, glowering at her, nostrils flaring. 'All right, darling,' Starlena would murmur. 'It's up to you.' She would lay down his food, before stepping back a pace, all the while murmuring soft endearments. After a while, cautiously, he would come to take the food or water, his big black eyes rarely leaving her face.

Everyone was fascinated by this state of affairs. Paddy would say, 'Sure, she'll never win the fella over that way.' Rona knew better. Jackson, mesmerized by it, thought that if the horse didn't fall in love with her, he himself was slipping deep enough beneath her spell for both of them!

During the second week, Stormer came to eat out of Starlena's hands. Two days later, he allowed her to slip a halter over his head and to tether him by the door where he could watch while she mucked out his stable, every now and then stopping to talk to him, or to softly stroke his neck. The next day, he was walked round the stable yard and very gently groomed before being returned. Yet in spite of these achievements, Starlena could see by the occasional flash of white in his eye and by that unpredictable throwing up of his head, that they still had a long way to go.

Into the third week, and the stallion responded when Starlena called his name, after which she would tenderly stroke his face and murmur to him while he ate the titbits she brought him. By this time he readily accepted body-grooming, being haltered and led, and showed aggression only once, when Starlena slid a blanket over his withers. At this point, he had risen up and brought his two front hooves crashing down onto the floor, splitting it asunder and fetching Jackson running with a shout of 'Jeez! What did I tell you?' Obviously he was greatly concerned for her safety, but when, somewhat shaken yet undaunted, Starlena reminded him that she still had over a week to go before he carried out his threat to 'bring in the meat-wagon', Jackson reluctantly conceded.

Now it was a week later and today was her last chance. In spite of the fact that she had made remarkable progress with the stallion, Jackson would not give her any more time. In less than three hours the meat-wagon would be here, and unless Starlena could prove to Jackson that Stormer was trainable and could be backed, he would be loaded onto that wagon and carted off as so much dogmeat. Starlena had no intention of letting *that* happen!

These past few days, Starlena had kept an old saddle over the stable door, allowing Stormer to sniff and lick it, and to nibble on it occasionally. At first he'd been shy of it, but now he had grown used to its sight and smell. When now she slung it over the rail of the paddock, he gave no hint of being startled. And when gently, she led him to it, saying, 'Y'see that, darling? It isn't such a terrible thing now, is it?' he did not pull away. All the same, Starlena was not fooled. She was well aware that should she slide that weight onto his back, he could just as easily trample it into the ground, and her along with it! 'I have to do it, though,' she told him softly, at the same time checking his head collar and calculating which way he might buck when both she and the saddle were on his back.

As she tethered him and began lifting the saddle towards his withers – all the while her voice low and gently murmuring – Starlena could feel the palms of her hands starting to sweat. Suddenly, she was trembling. 'This is it, Stormer, old fella,' she whispered, breathing gently up his nose and 'brekkin' him under' the way she had learned from her mammy. 'It's now or never.' It didn't help that, just at that moment, a sombre-looking wagon was driven into the yard. Out of the corner of her eye, Starlena saw Jackson order that it be backed right away out of sight. Afterwards, both he and two men came to watch from the rail where already Paddy and Rona were standing, Rona with the boy pulled tight against her.

'You have an audience, darling,' Starlena told the nervous horse. 'Now don't you let me down, will you?' The stallion snorted, rolling an eye in the direction of the onlookers. Not one of them made a move, as all eyes were on her, and on that magnificent beast which had the instincts of a killer! Now, as Starlena slid the saddle over the stallion's back, there was not a sound, save for a low trembling snort, which warned Starlena to be wary.

'Easy there,' she whispered, stroking the flat of her hand down his neck, her dark eyes gazing into his and her warm breath mingling with his own. 'Nobody's going to hurt you. It's just you and me. Just you and me.' She looked deep into the rich black eyes which followed her every move. Then, slowly now, Starlena drew the girth tight beneath his belly. Still quietly murmuring, she drew him round and raised herself on the rail. With her heart in her mouth, she simultaneously slipped the tethering knot and eased herself into the saddle.

For a second, all was deathly quiet and still. Then Starlena felt him tremble beneath her. With a toss of his head and a great nerve-rending volley of whinnying, he began writhing and twisting in every direction, throwing out his front legs and half-sitting on his rear, all the while tossing his head and rolling his eyes like a mad thing.

'God almighty!' Jackson shouted. 'Hang on in there!'

There was a burst of calls from every man watching, all enthused by the battle going on in the paddock. 'Jesus, it's a twister all right!'

'Keep him down!' 'Ride the son of a bitch. Ride 'im!'

'Woo-ee!' shouted Paddy. 'The bugger's gorran Irish temper, sure he has!'

Only Rona made no shout, for though greatly excited by it all, she preferred instead to whisper a prayer that Starlena should not forget the teachings of a lifetime, for if she did, it could mean her being crippled, or worse!

Hanging on for grim death, Starlena felt sure that his energy, like hers, must be nearly spent. Even as the thought entered her mind, there came a moment when he reared high in the air, before crashing down and racing like a fiend round the paddock!

'Lord love us. She's done it. Praise be to all the saints above, she's bloody well done it!' Paddy was jumping up and down to see that great beast running flat out. There came a warning shout from Jackson. But Starlena was ready. When the stallion launched himself into the air, she kept her grip. In a moment, they had cleared the paddock fence and were racing away over the fields. From behind her, Starlena could hear the whoops of laughter and the shouts of admiration. The palms of her hands were raw, and the sweat was trickling down her back. But oh, she felt wonderful! There was never a feeling so exhilarating as this! As the stallion carried her at furious pace over field and ditch, she gave thanks and praised him for the glorious creature he was!

When, some time later, Starlena brought him home, the pair of them bedraggled and exhausted, it was to tumultuous applause, with Jackson coming to help her down and to take her in his arms, saying as he gazed deep into her shining eyes, 'You're magnificent! In all my experience, I've never seen anyone – man or woman – handle a stallion like that.'

'So I'm worth the money you pay me?' she asked with a cheeky smile.

'Bringing you here was the best thing I ever did in my life,' he replied. The smile slid from her face, and in its place there crept a fierce blush. Feeling desperately self-conscious beneath Jackson's sensuous emerald gaze, Starlena turned to Rona, who had rushed up to hug her 'darlin' lass'.

When the meat-wagon had been sent on its way and everybody had returned to their respective duties, Starlena set to grooming Stormer and seeing that he was comfortable. 'Oh, you're a darling lovely horse!' she told him, both arms round his neck, laughing when he returned the compliment with a warm nuzzling of his nose.

As she went about her other work, Starlena's thoughts were for Jackson only. Surely she had not imagined that look in his eyes today? That wonderful tender look, which told her that he loved her?

At the end of a long and exhausting day, Starlena came into the big barn, where she hung up the bridle and halter and gave a great inward sigh. She thought she might just look in on young Danny before spending an hour or two with her mammy over a welcoming drink and a bite to eat. She wouldn't be at all surprised if there was a plate of Paddy's delicious muffins on the table. Here, Starlena gave a little smile. Rona had a knack of spiriting them away right from under his very nose.

Undoing the ribbon which had secured her wilful locks at the nape of her neck, she thrust it into the pocket of her skirt, and shaking the hair to fall naturally about her shoulders, she began making her way to the house. Even though the day was not yet ended, there shone a light from the main living-room. Starlena wondered at it, thinking that maybe Jackson had moved his son from the confines of the bedroom into the front of the house where, from the window, he might watch the comings and goings of the horses. She was not to know that inside that room at this very moment, there had begun a series of events which would dictate the course of her life from that day on.

Pausing for a while, Starlena self-consciously patted her hair and drew her hands over the folds of her skirt, smoothing them into place and hoping, as she always did when about to face the possibility of seeing Jackson, that she at least looked presentable.

It was then that the two figures moving about in the lighted room caught her eye. There was Jackson, serious-faced and uncomfortable, and a woman, who seemed to be pleading with him and was obviously distressed. Starlena took the woman to be in her late twenties, tall and excruciatingly thin, and even from where she stood some six yards away, Starlena could see that she looked very ill. In the light from the lamp her face was almost ghostly, although, judging by her finely-chiselled facial structure and the elegant manner in which her blonde hair was swept up, the woman must once have been a real beauty, thought Starlena.

Greatly curious though she was, Starlena felt acutely conscious of the fact that she had Jackson and the woman at a disadvantage, for although they could not see her, camouflaged as she was by a patch of shrubbery, she, on the other hand, could see their every gesture, their every expression, and when, as now, their voices were raised, she could hear a raging argument, which to some extent involved young Danny.

Turning swiftly away, Starlena hurried back through the shrubbery and across the vegetable garden, then on past the big barn to where Rona sat in contented fashion on the porch, her mending in a heap by the feet of her rocking-chair and the little clay pipe between her teeth puffing out spasmodic explosions of grey smoky rings. Seeing Starlena approach, Rona stopped rocking and took the pipe from her mouth.

'Where've yer been, lass? Will yer never learn when to stop work, eh? There's a pan of good wholesome stew made, and a few o' Paddy's muffins,' she said with a smile, before chiding, ''Tis a wonder it's not all spoilt!' Then, seeing the troubled look on Starlena's face, she was quiet for a moment, before asking in softer tone, 'Some'at wrong, is there, me darlin'?' Now she was on her feet. ''Ave yer been to see the lad? Is 'e all right?'

It was the panic in her mammy's voice that distracted Starlena from the memory of what she had just seen. She was greatly intrigued to learn the identity of the woman, and why she and Jackson should be engaged in heated argument, with the boy in the middle of it all?

'No, no, Mammy. Danny's fine, I'm sure,' she replied, coming up the steps to peck Rona on the cheek. 'Come on then, where's this meal you've kept waiting for me, eh?' she went on with a disarming laugh. 'I'm *starving*!'

In the event, Starlena could manage no more than the smallest helping of Rona's truly delicious stew, although she did finish off a whole muffin, covered in homemade loganberry jam and crumbling enough to melt in the mouth.

It was just as they were seated on the porch, sipping their coffee and enjoying the last remaining light of day when the familiar white shock of hair appeared round the corner. By the look of his bright purple nose and his unsteady gait, Paddy Riley was not the most sober of visitors.

'Yer ol' bugger!' chastised Rona. 'Yer've been at yon bottle agin! I'm tellin' yer, Paddy Riley, the booze'll finish yer off, else my name's not Rona Parrish!' She shook her head at him and clicked her lips together in a loud tutting noise.

Preparing herself for yet another slanging match between the two and laughing softly to herself because of it, Starlena rose from the hard slatted bench and started back into the shack, with the idea of getting old Paddy a mug of coffee – black and strong, she thought. She had gone no more than two steps, however, when she was stopped dead in her tracks by the Irish fellow's reply to Rona's warning.

'Be Jaisus! 'Tain't the booze that'll do fer me, Rona me beauty. 'Tis the woman!'

'What woman's that?' demanded Rona, thinking he was talking from the top of his head, for she had seen no woman.

'Oh ho! Ye've not 'ad the pleasure of her, then?' Paddy Riley scrambled up from the porch-step on to which he had ungraciously fallen. Bending at the middle in subservient fashion, he swept out his short stubby arm in a comical and extravagant fashion, telling Rona in a mock whisper, 'Sure, ye must know that the missus is back? The one as took herself off some five years ago? The one as ran off wi' a knight in shining armour – who dumped her when he found out she'd a crippling illness?'

Starlena was shocked. 'Do you mean Jackson's wife? She's back?' She waited for an answer, but knew it already.

'The very same!' confirmed the Irishman. 'Mrs Deandra Grand! The very same who left her husband and her babby and didn't give a josh fer either of 'em. Yet the very same who wants to come back to the arms of her family afore the Good Lord calls her to account.' Here, he fell back on the step, moaning about how he'd gotten used to not having a woman under his feet and how she'd be poking her nose into this and that and making his life a misery!

Mine too, thought Starlena, with a stab of regret, mine too. But, she made no comment and, kissing Rona goodnight, she suggested to the Irishman that he would soon get used to the new situation. She went to the scullery, where she had her nightly strip-down wash over the big tub. Then on to the bedroom which she and her mammy shared. Climbing into the hard bed, she lay thinking, devastated by what she had just heard and too stirred up to go to sleep. How could she stay here now, loving Jackson as she did? So many questions presented themselves, so many anxieties filled her heart, that suddenly Starlena was moved to tears. Burying her head in the pillow, she sobbed with the frustration of it all, until, physically exhausted from the exacting day's work and so unhappy in her heart, she fell asleep.

The tears were still wet on Starlena's face when, after sending Paddy on his way, Rona came into the bedroom. Stooping down to stroke the ruffled black hair back from Starlena's sleeping face, Rona gently brushed dry the tears. 'Oh, yer darlin' gel,' she whispered, her voice trembling with emotion and her own dark eyes blinded by a mist of tears. 'Did yer think I wouldn't guess? Did yer truly think that when 'er precious child was suffering, her ol' mammy couldn't tell?' She gazed at Starlena a moment longer, before sniffling hard and wiping her nose with the back of her hand. Then, crossing to her own bed in the corner, she murmured quietly, 'Some'at tells me in here . . .' she tapped her chest gently, '. . . that it's time, me darlin'. The Good Lord ain't yet seen fit to give you an' me the right to set down roots.'

She became quiet for a while, then, having undressed and climbed into bed, she whispered into the dark, in a voice as though praying, ''Appen the lie yer ol' mammy's forcin' yer to live, is the whip that drives us ever on. I don't know, child. I just don't know. All I *do* know is I'd travel the world one end to the other to keep yer safe.'

Two days later brought the end of the month and a busy time. The sales at Dorchester were already under way and Jackson had earmarked four yearlings and a gelding to be taken into the sale yards, together with a batch of old harness. Starlena had worked alongside Jackson since early light, preparing the yearlings and polishing up the harness till it looked a little less old and worn than before.

'Is this the lot?' Jackson swung the saddle and string of head-halters over his arm and, as it had been since the night when he'd kissed her so intimately, his voice was formal, his manner forbidding.

'Yes. That's it.' Starlena kept her back to him, deliberately intent on sweeping out the stable, her own voice equally stiff and unfriendly. From the window of the stable, she could see Deandra Grand seated out on the verandah, her legs wrapped up against the keen breeze and her son Danny happily chatting to her from the window of the house where he had been confined for at least another week. She smiled as she thought of the Irish fellow. Starlena was glad that his fears had been unfounded for Jackson's wife had not interfered with the running of the house, seeming only too pleased to be near her husband and son and to share once more in their lives. Yet, for all that, Starlena thought the woman to be no better in her health and she was painfully sorry for her.

'Starlena,' Jackson had come up behind her. He laid down the harness and, looking over her shoulder to where his wife and son laughed together, said in a tender voice, 'You see how contented they both are?'

His sudden nearness had both startled and excited Starlena, who at once began feverishly sweeping, until the straw-dust was whipped up into great choking gusts. 'They do seem very happy in each other's company,' she acknowledged, not daring to turn and look at him.

Taking the broom from her hand, Jackson placed both hands on her shoulders then, swinging her round to face him, he lowered his gaze to hers and said in a quiet voice, 'Starlena – if things had only been different, I could have loved you till the end of my days. You must believe that. Deandra was wrong to do what she did and I'd be a liar if I said I didn't find it hard to forgive her – I don't know that I have altogether forgiven her. But, she is my wife and she is Danny's mother.'

He paused when Starlena lowered her gaze, overcome with emotion at the beauty of his dark green eyes, which to her seemed as filled with pain as was her own heart.

'No, look at me, Starlena,' he pleaded. With every nerve-ending on fire, she did. But it was a while before he went on, his gaze locked into hers and seemed to draw strength from that vivacious and stunning beauty which always struck right to his heart. 'She's very ill. There was no other choice. You do see that, don't you, Starlena?'

Starlena did. And in a calm clear voice, which belied the frantic beating of her heart, she told him so, thanking him when he explained that of course, she and her mammy were welcome to stay just as long as they wanted.

'And I hope you will,' he said, before giving her a last long look. His strong sensitive hands gripped her shoulders in a firm yet tender embrace, then in a moment he was gone. And Starlena was left feeling drained of emotion.

Stay, he had said – *as long as you like. I want you to*! Oh, and so did she. But clearly she could not stay. On the morrow plans would have to be made and her darling mammy would have to be told that the life she had come to enjoy in this lovely place must come to an end. Starlena was confused and saddened at such a prospect, yet she could see no alternative. In her deepest heart she felt that staying here could only lead to trouble and more heartbreak. Yet, for all that he had shattered her dreams, she could not help but admire Jackson Grand, for he was a man amongst men – a man of sacrifice and principle, a man of compassion. A man to be loved, but someone else's man. Not hers!

Starlena could not know that, as he walked away, Jackson's regrets were as deep as her own, or that his lonely heart ached with the same hopeless love.

* * *

274

Dorchester Sale Yards on a market day was an exciting and adventurous place. A wonderland where both Rona and Starlena loved to spend many a happy hour. Today was no exception, although Starlena was on her own, having delivered the last wagon-load of paraphernalia to be auctioned – the flat-wagon included, for it was an old article, rarely used about the farm and just gathering dust in the big barn. Starlena drove the wagon into the sale yard, parked it in the directed bay, to await the auctioneer's hammer. After which, she wandered about, enjoying the busy exciting atmosphere.

These farm sales were an annual event. Farmers from miles away would travel in to take the opportunity of ridding themselves of surplus animals, machinery and any other outdated and unwanted items. The result was mounting excitement, noisy people bartering before the formal auctions and myriads of other people with wares to sell setting up makeshift stalls, or even just spreading their goods over the ground. Then, at the tops of their voices, waving pieces of merchanise under the noses of passing potential-customers, each and every one would proclaim the virtues of buying from them. Starlena loved it all. And with so much on her mind, it was good to be distracted for a while. There'd be time enough later for unpleasant decisions.

The 'decision' however, was forced on Starlena some forty-five minutes after she had returned to watch the four yearlings sold, and it was even more unpleasant than she had imagined.

Precariously perched on top of a railed fence, the easier to view the proceedings, Starlena had watched with interest as bidding for the yearlings swiftly reached reserve price and then rose above. Yet from where she sat, able to see Jackson's tall familiar figure, Starlena could detect no note of satisfaction on his handsome face. Instead, he seemed not to be taking much interest in the sale at all, looking serious and decidedly preoccupied.

Swinging down from the fence, Starlena left the auction yard and began making her way through the crowds of spectators towards the outer field and the track which she and her mammy always followed when coming in on foot. She had seen enough for today, and the sight of Jackson looking so dejected had reminded her of what she must do. Her only thought now was to talk things over with her mammy, for she had always been a source of wisdom and great consolation.

So alive was her mammy in her thoughts at that moment that when she saw the figure of Rona approaching from the distance – one arm weighed down with a huge bundle and the other frantically waving to her – Starlena thought she must be imagining it. But no! Her mammy was shouting to her and, on seeing Starlena, had begun to run, tripping over the bundle she dragged along.

'What is it, Mammy?' Starlena, alarmed at what she saw, ran to meet her. Rona was in a dreadful state of panic and she wrapped both her arms about her for support.

'Oh, child, quickly – we've got to leave this place . . .' Rona's face was pink from hurrying with the dead weight of the bundle and suddenly, she was sobbing in Starlena's arms.

'What do you mean, we've to leave?' Starlena took the bundle from her mammy's grasp. 'We're going nowhere until you've told me what all this is about.' Then, in an effort to relieve the situation and bring a smile to Rona's tear-stained face, she said, 'You've not been pinching old Paddy's muffins again, have you?'

But there was no consoling Rona, who, grabbing back the bundle, told Starlena, 'We're in danger 'ere. We *must* go – now!' With every other word, she stole a furtive glance over her shoulder in the direction from which she had come. 'Aw, child. Believe me, there's no time! I'll tell you on the way.'

'On the way *where?* Mammy, you'll tell me right away – who is it you're running from? What danger are we in?' In spite of her concern and because she was angered that her mammy should be frightened so, and because somewhere in the back of her mind she wondered whether it had anything to do with her and Jackson, Starlena stood her ground and waited.

Driven by panic and seeing that Starlena would not budge until her questions were answered, Rona poured out enough of the story to satisfy her of their dreadful predicament. She told how, on being curious when a buggy had swept up to the house, she had watched its occupant step down. The occupant was a woman she had known many years ago – a woman who must have come to America to hunt her down. 'Oh, darlin' gel! If she finds me – I'm done for, don't yer see? I'm done for! Aw, an' what'll 'appen to you? Aw, child, I'm an old woman – an' greatly afeared.' Her voice and her body were shaking violently.

Starlena was shocked. Into her mind came things from their past – a man of gentry searching Gypsy Hill for them – the one whose life she had saved in that terrible shipwreck, who had confessed that his errand was to kill both her and her mammy . . . The brooch, which for years had been hidden from sight, and which she was convinced had been stolen from someone whose quest for revenge knew no bounds . . .

Suddenly, Starlena was filled with a fury at such vindictiveness. She would rather face the villain and work the years it took to pay for the wretched brooch than have her mammy hounded another minute. 'You find a comfortable place to rest!' she told Rona, 'I'm going back to the farm. Is the woman still there? I must talk with her . . .'

'Oh, God above! No! You must not – you must *not*!' Such desperation struck Rona's heart at Starlena's words that she felt her very life leaping out of her. Quick! How to stop her?

'There's things I've not told yer, lass – dreadful things yer ol' mammy's done. I'll be thrown in prison. I'll be 'anged fer sure!'

'All right, all right, don't take on so.' Starlena looked into her mammy's wide fearful eyes and her heart was torn by the terror there. 'All right, darling – ssh, now.' She caught the dear woman into a close embrace, rocking her in comfort as one would a child woken from a nightmare. 'Ssh – it's all right, Mammy. We'll do as you say and leave this place. There's nobody going to put my mammy in prison – nor hang her. Not ever!' She too was moved to tears.

'Now? We'll go right now?' Rona was in a panic. Each minute brought disaster nearer, she was sure.

Starlena paused only for a second. They had little enough to take with them – their only possessions no doubt hurriedly packed into the bundle her mammy had fled with. And sadly there were no goodbyes that, unsaid, would be missed. Maybe it was all for the best, reasoned Starlena.

'This very minute!' she agreed. 'If that's what will make you happy, darling, we'll away this very minute.'

At this, Rona relaxed, took Starlena's free hand and, turning towards the south, the two of them trudged across the fields, each deeply occupied with her own troubled thoughts.

Starlena was still riled enough to want to storm back to the farm to face that woman who had caused her mammy so much pain. It went against her very nature to understand how anyone could be so eaten with revenge as to hunt down a poor helpless gypsy whose only crime was to steal a brooch – however valuable. Ah, Starlena reminded herself, her mammy had confessed just now that she had been guilty of other things. Dreadful things she had said, yet Starlena did not believe her. Such a confession was surely a ploy to escape the woman who had come looking for her. Her mammy wasn't capable of committing dreadful things – never!

Starlena however was convinced by one claim her mammy had made in such fear. There was no doubt that she would be thrown in prison for stealing from the gentry. Not hanged as her poor mammy had threatened, but left to rot. Oh, yes, leaving a body to rot in jail would suit the owner of that brooch, she had no doubt.

Starlena was certain of one thing. If ever the opportunity came when she could return the pain and punishment this particular 'gentry' had meted out to her and her mammy, she would repay it tenfold. And Starlena was convinced that day would come.

Rona also, was thinking of these 'gentry'. She had not enjoyed lying to Starlena – making her think there were terrible crimes she had committed. It was cruel to let her go on believing that they were being pursued because of the theft of a piece of jewellery. Yet, all of that was necessary because Rona knew in her heart that Starlena was in the most terrible danger. The man in the shipwreck had told how he'd been sent to murder them. And now! Oh, dear God, what a frightful shock Rona had suffered when seeing the occupant of that buggy step down. The face was over twenty years older, yes. But the small bright eyes, the prim taut figure and that special fancy upright way she had of walking. There wasn't the slightest doubt in old Rona's heart. That woman, who had traced her and Starlena to America – to Grand Farm – that woman was the same woman who had tended Starlena's real mother on the night she gave birth.

Why was she here – the one Starlena's father had called Freya? Why was she here, if not at the man's bidding, to finish the job which was not finished on the ship?

The answers to her own questions frightened Rona and, taking Starlena with her, she hurried them on even faster.

Starlena made no complaint, nor gave Rona any cause for further heartache. She loved her mammy and would follow her to the ends of the earth if needs be.

'We're sure to get work here, Mammy!' Starlena clapped her hands together as, laughing, she directed Rona to a large wooden board on stilts, whose bold letters read:

> United Textile Company
> Fall River,
> Massachusetts

'What's it say, lass?' The writing meant nothing to Rona, who had never seen the need for learning to read. When Starlena explained she merely snorted, got to her feet, yanked her shawl tight about her and, in surly mood, said, 'Don't be so sure, my gel! But we can try. We can try.'

Collecting the bundle in one arm and her bad-tempered mammy in the other, Starlena set a path towards the huge grey monstrosity of a building. With its forest of tall chimneys and myriads of long narrow windows it presented an awesome spectacle indeed. Strange, thought Starlena, how this town called Fall River held an eerie resemblance to the many cotton mills through Lancashire. Even down to the six a.m. mill hooter which roused an entire community from their beds to come pouring out of miserable little houses arranged in long tight rows of the kind she had seen in the mill town of Blackburn. Why, she had even detected many a homely dialect as the rushing, pushing, hordes of workers thronged past them to their day's labours. It was almost as though she and her mammy had fallen asleep in the land of America and had woken up in old England, for it seemed like a piece of old England to her – definitely a piece of beloved old Lancashire.

Rona also, had made the very same comparison, telling Starlena, 'By, lass! This is some'at an' all. I'm blessed if we ain't been transported back 'ome!' Then, on realizing they had not, she relapsed into one of the surliest moods Starlena had ever seen. Knowing how both their spirits were flagging, Starlena chose to ignore it, believing that there were better things in store for them both. Surely to God there *must* be!

It was no wonder they were down in heart, reasoned Starlena, for these past three days had tested them well. She and her mammy had travelled a long hard road since leaving Dorchester behind. Having left in such a hurry without map, direction or plan of any sort and, knowing next to nothing of the countryside they found themselves in, they had resorted to the only course possible in the circumstances: to keep on going and follow their inbuilt gypsy instincts. Their journey had brought them to this town of Fall River, some fifty miles south of Boston, through isolated sleepy towns and open countryside which offered them nothing but the desire to trudge ever onwards, surviving on the supply of fruit and muffins which Rona had thrust into the bundle – supplemented by the odd egg or two stolen from beneath an unsuspecting hen, a cup of warm milk from the farmer's churn and, on one occasion, two delicious chubby fish, caught by Starlena in a winding brook. The nights had been the worst. On the first evening and again last night they had been obliged to steal a hard uncomfortable bed amongst a consignment of large wooden crates stacked in a warehouse along the wharf of this town. Had they been discovered, they would surely have been unceremoniously evicted.

The shriek of the mill whistle startled them awake in the early hours when, undetected, they emerged from the warehouse, quickly splashed their hands and faces in a nearby stone horse trough and then, like all the other bleary-eyed and silent folk, made their way to the mill, bent on doing a day's work for a day's pay.

As Rona had clearly anticipated, Starlena's hopes were shortlived when the gruff-voiced and hostile foreman demanded, 'Ever operated a weaving loom, have you?'

To this, Starlena replied that she had no experience, but could very quickly learn.

'Are you familiar with spinning machines?'

'No, but . . .'

'Any idea of carding? Doffing? Gaiting?'

'Please, sir!' Starlena's heart fell to her boots with each question, 'I'm young and strong. What I don't know, I'll be quick to pick up . . .'

'Not in *this* mill, you won't!' His sour eyes raked them both, fleetingly over the older figure, crooked and tired with her nutmeg-coloured skin and grubby blue gypsy-turban. Then, more lingeringly, over Starlena, whose dark beauty was strikingly vivacious, and whose proud bearing raised, even in such an uncouth lout as he, a glimmer of admiration. Yet he was not moved to relent as, flinging open the door of his office, he instructed, 'Out! Damned gypsies! I've sure as hell had it with your kind. Jesus, I even had one go stir-crazy on me. You lot can't be shut up in a mill, hour after hour, hemmed in by noise and machines. I've seen it, I tell you! And I'm not about to have any more gypsies running wild in here!' Bending his thin lips into a sneer, he put a hand on Rona's shoulder as though intending to help her on her way, 'You heard. Out! Before I get you thrown out!'

'You take your grubby paw off my mammy!' Starlena pounced forward, wrenching his hand from Rona's shoulder and for good measure fetching him a sharp kick to the shins with the toe of her boot. 'We wouldn't work in your mill if you paid us twice the going rate!' she told him, at the same time propelling her mammy out of there at some speed.

'That's a real spitfire you got there, lady!' the foreman called after Rona, a reluctant smile replacing the sourness on his face,

'Sorry I can't help you – you gypsies are too much of a risk. Look! Why don't you do what you know best, eh?' The smile slipped from his face as he bent to stroke his painful ankle, 'Go and sell a few pegs – hawking and selling! That's about your measure! You're good for nothing else.'

'Come on, lass.' Rona would have kicked the man herself had she been younger and more full of fettle. But she knew what he was saying to be the truth. A gypsy's free soul could be tortured by being confined in such a prison as this. 'Twas a fact and there was nothing to alter it.

The foreman's cruel words were ringing in Starlena's ears, 'Do what you know best,' he had said, before with a laugh he had slammed shut the door after them. Unintentionally his jibes had set Starlena thinking. There were *two* things she knew best – other than living the gypsy life in a wagon – and they were breaking horses and dancing to the tune of her mammy's flute. Just now, it might be dangerous to look for work with horses, for that might be the very occupation to lead any curious body right to them.

'Take heart, darling,' she told Rona, putting down the bundle and easing her weary old mammy onto it. 'We're not done for yet – not by a long shot. Now, you take a few minutes' rest, then we'll be on our way again.' Her voice was deliberately cheerful, designed to raise her mammy's flagging spirits.

It worked for, taking out her little clay-pipe, Rona packed it with the remains from her baccy pouch, struck a match against her boot and, drawing life into the pipe, she began merrily puffing. 'Let's be off then, lass,' she said. Then, with a crafty wink, 'Even a fox may outwit a pack o' hounds if 'e's a mind to!'

That was Starlena's thought too. Often, when a fox was close to capture, he would double back, covering his tracks in the obvious way, for a hiding place was even more secure once it had been searched and found to be empty.

Starlena and Rona were long gone when the black Ford car came to a halt outside the Fall River cotton mill and from it stepped the slim figure of a man with fair hair and a prominent limp.

Lester Judd made his way to the manager's office then, after a lengthy conversation regarding various business transactions and detailed scrutiny of the books, the two of them went down to the mill floor where they found the foreman occupied in matters of a baser nature, concerning the discipline of a rebellious worker.

'Gypsies is trouble!' came the retort to Lester Judd's initial questioning.

'I'm not concerned with your opinions, man!' Elizabeth Judd's husband had taken an instinctive dislike to this fellow. 'I'm asking – have you had any gypsies here looking for work? *Two* gypsies to be precise. A young woman, an unusually beautiful creature, with black wavy hair and large dark eyes? She has with her an older woman – more gypsy-looking. Their names are Starlena and Rona Parrish. Now then! Think, man. Has there been an enquiry for work from any such persons?'

The foreman had only to cast his mind back these four hours and, being the crafty fellow he was, his instincts told him that he must be careful. This Mr Judd was a big noise from England – the owner of this mill and, by the concern on his face, a champion of gypsies. And, as such, he would not take kindly to his foreman turning such sorry creatures away.

'Nope! Can't say as I've come across such persons as you describe.'

He felt he'd said the right thing when, visibly disappointed, Lester Judd turned to the manager. 'If they turn up here, either my wife or I must be informed at once! What *is* your policy regarding gypsies?' he added. Lester Judd was aware that, not too long back, a gypsy might be snatched from the street, accused of theft or such-like and there and then be strung up high by a rampaging mob.

Before the manager, a small sharp man of quick and nervous movements, could voice a reply, the foreman offered with some vehemence, 'Like I said! Gypsies is trouble. They're not cut out for this sort o' work. Hell! They cause more aggravation than they're worth!'

Without acknowledging the foreman's outburst, Lester Judd

283

demanded of the manager, 'I asked – what is your policy regarding gypsies looking for work?'

In the face of Mr Judd's obvious concern, the manager felt the need for caution. 'Our policy is the very same for *everyone*, Mr Judd. We'll take them on if the work's there.'

'Good. Because if it comes to my notice that certain parties are discriminated against, the one guilty of denying them work will very likely find himself denied work. Do I make myself clear?'

He looked first at one, then the other – both of them vigorously nodding their understanding. 'Good!' he exclaimed, going towards the door and requesting that the manager accompany him, 'I'd like to take a look at the turnover of labour, if I may.'

Lester Judd didn't expect that he would discover there the names of Starlena and Rona Parrish. In fact, he had told Elizabeth that very morning that this impossible mission was like finding a needle in a haystack. But she had made herself quite ill, obsessed with the idea that she must find this gypsy girl, this Starlena and her mother. Other than charging him with the urgency of locating the two gypsies, Elizabeth had confided very little, entreating him not to talk about it to anyone, except to those who might know of her whereabouts and, especially not to discuss the matter with his sister, Freya.

Lester Judd sighed. And there was another source of mystery! Not only had Elizabeth suddenly wanted to accompany him to America, where there was much ground to cover and ongoing business to monitor – but his sister had also developed a sudden interest in making the trip; only to have gone her own way from the very minute they had set foot here.

It was all most odd, most odd indeed! But women were strange unpredictable creatures. It did no harm to pander to their whims on occasion. It was just as well that he had a first-rate overseer, in whose very capable hands he had left the running of Whalley Grange. All the same, though, he had no intention of prolonging his trip. When the business was done he intended to get back home as quickly as possible – gypsies or no gypsies! In any case, he questioned whether the journey here had helped Elizabeth's somewhat deteriorating health. Only this very morning she had been confined to her bed by the hotel doctor. No! She must not concern herself too much with the plight of others. Of course, he would do what he could, regarding the gypsies, but when it came right down to it, Elizabeth must be the first priority. Especially now he had just learned that she was carrying their child.

In actual fact, Elizabeth Judd's poor state of health prompted their departure from America some few days before Lester had intended. In spite of protests from both his wife and his sister, Lester arranged that they sail home on the first available ship. When Freya suggested that she at least might stay on a while, he became adamant that it was he who had brought them both out here, and it would be he that took them back again.

Freya Judd would not have been so dominated by any other man. But in her beloved brother's hands she was always flexible. After all, she told herself, good money will buy a first-rate investigator who knew this land of America far better than she.

It was necessary for them to board the ship on the evening prior to sailing, so Lester Judd secured a carriage, as opposed to the increasingly popular motor-car, because of Elizabeth's intense dislike for what she called 'noisy, smelly articles'.

'You do promise to bring me back?' Elizabeth begged of her husband.

'I promise. But only when you're much stronger, my darling.' Lester would keep his word. They would come back and, as this business of the gypsies was so important to her, he would devote far more energy to it on their return. He had the distinct impression that were he not to bring her back she would make the journey on her own.

From Charlestown, the carriage travelled to the docks, via the Charles River bridge, skirting the perimeter of Boston's West End, then through the poorer North End, where had grown up little independent states – populated by immigrants from all corners of the globe.

It seemed, as the carriage swept past a brightly-lit and crowded club, that half the population had gathered for a night of drinking and merriment. The sound of laughter, clapping and music made an uproarious din.

'Sounds as though someone's having fun,' Lester remarked, in an effort to draw out the two brooding women.

Inside the building, which was perhaps not as grand as a club but a little more prestigious than an ale house, there were many who would agree. Now, they shouted and whistled encouragement to the ravishingly beautiful gypsy girl who someone had brought in from the pavement outside. They swung her up onto the bar where her dainty feet and agile figure danced to the music and the sound of silver coins being thrown from every direction.

Starlena loved to dance and, in spite of the circumstances which had forced her to it, she spun and twirled, threw back her dark head and kicked up her heels – her black laughing eyes torturing the dreams of every man there. One in particular, the handsome and charming Jake O'Malley, Irish-American by origin, womanizer by design and landlord by trade. He looked around to see the excitement on his customers' faces. An excitement put there by this tantalizing gypsy girl. A girl who moved him to his very roots. A girl he'd be a fool to let go!

Only Rona was saddened by the sight of Starlena, elevated for all to see, dancing with such vigour to the music of the accordion, all eyes riveted in her direction. Everyone clapping and stamping and showing their appreciation by tossing silver coins beneath her feet. Her heart was heavy, yet strangely proud. Her deep love for Starlena was never stronger than it was at that moment. They must look after each other, she and this darling girl who had always been God's special gift to a lonely gypsy.

286

Chapter Seventeen

'I'm buggered if I'll let an addle-brained chicken get the better of me!' Jemm, the gypsy man, lunged at the fleeing creature, chopper in hand and a look of determination on his face. Each time he came close enough to grab its scrawny neck, the chicken gave out a mighty squawk, flapped its wings and, as much intent on escaping its fate as the gypsy was to seal it, took off in a flurry, leaving its pursuer more frustrated than before.

'Sod an' bugger it!' exclaimed Jemm, pausing for breath. In a fit of pique, he grabbed the flat cap from his head and threw it angrily to the ground. 'Yer'll not escape me, yer bugger!' he yelled at the chicken, who by now had taken refuge behind the makeshift hen-house and was peeking at him with a 'get me if you can' look.

From their respective vantage points – one seated on a fallen tree and the other at the door of his bow-topped wagon – Celia the gypsy queen and Anselo were in fits of laughter at Jemm's antics.

When, suddenly, both chicken and man disappeared into the spinney, the laughter subsided.

'Must you leave us again, Anselo?' Celia had turned to gaze on the figure leaning nonchalantly against the wagon door, a handsome figure, attractive in the dark green cord trousers, black shirt and scarlet waistcoat. 'Your father wants you to stay,' she added, hoping that such an observation might persuade him to remain.

'Father has you. You'll both be fine without me.' Anselo's reply was in a clipped impatient tone. The smile had gone from his face and his dark passionate eyes were troubled when without another word, he went into the wagon, moved noisily about as he secured it for life on the move, then emerged with a sense of urgency. Snapping shut the door, he jumped from the platform then, deliberately keeping his glance from the watching woman, he slung the water-jack up above the wheel and strode to the front of the wagon to check that horse and shaft were also secure. When he was satisfied he swung about, to come face to face with the gypsy queen.

'Anselo, how much longer before you make me your wife!' she asked, a kind of impatience in her voice but, this time tempered with persuasion. Celia was no fool. She knew from old that a man like Anselo would not be dictated to – nor would he be hurried. She knew that his heart and his love eluded her now as much as they had ever done. Yet, of late, she had sensed a weakening in him, a facet of his character that she must handle with extreme care were she to draw his mind and heart from the one called Starlena. As always, whenever that name came into her thinking, she felt murder in her soul. It was Starlena who had bewitched the man meant for her. Starlena who even now – wherever she might be – was the only barrier between her and this man whom she craved with every fibre of her being. Yet, for all that, Celia had learned the art of cajoling well.

'They say she and the old one went to America. Let them go – let her go! It's me who loves you, Anselo! Me who'll wait for you – no matter how long it takes.' So strong was her need for him, she was moved to tears.

Anselo, looking down on her, felt a pang of compassion. His dark handsome eyes gazed into hers; the fiery hazel strength of her gaze glinting in the bright sunshine of a lovely April morning and her deep longing for him so naked there. He had long ago ceased to look on Celia as his sister. She was not. She had gone to great pains to wean him from such a misconception. No-one knew her shortcomings better than he; Celia the gypsy queen was pampered, vain, spiteful of tongue and, at times, dangerous. But Anselo knew also that the love she had for him was fierce and loyal. He could not deny that. Nor could he deny his own longing for Starlena. She had become an obsession with him. His mind and heart were filled with nothing else and, wherever she was, he felt in the depth of his being that she would come back to him. One day, he would look up and there she would be. It was the dream which kept him going. The dream he would – must – hold on to, for as long as it took.

'I know there's talk of them having gone to America,' he told Celia, placing his two hands on her shoulders and looking deep into those brilliant eyes, 'but it's no matter, for even if it is so – she'll be back. I know it, and when she does return, I'll be waiting. She knows that.'

'Then you're a fool!' Celia spat out the words, her mind returning to the evening when Anselo had come into the camp some four nights ago. He had been weary of spirit and sad of heart. In his vulnerable state, she had seized her opportunity to seduce him with tender loving words and a woman's wiles. It was a night of passion she would never forget. Its intensity had made her all the more determined to possess him. In gypsy tradition, being gypsy queen she could have forced his hand in marriage after such a night. But such an arrangement would not bring satisfaction. She wanted Anselo, yes. But she would settle for nothing less than having him body and soul. Yet, all was not lost in her eyes, for on that night he too had found pleasure in passion's embrace. It was in her arms that he had enjoyed such ecstasy, such consuming delight. And it would be in her arms that he must eventually find lasting happiness and fulfilment; she must work to that end, and she would.

'Forgive me, Celia, but I need to be alone on the road. I wouldn't make good company, I promise.' Anselo bent to kiss her lightly on the mouth, 'Take care of each other,' he said, glancing towards the spinney. 'We'll meet up at Appleby in June, eh?' Then, without waiting for an answer, he turned away to climb into the front of his wagon, where, settling himself into the seat, he gathered up the reins and took to the road.

The gypsy queen, watching as the wagon became a moving speck on the horizon, spoke out loud, her bold eyes defiant and the look on her face terrible to see, 'You're mine, Anselo!' she hissed after him. 'You say when she returns that you'll be waiting. Well, so will I, my darling – so will I!'

289

* * *

Some time later, when the morning had become afternoon and the light of day had lost its brilliance, two more wagons lumbered into camp. Soon, they were comfortably pitched and the horses contentedly grazing, after which everyone gathered about the campfire for a tune on the accordion, a song and what Jemm described as 'a good old chinwag'.

It was during this 'chinwag' that certain titbits of gossip emerged. Titbits that made the gypsy queen sit up and take particular notice. The talk was of Starlena and Rona Parrish.

'Oh, aye!' mumbled the old toothless one with a lazy fat tabby cat on her lap. 'They were seen leavin' the docks – bound fer 'Merica t'were said.'

''Appen in search o' that brother of 'ers?' suggested another. 'Y'see – Rona Parrish is Rona Canaar as was – afore she married that fellow Leum Parrish. 'Er brother were Callum Canaar – took off for 'Merica some twenty-odd years back.'

'True is that!' interrupted the ancient husband of the one with the fat lazy cat. 'Known a lotta tragedy though, 'as Rona!' Here, he wagged one gnarled hand at Jemm, while with the other he picked the cap from his head and proceeded to scratch the bald patch beneath with vigorous delight. 'Y'remember Abe – the best poacher as ever was? Out Shillington way?'

After a moment's consideration, Jemm replied, 'Aye. Go on, then.'

He continued with the relish of a true storyteller, 'Well – seems 'e told the tale that 'twere 'e an' another who found Rona – an' the broken bodies o' Leum an' the child.'

'What child?' Celia's interruption caused all eyes to look her way. Now, the ancient one directed his story-telling to her.

'Why! Rona and Leum Parrish only ever 'ad one child. A lovely girl – babby, some two week old. Well – o' course, Rona must 'ave married again though. 'Cause it's said 'as she went to 'Merica with 'er daughter. So, like I said – she must 'ave married again.'

This time it was Jemm who spoke, quietly and with some deliberation. 'No. She did *not* marry again. Leum was the one and

290

only in her life. An' I were allus given to believe that Starlena was Leum's offspring. That, although the man perished in the tragedy, the child survived.'

'Not the case!' confirmed the old toothless one with the lazy fat tabby cat on her lap, 'Yer've got it wrong. But she's a deep 'un is that Rona Parrish, all the same. There's funny things goin' on an' that's fer sure!'

'What "funny things"?' asked Celia, confused and curious as to all that had been said.

'Well! There's a fella – no, a *gent*, if yer ever did – 'awkin' a water-jack round the camps. Wants ter know whose initials are carved into it. 'Tis plain whose they are. Everybody knows Callum Canaar's mark!' Here, she made out two large Cs in the air with the tip of her fingers. 'Took 'im ages to learn 'ow to put the mark of 'is name on that there water-jack!' She broke out into a toothless grin. 'The gent says if anybody wants ter earn a tidy penny they've ter go to Bessington Hall near Whistledown Valley, an' ask fer Mr Redford Wyman if they can tell whose initials are on that water-jack. Well, o' course, the gypsy ain't yet been born as'd shop one o' their own. Nobody wants that sort o' blood money, eh?' – an observation spoken with force and greeted by a rumble of assent.

The gypsy queen also nodded, perhaps more fervently than did the others. She had made a mental note of the name – Redford Wyman – and the address, Bessington Hall. She was greatly confused but greatly excited. And the more she thought on the puzzle, the clearer it became.

Rona Parrish had claimed Starlena to be her own flesh and blood when possibly she was not. So two questions arose from that. Why did Rona – and Starlena – tell the world that they were mother and daughter? And secondly, if Starlena was not Rona Parrish's daughter, then whose daughter was she? And, more importantly, was she even of true gypsy blood?

The next little puzzle was the water-jack bearing Callum Canaar's mark. How did it get into the hands of a gent? And why should that same gent be offering money to find out who it belonged to? Strange how it was Rona Parrish's brother that the gent was after. For what reason? Did the whole thing have anything to do with Rona? Or even, with Starlena – the imposter.

Celia was in such a state of excitement that she could not sleep, even when the night was melting into the first light of morning. Getting from her bed, she crept out of the wagon. Pacing feverishly round and round the cold dead ashes of the campfire, she came to a decision. She would go to Bessington Hall. She would speak to this gent, Redford Wyman, but be careful to guard her words and to learn more from him than he did from her.

As she made her way back into the wagon, a memory awakened in her revengeful mind. The memory of a terrible thrashing she had endured at the hands of Jemm. One she had never forgotten. And all because of her craving to own a glinting, glittering, bejewelled pin. She had often wondered since how such finery came to be in Rona Parrish's possession, for it was so obviously the ornament of a fancy lady. Here, the gypsy queen smiled to herself. A fancy lady, perhaps belonging to a fancy gent. Maybe the fancy gent's name was Redford Wyman. Oh, ho! There were stones to be upturned here, she told herself with glee. And secrets to be uncovered. And maybe, along the way, the chance to be rid of the woman Starlena after all!

'Hawkers round to the back door – if you please!' Freya Judd's successor as housekeeper at Bessington Hall was a pompous woman of middle age, forbiddingly large appearance and frosty face. The look she thought fit to bestow on the slight gypsy woman, whose vivid red turban was matched only by the brightness of her hazel eyes, was enough to send a grown man scurrying.

The gypsy queen stood her ground, replying in equally frosty manner, 'I *ain't* hawking! I'm on business! – to see a Mr Redford Wyman.'

The woman snorted disdainfully and would have slammed shut the door there and then. But the gypsy said in a warning voice, 'Yer master won't thank yer if yer turn me away. I have news concerning a certain . . . water-jack.'

The housekeeper stopped in her tracks. It was common talk below stairs that Mr Wyman junior was obsessed with wanting to know the owner of a battered water-jack, of the type used by gypsies. 'Wait there!' she said in a sour voice and with even sourer expression. She shut the great heavy door with a resounding clatter, leaving Celia the gypsy queen laying a vehement curse on her.

In the drawing-room Redford Wyman was deeply immersed in a conversation with the good Doctor Morley, who was here on one of his regular visits during which he had examined old Edward Wyman most thoroughly and, much to Wyman junior's disappointment, had expressed his opinion that the patient was continuing to make painfully steady progress – being not markedly better but not markedly worse either.

At the point when the knock came upon the door the conversation turned to other controversial matters. Not the least of which were the moral and economic issues arising from the alarming drift of agricultural labourers from the farms into industry, where the financial temptations were proving to be profitable for the labourer and extremely aggravating to the landowners.

'They'll run back quick enough when the depression stops the factory presses, you mark my words!' Redford Wyman stood with his back to the huge open fireplace, moving with pleasure against the small rays of warmth emanating from the meanest little fire, his good eye looking upwards and raking the panelled ceiling, 'And when they do, they'll find themselves paying hard for their lack of loyalty!'

'So! You're convinced there'll be a depression, then?'

'No question! The signs are already there. But the fools who think to better themselves in this present burst of prosperity had best be ready to count the cost!'

'This is 1919, man! Not the eighteenth century. The days are long gone, thank God, when employers use their labour force as they please.'

'You think so?' Redford Wyman took a puff of his expensive cigar, then, blowing the smoke out in fast and furious manner, he added in a menacing voice, 'We shall see. When the work comes few and far between, and industry gasps for breath – we shall see.'

It was at once clear to the doctor that with such a statement, the conversation had been brought to an end. So when the knock came upon the door more urgently for a second time, he collected his battered black bag from the sofa table and with his other hand tapped the crown of his short topper, as though to ensure it was secure upon his immensely dignified head. With a curt, 'Good day to you,' he departed the room, nodding slightly to the fidgeting housekeeper as he passed.

'Don't stand there bloody dithering, woman!' From his place at the fire-side, Redford Wyman waved an impatient hand at her, tracing a confusion of smoke from the cigar between his fingers, which wrapped itself round his face, causing him to cough and become even more agitated. 'What is it?' he demanded, taking a step forward to escape the fumes.

'There's a gypsy woman asking to speak to you, sir.'

'A gypsy woman?'

'To do with a certain water-jack,' she said.

Suddenly the fierceness was gone from Redford Wyman's expression. With a sickly smile which was no improvement, he suggested, 'What are you waiting for? Bring her in at once.' Then, as an afterthought, 'Wait! It could be foolish to show these lowly creatures the inside of a gentleman's domain.' He swept his good eye over the wood-panelled walls, the tapestries and paintings, the silver candelabras gracing each side of the magnificent long dresser and lastly, over the rich deep leather furniture, where he might be obliged to offer the creature a seat. 'No doubt they leave a particular smell of their own, being so unaccustomed to regular washing and general cleanliness.' He strode across the room past the waiting housekeeper, 'I shall make my way out to the stables. Direct her there!' He would have made his departure through the front of the house, until, in a state of distress, the housekeeper rushed after him, 'Oh no, sir! Not that way, if you please!'

Redford Wyman was brought to a halt and staring round at her he said, 'You don't mean to tell me that the creature had the gall to come to the front door?'

The housekeeper gave no reply, but nodded feverishly. Where-upon Redford Wyman gasped out loud and, turning direction, made towards the rear of the house, bouncing past her in such a temper that he almost knocked the poor woman to the ground.

'Could it be that the owner of the water-jack stole a valuable brooch from you?' The gypsy queen waited for an answer.

'Brooch?' Redford Wyman was all attention. 'What do you know of any brooch?' he asked, coming closer and eyeing her most severely.

'Ah! Struck a chord, have I, gent?' With a laugh, Celia went on to describe the brooch in great detail, together with the shawl which she had found it wrapped in.

Redford Wyman viciously grabbed her to him and demanded in a whisper, 'The one who had these things – was it a man? Or a woman?' He was trying her – testing the extent of her knowledge. When, laughing, she replied, 'An old gypsy woman and a girl,' he threw her from him as though the very touch of her gave him pain.

'You're not looking for the owner of that water-jack, are you?' Celia prided herself on being able to read a body's moods. And, this one was frightened – desperate! 'It's them ain't it? You're looking for the girl and the woman.'

'Don't think to bleed me dry,' Redford Wyman warned, 'but if you know where I can find the two you speak of, I'll make it well worth your while.'

'You do that, gent,' came the reply, 'and when you have, I'll give you the names of them two.' Now she was looking directly into his good eye, her own expression as devious as his, 'And mebbe you can tell me something, gent? Why is it that a gypsy woman should call a girl her own daughter when, by all accounts, that girl is not her own daughter?'

Watching the colour drain from Redford Wyman's face, the gypsy queen knew she had struck home. There was a mystery here. A deep and fascinating mystery which intrigued her greatly.

'I want names! And I want to know where these two are to be found. You'll be paid good money. That's all you'll get, do I make myself clear?'

To the gypsy queen, who had relished the vehemence in his voice, knowing that it was directed not at her but at Rona Parrish and Starlena, it could not have been clearer.

In the few moments it took Redford Wyman to return to the house for a wad of notes, Celia felt more content than she had done for some long long time. Taking the money and pushing it deep into the pocket of her skirt, she told him everything she knew. She explained the initials on the water-jack, revealing that Callum Canaar was the brother of Rona Parrish. He had been gone to America these many years to seek his fortune, so it was said, although she knew nothing more of him and neither did anyone else. Rona Parrish had followed him to America some six years back, taking with her the one she had passed off as her daughter. This one by the name of Starlena.

When, growing more excited with each revelation, Redford Wyman entreated, 'Describe her to me – this Starlena,' she went on grudgingly to admit that Starlena was indeed very beautiful by any standards, slight of build, with a graceful, desirable figure, thick wavy hair as blue-black as midnight and long enough to sweep about her hips. Then, thinking how besotted Anselo was, she went on to say how Starlena's large black eyes were able to bewitch a man 'and swallow him whole!' she finished, the vehemence thick in her voice.

Redford Wyman was beside himself with excitement. It was she! The very same petite and graceful figure as his mother Kathleen. The same eyes – dark and attractive. It was she. His sister! The Wyman foundling who stood between him and all that mattered to him – the Wyman fortune. At last he had names by which she and the gypsy woman with her were known. Now it would be only a matter of time before he was rid of her once and for all. This time he would not make the mistake of entrusting the job to another. He, Redford Wyman, would dispose of the pair. That way, he could be sure it was done.

Turning to stare at the gypsy before him, he let her last vicious words reverberate in his mind. 'You hate this Starlena,' he remarked with a sly grin. 'Loathe her, don't you? It oozes from you – you really must learn to disguise your feelings, my dear. To show them to another is to leave yourself open to mischief.' He turned away from her, laughing out loud and jubilantly throwing his two arms above his head. Then he suddenly became silent and, coming back to stare at her once more, said in a frightening voice, 'Whatever your reason and however much you loathe the one they call Starlena – the reason cannot be more crippling and tormenting than mine. Nor can your loathing be as deep – so very deep that it tears at your soul and disturbs your sleep like a black, clawing nightmare.'

His revelations, spoken in that devilish way and the awful effect his blue eye had on her as it stripped its way into her soul made the gypsy queen feel such terror as she had never before experienced. Backing away, she told him, 'Our business is done. You have the information you wanted – I have the reward. Kill Starlena if you must, and the old one, if you've a mind. I won't be sorry, you can be sure of that. Only one thing though . . . if on a day in the future I should come seeking the outcome . . . you'll tell me?'

'I make no promises but one. That being that should you speak a single word of our encounter here today, I will search you out and finish you.' He gave the most terrible smile, 'You do understand?'

The gypsy queen, already nervous lest she was discovered here by her own kind, betraying one of their own, quickly assured him of her silence, adding as she swiftly retreated, 'I have my own reasons for not wanting our meeting made known.'

As she slipped away into the camouflage of the spinney beyond the stables, Celia had small regret for her actions. She thanked her lucky stars that the 'mad gent' was pursuing Starlena and not her.

From the window of Edward Wyman's sick-room, where he had regained health enough to move his fingers and hands and to speak in a broken pitiful way, the sight of the gypsy woman stealing from the barn, followed soon after by the darkly-smiling figure of the man who was his son in blood only, caused Edward Wyman to become greatly agitated. He was transported back over the painful span of more than twenty years to this very house – indeed, this very *room* – where he had insisted on being moved during the latter

297

part of his illness. He carried in his sorry heart a deal of deep regret. Yet, in spite of it, he still suffered terrible jealousies and such guilt which, till now, had prevented him ever making amends. He was aware of the great flaw in his character which had made him the arrogant, mean and unloving man he had once been. He bitterly regretted all those traits which had surfaced uppermost in his son Redford. Of late, when he had felt near to leaving this world, Edward Wyman saw the need to put right what he knew always to have been wrong. Yet he could not! He could not embark on an all-out search for his daughter because he felt in his heart that she would never forgive him. Any child would hate a father who had first given her away at birth and thereafter denied her, and then to have committed her sane mother to a hellish institution for the insane. For those reasons, he could never face the child who, by now, was undoubtedly a magnificently beautiful woman. Nor could he have his wife, Kathleen, brought home – for the very same reasons.

Ah, but there was one thing he could do to make amends, thought Edward Wyman. In his confused state he had toyed with such an idea, but had not gathered the strength or will-power to put it into motion. Now, the sight of that gypsy woman running away had re-awakened the whole episode in his mind. He would do it now. He must! Before being called to his maker, he must rectify his cruel actions. How close he had been to doing what he should have done long ago, when it was confirmed to him that the fellow Durnley had no stomach for women – having relationships with men only – how close he had been then to bringing Kathleen home and to finding his only daughter. But his own arrogant pride and weakness had prevented him from having to face the truth in his wife's and daughter's eyes. He could not bring himself to do it. He could not and, oh, so soon it would be too late.

Beneath the weight of his terrible guilt and loneliness, Edward Wyman began to moan, softly at first, like a small child waking in distress. Then, the moan became a loud pitiful crying. And when the nurse rushed in to wheel him away from the window, he began to sob uncontrollably, until the tears ran down his face to mingle with his coarse grey beard, and the pain in him became so unbearable that the nurse could hardly hear him when, in the midst of his anguish, he asked for two men to be sent for – one a lawyer, the other a confidant who would give him the strength he needed, to tell all.

'Lester . . . I must speak to Lester Judd,' he begged. Only when the nurse assured him that the arrangements would be made, did he seem calmer and, in a still tearful voice, say, 'They may never forgive me . . . how can they? But, I must be sure that when I'm gone, they will have what's rightfully theirs. And, they will have each other, at last. Please God!'

Chapter Eighteen

The Boston Elevated streetcar rumbled towards Commercial Street and Hanover, carrying Starlena and her mammy back into the North End of Boston. They were returning from a short trip to the shops where Starlena had purchased a small quantity of cheap but cheerful calico with which to make them each a new dress. Rona had chosen a dark brown colour. Starlena had preferred the mid-blue with a dark speckle in it. Neither were particularly attractive, either to the eye or the touch, but the price was within their reach and that had dictated the choice.

'All right, are you, lass?'

Jolted out of her deep speculative thoughts, Starlena turned her attention away from the window and, with a gentle, appreciative smile, tapped Rona's hand reassuringly, 'Of course! Why shouldn't I be?'

'No reason! No reason! 'Tis just that yer've been so quiet all the day, that's all.' Rona looked long and hard into Starlena's lovely dark eyes. Much as Starlena might try and deceive her into thinking nothing troubled her, Rona knew otherwise, for the eyes lacked their usual lustre – indeed, there might even be a tear lurking there, she thought with a pang of compassion.

'Don't be silly, Mammy. I'm just fine.'

'If you say so! But look now, lass. If there's owt … owt at all that's playin' on yer mind, I want to know, yer'ear me?' she added, her voice kind but reproachful.

'I hear you, Mammy.' Starlena reached over to kiss Rona hard on the cheek, 'You're an old fusspot,' she said in mock reprimand, after which she returned her gaze to the street below, where life was teeming on this fine sunny day in the month of May, 1919.

The street over which the rail structure was constructed was still scarred here and there by a most dreadful incident which had taken place at the beginning of the year. Some two million gallons of molasses belonging to a distilling company had erupted in an explosion, bursting the confines of its tank to spill out in a deadly mountainous wave more than fifteen feet high and as broad as the street itself. In a relentless surge, it had careered down the street, sweeping all before it, pulling down a section of the Atlantic Elevated near Copps Hill Wharf and killing a number of poor innocent souls. What a tragedy for their families, Starlena thought, wondering how the Good Lord could see fit to punish folks who already endured a miserable existence in these pitiful slums.

But for all that, there prevailed an air of bustle and comradeship throughout the North End of Boston; somehow the unfortunate always managed to rise above even the most cruel adversity. In times of greatest stress, whether caused by loss of a job, illness or grief, everyone rallied round like one big family to help each other over the crisis. It had been that way for almost a hundred years, when the influx of hopeful souls to America congregated here, close by the docks, to find their bearings in a new land. Some – like the vast majority of the Irish settled in Boston's North End for as long as it took them to acclimatize – then moved out to Charlestown. From there they went to Medford and Stoneham; others progressed to even more adventurous destinations throughout the United States. There were many, of all nationalities, who followed suit. Many others though, perhaps through no real fault of their own, found themselves trapped in the slums of Boston. The North End was as far as their ambitions and dreams had brought them. So they made the best of what they had, assisted by the many organizations whose sole purpose was to cushion their bitter disappointment and make life tolerable at least. Strangely enough, many of those who moved out soon came scurrying back, claiming that they were only happy in the close supportive community of Boston's North End.

Looking back over the past two months since Jake O'Malley

had taken in her and her mammy, Starlena supposed she too had found a small degree of contentment. It was an uneasy contentment, she had to admit, but it had given her a precious breathing space during which she had been able to assess her life so far. There were times when her soul felt agonizingly suppressed – when each day merged into the previous one and the one yet to come. When her heart was sore with regrets and filled with an overwhelming need for things of the past, for the uniquely beautiful landscape of Whistledown Valley, and for the sight and sound of the one who had befriended her in the time of need. Oh, she had wondered many many times why Miss Elizabeth had turned her back on that friendship, ignoring all the heartfelt letters which Starlena had painstakingly written. When, long after the last one had been dispatched, there was still no reply, Starlena sadly concluded that Miss Elizabeth wanted nothing more to do with her. It had been a most painful conclusion, but she could see no other explanation. Anselo, too, played a special part in her regrets. Starlena supposed that by now he and the gypsy queen must be wed. Thinking of it brought a sadness to her heart, for he had been her first love – her only love in truth – and more than once she had cried herself to sleep because of it.

But the man who had left the deepest impression on Starlena was Jackson Grand. And because her feelings for this man went so very deep she kept them there, forbidding herself to think too long on him and the wonderful times she had experienced in his company. She had loved him in a very special way, for he was a very special man.

Now, there was Jake. A warm and charming fellow who had given her and her mammy a home in the basement of his club. Starlena was paid wages of twenty dollars a week for dancing, and her mammy was paid fifteen dollars a week for washing and cleaning – although Starlena had taken most of that work onto her own shoulders, since her mammy had been smitten with recurring attacks of gout. Starlena had worked out a sensible budget, spending her own wages on food, clothes and other necessities, and putting by the remaining fifteen dollars. The coins thrown at her feet were fairly divided between Jake and herself. It didn't amount to much, but this also was put carefully by, for Starlena had the most driving urge to save every cent she could. Never a day went by when she wasn't afraid of the future. She had dreadful nightmares where she and her mammy were thrown onto the streets, with never a friend and no place to lay their heads.

Starlena had decided that if she and her mammy were to be safe and secure, it was up to her to make it so. And, she would – whatever it cost.

'Look yonder, lass!' Rona gave a small laugh and prodded Starlena on the shoulder. 'Could you see yer ol' mammy in a titfer like that, eh?' She pressed a hand over her wrinkled mouth to stem a spurt of the giggles. 'I'm buggered if it don't look like a piss-pot!'

'Shame on you, Mammy!' Starlena chided playfully, seized by a fit of giggling as her quick glance alighted on the hat in question. It adorned the head of a trim, carefully dressed figure emerging from one of the houses below. Starlena recognized her as being one of the few who stalked the better streets, looking for clients who might pay for a few hectic minutes of her time. But, unlike others who might condemn such wretched women, Starlena thought them a breed with special strengths, who coped with life in the only way they knew. Besides which, they made enough money to dress in the most up-to-date fashion. Deep cloche-type hats came down to their eyebrows and finished in a smart little brim, often adorned with a perky feather or a silk rose. Skirts had risen way above the calf and brighter colours were now evident in styles which were more feminine and drawn into the waist. It was mainly the younger, more adventurous women who pioneered such fashions; the older ones stayed loyal to their straw boaters, blousy tops, fringed shawls and ankle-length skirts. The men, always the dandies, were loath to part with their light-coloured boaters, banded with ribbons of red or blue – although their suits and coats remained of dark and sombre appearance.

Starlena thought it must be the gypsy in her, for she did not favour the shorter skirt, neither did she want it flowing over her ankles. So she had settled for a happy medium between the two.

Her own style never changed. She always felt comfortable in bright feminine tops with full swinging skirts and small heeled shoes. In all her life she had never worn a coat and she never wanted to. Just having the cherished shawl about her shoulders was enough – although it had been delicately patched so often that there was little of the original left, except the fine exquisite embroidery worked here and there on silk backing.

'I shall mek us a hot brewin' o' tea when we gets 'ome, my gel.' A little smile curled up Rona's mouth at the thought of it.

'We'll be getting off in a minute,' answered Starlena, her dark eyes roving the inside of the streetcar where the slatted wooden seats, hanging leather handholds and window-shades, were all now a familiar sight to her. There rose a general hubbub of conversation from the passengers inside – some concerned about the failing health of President Wilson, others vehemently condemning the European power politics and some acutely concerned that Prohibition was looming close.

'Shut the ale-houses,' said one middle-aged man with a portly beer belly and a broken nose, 'and sure as hell there'll be trouble on the streets of America!' Starlena knew that particular argument well. Most nights the men drinking in the Club echoed the very same sentiments and it was a threat which greatly troubled Jake.

Walking down Hanover Street towards Jake's Club, which straddled the corner into Commercial Street, was always a fascinating experience. Early on a Friday evening the street practically throbbed with life and even on a sunny day like this, the two-and three-storey wooden houses stretched tall into the sky, so closely packed that the daylight was almost obliterated. It was a noisy street, full of dogs, children, and women breast-feeding, while their husbands stood about in busy groups, discussing this or that, and putting right the world at large. Some of the houses had been divided up by the greedy landlords and, as a result, families of eight, nine or even more were squashed into two rooms, where they survived under the most miserable conditions. Lingering over the entire street was a particular odour – heavy and clinging, yet strangely comforting, like an embrace of bodies long huddled together and giving off a warm, cloistered aroma. The very same aroma that was brought into Jake's Club night after night, mused Starlena.

The Club was nothing grand, being little more than a covered dwelling, with a bar inside and a small area where the men could sit at the tables to watch the dancing and join in with the music. But it was a place of refuge to the folks who came through its doors, and to Jake O'Malley it was a monument to his ambition. An ambition to own a string of such clubs, if only the threat of Prohibition would stop rearing its ugly head.

As she and her mammy wended their way through the bar to the back store-room, from where steps led to the basement, Starlena could hear Jake clattering about in the backroom. He was whistling in that jolly fashion which always brought a smile to her face. Rona's cynical sideways comment of 'Anybody'd think'e were fed on bloody bird-seed!' made her laugh out loud. She gave her mammy a playful push, urging, 'Get a move on, darling! I'm not in the mood for one of Jake's long conversations!'

He was a nice enough fellow, she thought, always polite and charming, already ready to brighten the day with a smile. But, somehow, he never failed to make her feel uneasy – he was too charming, too obliging and his persistence in asking her to marry him was wearing her down. She did not love him. She had told him so many many times, but still he wouldn't give up, saying, 'I'll look after you and your mammy. You'll both have a good home here and you'll want for nothing.' Starlena couldn't help but smile. Jake was a man used to getting his own way, that was plain to see. First he had showered her with little gifts, of no value but extremely decorative – like the blue straw hat and the pretty bunch of artificial flowers. Then had come the wooing and the relentlessly persuasive methods to get her into his bed. After which, seeing that he had misjudged his quarry, the charming Jake finally let down his last defence and proposed marriage as soon as possible.

Starlena's answers would have dissuaded a less forceful character, but not Jake O'Malley, who, to an outsider, might seem a strong, loyal and wonderful fellow any girl could be proud of. But Starlena had no feelings for him other than friendship and gratitude. Besides which, she sensed him to be a bit of a rogue beneath that dashing and handsome exterior – and if ever his back was forced to the wall, Starlena was in no doubt whatsoever that he would surely take the coward's way out.

'By 'eck, lass!' Rona stumbled in the door, making a beeline for the wicker armchair by the rusty iron stove, and falling into it with a thud, her arms dangling over each side of the chair and her whole body seeming to shrink right into the squashy floral seat, 'I'm beggered! Truth is . . . I'm a bit old in the bones to be trudgin' about the streets.' She gave Starlena a cheeky wink, 'Be a good' un fer yer ol' mammy, darlin'. Mek us a brew, eh?' Then, with a great sigh, she closed her eyes.

For a moment, Starlena made no move. She smiled back at the exhausted figure in the chair, her dark eyes full of love. She saw the same little lace-up boots, the same long grey skirt sweeping the floor and the very same black fringed shawl that had covered her mammy's shoulders these many long years. The gypsy bandana, still of her favourite blue colour and still covering her long thinning grey locks, was knotted in the same familiar way – drawn tight across the forehead and neatly knotted at the base of her neck, catching the hair inside. None of these things had changed and Starlena knew they never would. Her beloved mammy, Rona Parrish, was gypsy through and through, steeped long in the culture and tradition of her own kind.

A mighty sadness moved Starlena as she continued to gaze on the snoozing figure. The clothes and style that labelled her mammy to be gypsy might not have changed, but there was a change in the hands which were now gnarled and speckled brown with age, and in the stoop which marked the way she walked, and which she tried hard but unsuccessfully to disguise. It seemed to Starlena that each day carved yet another deep wrinkle into that familiar darling face. Until now, the laugh lines and the cry lines had met each other in a hopeless tangle which criss-crossed the nutmeg weathered skin like lines on an old parchment map. Starlena smiled when her mammy let out a little snore, the mouth falling open and showing that Rona Parrish, old and worn as she surely was, still boasted most of her own teeth, and they were as white and straight as anyone's less than half her age.

Intending to let her mammy sleep on, Starlena began creeping about when, of a sudden, there came the sharp reprimand, 'Ain't yer made that tea yet, gel?' Turning round she was met by two bright wide-awake brown eyes, 'By! Yer that slow!'

Shaking her head, Starlena took the shawl from her own shoulders, threw it over the only other chair in the tiny room and, going to her mammy, she leaned down to kiss the top of her head – at the same time collecting one of the gnarled brown hands into her own. 'You're a slave-driver, Mammy Parrish!' she laughed. Then, with all the great love from her heart showing in her voice she said, 'But I do love you, darling.'

'Aye! I love you an' all. But me throat's closed up, it's that thirsty, gel! A brew o' tea'll put it right.'

And it did! In no time at all Rona was revived enough to lend a hand in rustling up a plate of potatoes, meat pie and gravy. After which, Starlena set to and washed up the crockery while her mammy sat in the chair, puffing away at her little clay pipe, every now and then humming a tune.

While she was clearing away, Starlena thought about the small room which she and her mammy called home, and which was as comfortable and welcoming as they could make it. She had every intention of changing the chocolate brown walls to a more pleasing and gentle colour, but as yet there had not been either the time or the money to do so. The same applied to the battered threadbare carpet square which she and her mammy had patched up time and time again, until now the hitherto floral pattern resembled something quite grotesque. The furniture consisted of two wicker chairs, a small square table, two upright chairs and a particularly ugly squat dresser, with a cupboard either side and three drawers down the centre. There was a small stove, a deep pot sink, whose messy underneath was prettily disguised by the creamy frilled curtains sewn by Rona and cleverly hung by Starlena. The bedroom had in it just two little iron-framed beds, a brown-stained chest of drawers and a walk-in cupboard built into the wall.

The two rooms were not much to be proud of. They were not too warm and there was a dampness in the air which aggravated her mammy's cough. But this was home! At least for now, thought Starlena, as she packed away the clean pans and plates into the dresser cupboard. She was determined to take her and her mammy out of here, just as soon as there was enough money saved. But, all that would come later rather than sooner. They had only just found their feet and started to save a regular sum each week.

At six o'clock, Starlena began her strip-down wash at the sink, afterwards rubbing her hair vigorously with the towel. Her wild thick hair was not easily dried and, as always, when her arms began to ache, she knelt in front of the stove and her mammy would pull up her chair and take turns at rubbing the towel over the long wavy strands in the gentle warmth of the fire.

Two hours later, Starlena was ready. 'By! Yer a picture an' no mistake, lass,' Rona told her. Every night she made the very same comment, with a look of fierce pride in her eyes. There was no doubt that Starlena did indeed look a picture as she twirled about for her mammy's approval. The skirt was one bought for her by Jake, being, as he said, 'part of your wages and necessary for the job'. It was ankle length, extravagant with yard upon yard of swingy material which seemed to dance all by itself, black in basic colour, but festooned with flowers of rich eye-catching hues. The blouse which Starlena had chosen to go with it was of the deepest sapphire blue, tight-fitting at the bodice, with deep revered neckline and full Spanish-style sleeves caught in neatly at the cuffs. Her legs were bare, as always, and though her shoes were very pretty, being a creamy colour, of dainty heel with a small crossover bar at the ankle, they never stayed on her feet for the duration of the evening. Starlena loved dancing. She loved dancing barefoot even more.

'Go on then, lass.' Rona ran her two hands down Starlena's hair, clicking good-humouredly when the wild black strands sprang out with a mind of their own, having been suppressed during the day by a pretty ribbon which kept it tidy in the nape of Starlena's neck.

Now it whispered about her lovely face in tight spiralling curls, the main mass forming deep black waves which fell about her pretty, trim shoulders like a glorious mantle.

'By! Thar a right beauty, that yer are!' exclaimed Rona, who suddenly began to cough – that small irritating cough which seemed hardly to give her any peace.

'All right, are you, Mammy?' Starlena had grown increasingly concerned of late, although Rona had constantly assured her, ''Tis nothin'! Just a tickle, which will be off on its own, I tell yer!' She said as much now, taking a deep breath and seeming to recover. 'Now, get yersel' out there, while I 'ave me bedtime wash.' She lifted her face for a kiss, after which she handled Starlena out of the door, adding, 'I'll 'appen 'ave an early night tonight, lass. Now, it's all right!' she interrupted, as Starlena began to comment, 'I know I allus watch yer dance . . . but, I'm just feelin' a bit whacked, what wi' all that blessed trudging round the shops.'

Starlena was not convinced and had half a mind to go and see Jake about giving it a miss tonight, if only her mammy had not read her thoughts.

'Be off! Am I not allowed a few hours on me own, eh?' Good naturedly she pushed Starlena right out of the door, which she then promptly closed on her. She stood there for some time after, gently coughing and wiping away the beads of sweat which had collected on her forehead in a broad glistening band. Her whole body was blowing first hot then cold. She felt most unwell. 'Aye!' she murmured to herself, ambling across the room towards the sink, 'a bedtime wash, then an early night.' A little smile lifted the corners of her mouth as she heard the club piano burst into a jolly melody and, in her mind's eye, she pictured Starlena, her white teeth flashing in a smile, her black eyes alight and her feet tapping out the melody to the added beat of a hundred clapping hands.

As usual, when Starlena danced, the Club was packed and every man there thoroughly enjoyed himself. With the exception of one.

From his place at the bar, Jackson found it hard to believe his own eyes. Starlena! Dancing in a place like this! So, it was true, what he had heard. And to think he'd called the guy a liar! As he watched her, all manner of emotions surged through him. Admiration for her striking beauty and obvious talent, curiosity as to why she had chosen to run away from the farm in the way she did, deep and abiding love which haunted his every waking hour and anger. Anger at the cruel way fate had thrown them together, only to tear them asunder again. Also, he could not deny that green-eyed monster jealousy, which stormed through him as he looked about at the enjoyment on these guys' faces when they gazed on Starlena.

He wanted to rush up there and grab her from their sight – hurry her away to where the two of them could be alone. He argued with himself that, after all, it was really none of his business. He had no right to tell her what to do, or what not to do.

Yet, when someone close to the makeshift stage got so excited that he made a grab for Starlena's ankle, Jackson crashed his way through the tables, and, leaping on to the stage, he grabbed her by the hand, saying through gritted teeth, his green eyes full of fury, 'I'm sure as hell not standing by while you flaunt yourself in front of a bunch of drunken bums!'

If Starlena had been shocked by what had happened, she was even more shocked to see who had caused the uproar. Jackson's grip on her arm was such that, struggle as she might, Starlena couldn't break free.

'Jackson! Let me go!' she yelled, her efforts puny against his determination to drag her away from prying eyes.

Suddenly there was pandemonium! From the side of the small stage, Jake O'Malley swung himself up between Jackson and Starlena, his determination to break her free every bit as strong as Jackson's was to hold onto her. 'Take your mitts off!' he yelled, landing a punch on Jackson's face.

'The hell I will!' came the reply. Jackson swung Starlena up with one hand, lifting her feet from beneath her as she dangled helplessly in his vice-like grip. The other hand he bunched into a fist, which he smashed into Jake's jaw. 'This lady ain't doing no more dancing,' he snapped.

It was then that the whole body of shouting men surged forward onto the stage. Within a matter of seconds there were punches flying left and right, and here and there the unmistakable crunching sound of noses breaking and chairs being smashed over some poor unfortunate who hadn't learned to duck.

Amidst the chaos, Jackson carried Starlena through into the store-room. The minute he released her she began thumping her two fists into his chest.

'You've no *right*!' she yelled, her eyes flashing fire and her fists flailing at him, until in a swift movement, he grabbed her small fists into each of his.

'I have *every* right! The strongest right of any man. I love you, Starlena . . . you know that, don't you?'

Calmer now, her heart beating fast at the nearness of him, Starlena lifted her eyes to meet the intensity in that dark green and beautiful gaze. He loved her! What wonderful yet sadly painful words. He could never love her more than she loved him. Yet, they both knew that nothing could come of it. There was so much she wanted to say to him – so very much that she wanted to give. There were words she would have uttered from her heart. But, they were stuck fast in her throat, choking her.

It seemed a lifetime passed as they gazed at each other. In that lifetime they lived through a range of emotions, so deep, so tender, so exquisite and filled with love, that it took her breath away. Starlena couldn't speak, nor could she tear her black tearful eyes from his. As though in slow motion, he bent his head forward, his hair the colour of rugged brown earth brushing her face, his gaze soft and compelling. When, in a sweet and riveting sensation, his mouth found hers, Starlena melted into him, her need of him every bit as strong as his need for her.

Murmuring against her lips, he told her how she haunted him and he promised her that life could be wonderful, if only things were different, 'Deandra is very ill,' he said, lifting his face from Starlena's. 'My heart and love is with you . . . but my duty is with her and Danny.'

'I know,' Starlena whispered, her heart breaking. How she wished he had not found her! Now all those emotions and regrets which she had learned to live with were clawing at her once more.

311

Lowering her gaze, she pleaded, 'Jackson, you must go. You've got to leave me be … there's no future for us. Please just go!'

'Why did you run away? A woman came looking for you and your mammy. She wouldn't leave her name or her business. Was *she* the reason you left?' He waited for an answer. Then, impatient, he shook her, saying, 'Don't live like this, Starlena! Come back to the farm . . . I *need* you!'

'No, Jackson. I can't do that!' Starlena stood up to him, her black eyes staring into his. How could she go back? There was only torment and heartache back there. Added to which was the woman who knew of that place and who might be watching and waiting. How could Jackson ask her to go back there, when he must know that just to be near him tore her apart? Oh, he must be a good deal stronger than her, if he could endure such pain.

'I want you out of this place,' he said, gently shaking her. Suddenly he was snatched from behind, as Jake O'Malley swung him round, warning, 'It's you who's getting out!'

In a minute, both he and Jackson were in the throes of a vicious fight, each man launching himself at the other, until both were split and bleeding, yet both determined to fight to the last. Starlena was held back from stopping them by the crowd who had gathered to watch.

'Let them get it outta their systems,' she was told as she was forced to watch helplessly.

It took only a matter of minutes before Jake was lying on the floor with Jackson standing over him, triumphant. When it became clear that his opponent was spent, Jackson stepped aside to take Starlena by the hand, 'Fetch your mammy,' he said. 'I'm taking you back with me!'

Starlena knew that it was time. Time to make one of the hardest decisions of her life. Yet, every instinct in her body shouted that it was the only decision she could make.

Shaking her hand free from his grip, she went to where Jake was struggling to sit up on the floor. Putting an arm about him, she looked up straight into Jackson's troubled green eyes, 'This is my place!' she told him, 'Here, with Jake.' Then, swallowing hard, she added in firmer voice,' Jake's asked me to marry him . . . and I've said yes!'

For a moment there was hushed silence before Jackson spoke, his voice low and accusing, 'If that's so, there's nothing for me to say!' Then, with one last lingering look at her, he turned away and was lost to sight.

Jake punched his fists together in jubilation, his face wreathed in smiles as he yelled, 'Drinks on the house!' simultaneously grabbing Starlena into his arms and showering her in kisses. As the men thronged back towards the bar, there began a muttering and a wave of laughter erupted soon after.

Starlena helped Jake to his feet, with a smile to meet his, although her heart was heavy. If she had been able to hear the whispered conversations going on in the bar at that minute, or had known what the bouts of sniggering signified, her heart would have been heavier still. For, though there was a strong Catholic community hereabouts, there were also men who found it amusing – even gratifying – to see a woman so cunningly used. And tonight many voiced their approval with low nasty sneers.

When a younger and more recent member made the observation, 'But I was given to understand that Jake O'Malley already had a wife!' he was swiftly silenced.

'True!' said one, 'But she saw fit to take herself off – on the arm of another fella!'

'Aye!' said another, 'I've yet to meet the woman that can be altogether trusted.' From the look on his face, it was plain to see that this one had suffered at the hands of some woman or other. 'There's more trouble in keeping a woman than ever there was in keeping a dog – ain't that right, lads?' he asked of one and all.

Back came a chorus of, 'True enough!'

'Bloody women'll do for you every time!'

'If you don't do for them first!' The fellow leaned towards the younger man, saying in a quiet warning voice, 'So you see, lad. What Jake O'Malley do or don't do – 'tain't none of our business! D'you understand?'

Looking sideways and drilling him with bloodshot and boozy

eyes, he waited for an acknowledging nod. When that was given he smiled from ear to ear, stood up straight and, giving the young man a hearty pat on the back, shouted to the barman, 'Gi' this fella a drink!' 'Cause, like the rest of us, he's learnt when to turn a blind eye.' A cheer rose from all about him and, in merry heart, the laughter and drinking went on.

On a bitter cold morning in January of the following year, Starlena woke early, rose from her place in Jake O'Malley's huge comfortable bed, then, after quickly washing and dressing, she crept out of the room and down to the basement, where her mammy was still fast asleep. By the time Rona opened her eyes, there was a cosy fire in the stove and a fresh brew awaiting her.

'Aw, lass!' Rona shifted her weight to raise herself on one elbow, her brown eyes following Starlena's every move. 'Yer shouldn't be rushin' about in your condition!' She let her glance rest on Starlena's bulging middle before lifting her gaze once more and chiding, ''Tis you as should 'ave a cup o' tea brought ter yer bed, lass. Over seven month gone an' still tearin' about like a pup wi' two tails. An' wearin' nowt but a night shift.' She made an effort to get up from the bed, but was taken with such a fit of coughing that she fell back into it, perspiring and exhausted.

'Take it easy, Mammy!' Starlena cast a worried glance over the little figure in the bed, her dark eyes sorely troubled. Since the onset of winter, with its relentless fall of snow and perishing conditions, her mammy had not seemed to rise above that niggling cough which constantly sapped her strength. Pouring out a helping of hot steamy tea, Starlena took it to Rona. She persuaded her to sit up and, perching herself on the bed, she waited patiently till every drop was drunk. 'That's my darling!' she smiled, taking the cup and putting it to the floor. 'Now, let's have you on your tummy, eh?' Going to the dresser, she opened the top left-hand drawer, from which she withdrew a small bulky bottle. After giving it a vigorous shake, she plucked out the cork and returned to where Rona was patiently lying on her front, with her face turned to Starlena and on it an exasperated expression.

314

'I don't like the stink o' that bloody awful stuff!' she protested, wrinkling up her nose and pouting her lip.

'You don't, eh?' Starlena laughed out loud at her mammy's baby face. 'Well that's just too bad, Mammy Parrish, 'cause I intend to give you a real good dressing of it!' Whereupon, she sat down beside the grumbling patient and without further ado proceeded to rub a good measure deep into the centre of her shoulder-blades. That done, she helped her mammy over and rubbed an equal amount into her chest, all the while thinking her mammy was right. The liniment did stink and was so potent it brought tears to her eyes.

'Eh! I've telled yer afore . . . I'm capable o' rubbin' me *own* front!' Rona retorted, each breath popping out with every rub of her chest, her head turned from the smell and every so often giving out a cry of 'Pooh! Lord 'elp us, a basketful o' rotten eggs smells better.'

'Stop your moaning . . . it'll do you no good,' warned Starlena. 'As for you rubbing your own front, we've already tried that as well you know. I'm up to all your tricks by now.'

She had in mind the time her mammy made a big show of rubbing in the liniment, when all the time the bottle was hid under the pillow. Starlena had been cleaning up the room and, if it hadn't been for the absence of that pungent odour, the crafty Rona might well have gotten away with it.

'Wouldn't need none o' this 'ere rubbish, if'n we were back *'ome*. There's all manner o' herbs and plants as'd mek short work o' this bloody cough!'

'Mebbe, darling . . . but we're *not* "back 'ome". We're here in the United States of America and we must get used to it.'

'Never! I'll never get used to it. Leastwise, not this part of it. It's so squashed in an' dark.' Her mood fell to one of melancholy and Starlena was hurt to see those loving brown eyes mist over, 'Oh, lass! I do miss the green rollin' meadows an' the sound of a cob's hooves clatterin' along a country lane.' On the last word, her old face crumpled and her lip began quivering, 'Oh, darlin' . . . what 'ave I done to bring us to this?' Now she couldn't hold back the tears as they brimmed her eyes and ran down the worn crevices of her face. 'Oh, Lord 'elp us!' she kept saying, 'Lord 'elp us!'

'Aw, don't take on so, Mammy.' Starlena quickly caught her into a warm comforting embrace, wrapping her two arms about the weeping figure and drawing her to her breast, 'You mustn't blame yourself . . . not for *anything*!' She rained kisses down on the trembling grey head, 'You've been the most wonderful, darling mammy anybody could ever have.' She also began to cry, for deep in her own heart were the very same sentiments, although Starlena blamed only herself. Never a day went by that she didn't question what could have been done to save the situation. Yet, the more she'd examined all options, the less likely they became. She and her mammy had taken the only road opened up to them. There had been no other. But, oh, if her mammy had regrets, they were never as many as she herself suffered.

Sniffing, Starlena wiped the back of her hand along her face to dry the tears. C'mon gel, she told herself, pull yourself together, for your mammy's sake! And, oh so tenderly, she lifted the little figure away from her. Then, placing a hand beneath the grey bowed head, she eased it up until the brown weeping eyes were forced to look at her.

'You and me,' Starlena whispered in a loving voice, 'we have each other's strength to lean on. We'll always look after each other, won't we, eh?' She patted the bulge beneath her nightie. 'Soon, there'll be another to share our love with, won't there?' When, sniffling, Rona nodded, Starlena caught her into her arms again, saying, 'All I want just now, darling, is to see my mammy well again. Fretting like this will only make you worse. And you know we could never go back to England . . . you don't want to end up in jail, do you?'

Secure in Starlena's warm loving arms, Rona wanted to cry out that they could go back, that she would not go to jail for thieving from the gentry, as she had led Starlena to believe. She would have cried out that unless they did go home, she would surely die of longing and heartbreak from being so far from the open fields and free roaming life they'd known and loved. She was a gypsy! She

316

had the heart and soul of a gypsy. All of these things Rona would have cried out, were it not for the belief that on England's shores death lay in wait for her beloved Starlena. So, instead she murmured, '*Why* did yer 'ave ter wed 'im, child? Why?'

Rona had voiced this question on so many occasions since her marriage to Jake. Starlena let her mammy sink back into the pillow, reaching out a hand to wipe the tear-stains from the wizened cheeks and to tidy the wayward grey strands of hair back into place. 'Don't let's go into that again, Mammy, please.'

'Yer don't love 'im. Yer *can't*!'

'He's kind to us, isn't he? Looks after us both, doesn't he?'

'Oh, aye! The bugger does that, right enough. But, there's some'at I don't like about 'im! 'Ow come there were no documents nor nowt to be shown when yer got wed?'

'I told you. When I asked him about that, he said there was a perfectly good explanation. Being as you and me have ducked and dived from the authorities at every turn, Jake saw to everything.'

'Well, I don't like it! I didn't like that preacher, neither. 'E were a shifty lookin' fella, if ever I saw one.'

'You're just being foolish. Why! Jake even took me into the office to collect our marriage lines. So, just behave yourself or I might find it necessary to give you another rubbing of this liniment.' She shook the bottle in front of Rona's face. It did the trick, although Rona could not resist one more question.

'Are yer 'appy, lass? Really 'appy?'

In all truth, Starlena could not answer that positively, for she was not 'really happy'. How could she be? Here she was, married to Jake and having his child, when her heart belonged to another. She was content to a certain degree, although she suspected of late that Jake was paying far too much attention to the new girl he'd taken on to sing in the Club. But Starlena didn't speak of her suspicions for, however poorly her mammy was, there'd be no stopping her from tearing his eyes out. Yet, it didn't bother her. If Jake paid his attentions elsewhere, it only meant that he was leaving her alone and that was fine, because these past few weeks she'd grown big and uncomfortable with the bairn inside her. And, oh, how she was looking forward to holding the darling little mite in her arms! In her secret heart Starlena prayed that it would be a boy, for life seemed kinder to the male of the species. But if the Lord saw fit to bless her with a girl-child, then she would call it Rona, after her darling mammy. Jake didn't seem to mind one way or the other, 'That's woman's business,' he'd told her. So, in answer to her mammy's question, Starlena replied, 'I'm happy enough,' at the same time getting up from the bed and going to the sink, where she washed her hands, rubbing plenty of carbolic soap in, to get rid of the smell.

During the next twenty minutes, when Starlena busied herself sweeping the floor and dusting all about, Rona pestered her with questions, the most persistent of which was the one that demanded whether they would ever find her brother, Callum.

'I don't know, Mammy,' Starlena answered dozens of times, 'We've tried all we can, without success. Jake even put that sign over the bar asking for Callum Canaar's whereabouts. He just seems to have gone from these parts altogether.'

'Aye, I know, lass,' Rona agreed sadly, 'It's just that 't'would do me ol' 'eart good to see the lad again.'

'Hardly a *lad* now,' Starlena reminded her, 'more a grown man … well into his fifties, Mammy.' To which Rona just quietly mumbled, 'Aye, that's so, lass. That's so.'

Within the hour Starlena was back upstairs, where she quietly dressed, creeping about so as not to disturb the sleeping dark-haired figure in the bed.

Seated before the oblong mirror above the dresser, Starlena brushed her mass of wavy black hair, the brush-strokes taking on a slow methodical action as she fell into a deep trance. Here she was, twenty-two years old, married to an Irish-American with a roving eye whom she hardly knew and, whom she did not love in the way a woman seven months pregnant by her husband *should* love. Downstairs lay the dear heart who was not only her mammy, but her friend, her adviser, her tormentor and her conscience. Oh, how it hurt Starlena to see the little woman so aggravated by that cough and so saddened at never being able to return to her own land and her gypsy way of life. Indeed, Starlena wondered whether the cough which plagued her mammy was only a symptom of what was really wrong. Did her ailment amount only to homesickness?

Starlena would never openly admit to her mammy's suspicions regarding Jake, but she had her *own* suspicions which, in view of the circumstances, were best left unspoken. All the same, Starlena wondered about the future, and the more she speculated on it, the more she wished she had not. Yet she always trusted that there was a future – for her, her mammy and for the child soon to be born. It was not in her nature to despair. It had never been.

'Awake already, my lovely?' The sleepy voice of Jake shook Starlena from her thoughts when, quickly gathering up her long tresses, she twirled them into a spiral, brought the spiral into her head and pinned it at the top with a curved ivory comb.

'Sorry, Jake,' she said quietly, 'I tried not to disturb you,' at the same time taking a last look at the misshapen form in the mirror. Not too much of a mess, she thought, regarding the pretty, white long-sleeved blouse and full dark skirt, which fell comfortably over the surge of her middle. The loose-fitting floral pinafore helped also to make the swelling less prominent. But her eyes told the tale of sleepless nights and worry. Though still incredibly dark and lovely, the brilliance in her eyes had faded. There was a quiet sadness about the gaze – this emphasized by the dark shadowy patches beneath. Yet, when Starlena smiled, as her very nature decreed that she must, whatever the torment in her heart, that smile lit up her eyes and gave her a particular glow, which might mislead the world into thinking that all was well.

'I'll away down and get the breakfast, Jake,' she told him, seeing that he had got from the bed and was standing just behind her, naked and so obviously wanting her.

'I thought you might come back to bed, sweetheart,' he suggested, his dark eyes boring into her, his two hands beginning to grope her body.

Starlena moved away, 'No, Jake,' she said firmly, without a trace of apology in her voice, 'I've told Mammy I'll be down shortly with her breakfast.' At the door, she turned to glance at him.

There was no denying he was attractive, with his slim, well-endowed manhood, dark shining hair and roguish brown eyes. But, even as she had on their first encounter, Starlena saw through the outward display of manly strength. It was just a display. For Jake O'Malley had no substance – charming yes, generous and handsome also; he had nothing in his character of any *lasting* value. But, Starlena reminded herself, he had been good to both her and her mammy and he was harmless enough.

Coming back into the room, she reached up to give him a small kiss, saying, 'Go back to bed. I'll call when breakfast is ready.'

Grunting as Starlena swiftly took herself out of reach, Jake looked at the clock on the dresser, saw that it was only eight a.m. and, shivering, he climbed back beneath the bed-covers, 'Jesus! It's bloody freezing!' he exclaimed, adding, 'Don't call me till ten. Don't let me sleep past that though! There's a meeting . . . some of the fellows are making their way here at ten-thirty.'

Oh, Lord! thought Starlena, not another blessed meeting, when voices would be raised and cries of anger would echo through the Club. There had been many such meetings of late, not just in Jake's Club, but in countless such establishments throughout America. And all to do with this Prohibition Bill, which, in spite of President Wilson's vote against, had been passed by Congress some months ago. Any week now, it was set to become actual law.

Starlena was no fool. The men who organized these meetings went to great trouble to keep them secret. Even Jake did not discuss what went on behind closed doors. Yet Starlena had learned enough to know that if and when Prohibition became law, these men and many like them would not take it lying down. There were plans being made – provisions, which, if drinking was forbidden in *public* places, would drive it into dark hidden establishments not so easily detected by the law. And, of course, if a commodity became scarce, the value of it would surely increase. There were fortunes to be made. And there were men desperate enough to grow rich on other's weaknesses. Jake O'Malley was one. Starlena had learned not to ask questions and to turn a deaf ear when necessary. She

320

made no mention of any of this to her mammy. What the mind didn't know, the heart wouldn't grieve over, she told herself.

All day Starlena was kept busy, keeping up with the cleaning and cooking, labouring hard over a sink of steaming hot water and piles of washing, in between which, she was up and down stairs seeing to the needs of her mammy. By the evening, her back felt ready to break in two, her legs ached and the weight of the unborn child across her middle pulled on her like a cartload of elephants.

At last, just as the clock struck ten o'clock, Starlena stumbled into the tiny sitting-room – which had been no more than a spill-over from the store-room when she and Jake were married, but which was now furnished with warm polished furniture. Over the windows hung pretty floral curtains to match the cushions Starlena had made.

When Jake came in from the bar at midnight, it was to find Starlena still asleep on the sofa where she had collapsed, exhausted. For a long poignant moment he gazed down on her face, the beauty of which seemed to him enhanced by her advanced state of pregnancy. The train of hair which she had coiled up tight to her head had loosened during her fitful sleep, the comb had worked its way free and now lay on the carpet. Such beauty, he thought, his dark eyes narrowing as they travelled from the slim pretty ankles crossed one over the other, to the dark splash of hair spreading across the pillow to spill over the sofa and down to touch the carpet. His eyes caressed her sleeping face, taking stolen pleasure in the fine classic features – the small straight nose, gently tipped towards the end, the high cheekbones, the perfectly arched eyebrows and those long sweeping lashes. More like a lady than a gypsy, he thought with some amusement.

Going towards her, he stooped to touch the deep shining waves of her luxurious black hair, and in the softest voice, he said, 'How am I to tell you? And when I *do*, will you ever forgive me, I wonder?'

Starlena stirred and sitting up with a start, she gasped, 'Jake! Whatever's the time?' Swinging her feet to the floor, she said, 'Oh, I must go down and see that Mammy's all right!' Still dizzy with sleep, she put her hand across her forehead and just for a moment, closed her eyes. 'Is it late?' she asked.

'Midnight. Rona's all right . . . I looked in on her just now,' he lied, thinking to get Starlena to bed all the quicker.

'Was she sleeping?' In a moment Starlena was on her feet. 'No, never mind . . . I'll feel better if I take a look at her,' she remarked before he could answer.

'Why won't she see a doctor, dammit!' Jake was beginning to feel peeved. The sight of Starlena lying there had set off a deep urge in him.

Starlena was already on her way out of the door, 'She's an old woman, set in her ways. Besides which, she's never seen the need for a doctor in all of her life . . . always finding a cure for every ailment by way of the plants and herbs that grow 'neath the hedgerows.'

'Then it's time she saw that there's no hedgerows round these parts!' he shouted after her as the door shut her from his sight. 'And don't forget to call me outta bed by ten in the morning . . . there's an important meeting.'

Over the next week, the frequency and mood of such meetings greatly intensified. There was much whispering, with furtive comings and goings at all hours of the day and night, making life difficult for Starlena and ensuring that not a night went by without her sleep being disturbed by Jake either creeping in or creeping out. On top of that, Rona's health took a turn for the worse. Her limbs ached so much that it was an agony to try and move them. She was shivering cold one minute, feverishly hot the next, and sometimes, when at her worst, she was delirious. Yet, through it all, she was vehemently adamant that, 'I'm 'avin' no bloody doctor pokin' me about!' Indeed, such was her agitation at the prospect that Starlena had to settle for the services of an old woman from North Street – a kindly creature who delivered all the little newcomers and said prayers over all those who were about to depart the world. She was a well respected person hereabouts, very knowledgeable in matters of a body coming and going one way or the other.

'Nearing her mid-fifties, you say?' she asked of Starlena, on this, her fourth visit. 'That's old. But she looks older. She's riddled with gout and has a touch of fever, that's for sure. But, to tell you the truth, I'm of a mind that it's something else we're dealing with here. Look!' she pointed a finger at Rona's sleeping face, 'Can you see? Her lips are blue! That's a sign of an ailing heart.' She shook her head from side to side, 'Little you can do but keep up with the soup, make her comfortable and be on hand should she want to make confession.' With that, she collected her dollar and was gone, leaving Starlena close to tears and reluctant to believe what the woman had said.

'You'd best buck up, Mammy Parrish!' she said, her voice trembling as she undressed and slid into the bed beside the still figure, '"cause if you don't I'll be left here on my own – and you wouldn't want that, would you?'

For what seemed an age, Starlena lay quiet, her dark sad eyes embracing that wrinkled old familiar face and her fingers tenderly stroking the long grey hair. Suddenly, the tears welled up in her eyes and with a heavy aching heart, she tore her gaze from her mammy's face – raising it as though to heaven and, in a broken voice, she pleaded, 'Please God, don't let her die! Not here . . . away from her fields and country lanes. Don't take my mammy from me.' She began to sob, 'I would miss her too much. Oh, how could I face the morning when she wouldn't be here to smile at me?' Her prayer fell silent, though in Starlena's heart it was still alive. In the morning she would fetch the doctor to her mammy and face the consequences afterwards.

When there came a moaning from the bed, Starlena made to take the little figure in her arms, but before she could, her mammy's hand took hold of hers, although her eyes stayed closed and she made no other movement. To Starlena, it was obvious that her mammy was in the throes of a disturbing dream. Now, she was muttering – then crying and beginning to tremble.

'Ssh, darling . . . it's all right. Starlena's here. It's just a dream you're having. Ssh, now!' Starlena told her, caressing her tightly.

'Starlena!' Rona suddenly opened her eyes and looked straight into Starlena's. 'Tek me 'ome, lass! I'm no thief. There's no gent after me for stealin' 'is jewellery. 'Tis you they want, me darlin' . . .

323

you! Yer 'ave the blood of aristocracy in yer veins, an' a fortune at yer fingertips. 'Twere me as snatched yer from it . . . for 'e would surely 'ave killed yer! Oh! They'll not find yer, I promise . . . but the buggers 'ave tracked us to 'Merica! Please God, tek us 'ome! We'll 'ide better there, I'm thinkin'.'

She began crying pitifully, until Starlena was forced to promise that she would take her home. After that she fell into a deep contented sleep, seeming to Starlena to be more at peace and breathing much easier than for a long time. Only once did she stir and that was to murmur in the old gypsy tongue *Rikker it adree tute's kokero see an' ker'll jin it'* – which meant in gorgio language, 'keep it a secret in your own heart. Nobody will know.'

Yet Starlena could not sleep. For a long time afterwards she paced the floor, up and down, round and round, ever thinking, ever searching. So! Her mammy was not pursued as she had thought. She was not a thief, after all. But what did she mean . . . it was she they wanted. Who were they? And why did they want her? Why? What did she mean about 'the blood of aristocracy'? Oh, Lord, what was to be made of it all? Starlena was more convinced than ever that what was really ailing her mammy was a severe and dangerous bout of pining – pining so badly for home that she might even prefer death to being forever away from old England. So steeped in nostalgia was she that her poor old mind was becoming affected.

From above there came the sound of clattering and banging. *More* meetings and secret whisperings, thought Starlena, her mind in a whirl and her tired aching body feeling as though it had been run over by a street car. Telling herself that she could have the whole thing out with her mammy in the morning, Starlena got back into the bed, making sure not to touch her mammy for a while. The cold had got to her bones and she didn't want to shock the sleeping figure with it.

The following week Starlena got no satisfactory answer to her questions, although it gladdened her heart to see how well her mammy's health was recovering under her own tender and incessant care.

324

Recovering enough to put Starlena smartly down with her answers, ' 'Twere *you* that were dreamin', lass!' she retorted each time Starlena broached the subject, 'I took the gent's precious jewellery sure enough. 'Tain't nowt ter do wi' you, lass! But the buggers 'ave found we've left old England. It does cross me mind ter wonder whether we'd fox 'em by sneaking back an' findin' a safer 'idey-'ole? Oh, but I don't know!' she began, frowning at this stage and pulling at her face, ''Tis all so dangerous, there's no escapin' that fact!' There had come a faraway look into the old brown eyes, 'I don't know this 'Merica. I'm like a wild creature out of its own territory 'ere.' Her voice had fallen to a whisper, as though talking to herself. 'I knows me own part o' the world like the lines on me face . . . better'n anybody! I'm of a mind they'd be 'arder put to track us down there than they would 'ere, eh? Eh?' she asked herself, time and time again.

Whenever Starlena intervened she fell silent, leaving her feeling as though her mammy had isolated her from an argument that only she herself could resolve. Starlena put it all down to the after-effects of her mammy's illness. Yet it was all so worrying and she felt very restless. But it was only three weeks from the birth of her child and just now she had not got the energy to cope with everything at once. So she left her mammy to her mutterings, thinking that whatever it was she insisted on 'chewing over' as she put it, would no doubt resolve itself. All the same, her mammy did worry her and, it was strange also, how Jake seemed to have taken an interest in what Rona had to say – to the point of keeping her company whenever he had a minute to spare. It was all very perplexing to Starlena, but with the baby ever quickening inside her she must prepare for its coming. After that, she and her mammy must clear the air of mystery which seemed to have risen up between them – with Jake somewhere in the middle.

The reason for all the mystery soon became clear. On the sixteenth of January – the very same day that Prohibition became law – the arrival of a stranger at the Club, heralded dire consequences for Starlena and Rona.

Being much improved in health and spirit, Rona had come up to the little parlour where Starlena was washing up the supper things, 'All right, are yer, lass?' she asked, taking up a cloth and beginning to wipe the crockery. 'Won't be long now, I'm thinkin', eh?' She cocked a cheeky little glance at Starlena's bulge.

'Two weeks and one day,' Starlena had it all worked out, 'and yes, thank you, Mammy. I'm feeling well.'

Rona became quiet for a while, as though ruminating on something. Her heart ached for this lovely soul who was more than life to her. She wondered how the lass would take the information that she must be told. Yet in her heart Rona was convinced that, like all the other adversities heaped on her darling innocent head, Starlena would find the strength to cope. But she must be spared until after the child was born, for that was more than enough trauma for the time being. Rona was not to know that even at that minute such matters had been taken out of their hands!

First, there came the sound of voices from downstairs, talking loudly to begin with, then yelling to the accompaniment of crashing glassware. Even as Rona and Starlena looked at each other – Starlena drying her hands on her pinnie and Rona taking a step towards the door – there came the sound of running steps and frantic warnings, as the argument carried itself up the stairs. Now, Jake's voice was clear above the woman's.

'Leave her be! It's *me* that's to blame, damn you!'

The door was flung open to reveal a woman standing there. A woman looking to be in her early thirties, brazen-faced with too much make-up and brassy blonde hair. She stood for no more than a second or two, her bright darting eyes raking the two women in the room. When her stare fell directly onto Starlena's swollen stomach, she lunged into the room, knocking Rona sideways and making a deliberate grab for Starlena, 'You trollop! You filthy bloody trollop!' she screamed, raising up her arm to strike the riveted and shocked Starlena, 'I'll finish you! Stealing my husband! I'll teach you a lesson you won't forget in a hurry!' The knife-blade was raised high to strike.

It was then that Jake sped into the room. Together with Rona, now recovered enough, he surged forward – Jake to prevent a murder, Rona with her heart in her mouth and a prayer on her lips.

Instinctively, Starlena stepped back as the knife was thrust towards her. Although it didn't find its intended fatal mark, the blade slashed a cruel and painful path down her shoulder, missing her neck by a whisper. As she reeled away, Jake and Rona were both on her assailant, Rona gripping her by the waist and Jake, having grabbed both her arms, which in spite of her struggling, he had well and truly pinned to her writhing body.

'You'll rue this little lot, Jake O'Malley,' she yelled, 'Our son's on his way. He'll deal with you, for sure!'

'Get the hell outta here!' Jake yelled to Starlena, all the while grappling to wrench the knife from the cursing woman, 'Go with your mammy! Go on! For Chrissake – get outta here!'

'Quick, lass!' Rona could see that not only was Starlena still shocked by the vicious onslaught, but that she was badly hurt. Going to where she had fallen back against the sink, her fingers to her shoulder and the crimson blood already seeping through, Rona put her arm behind and around her, 'C'mon, child – we must away, quickly!' she urged.

Leaving Jake O'Malley struggling with his manic wife, she hurried Starlena out of there, swiftly grabbing up both hers and Starlena's shawls on the way out. And grateful to the Lord that the money and address given to her by Jake O'Malley was secure in her skirt pocket.

Through the dark narrow streets the two of them sped – Rona frantically looking back for fear that they might have been followed, and Starlena, growing weaker by the minute, feeling the baby agitating inside her and murmuring over and over, 'He was married all the time, Mammy. Jake was married – and I'm carrying his child!'

On they went, out of Hanover Street towards Prince and Endicott, on to Salem Street. Here they would find the Jew whose address was on the paper given to Rona by Jake O'Malley. Knowing she could not read, he had obliged by making a drawing and explaining the position of the house more carefully Rona had memorized every detail. Jake had been most eager to rectify the wrong he had done Starlena and, were it not for that, Rona would have torn him limb from limb. As it was, she had whipped him most viciously with her tongue – laying on him the most devilish gypsy curse she could muster. He had been warned of his wife's vindictive approach, which was why he had played on Rona's longing for old England, and together they had prepared for such an event. Yet, hoping that at least Starlena need not know until after the child was born, Rona had extracted a promise – eagerly given – that he would make no effort to lay claim to the child, for Starlena must not be punished any further.

The distance between Hanover Street and Salem Street, where the Jewish man lived, was little more than a mile. Yet to Rona it seemed like a hundred. Starlena was bleeding profusely, and judging by the painful groans escaping her, it seemed that the child inside her was struggling to find an early way into the world.

Starlena, though riddled with pain and her senses ever slipping from her, made no complaint. Upon Rona's assurance that, ''Tis all right, lass. There's 'elp not far away now,' she merely whispered, 'Oh, Mammy, thank God. Thank God!'

Chapter Nineteen

For three days and nights Starlena's life hovered between that delicate line where a heartbeat one way or the other would decide whether she lived or died.

To Rona it was the very worst time she could ever remember. From the minute they had arrived on the Jew's doorstep, when he and his family had taken them in with the utmost urgency and kindness, she had not had a single wink of sleep. Every precious minute of her time had been spent by Starlena's bedside, wiping her brow, tending the deep gashed wound on her shoulder, murmuring words of comfort and praying that if there was a God above, he would not be so cruel as to take the life of Starlena, who in her twenty-two years had been dealt more than enough tragedy and misfortune.

Rona's prayers were answered, as were those of the Jewish family who every evening gathered in their own special way to offer up sincere and heartfelt pleas on behalf of the young woman so desperately ill.

On the fourth day after Rona had brought Starlena to this friendly sanctuary, there came into the world another being. A tiny little bundle of pink flesh, with enormous dark eyes and a shock of black hair. 'A little Starlena in miniature!' Rona had declared with a burst of pride. 'Oh, lass!' she told the exhausted but smiling Starlena, '. . .'tis a little girl-child. See!' Holding out the squirming child, whose cries filled the room with joy and wonder, she watched, beaming from ear to ear, as Starlena took the bundle.

'Oh, Mammy – she's so beautiful!' Starlena gazed at the child's tiny face and in her black eyes there was such joy that Rona started crying again. 'Aye! She is that, me darlin',' she sniffled, wiping the back of her hand across her wet face, 'she is that!'

All manner of wonderful emotions swept through Starlena, her heart swelling with such pride and joy that she felt it must burst. Of a sudden she was both laughing and crying at the same time – burying her head in the baby's warm pink face and thanking God for such a wonderful gift. After a moment, she cuddled the child to her breast and, holding out her hand, she said to the little figure looking down on her with tears of joy in her old brown eyes, 'Come here, Mammy, darling.' And when Rona came close, Starlena caught her fast in a loving embrace. 'What would I ever do without you, Mammy Parrish, eh?' Then, looking again at the girl-child, she said tenderly, 'I shall call her Ronalda! Would you like that, Mammy?'

'Oh, lass! That's grand – right grand – a little Rona, eh?' she giggled like a young girl and Starlena was most surprised to see her mammy actually blushing pink with pleasure.

All too soon, there were urgent matters to be decided. Mrs Cohen, the chubby likeable wife of the Jewish man, rushed in the next day after a visit to the shops, highly agitated and quickly relaying what she had heard to her husband. He, in turn, went straight to Rona, importing the terrible news that a body – thought to be Jake O'Malley – had been discovered in the Club on Hanover Street, and a hue and cry had gone up on every street corner.

'You must go at once, my dears!' he entreated, pulling from his wallet a cache of documents. 'There's no time to arrange papers for the child. It's more than I dare, to venture a further bribe. Prepare to depart in two hours . . . there's passage arranged on the next ship. There'll be no questions asked, my dears, nothing to worry yourselves about.' Here, he stopped to frown deeply, 'But you must keep the little one hidden from sight until you're safely back in England. Do you understand? Keep the little one hidden!' He handed over the sum of money remaining, tickets for the voyage and other documents that might need to be shown.

Within the hour, Rona and Starlena were ready to leave – Rona

330

fussing that *she* should hide the baby beneath her shawl. 'Yer look so tired an' weak, lass!' she told Starlena, who did indeed, appear ashen-faced – although her stance was upright and her resolve to keep the newborn close to her own breast was unshakeable. There was, however, one matter which deeply troubled her. If they were embarking on a long sea journey, and bearing in mind the many hazards which might await them, she felt in her heart that little Ronalda should be christened. Unable to suppress her fears any longer, she made mention of it to her mammy within the hearing of Mr and Mrs Cohen and their young son – all of whom unanimously confirmed that the child must indeed be christened.

And so she was. With a group of loving people around her, the child was given the name Ronalda Parrish and offered up to God's safe-keeping for the whole duration of her life – which everyone prayed would be a long and happy one. It saddened Starlena that her child would never know her father – nor his name. But then, *she* had never known her father, except through her mammy's fond telling of him. Little Ronalda might not even have that, for, feeling bitter towards Jake O'Malley as she did, there was no desire in her heart ever to speak of him again – fondly or otherwise.

After a hurried round of hugs and kisses, the two families parted company – the Cohen family to continue with their life, ready, always, to help any less fortunate than themselves, and the Parrish family to the docks where, with the tiny newborn bundle kept warm and hidden close to Starlena's body, they would sail for England – there to find a safer haven, God willing. And looking at the smiling countenance of her mammy, Starlena was even more convinced that it was a great and desperate longing for home that had brought the old gypsy close to death's door back there in Jake O'Malley's place. She herself had only one searing regret, and that was bound up with a man by the name of Jackson Grand – a man she could never forget.

Some short time later, Lester Judd disembarked from the ship which had carried him to these shores of America. The errand he had come on was of the utmost urgency. At long last he had persuaded Edward Wyman to bring Kathleen, his wife, out of the hellish asylum to which she had long been confined. It was only following Lester's dogged investigations that her whereabouts had become known.

Edward Wyman had been pitifully adamant that he should not be made to come face to face with his estranged wife at Bessington Hall. He agreed instead that she could be transferred to a home of gentle nursing and pleasant surroundings, where she would be afforded the very best of treatment.

Lester Judd had been horrified to hear from Edward Wyman's own lips how, in an unjustified fit of jealousy, he had given away his own child and afterwards forcibly committed his faithful wife to an asylum, for reasons known only to himself and later much regretted. Now, as he strode in an uneven limping gait from the docks, it was with *two* purposes in mind. Firstly, to find Edward Wyman's daughter, and secondly, to reunite her with Kathleen her mother – who even now cried pitifully for the child who was cruelly snatched away at the very moment of birth.

Lester remembered with affection Elizabeth's part in piecing together a section of this horrifying but fascinating jigsaw. It was she who had suspected that Starlena and Rona, the two gypsies from Whistledown Valley whom she had befriended, were possibly the same two he must now find here in America. She had given a vivid description of them to Edward Wyman and he showed her a portrait of Starlena's mother, Kathleen, which left no doubt. The similarity between the lovely gypsy girl she knew as Starlena and the portrait of Edward Wyman's beautiful young wife – both of which he had kept hidden all these years – was startling and uncanny.

As Rona hurried Starlena into the docks, she caught sight of the well-dressed figure which swept past. In spite of that ungainly limp, he had the upright and confident manner of a wealthy aristocrat, the sight of which turned her stomach with nerves. 'Quick, lass!' she murmured, 'Keep the child tight to yer an' let's be gone with all speed!'

'Don't fret, darling,' Starlena smiled, the child warm and

throbbing and only the smallest painful ache in her shoulders. 'Don't fret!'

But Rona did! And she would not stop fretting until they were on that ship headed for home, and perhaps not even then.

Part Six

1920
England

'Red Fire burns autumn
An instant of me.
Fells autumn trees and I
And hazy dreams
In emptied leaves,
Brush trodden grey pavements.'

Spenser

Chapter Twenty

On a warm sunny day in the month of March 1920, Lester Judd turned off the main Preston New Road towards the lovely hamlet of Salmesbury, some four miles distant from the town of Blackburn in Lancashire. After driving along the pretty winding lanes, flanked either side by thick wild hedgerows already festooned with myriads of flowering blossom, he came upon a wide open gateway, enclosed by two stout pillars of stone – one bearing the sign:

Salmesbury House
Rest Home for Gentle Ladies

'Here we are, darling,' he remarked, turning to Elizabeth with a smile and thinking how lovely she looked in her pale blue cloche hat and loose-fitting two-piece suit with that attractive sailor collar which suited her so admirably.

Returning his smile, Elizabeth touched his hand, her voice a little tremulous as she remarked, 'Oh, Lester . . . I do hope Kathleen has greatly improved since our last visit.'

'I'm sure she has,' came the confident reply.

But not reassured, Elizabeth continued, 'If only we had more positive news to bring her. Oh, darling . . . if only we could have Starlena here, in the car with us.'

'And we will! I promise we will. Soon! At least we know that she and the old gypsy are back in England. Our investigations tell us that much, at least. It was a bad business . . . that landlord being murdered and his wife being arrested for it. Then again, if it hadn't

337

been for that, we might not have been so fortunate.' Here, he paused awhile, seemingly turning something over in his mind before at length he added, 'Pity we never discovered who this American fellow was . . . the one who also made enquiries after Starlena. Still, if as we suspect, the two of them returned to England some four of five weeks back, it's only a matter of time before she turns up at Whistledown Valley. You've said yourself, Elizabeth, how very much Starlena loved that particular place. Besides which . . . we do have people looking for her.'

'Yes! Yes! I know, darling.' The blue eyes were still alarmed, 'But, are you sure she's in no danger from her brother, Redford?'

'Look! Enough of that nonsense, Elizabeth. Don't let your imagination run away with you!' How many more times must he reassure her, he wondered? 'In view of your suspicions regarding Redford Wyman, I've talked with him. Explained how desperate his father is to make amends . . . to have mother and child reunited and to restore what he so cruelly took from them. Of course, Redford Wyman will not altogether lose out, he knows his father will leave him adequate funds to maintain a "certain" lifestyle. He has assured me that he also wishes most earnestly that his sister and mother be reunited. He isn't altogether heartless, darling, believe me!'

'You're far too trusting, Lester. Always ready to judge others by your own standards. If, as you say, Redford Wyman isn't altogether heartless, why has he not visited his own mother? Tell me that!'

She was not convinced that Redford Wyman had any good in him whatsoever and, after the strange conversation she had overheard between him and Lester's sister, Freya, how could she not worry until Starlena was safe in her sights? Elizabeth had not burdened Lester with details of that conversation, because to implicate Redford Wyman would also necessitate Freya Judd being named as accomplice. She could not be so cruel as to hurt Lester in such a way, for, in spite of her malicious character, Freya Judd was his devoted sister. And he loved her!

Salmesbury House was an elegant building of Regency design. Its long casement windows gently arched at the top and leading out onto a great expanse of elevated terrace lent an air of grandeur. Even on the dullest of days there was about the whole place an overwhelming sense of light, beauty and great tranquillity. Set in four acres of exquisite landscaped gardens, it seemed like a small piece of heaven to all who stayed there. The strikingly handsome front entrance, with its sweeping steps and classically simple arched doorway, led into a great open hall beyond.

They were greeted with a smile and an observation that the two of them were very welcome. 'Mrs Wyman will be most pleased to see you,' said the slim, pleasant-natured woman, as she led the way through the hall, up the curving stairway where, at the top, she veered off to the left, coming to a halt at the second door along. 'We've moved Mrs Wyman to the front of the house . . . she so much wanted to be able to look out over the drive.' Here she gave a little good-natured click of the tongue. 'Whenever she's allowed out of bed, it's to ask that she be seated by the window. It's almost as though she's keeping a constant watch out for someone . . . yourselves, I expect,' she added, though seeming not entirely convinced, if only because of Mrs Wyman's repeated and anguished references to her 'daughter'. She was curious, because there had been no other mention made of any 'daughter' and something warned her not to raise the matter further – not yet anyway. She had been in the nursing profession long enough to know that it was always preferable to wait for the patient to confide in you – rather than to pry where it might create pain.

'In you go. She's waiting for you.' The woman gently eased the door open, gave a little smile and promising 'I'll have a tray for three sent up,' she went away at a smart pace.

They entered a large sunny room, beautifully furnished with cream furniture festooned with delicate little cameos and prettily curved brass handles. The figure seated in a large high-backed chair set by the window was not immediately apparent, because of the strong sunlight which poured in from beyond, blinding the visitors.

Blinking against the light and drawing Elizabeth to one side, Lester Judd approached, both hands outstretched, towards the moving shadow. 'Kathleen!' he said, his voice warm and concerned,

'How are you, today?' As he and Elizabeth drew close, the sun was wrapped in a blue haze of passing cloud, which enabled them to see the woman more clearly.

Making no move to lift her feeble hands to join his, Kathleen Wyman looked up into his face. Her large dark eyes, a picture of sorrow seeming incredibly beautiful set against the pale canvas of her delicate skin, were the most remarkable feature amongst the fine classical lines of her face. There was an almost ethereal, translucent quality about her which made one react most tenderly towards her. But more moving than her pitiful beauty was that aura of suffering which hovered about her like a clinging perfume.

Only for a fleeting second did she let her gaze rest on Lester Judd's face, then she tore it away to look upon Elizabeth, a gleam of expectancy in her eyes which quickly faded. 'You haven't found her? You haven't brought my child to me?' Her voice, strangely rich in tone, faltered, and with a sob she looked away. 'I must watch,' she whispered, returning to gaze out of the window, to the long winding drive below. 'She *will* come, I know she will. My baby . . . my daughter . . . she will come!' In frantic movement, she picked at the black and greying strands of her short bedraggled hair.

Moved to tears at such dreadful pain and at the ever-fervent belief which kept this long-persecuted woman alive, Elizabeth Judd gentled her husband to one side, leaving him to seat himself on one of the two chairs so thoughtfully placed there by a member of staff. Stooping low, she took up the woman's slim fragile hands in her own saying gently, 'Yes, Kathleen. Your daughter . . . Starlena . . . she will come to you. I give you my word. Lester will find her, please believe that.'

At the mention of the name Starlena, Kathleen Wyman gave a little start. Drawing her gaze back, she looked intently into Elizabeth's soft blue eyes. 'Starlena?' she said, a deep frown etching its way into her forehead. Somewhere in the darkest, most fearful shadows of her mind, that name stirred up a memory – a confused picture, which showed a long dark dormitory, grim-faced wardens and terrors she could not forget. That name Starlena brought a light into her heart, to cast a warm glow which made the awful memory less dark, less frightening. It conjured up a face also. A little smiling face, with huge black eyes and a lovely mass of blue-black hair. She saw it all in her mind. She saw those big black eyes peering up from beneath the bed at her, loving and compassionate. She had felt, ever since, those small hands stroking her hair and comforting her. She could feel it now! But, oh, how confused became the picture in her feverish mind.

'Yes, Kathleen. Your daughter is known by the name of Starlena . . . a beautiful, striking name. As lovely as she herself is.' Elizabeth stroked the limp hands up and down in her own, as though in an attempt to bring life into them, 'You'll adore her, Kathleen. She looks so like you, and she is a wonderful loving person. I know she'll make you so proud.'

Elizabeth waited patiently as Kathleen Wyman continued to stare at her, her large dark eyes quizzical and her lips softly mouthing the name 'Starlena . . . Starlena', over and over. Of a sudden, she became quiet. Her mouth began trembling and her hands gripped Elizabeth's hard. Yet, still she gazed deep into those gentle blue eyes, as though attempting to find there the answers to all that had gone before. Slowly, there came into her dark gaze a moistness, which quickly thickened and gathered into a pool of tears, until slowly they swelled and spilled out – to run down her trembling face and onto her hands, so fiercely joined with Elizabeth's.

At this point there came a knock on the door, followed by the same woman who had shown the visitors in. She had with her a tray, upon which were sandwiches, a plate of delicate little cakes and a large white teapot, with matching sugar bowl, milk jug and three cups with saucers.

'Oh dear! Mrs Wyman, whatever's the matter?' she exclaimed, placing the tray on the dressing-table with all haste and rushing to separate Elizabeth from the patient, 'I think it best if you go,' she remarked kindly to both Lester and Elizabeth, 'she'll be all right, don't worry.'

When her concerned visitors kissed her each in turn, Kathleen made no response, her sorry eyes turned once more towards the drive outside.

Downstairs, waiting in the reception area in order to have a brief word with the Matron regarding Kathleen Wyman's progress, Lester and Elizabeth were drawn into conversation with two gentlemen who also appeared to be waiting. As their talk rambled on, about such things as the League of Nations, the great mood of depression throughout the country and the declining popularity of Lloyd George, the Prime Minister, both Lester and Elizabeth wondered how the world could still keep marching on, when for that poor wretched woman upstairs, life had come to a standstill until the child that was hers was rightfully returned.

In their hearts, both Elizabeth and her husband vowed to double all efforts in order to bring that about.

Chapter Twenty-one

'Get away! Keep away from here! What do I care if she does die? Jemm was took, so why shouldn't *she* be took, eh?' Celia the gypsy queen was beside herself with rage.

'Tell me where Anselo is!' Rona pleaded, 'I'm sorry about Jemm. I didn't know. Please, tell me where to find Anselo!'

'Anselo's gone into mourning. You won't find him . . . you'll never find him,' came the vehement reply, 'And, she won't have him, I tell you. I'll *kill* him first!'

Rona could see that the gypsy queen was almost out of her head with grief – as well as driving herself crazy because of her obviously unrequited love for Anselo. So Jemm was gone, and Anselo had taken off in the way of a gypsy, to grieve in solitude. As she stumbled away, Rona gave a backward glance to where Celia was seated on the steps of her bow-topped wagon, head in hands and shaking with a fit of sobbing. Even though there had been more animosity than love between them in the past, Rona felt sorry for her. 'Twas a bad thing to be so alone in the world, that it was.

But if the gypsy queen had her share of troubles, Rona had more. She must get help for Starlena, or as sure as God was her maker, the lass would die.

It was an unusually hot April day, muggy and claustrophobic like a clammy day in the hottest of summers. As Rona stumbled back towards the tumbledown shack which she and Starlena had come across in their trek across the lovely but harsh Lancashire countryside through Freckleton, some short way out of Blackburn town, her heart was in her mouth.

Pausing only to collect a discarded bucket with a hole some halfway up towards the brim, she quickly part filled it with a small amount of water from a nearby brook and went on her way.

Once in sight of the shack, set down in a valley for the purpose of sheltering sheep who had recently given birth to their lambs, Rona breathed a sigh of relief. She was uncomfortably hot, her arms felt pulled from their sockets by the weight of the bucket – which she carried first in one hand then the other, to balance the burden more evenly – and she was desperately worried.

In the eight weeks since returning home, she and Starlena had trekked many long and weary miles, selling a few pegs here and a bit of firewood there – making sure all the while to stay away from the beaten track and the haunts of other gypsies, for Rona had learned to trust no-one. A harder time, though, she could hardly recall. Starlena had suffered badly, what with not having been given the chance to recuperate following the birth of little Ronalda and the sore effects of that wickedly-inflicted gash to her shoulder.

It was the latter which had been the most trouble. Flaring and festering in a way that even her knowledge could not cure. Rona had gathered and applied every plant or herb that might combat the rapidly spreading infection – but all to no avail. The creeping poison would not be stopped and she was at her wits' end.

In desperation Rona had read and followed the tracks of a gypsy wagon – only to find that it was the wagon of Celia, the gypsy queen, more embittered by the years and following the passing of the one who had raised her as his own, all alone and, Rona believed, terribly frightened. Rona had got no help there – she would not have expected it. And as God was her judge, she did not know where next to turn.

Starlena could feel the child nuzzling hard into her, searching for a teat on which it might draw comfort and nourishment. Struggling to a half-sitting position, she dragged herself backwards, to support herself against the dry rotting wall of the shack. Every inch was excruciatingly drawn-out and painful, her whole body racked with agony, and the sweat trickled down her back – not only from the clammy heat both within and without her body – but from the sheer effort of moving at all. When she was propped up against the wall, Starlena opened her blouse top and, drawing the crying child into her, she steeled herself for the punishment she knew must follow. She had not envisaged the severity of pain which seared through her as the child found her breasts, then began greedily sucking and tugging with the energy and desperation born of hunger.

For as long as she was able to bear it, Starlena held the infant to her. But, weakened both by her own hunger and the torturous pain which riddled every inch of her poor body, she could keep her senses no longer. Slipping into merciful unconsciousness, she fell to one side. The child rolled to the ground, still with her appetite not satisfied, and crying lustily.

This was how Rona found them on her return. 'Dear God!' she cried, dropping the bucket at the door and rushing inside. 'Oh, dear God . . . let her be alive!'

On quick examination, Starlena was found to be alive. But only just. It was then that Rona made the decision which had been tormenting her this past week, since Starlena's worsening state of health had brought them to this shack. As Rona pleaded with God for Starlena's life, she gave thanks also for her own improved health since returning to England. It was almost as though in just setting foot on its soil she had herself been given a new lease of life. In her heart she was so much stronger.

Using the clear brook water to bathe the now hideous and festering wound over Starlena's shoulder, Rona tore off yet another strip from her now ragged petticoat. Then, with the gentlest touch, she re-dressed the gaping wound and made Starlena as comfortable as was possible. Next, what to do about the child, who, in frustration, had cried itself to sleep? She would have carried it with her, but she had not the strength. Such a foolhardy plan would only slow her down and speed now was of the very essence. Whistledown Valley was some four miles away. If Starlena was to be saved, there was no time to waste.

Covering over both the child and its mother, Rona crept outside, drawing heaps of loose bracken and such-like up to the doorway

345

and across it. She didn't want animals straying in here. She wanted her darlings kept safe until she made her way back – God willing – with help.

Having secured the precious contents of the shack, Rona put her gnarled old hands together, raised her anxious brown eyes up to heaven and asked, 'Please, Lord, keep them safe, and give an ol' gypsy the strength to find the 'elp they need.' Whereupon she gazed upwards just a moment longer, as though helping the Lord to recognize her amongst all those other desperate souls who might be praying. Then, gathering every ounce of strength left in her tired aching bones, she turned away from the shack.

Gathering her long skirt up from her ankles, Rona made all haste towards Whistledown Valley towards Whalley Grange and towards the only one left to turn to – Starlena's friend Miss Elizabeth.

Following the initial shock and delight at seeing Rona Parrish at her door, Elizabeth Judd was filled with horror at her story. After telling it to her, the exhausted old gypsy collapsed in a ragged heap at her feet.

Arrangements were swiftly made. Rona was carried inside by Lester, to slowly recover from the trauma of her journey there. Searchers were instantly dispatched and medical assistance summoned straight away. A bedroom was made ready – the very same where Starlena had stayed once before – and all the while she rushed about preparing for Starlena's arrival, Elizabeth fervently prayed they would find her and the infant safe.

Having heard the news from Lester, who had led the party to bring Starlena and her child back, Freya Judd made no comment. Instead, she looked first stunned, then shocked. Before sweeping away upstairs in a strange surly mood she had expessed her opinion that, 'It's most inadvisable to entertain the likes of gypsies in one's home!' Upon being reminded by Elizabeth that Starlena was no gypsy, Freya Judd merely gave a snort, displaying her distaste for the whole matter and making the crushing remark, 'My own belief is that it's not what runs through one's blood that dictates a person's behaviour, it's the environment they're raised in and the standards they live by. You will never make a lady out of this . . . gypsy! Mark my words.'

To this cutting observation, Elizabeth gave the curt reply, 'I will not mark your words. They mean nothing to me!' After which, she looked in on Rona to see that she was receiving every attention. Then, satisfied, she hurried away to arrange for a wet nurse. Starlena was obviously in no fit state to feed the infant, so a good old-fashioned wet nurse was the answer. The very same one who had nursed her own son, David, when he was not long born.

Over the following two weeks the infant Ronalda positively thrived. Starlena grew from strength to strength and Rona never left her side, except when nature called, and on one occasion when Miss Elizabeth had badgered her into the next room, where was situated a long coffin-shaped container which had been filled with hot soapy water.

'It's a bath,' Miss Elizabeth had explained on seeing the old gypsy's wide astonished eyes, 'If you don't wash some of that country smell off it's probable that the maids who come in and out of Starlena's room will up and rebel!'

'They're sayin' I stink, are they? Show me the buggers as said that! They'll not say it again!' Rona retorted in fighting voice. But Miss Elizabeth had been most insistent, so, as quickly as she could, Rona had gone into the room – handing out her clothes one by one to a somewhat sour-faced kitchen-maid.

'Don't throw my faithful rags away!' warned Rona, with an idea of what that sour-faced creature had in mind. Only upon Miss Elizabeth's assurance that they would be washed and returned did she give over every single garment. Left on her own, she had no intention of sitting in that 'coffin'. Oh dear me, no! Instead, she took the bowl from the wash-stand up in the corner, and scooped up a great helping of the hot soapy water in it. Then, placing it on the floor, she knelt before it and, with the utmost precision, vigorously washed every inch of her body and hair. Following that, she wrapped herself in the huge towel from the rail and, feeling just a little foolish, she padded back to sit by Starlena, and there to await the return of her familiar garments.

There was an air of expectancy about the big old house. There was also a mood of disapproval from below stairs, this cleverly stirred by a series of comments purposely delivered by the acid-tongued Freya Judd who went about her business in the same haughty manner as always, choosing to pretend that the whole matter was decidedly beneath her. On the surface it appeared she was ignoring the entire episode, while underneath, in that sinister and evil part of her, she abhorred every moment the visitors remained under the same roof as herself. Her disposition was not improved by the business of Edward Wyman's daughter having been brought into the open. To her way of thinking, she had been cheated out of yet another opportunity to add to her ill-gotten gains which would ensure a sound, secure independence for her old age. However, the unforseen developments did afford her the old crooked smile now and then, for if the return of Edward Wyman's daughter had thwarted any plans *she* might have devised, how devastated at this very moment must be the greedy avaricious Redford Wyman. Oh yes, indeed! The thought gave her some small grudging comfort.

Of course, it had been Freya Judd herself who had made haste to Bessington Hall at the very first turn of events. She had been unable to resist imparting the news of his sister's discovery to Redford Wyman. He had taken it as she would have expected – in a rage at first. After which, he had been struck by a terrible silence, during which he pounded the carpet with furious pacing, as though in a frantic effort to beat from it the solution to all his problems.

Seeing him thus had delighted Freya Judd. Soon the servants caught up with the news and swore they would go on the streets rather than have a gypsy for a mistress! Then, the tidings spread over the estate on the wings of titillating gossip and before long everyone was aware of the situation, except those at its heart: Edward and Kathleen Wyman, Starlena, their true daughter, come home with a grandchild for them, also the old gypsy woman, Rona Parrish, yet another innocent enmeshed in a tragedy which had been created by greed, jealousy, hatred and revenge.

In such a tragedy, only love can triumph. Love, such as Kathleen

Wyman's for her newborn child. And love, such as that shared between two people like Rona and Starlena. The one idolizing her mammy and knowing no other, the second fiercely dedicated to the helpless babby whose life she believed herself to have saved – then to the growing child and the blossoming woman, who was now a mother herself. Rona Parrish had given her all to the one she had named Starlena and over these many long and tortuous years the old gypsy woman had almost come to believe that the child had been hers. But, always, she was reminded otherwise by one dreadful means or another. Always, she had been haunted by that knowledge and had fled from it – across mighty oceans and to the far side of the world.

In her heart, Rona Parrish knew that the day of reckoning must surely come. She did not know how close to her it had crept. Yet, had she but once set eyes on Freya Judd, who went to great pains to avoid being in close proximity to the old gypsy, Rona Parrish would have known instantly.

Chapter Twenty-two

Rona was devastated! She could feel her darling Starlena slipping out of her life and her old heart ached. That same bitter agony was alive in her brown eyes as she gazed upon Miss Elizabeth.

'No . . . oh, no, it mustn't be!' she protested, her voice broken and weary, as was her aged body, 'How can it be?' she asked, quietly crying, '. . . is this the end of the road, Miss Elizabeth? . . . for I have no strength to go on.' Rona thought it strange how life had come full circle, and foremost in her thoughts was Starlena's safety. 'You tell me that Starlena's father is Edward Wyman . . . and that he wants Starlena reunited with her mother. Yet, 'twas he, this very same man, who threatened to squeeze the life from his newborn. 'Twas he who had the darkness of murder in his eyes. And 'twas the very same monster who treated his own wife in the awful way you have described.'

'Edward Wyman did commit these terrible wrongs, Rona . . . that is true. But he's old and crippled, with not long to go before he's called to account for what he did. He's truly sorry and is desperate to make amends . . .'

'How am I to believe such a thing, tell me that! When 'twas he who sent murderers after us!'

'No, not he. Not Edward Wyman, I know.'

'Then who? If not this one, then who wanted the lass dead?' Rona rubbed her hands together, frantic and confused. 'Oh, I'm afeared, Miss Elizabeth! I'm awful afeared!' The ingrained terror of the bearded monster she had seen on that dreadful night a lifetime ago – the man who would have killed his own child – would not be so easily quelled in Rona's tender shaking heart. She must be sure! If she was not, then no power on earth would make her hand over her darling Starlena to this man! 'Take me to him first! Then, if I'm satisfied, be kind enough to let it be me who tells it all to Starlena. And, oh, if the hour comes, I pray 'twill not be too much of a shock for her!' The very prospect of telling that darling lass that she was not her real mammy put a crippling fear into the old gypsy's heart. So much so that, of a sudden, she broke into a fit of sobbing. 'How can I part with her now?' she cried, bringing the corner of her shawl up to her face and covering it completely. 'The lass is my life! Without her to face each day with, I don't want to go on. Oh, I love her so! I do love her so, Miss Elizabeth.' Her tortured words were lost in the great rending sobs which engulfed her.

Moving closer along the bench to the bent shaking figure, Miss Elizabeth said nothing, only put a comforting arm around the small shoulders, her gentle blue eyes gazing over the beautiful sun-bathed gardens which stretched before them. There was nothing she could do or say to ease the old gypsy's distress. The kindest thing was to let her cry herself out. Yet something that Rona Parrish had said deeply disturbed Elizabeth Judd. So! There had been messengers sent after Rona and Starlena? Messengers on an errand of murder! Elizabeth knew it could not have been the old Master Wyman. But, her every instinct – together with the recollection of a certain discussion she had overheard between his obnoxious son, Redford, and the ever-devious Freya Judd – told her a story she did not like. Did not like at all! Redford Wyman, of course, would have had every reason for preventing his sister's return to the family home and to the family fortune. Freya's part in it was no doubt motivated by greed, Elizabeth was certain. It had been a most dirty and shameful business, she was sure. But she was equally convinced that now Starlena was home to claim her rightful place there was little question of her being in any danger. On the contrary, if Redford Wyman had any sense, he would surely see that it would be in his own interests to be a proper, warm and loving brother to his long-lost sister.

Elizabeth Judd, with her gentle trusting nature, could have no

351

real perception of the black evil ways of a creature driven by all-consuming greed. But Rona Parrish suffered from no such illusions; although her instincts warned her only of Starlena's father. She knew next to nothing of her brother.

That same afternoon, Lester Judd, his wife Elizabeth and Rona Parrish were admitted to Edward Wyman's sickroom. From a safe distance, Redford Wyman skulked in a doorway, his one blue eye riveted on the party as they disappeared into his father's room; the look on his face would have frightened the devil himself!

All the way across the hall, then up the stairs and along the galleried landing, whose eerie procession of paintings gave her the same shivers they had done on a night some twenty-two years ago and more. Rona was made to relive it all over again. It seemed to her uncanny how she was transported back through time. Outside the world had continued to change, yet here, in this luxurious mausoleum, every little detail remained the same, cocooned, mummified almost – every inch of the way and every step she took, raising up such terrible ghosts in her, that set her trembling. She wanted to turn and flee from this place of memories, to grab Starlena and the infant, Ronalda, and to escape where they could never be threatened again. All these things set her instincts racing. Yet, there were deeper, more compelling instincts, which told the old gypsy that the time for running was past. On that night when she had fled from here with the new, warm bundle in her arms, fate had already decreed that one day she must return that child which she took. Today was that day. A glorious, sunny day in May 1920 – as stark in comparison to the evil black night when she had been brought here as God and nature could make it.

When Rona set foot in that same bedroom where Starlena had been born, a very strange and unexpected thing happened. Instead of being cloaked in darkness with only a lamp to give light, the room was filled with brilliant sunshine. There was no sense of urgency, or of fearful murder, as there had been on that terrible night. There was no anguish, no cries of violence and no terror there. Instead, there was a quiet aura of peace. There was suffering,

352

yes, and there was pain. But it was pain and suffering which only love could bring about. Love, and a sense of desperate crippling remorse. And, deep into Rona's heart, there came an uneasy sense of peace.

Rona could not bring herself to look upon the man lying in the bed. Convinced, however, that the issue must now be faced, she turned to Miss Elizabeth and said, 'Tek me back to the lass. Let me speak to 'er.' She turned from the room and waited outside while Lester and Elizabeth Judd spent a while with the ailing Edward Wyman. After which, Lester Judd drove them back to Whalley Grange. There, while Rona told all to Starlena, he had a long telephone conversation with the matron at Salmesbury House for Gentlewomen. Now that Starlena and her child were both strong again, there was much to do. At long last Starlena would be reunited with her family and restored to her rightful place. Yet, in all their joy of the situation, neither Lester nor Elizabeth could help but feel the greatest compassion for the old gypsy. It was she who was called on to make the greatest sacrifice.

When, after they arrived back at Whalley Grange, Rona went slowly upstairs to where Starlena was almost fully recovered, their hearts went with her!

'Oh, there you are, Mammy!' Starlena threw open her arms. 'Took an early walk did you?' She felt wonderful. Today she was to be allowed out of her bed and could actually walk about the gardens, the doctor had said. It would be a wonderful treat for her and little Ronalda and, oh, she was so looking forward to it. Already she was seated in the rush chair, with the child sleeping in a cot nearby. She had taken a bath and, when her hair was dry, she would don the clothes already being prepared for her. After which, she would enjoy that long leisurely stroll about the grounds with her babby and her beloved Mammy Parrish.

'Miss Elizabeth has been so kind,' she beamed at Rona, after the two of them had hugged and Rona was seated on the edge of the bed close by, 'and I'll be sorry to leave. But we must be gone quite soon. Oh, Mammy! I have such plans, now that I'm strong again!

We'll soon have our own wagon, you'll see . . . and we'll search out Anselo. He'll give us help I'm sure. Oh, it will be good to see him again!' On and on she went, bubbling with plans for the future, her heart already out on the open road and the prospect of seeing Anselo again bringing a ray of sunshine to her heart.

During these past two weeks when she had lain in that bed which, when she was at her weakest, Starlena had believed would be her death bed, all manner of things had come into her feverish mind. There had been images conjured from the depths of her subconscious: images and confused memories to frighten and torment her, images of Jake, struggling with a figure, and amidst it all, such searing pain that it made her cry out. Then there had been a picture of Anselo, down at the lake where they had made such young and passionate love. And Jackson! Oh, that was the one to cause her the greatest pain. Jackson, with his strong, dark green eyes, hair the colour of rugged brown earth and a slow, deliberate way of talking. Jackson, first serious, then laughing, beckoning to her and, even as she ran towards him, the figure of a woman stepping between them, before spiriting him away. Jackson, loving her, wanting her in the same way she loved and wanted him. And, both of them knowing the futility of it.

When the fever passed, Starlena had put behind her all of these painful images for she had a mammy and a darling child who loved and needed her. These two were ever constant in her thoughts – the anchor she desperately needed. All her energies would be devoted to making them happy, and in this way she also would find the greatest happiness. She felt it in her heart.

Now, as she gazed on the solitary little figure perched on the edge of the bed, looking so forlorn and unusually quiet, Starlena was quickly concerned to assure her.

'It's all right, darling. I know how you hate to be cooped up, bless you. But it won't be long now before we're out under God's sky again. Out along the open roads you love so much.' And which I also love, she thought.

'Nay, lass,' came the dejected little voice, 'You've more important paths to take just now. 'Tain't so simple any more, I'm afeared.'

354

Starlena would have laughed in good humour at her mammy's peculiar remarks. But something in the weary stoop of her shoulders and in the heaviness of those worn brown eyes, pulled her up short. 'What is it?' she asked softly, the smile now gone from her face, and her black eyes troubled. Somewhere deep inside her was an inexplicable feeling of dread. 'Mammy! What ails you, making you look so sorrowful, when we've so much to look forward to, now that we have another soul to give us joy, and me so well again?' Starlena leaned towards her mammy, bending her head to draw the little woman's gaze, which was now fixed on the floor in a bid to avoid Starlena's perceptive black eyes – which Rona knew could easily read her every mood.

'Aw, lass . . . there's things to tell yer. Things yer 'ave a right to know. Things I've wickedly kept from yer all these years.' Rona had never been so afraid in all of her life! Not when under threat of being murdered. Not when driven across the world to wander a strange land. Not when caught up in the nightmare of a terrible shipwreck. Never, never had such feelings of dread swept through her as they did now. Not even when she thought Starlena would be taken from her in illness, for if that had been the case, then somehow she would have found the strength in her terrible sorrow and loneliness to trust that it was the wish of God, and His hand that had brought it about, for reasons only known to Him. Now, in this very moment before she must confess everything to Starlena, Rona still felt – however much she craved for reassurance – that these circumstances were writ by the devil. She prayed her faith in God and His divine help would see them both through.

So acute was the old gypsy's guilt that she could not lift her gaze to look into those big trusting black eyes. 'Yer must listen to me, lass. Listen 'ard, won't yer? As much as I've prayed that yer need never know . . . I can see that there's no other way. Not now. I must tell yer, for if I don't, somebody else will. And while I'm tellin' yer, don't say a word. Or I might lose the strength to go on.'

'Tell me what?' Starlena came to sit on the bed beside her mammy. Placing a loving arm round her shoulders, she asked again, this time more gently. 'What must you tell me? If there's something lying heavy on your mind, darling . . . then of course you must tell me.' She gave a nervous forced laugh, 'I promise I'll not bite your head off. It can't be all that bad, eh?' Yet Starlena had a feeling that it was, for in all her life, she had never seen her mammy so deeply troubled as she was at this moment, 'Come on. Out with it!' she coaxed tenderly.

And Rona did just that. Carefully and tenderly as she could, she told the young woman that she was not a gypsy, but a true-born lady. That the woman she had known all her life as her mammy was not and never had been such. That her father was a phenomenally rich man, and consequently she too was vastly rich. That her father, that same wealthy personage, in a misguided fit of jealousy had given her to a gypsy before even the umbilical cord was cleanly cut, afterwards forcibly committing her poor innocent mother to an asylum, where, for the best part of Starlena's life, the wretched woman had been left to rot, only lately having been released into Lester and Elizabeth Judd's loving care.

Rona revealed to Starlena how her father, Edward Wyman, was dying and wished to make amends. It was his intention that mother and daughter be brought together in a more kindly and civilized way than when they were split asunder by his vindictive hand.

The whole time Rona was spilling out the story, her gaze fixed fast to the floor, as though she was afraid to look up and see the havoc caused by it, Starlena spoke not a word. Having recoiled in horror as the whole awful sequence of events unfolded, she sat with her two hands fiercely gripping the bed edge, her knuckles as stark white as her face. There was no emotion in her quiet expression – only a reflection of the numbness which had squeezed at her heart, leaving her weak and shocked.

Starlena consciously forced herself to remember mundane things, such as her clothes which should be arriving soon and the fact that Ronalda was sleeping well after her feed. These were events she felt she must cling to. They were real to her, whereas Rona's shocking revelations were not. How could they be? she asked herself. How could it be that all of her life was a lie? She had been a trespasser! She had no rights, no roots – no future as she had planned and no past as she had believed. No! It was *not* true! It *could not be* true. Yet – fight against it as she might – Starlena's instincts told her that it *was* true. So many things were explained because of it. So many incidents over which she had puzzled were now made clearer. They came rushing back, reeling into her memory one after the other with sickening force. Always they had been running, hiding, and often as a tiny child she had been snatched from her bed at the merest sound in the dark. Always, there had been that feeling of being driven – on and on, day and night – as though the very devil were on their heels.

Suddenly there came into Starlena's mind a train of thought to alarm her. Who was the 'gent' looking for them on Gypsy Hill in Appleby at the time of the fair? Why had there been a man sent to murder them on board ship? Who was the intruder who had frightened them away from Jackson's farm in America? If she had been given away freely by this wealthy landowner who by all accounts was her father, why was she then pursued all the way to America – and, worse, why did he want her killed?

The torment in Starlena's mind showed on her face and, seeing it, Rona guessed at the questions there. Now, she went on to explain to Starlena her own conclusions on this matter. How it was reasonable to suppose that Edward Wyman had slowly come to realize that his daughter could come back and claim her inheritance if there ever came a time when she learned of her true identity – no doubt creating much mischief if she was possessed of a vindictive soul. Therefore, he had possibly for that reason sought to silence her forever – sending out various emissaries to track them down. 'But, 'afore the deed could be done, lass, the man 'isself was struck down! By the 'and o' the Lord, I'm thinkin' – and from that day, it would appear there came over his black heart a great remorse to change 'im fer the best!' Rona explained how only that very morning she had seen Edward Wyman with her own eyes. 'Broken, 'e were! A broken, sorry fellow . . . afeared to meet 'is maker wi' such a sorry load o' guilt weighin' 'im down.' Rona could not help but add in a low private voice – but not so private that Starlena did not hear, 'Aye! An' so 'e should be. So 'e should be!'

In that moment Starlena's mind was made up. She would leave here this very minute. There was nothing here that she wanted except the two things that meant everything in the world to her – the babby Ronalda and her mammy. Yes! Her *mammy*, for there could never be another by that name – not for Starlena. *Never*! She wanted no other. Neither did she want any part of a past that made her a stranger. Not riches, nor anything that belonged to a man whose heart was so like stone and so eaten with black jealousy and hatred that he had committed such dreadful deeds. It mattered not that he had come to repent. A fiend like that one should be swiftly dispatched to hell and there left to burn forever.

Starlena had no feeling for this Edward Wyman, for he had been *bad*. So deeply bad, she could never be made to believe that his evil would be washed away in a wave of frightened remorse. All those years ago he had acted according to his own corrupt instincts. He was still responding to those same corrupt instincts. Starlena believed that with all her heart. Edward Wyman was not repentant. He was merely afraid. Afraid for his own wicked soul. As far as she was concerned, it could burn and shrivel in the fires of the devil's house – for, that was where it belonged.

In direct contrast to the harsh thoughts racing through her mind, Starlena's voice, as she turned to the anxious Rona, was quiet and strangely calm. 'I hope you're ready, Mammy!' she told the old gypsy, whose brown eyes lit up with surprise and delight on hearing herself addressed as 'Mammy'. 'The minute my clothes are brought, we're leaving for good.' Rising from the bed, Starlena went to the cot. In a great rush of love which over-rode all else, she reached her long sensitive fingers beneath the frilly canopy, to caress the pink sleeping face of her child.

'Leaving, yer say? What do yer mean, lass . . . leaving?' Rona's heart was stirred but she dared not hope too much.

Starlena gazed into the cot for what seemed an age to the watching gypsy. Then, turning only slightly, she gave a half-smile which could not disguise the trauma in her startling black eyes, 'We'll go from here,' she asserted. 'I have no wish to see this stranger, Edward Wyman.'

'Indeed!' Neither Rona nor Starlena had heard the door softly open to admit Miss Elizabeth. It was obvious, from her stern expression, that she was most disappointed in what she had innocently overheard. 'And have you no wish to see your real mother – an innocent in this whole dreadful tragedy, who loved her baby as surely as you love yours. And who, for almost twenty-three years, has lived through a nightmare – a nightmare not of her own making. Through it all, the one idea which kept her sane – kept her alive – was that one day she would see her child again. One day that same child who was snatched from her would be returned!'

Here, Elizabeth Judd ventured into the room and after laying Starlena's clothes on a nearby chair, she came to Starlena. The anger had gone from her blue eyes and in its place was a look of anguish, as she beseeched, 'Oh, Starlena . . . I know how you must feel. But, please, don't turn your back on a poor woman whose crime was no more than your own to be treated so.'

Starlena was ashamed. In her bitterness towards the man whom she could never in all conscience come to forgive, she had not thought of the woman he had shut away – the woman who, whether she herself cared for it or not – was her real mother. A poor ill-treated creature who had done no harm, yet had been punished most dreadfully. Oh, dear God! How would she herself feel, if some stranger hurried in through that door now and snatched little Ronalda from her. Just as her Mammy Parrish had been obliged to do on the night she herself had been born? Oh, how would she bear such a thing? She could not! And her heart was filled with compassion for this woman who had lost her child in such a monstrous way.

Rona also was filled with compassion for the woman who had given birth to Edward Wyman's children on that fated night – one, a boy, stillborn, the other a magnificent girl-child whom she herself had raised as Starlena. Rona recalled how the tending servant had told her that Starlena's mother had gone from this world and, gazing at the woman lying so deathly white and still, she had been convinced that it was so. She was not to know of the awful series of events which later erupted, but it was a hard and cruel set of circumstances, that was for sure, thought Rona.

Now, seeing Starlena so moved by Miss Elizabeth's plea, she added her own, 'Aw, lass! What that poor woman's been through don't bear thinkin' on! Both on yer were cast out, it's true. But yer 'ave ter remember, darlin' – you 'ad me, an' she 'ad nary a soul to give 'er peace in that 'ell 'ole where 'e threw 'er.'

When the old gypsy had finished speaking – her brown eyes so sad and an air of dejection about her – Starlena could not hold back her churning emotions. Rushing towards the weary little figure, she fell on her knees crying, 'Oh, Mammy! What kind of monster could do such a terrible thing!' Her black eyes were uplifted towards the kindly wizened features that she knew and loved so well.

Rona gazed down into those spellbinding dark eyes running fast with tears and pleading with her for an answer she did not have. She wound her arms about Starlena's shoulders and, drawing her close, she murmured, 'What kind of monster, lass? A foolish and jealous one, brimming over with a terrible hatred.' Here she eased Starlena's dark head away and, cupping the sorry face between her two hands, she lifted it to gaze deep into those black dewy eyes when, in a quiet wise voice, she told her, 'Or, a monster driven by a deep and abiding love. We'll never really know the truth, will we, lass?'

Starlena knew well enough what her mammy was saying. Love was a powerful emotion which could drive a body to terrible things, she was sure. Oh, but that didn't mean you had to forgive those things. And, where this Edward Wyman was concerned, she had not changed her mind on that score. Now, when Rona asked, 'Yer will go an' see 'er won't yer, lass?' Starlena answered from her heart, 'Yes I will. I must!' And having said it, she felt better in herself. She felt more contented at last.

'Oh, Starlena!' Elizabeth embraced Starlena as she got to her feet, 'That's wonderful! Oh, your mother will be overjoyed.' Her blue eyes were bright with tears as she drew away to regain her composure before, with a little embarrassed laugh, she added, 'You don't know – you can't possibly know what this will mean to Kathleen. She's been through so much and she is still very ill, I'm afraid.' Elizabeth broke off as she perceived the look of puzzled astonishment between the old gypsy and Starlena. 'What is it?' she asked, glancing nervously from one to the other.

Starlena could give no immediate answer, for she herself was not certain why her heart had suddenly beat faster at the name Kathleen. Before she could ask Miss Elizabeth to repeat the name, Rona voiced the question, 'Did you say "Kathleen"?'

'Yes. Kathleen Wyman. She is Starlena's mother,' returned Elizabeth, her blue eyes startled and a quizzical frown written into her high and delicate forehead.

Starlena gave a little gasp as the memory came to her. Her hand flew towards her throat as though to ward off the great painful lump which was threatening to choke her breath. 'Kathleen!' she whispered. 'Her name – my mother's name, is Kathleen?' She looked into Elizabeth's face, her own eyes astonished and deeper black against the pallor of her skin which, of a sudden, was like the colour of parchment. 'Tell me, Miss Elizabeth, please. Which asylum was Kathleen Wyman kept in? Was it a place in Liverpool? A terrible grey place by the name of "Kingston"? The man in charge there . . . going by the name of Mr Drew?'

Now it was Elizabeth's turn to look astonished, 'Why, yes! According to her records, Kathleen was detained there for some years. What makes you ask, Starlena? And how very curious. How did you come to know of such a place?' Starlena's questions had raised up a most uneasy question in Elizabeth Judd, since discovering that Kathleen Wyman had indeed been incarcerated there at the very time when she herself paid a visit while looking for her own late mother. She had often wondered whether she had innocently swept by that poor creature and never known it.

Elizabeth's questions went unheard. It registered only with Starlena that it was true! Kathleen Wyman, her mother, and the sweet, tortured woman she had befriended while scrubbing the floors of that dreadful place were most probably one and the same.

Starlena sat beside Rona and, taking a weatherworn hand into her own, she said in a voice trembling with excitement, 'It *is* her, isn't it, Mammy? I just know it is!'

'I don't know, lass,' Rona replied, thinking how cruel and unpredictable fate could be. ''Tis a strange thing, there's no doubtin' it! A very strange an' peculiar thing.' She was suddenly now even more afraid, because she still remembered Starlena's great affection for that woman.

For a while Starlena let her mammy's words sink in. It was a most peculiar thing, if indeed Kathleen, her mother, was the same woman. How many years ago was it now? Eight? Nine? A long time, she knew. Of a sudden, she had to find out. She had to see for herself. Enthused, she got to her feet, hurried to where her clothes had been most carefully placed and feverishly dressing she told Miss Elizabeth, 'Hurry! We must go to her straightaway. Oh, Miss Elizabeth . . . Mammy and I worked a while in this place called Kingston. There I grew fond of a darling creature with a haunted face and gentle frightened manner. She must have once been very beautiful, Miss Elizabeth, for it was still there . . . in her nervous smile and in her lovely eyes. Is it possible that she was the one who gave me life? Hurry Miss Elizabeth! Hurry, Mammy! We must go to her at once!'

All the while she rushed about, Starlena's heart was both heavy and excited. She had never forgotten Kathleen from the asylum. Often in the years after they had left that place for good, she would dream of that sweet lovely face, and her heart was sore. Many times she had puzzled over the reason why such a gentle and loving lady was closed up in an institution not fit even for animals. There had been many agonizing moments when she would have liked to have gone back there to see her new-found friend, to give her some small comfort and to bring a little smile to those big soulful eyes. Oh! could it be? Could it possibly be? She dared not dwell on it too deeply, nor raise her hopes too high.

Swinging about, she caught sight of Rona's dejected face and, looking first at Miss Elizabeth, who was still coming to grips with all of this, she went to Rona. Sitting beside her, she said in a quiet reassuring voice, 'If it *is* she, Mammy . . . it will make no difference. None of it will make any difference to you and me. You are my mammy . . . you always have been and you always will be! There isn't a single thing in the world to change that. You and little Ronalda are everything to me. I love you both so much. You do know that? You do believe that with all your heart, don't you, Mammy?'

If Rona had any doubts at all, they were blown away on the loving strength of Starlena's words. Suddenly, the world looked a brighter place where, only moments before, it had seemed a very bleak and lonely place. She had long given up hope of ever seeing her brother, Callum again, assuming that his terrible temper and his sledge-like fists had mebbe got the better of him one dark night. It was something she had come to accept. With him gone there was left only her darling Starlena. Without her and that little babby, Ronalda, she was all alone in the world. It had been a terrifying prospect, which was less threatening after Starlena's declaration of loyalty and love. All the same, Rona felt there were still hurdles to be got over, for, she knew well enough how often Starlena had cried in her sleep because of that poor creature in the asylum. Starlena had grown to love her very much. And, if it should now turn out that the woman was her own flesh and blood . . . her own mother . . . Well, we shall see, reflected Rona, her heart lighter, but still a little afraid. We shall see!

'When are we to see Kathleen Wyman?' Rona asked Elizabeth, 'And where is this nursing-home?'

'She's no longer there, Rona,' replied Elizabeth, going to the door and turning to look from one to the other, 'Starlena's father was finally persuaded by Lester that his wife should be brought home to Bessington Hall.'

Glancing at the china clock on the dresser, she saw that it was almost noon. 'She should be there by now. When she has been settled and made comfortable . . . and her private nurse installed, Lester will bring us. Within the hour, I'm sure.' Smiling warmly, she asked, 'Till then, shall we all wait on the terrace in the lovely sunshine?'

After the initial excitement with so many revelations and possibilities to contend with, Starlena had begun to feel a little apprehensive. Her own mother! What would she say? How would they feel on meeting? After all, they were strangers, were they not?

Kathleen Wyman had lost a newborn child and it was a grown woman who was coming back to her. Suddenly Starlena was anxious and even a little afraid.

One pair of devious eyes watched the little group depart from Whalley Grange. Freya Judd positioned herself on the landing over the hall, undetected by her brother and the three women, Starlena with the babby closely cradled in her arms. On their arrival at Bessington Hall, it was not a pair of eyes that monitored the group's arrival, but *one* eye, deep blue and more cunning than any pair. In the acute and narrowed vision of that one eye, Redford Wyman noted every small detail of the woman who was his own kith and kin. He admired the excellent cut of the lemon silk blouse she wore. He liked the way that expensive black skirt moved with her every elegant step and, he coveted the delicious manner in which it swung about those shapely trim ankles as she walked. Not for a moment did he believe those expensively tailored clothes were hers. No doubt they were from Elizabeth Judd's extensive wardrobe – probably discarded in favour of the newer fashion which displayed far more of a woman's delicious attributes. Yet these longer-style clothes suited the one they called Starlena – accentuating her air of mystery and flattering her particular dignity. Redford Wyman had never seen a more beautiful woman. Even from where he skulked at a safe distance and out of sight, he was amazed at those large black eyes and wild profusion of coal-coloured hair. 'The woman is magnificent!' he murmured. And, sister or not, he fancied that it would be an exciting and gratifying experience to wrap his legs about her and taste of that exquisite loveliness.

He would introduce himself to her at a later date, making a convincing show of brotherly affection. When all the while there was forming in his calculating mind a devious and devilish plan to restore himself to his rightful position at the head of the Wyman fortune. Oh, but carefully! If this plan was to come to fruition, he must be infuriatingly patient. He must bide his time, at least until his father had drawn his last breath. He fingered the scar on his cheekbone. His mother also would get her come-uppance!

The enormity of her father's house, the unabashed elegance and vastly expensive objects displayed throughout were a source of both fascination and astonishment to Starlena. On the two occasions when Miss Elizabeth had welcomed her into Whalley Grange, Starlena had been jolted at the beauty and luxury there. But little at Miss Elizabeth's house had prepared her for Bessington Hall. From the moment when Lester had driven through the wide ornate gateway, along the seemingly endless drive – lined by weeping willows, age-old oak trees and flowering shrubs – Starlena was mesmerized by such grandeur. Yet, if the way up to Bessington Hall was in itself an experience, how much more in awe she had found herself to be when first glimpsing the magnificent dwelling itself – a splendid building which took her breath away.

Inside she was instantly surrounded by sweet-smelling leather, aged and beautiful tapestries, and wood-panelled walls adorned with most impressive paintings. All about her was that particular aura associated with timeless elegance, great wealth and aristocracy and Starlena felt curiously subdued, yet at the same time rebellious and filled with a daring to venture further.

'I'll bide 'ere, lass,' Rona declared, looking about her and shivering, though not from the cold for, with the sun streaming in through the long windows either side of the great door, the hall was pleasantly warm and comfortingly bright. 'D'yer want ter leave the babby wi' me?' she asked, searching out a chair where, settling herself beneath the indignant eyes of the house-keeper, she made ready her lap to take the child.

But Starlena preferred to take little Ronalda with her. Having the child close to her breast gave her a feeling of warmth and security in a place which made her exceedingly apprehensive and most insecure.

Lester also hesitated, telling Elizabeth, 'I think it might be better, darling, if I make myself scarce.' Then, turning to the house-keeper, he asked firstly that Rona Parrish should be sent a reviving drink in such warm and thirsty weather, and then: 'If you'll direct me to Master Wyman's whereabouts, I'll make haste to join him.' Upon her reassurance that he would no doubt find Master Wyman in the West Meadow, attending to a matter with the foreman who had reported the brook to be dangerously low, Lester fondly kissed Elizabeth and wished Starlena 'a most rewarding reunion with your mother, Kathleen'. Then he set off in the direction of the West Meadow, where he intended to have a quiet talk with Starlena's brother, Redford. There were still small aspects of the whole business which slightly disturbed him.

Kathleen Wyman was established in the quarters directly facing the head of the stairs. Lester Judd had supervised that particular arrangement, bearing in mind the need for a nurse who must by necessity be constantly climbing up and down the stairs, together with the fact that if Kathleen Wyman, who was still incredibly weak, should feel the urge to come down below, there would be less distance for her to travel. Edward Wyman, languishing in his sick-bed some way along the landing, had no such problems, for his days were numbered few.

As she walked up the stairs beside her dear friend Miss Elizabeth, Starlena's thoughts were surprisingly calm – although her heart was beating with such force that she could hardly breathe. Her emotions and loyalty were torn in two, half of them desperately clinging to her darling mammy, left sitting so patiently downstairs – the other half reaching upwards to where there waited a woman. The woman who had waited so very long for her stolen child to be returned. The woman who was her true mother, and who might even be the same one she had befriended in that dreadful asylum. Only once, as she neared that room where Kathleen Wyman watched the door so anxiously, did Starlena hesitate. At that point she felt the encouraging touch of Miss Elizabeth's hand on her arm. When her courage strengthened, she went on, unsure of what she would find behind that great dark wood door which now loomed up before her, but knowing that there was no way back. Inside that room was a soul who had loved her and pined for her since the day of her birth. In the face of such devotion and suffering Starlena could never have denied this meeting and, the closer she came to it the more her heart was filled with a deep compassion and the beginnings of love.

'Ready?' Elizabeth put her hand on the doorknob, an encouraging smile in her bright blue eyes as she waited for Starlena's affirmative nod. Then, when it was given, she looked to the housekeeper, saying, 'Thank you. You can leave us now.' She watched until the woman began to make her way back down the stairs, whereupon she gave Starlena a gentle pat on the arm, then opened the door and went slowly inside. Starlena followed, waiting nervously until Miss Elizabeth had closed the door and the two of them approached the bed – beside which sat a kindly-faced nurse. She came forward to greet them with a warm smile.

'The journey from the nursing-home was a bit too much for her, I'm afraid. She so wanted to get out of bed for you . . . but I thought it best to be firm about it . . .'

'It's all right. Thank you,' Starlena assured her, going towards the bed, where Kathleen Wyman was sitting upright, supported by a number of bolsters and pillows, her two delicate hands fidgeting and plucking at the silk bedspread, her eyes fixed on Starlena, every step she took.

There was a deathly hush in the room. Elizabeth and the nurse kept their distance as Starlena, holding tight to her baby, reached the foot of the bed. And, as she did so, a small cry escaped her lips, her eyes growing wide with astonishment as they gazed on the woman in the bed. It was she! The dark hair more greying and less ragged, the facial features not so peaked and jutting, her whole countenance less desperate and the mad frantic look gone from those big dark and soulful eyes. But it was the same woman Starlena had befriended in Kingston Asylum. The realization sent a great painful lump into her throat and, with tears of emotion rising to her eyes, Starlena moved towards the bed-head, a gentle smile on her face.

So, *this* was Kathleen Wyman? This lovely creature was her mother? Starlena was overwhelmed. So many images careered through her mind as she came closer. When, in a moment, she was seated on the edge of the bed, Starlena was moved by an overpowering urge to take Kathleen Wyman in her arms but she was already holding the child, Ronalda. Instead, she balanced the fidgeting bundle on her knee, holding it with one encircling arm, while with the other, she reached out to caress Kathleen's face.

At the first touch, Starlena felt her cringe away. She was trembling, her dark eyes locked on to Starlena's gaze, with a strange quizzical expression in them, as though she was desperately trying to remember something. 'Kathleen,' murmured Starlena, her voice soothing and gentle, 'do you not remember me? When you were in your bed at Kingston and I scrubbed the floor there? Don't you recall how we used to talk together?' There was no response, save for those dark staring eyes which never left Starlena's face. 'We were friends, you and me. Do you recall my name – Starlena?'

Of a sudden, something stirred in the other woman's memory and her eyes first grew softer, then became filled with tears, as she repeated in a low croaked voice, 'Starlena . . . you were my friend.'

As Starlena squeezed the hand in hers and tenderly nodded, Kathleen's gaze grew less intense. Now she drew it from Starlena's face. Slowly, her dark troubled eyes travelled to where the baby was playfully entwining the shawl about its finger. Then Kathleen Wyman gazed on the shawl, and saw that the embroidery was the very same as on the shawl which had swaddled her own newborn, and a dramatic change came about her whole countenance. In an instant and, much to Starlena's astonishment, she had wrenched the child from its mammy's arms and was hugging it to her so fiercely that at first the child gave a startled cry.

'Oh, oh! You've brought my baby! You've brought my baby!' she sobbed, rocking the infant back and forth, back and forth as though her very life depended on it, the tears falling fast from her happy eyes and a deal of laughter amongst the sobs. 'Oh! . . . my baby. I have my baby at last!' She was raining kisses on the child's head, on its face, its hands – her two arms clasped about it and a look of such incredible joy on her face that Starlena could not help but sob with her. And, from the back of the room, where stood the nurse and Elizabeth Judd, there came also the sound of soft crying and sniffling.

'See! The child has my features!' Kathleen laughed, half-turning the infant to reveal her dark eyes and jet-black curls, 'They'll not take my baby away again! Never!' Now there was desperation in her voice as she stared at Starlena, 'You're my friend! We won't let them take my baby away, will we?'

For a moment, Starlena was lost for words. Her own heart was moved by a mother's love and she too wanted the child back in her own arms. Ronalda was her child! Hers! But, if her heart was moved by a mother's great possessiveness, it was also breaking for this poor misguided and tortured woman who in her desperation had lost all sense of reality and passage of time. Could she tear the child away, who was now contentedly gurgling into Kathleen Wyman's enchanted eyes? Could she tell her that the child was not hers? That the newborn infant she had lost was gone forever – grown beyond recognition into a woman? Could she be so heartless as to take little Ronalda, turn her back on Kathleen Wyman and condemn her to the same tortuous sufferings as her father, Edward Wyman, had so cruelly done?

Every instinct in Starlena's being cried out in protest. No! She could never do those things. On the way here, Miss Elizabeth warned her of the doctor's diagnosis. Her mother, Kathleen Wyman, would never regain her full senses. Neither would she ever regain her full health. He had said that in his opinion she would not see out the year. That was the way of things, and he was truly sorry. So was Starlena. In response to the great surge of love which had filled her heart, she came to sit close beside Kathleen Wyman, where, enclosing both woman and child in her two loving arms, she promised, 'No, Kathleen! We won't let them take your babby away.'

'And you'll stay with me also? You'll keep watch?'

'I'll stay with you, yes,' replied Starlena, thinking that a few months out of her life, when she must share Ronalda with Kathleen, who was after all the child's grandmother, would not be so great a sacrifice or cause her the terrible anguish endured by this gentle harmless creature. 'And I'll keep watch, I promise!' she assured her, tenderly wiping away the tears from her mother's eyes.

* * *

Later, when Starlena told Rona what had taken place, the old gypsy put on her most enigmatic smile and, in a sad voice, she told Starlena, 'I knew it, lass. I knew I'd lose yer.'

It took all of Starlena's powers of persuasion to convince her otherwise. After a while, and in the face of Starlena's very real and genuine love for her, Rona was talked into staying also. 'Well, all right, lass . . . till the poor soul draws 'er last. But *I* ain't bidin' in yon 'ouse! Not me! I'll be far more content in a corner o' that there barn.' She was adamant on that issue. However, when it was pointed out by Miss Elizabeth that there was an untenanted cottage close to the rear of the house, Starlena persuaded her mammy into a compromise. She also would have preferred not to stay in the great house, but she must be close to little Ronalda. There were times, according to the nurse who had answered Starlena's searching questions most thoroughly, when Kathleen's mind wandered and her span of concentration was short-lived. As far as Starlena was concerned, the situation must be carefully monitored and her baby watched over all the while.

'And will you still not go in to see your father, Starlena? Elizabeth Judd begged.

But Starlena's mind would never be changed on this score 'No!' she said, 'and please, Miss Elizabeth. Don't ever again ask me to!'

Chapter Twenty-three

'Your precious Starlena's a great and wealthy lady. She won't waste time on the likes of you.' Celia the gypsy queen had at long last found a direct route to Anselo's aching heart and, whether or not it caused him anguish she used it again and again to drive home the impossibility of his great abiding love for Starlena.

With the winter now beginning to set in, Anselo's period of private mourning for his father was drawing to an end. Four days ago, on a bitter afternoon in October, he had drawn his wagon into Whistledown Valley – there having tracked down Celia. With Jemm gone, Anselo now accepted her as his responsibility. But she had given him no peace. Starlena's sudden and dramatic turn of fortune had spread amongst the gypsy community like wildfire. The story was live round every camp-fire, about how she was not of the true gypsy blood, but was the only daughter of an important and wealthy landowner. Now Edward Wyman, her father and the powerful squire of Bessington Hall, had passed on – leaving behind him a will that left his surviving wife, Kathleen, and daughter, Starlena, an immense fortune. The talk was that although the son, Master Redford Wyman, was bequeathed a handsome legacy, he was rendered a pauper in comparison.

'Aw, Anselo . . . will you not put her out of your heart?' Celia pleaded, 'She's not our kind. I've known it all along. That one was allus different . . . never fitted in. Now, she's back where she belongs. Out of our lives for good, don't you see that? She's a rich and powerful lady, Anselo, and not meant to stoop to the likes of us. Oh, Anselo, don't waste your life pining for some'at that can never be yours. *I'm* the one as loves you. I've loved you all my life and I'll go on loving you, Anselo.'

Celia rose from her place by the camp-fire where, for the past hour, she had used every means at her disposal to persuade Anselo that in his obsession with Starlena he was fighting a losing battle. Now, she threaded her way towards where he sat on a tree-stump by the edge of the spinney, six or seven yards from the fire, his head slightly bowed and the handsome dark eyes flashing in the light from the flickering flames. His arms were crossed loosely on his wide apart knees and in his face was a look of absolute despair. He loved Starlena now as much as he'd ever loved her! Her black eyes, that glorious mantle of raven-coloured curls, her slim perfect figure and that wonderfully captivating smile that could bring sunshine on a dull day, were all embedded too deep in his memory and in his heart for him ever to forget. On cold lonely nights he had grown warm and alive in the magic of that night at the lake. That wonderful, unforgettable night, when he had taken her wet and naked body in his arms, when he had carried her gently to the bank and there, beneath the quiet moon, they had made love. Such glorious love before which everything paled into insignificance. On that magical night when he had taken Starlena's virgin innocence, he had come alive – for the first time he knew the true meaning of love in all its completeness. In that moment, Starlena had entered his heart. She had captured it for all time. And ever since he had been powerless against the fury and depth of his longing for her. Now he felt that she would never be his! For she had discovered her true heritage. She was no gypsy, but a woman whose veins were flowing with the blue blood of aristocracy. A woman who was now wealthy beyond her dreams. A woman whose vivacity and great beauty would ensure that she was never without the company of rich and eligible bachelors – one of whom she would no doubt wed. Celia was right! The idea of Starlena taking him, a vagabond gypsy, as her husband, *was* an impossibility. In fact, the more he thought about it, the more laughable it became to him. And because of it, Anselo had never before known such heartache.

Now, as Celia came to kneel beside him, Anselo was made to

372

look on her as she pleaded, 'Forget her. Marry *me*, Anselo, for I'll be a good and loving wife and I'll give you many sons. Oh, will you not see how you're punishing yourself? Will you *never* see?'

In the glow from the fire her uplifted eyes shone richest hazel, her long loose brown hair fell attractively about her shoulders and in her face Anselo saw such passion, such aching love, that just for the briefest moment his own painful heart was at one with hers. It was strange, he thought, how very much she had changed over the years. At one time she had pursued him with a vengeance which almost frightened him. There had been an intense and terrifying jealousy in her heart, which at times seemed almost evil. But since losing Jemm who had been like a father to her, she had become less threatening in her love. She, like him, had suffered terrible loneliness. She, like him, was besotted with a hopeless love and his heart went out to her because of it. For he knew that in spite of her mellowing attitude, her love was stronger now than it had ever been. Like his love for Starlena, the first fury was spent. It had burst in a great explosion of emotion, to settle more gently and more deeply into every corner of their being.

'Do you think I don't know how you feel, Celia?' he asked, gently stroking her hair, 'Oh, I know. I *do* know.'

'Is there hope for us, then?' she asked, her old hatred of Starlena having been tempered by the passage of time and by her deep love for Anselo. She knew now that whether or not Anselo would ever be hers would not rest on Starlena being alive or dead – but, on Anselo himself. Only he could make that decision.

For now, in answer to her question, 'Is there hope for us?' he simply murmured, 'Is there a God above?'

As they sat there, in the fading light from the fire embers – she at his feet and he with a comforting arm about her, Anselo felt no peace in his heart. He knew he must seek out Starlena, for there would be no peace till then. But he must wait a while first. Starlena must be allowed to savour the fruits of her inheritance and her new identity. Only then would she be able to assess its true value. But he and his love would never be far away.

373

Chapter Twenty-four

'What's taking so bloody long, man!' Redford Wyman glared furiously at the diminutive and somewhat nervous Mr Sanders. This poor unfortunate appointed legal representative of his late father had arrived at Bessington Hall on a certain errand which he had rightly anticipated would sink him even deeper in Redford Wyman's disfavour. In desperation, he cast an appealing look in Starlena's direction – hopeful that perhaps she might encourage her rather aggressive brother into a sweeter disposition.

'Dealing with such a vast and complex estate as your late father's takes time, Miss Wyman . . .'

'Parrish!' Starlena corrected, 'Miss Parrish, if you please.'

'Oh, of course. Yes! Miss . . . er . . . Parrish.' The little man could feel Redford Wyman's one eye burning into him – so much so that it was more than he could bring himself to look into it even one more time. With the beads of perspiration glistening on his forehead, he went on, 'Tax . . . duties . . . probate, it all takes a deal of time, I'm afraid. Of course, in the meantime, all three of you are receiving a handsome allowance. If it is not enough, then please say so. When everything is settled, your father's wishes will be swiftly executed . . . his entire estate divided equally between the three immediate members of his surviving family . . .'

'Yes! Yes!' Redford Wyman stamped his heels into the carpet, leaning forward from where he had been lolling against the fireplace and throwing his two arms up in despair, he thundered, 'We know all that, damn and bugger it! What I'm saying is, get the business

374

concluded! And since you mention it, the allowance I've been afforded is a bloody pittance!'

At this, both Mr Sanders and Starlena threw him a disdainful glance.

'A man of my standing has overheads . . . commitments. Look here! If you can't handle this business, then perhaps my father was misguided in his choice . . .'

To a conscientious man who took great pride in his professional expertise, the very suggestion was an outrage. 'If you don't mind my saying so, Mr Wyman,' Mr Sanders pointed out with surprising vigour, 'my family has dealt with matters of probate for many generations. And I might also venture to add that, although your father's estate is exceedingly large and therefore complex, it is not the largest to be handled by the firm of Sanders and Sanders.' His whole manner was most indignant and his shrimp-like features had grown quite purple. Not able to handle it! Why! The very idea! 'If you care to make arrangements to call at the office, the matter of increasing your allowance will most certainly be looked at.' He turned to Starlena, 'The same will of course apply to you, too.'

'Thank you kindly, Mr Sanders, but there is absolutely no necessity . . . not as far as I'm concerned.' As it was, she had barely touched the money, save for the small amount pressed on her by Miss Elizabeth, and which she had given straight to her mammy. The only other indulgence she had submitted to was the charging of clothes – chosen on the two occasions when she and Miss Elizabeth had gone into nearby Manchester to acquire certain necessities for little Ronalda.

'Well, if you reconsider, please let me know,' Mr Sanders reminded her. He had taken a liking to *this* Wyman offspring. He knew the full story concerning the circumstances surrounding her birth and upbringing and he had come to a conclusion regarding this beautiful and considerate creature. If he had to choose the better-bred between her and her obnoxious brother, he would not hesitate in choosing Starlena, for he was never a gentleman – while she was every inch a lady. He had not been surprised when Redford Wyman had complained of his most generous allowance, seeing that it had gone almost as soon as he received it. On the other hand, Wyman's daughter had hardly scraped at her allowance. Indeed, it seemed of little importance at all to her. And Kathleen Wyman's allowance was untouched. But then, considering the circumstances of her failing health, that was understandable. All the same, she was a fortunate woman indeed to have such a loving and compassionate daughter in attendance. The two of them were no doubt making up for lost time. It gave Mr Sanders a little squirm of pleasure to see Redford Wyman disgruntled. What with his mother due one third of the estate and his sister another – that left him with his one third less say in matters of the Wyman estate than he would no doubt have preferred. This brought him to the issue at hand and which now, after Redford Wyman's outburst, he would present with relish.

'I can assure you, Mr Wyman, everything is proceeding most satisfactorily.' He patted the briefcase on his knee and got to his feet. 'I have the signatures I came for, and now, if you're ready, I would like to introduce Mr Fairley to you. He is the newly appointed manager, in accordance with your father's will. As your father was advised, Mr Fairley comes with the highest recommendations and has proven experience in all aspects of running an estate of this size.'

'Oh! He *has*, has he?' Redford Wyman smirked, 'then by all means, introduce the fellow to Miss *Parrish* here!' He took delight in labouring the pronunciation of Starlena's name. After which he stormed towards the door and out of the room, calling behind him, 'I have better things to do!'

Starlena took an instant liking to Mr Fairley. He was a kindly-faced man of medium build and quick intelligence, who, as Mr Sanders had claimed, did seem to know what he was about. Starlena was grateful for his appointment – which would have been sooner had he been immediately available. Little as she knew about matters relating to this estate, she had been quick to notice Redford Wyman's lack of attention to it. The constant rows between him and the foreman had become painfully evident to everyone who lived and worked on the estate. There had been problems relating to the animal husbandry, the dairy herd – which ran into hundreds – the maintenance and replacement of machinery, together with the programme of crop-rotation and forestry matters. It seemed that nothing had run smoothly since Edward Wyman's demise. Ill as he had been, matters of the estate were supervised from his sick-bed for as long as he had been able; thereafter left to the sorry hand of his son. To the end, Edward Wyman was no fool. He had seen the need for putting a general manager in and had written the clause into his last will and testament, the situation to be closely monitored by the appointed executors.

Some short time later, Redford Wyman saddled up his prize stallion – a dark beast with equally dark temper. Coming out of the courtyard at a gallop, he almost careered into the little group emerging from the house. Cursing loudly, he dug his heels hard into the horse's underbelly and sent it away at furious pace towards the open end of the woods.

'Dangerous fool!' muttered Mr Sanders, kicking away the loose gravel which the horse's hooves had sprayed up onto his shoes. The young maid – a regular and willing bedmate of the master – gave herself up to a fit of giggling, which could have been prompted by the fright she had just received, or possibly by a particularly vivid image of the master stripped bare of his clothes and playing games with her, as on the previous evening. Whatever the reason, her spurt of giggling was abruptly stopped by a direct and disapproving look from Mr Fairley.

'Shall we proceed to the lodge house?' he asked with stressed politeness. 'The sooner I'm settled in, the quicker I can get started.' As he moved on, his eyes were following the swiftly disappearing figure of Redford Wyman. The solicitor had called that one a 'dangerous fool' and he had to agree most fervently. Although something warned him that Redford Wyman was no 'fool'. Dangerous, certainly, a man to be wary of, should you find yourself on his wrong side. But, fool? He didn't think so.

Once out into open countryside, Redford Wyman drove his mount on like a demon possessed. 'Bastards! The lot of them!' he yelled into the wind. 'They'll all be sorry!' His father's will had revealed too many shocks for him to take with any degree of graciousness. He had suspected that his mother and sister would be restored to favour . . . that much had come as no surprise. No! What had been the real shock was the extent to which his father had compensated them in his dying remorse. How dare he put those two women on equal footing with himself? More so, because between them, they held the upper hand. He had been frustrated in his attempts to dispute Starlena's true identity. There had been the shawl – unmistakably the one that had belonged to his grandmother, Kathleen's own mother. Then, the word by word correlation by Edward Wyman of the old gypsy's story. And, most damning of all, the uncanny likeness of Starlena to Kathleen Wyman. Then, adding insult to injury, the old bugger had directed that the third of his estate bequeathed to his son would be forfeited unless he not only agreed to the appointment of a general manager and the close monitoring of the estate-management by the legal executors, but he must also be seen to be working amicably with them.

'Bastards!' he screamed, kicking the horse on faster and faster, until both horse and rider were covered in a film of sweat, gasping for breath and their fury spent. Redford Wyman reined him in to drink by the brook's edge. Swinging to the grass, he lay down to scoop his hands into the water. Then, flinging the pool of wet cool liquid over his face, he scrambled to his feet, slapped the horse's neck in a rough gesture of affection and, throwing back his head he roared with laughter.

When he climbed back into the saddle, his face was a picture of deep cunning. 'First the sister and the brat!' he murmured. 'With the other one already three-quarters of the way to her grave, the rest will be all downhill. Redford Wyman to be beaten by two women and an old man's will? I think not!'

It was all planned . . . had been for months now. Tomorrow was the first step. Tomorrow, at the shoot. Here he gave out another laugh and, slapping the horse's neck again, he addressed it with some humour, 'Tut! Tut! Isn't it just dreadful, the easy manner in which accidents do happen at a shoot?' This time tomorrow night, he thought desperately, he would be well on his way to taking back what was his. His once handsome features crooked themselves into a devious grin. The old fool had slipped up but once in the making of his will. In the last paragraph he had stated that, should his wife be the first to die, her share must revert to his daughter – and vice versa. Of the remaining two, the last survivor was to inherit all. Redford Wyman was in no doubt that he would be the 'last survivor'. He was anticipating the prospect with great relish.

'Are you content here, Mammy?' Starlena looked up from the mat, where she was playing with the laughing child.

Rona smiled down on her from the wooden rocking-chair where, in the cosy glow from the fire, her old lined face shone a warm shade of pink. For a moment she gave no answer, letting her brown gaze wander over Starlena and little Ronalda, now seven months old and every bit as darkly handsome as her mammy. Starlena looked wonderful in a dark blue dress of soft woollen material, with a plain high neck, long close-fitting sleeves and flared skirt which fell to just below the knees, revealing her long exquisitely shaped legs. Her shoes were black patent, with a small square heel and crossed over at the ankle with a dainty buttoned bar. Her magnificent hair cascaded over her shoulders, so long that it brushed against the mat, and now, as she waited for an answer, her opaque eyes were stunningly beautiful in the firelight's glow.

Rona, thinking she had never seen her darling Starlena look more lovely, gave the answer always in her faithful heart, 'I'm content wherever I am lass . . . so long as we're all together an' safe from 'arm.' Bending carefully and with a little groan, she chucked the baby under the chin, laughing out loud when it began gurgling and giggling. 'And you, lass?' she asked, easing her bones back into the safety of the chair and re-arranging the shawl which had slipped from her shoulders, 'are you content?'

'No, Mammy!' came back the forthright answer, 'I'm not content.' How could she be? Over the past few months so many things had happened to pull her in so many different directions. It had been a very strange and revealing period of time, when by the very circumstances which had first delivered her to Bessington Hall and thereafter kept her there, she had been forced to find in herself the greatest strength. Not only had she had to adapt to the fact that she was not a gypsy but a lady and as such held title to riches beyond her most fanciful dreams, but there had come into her life new faces, new names and new expectations – so many strange values, standards and avenues down which she might be drawn, never to return. There were times, oh so often of late, when she felt deeply afraid – in danger of being cheated out of all that she held dear. Far from gaining a whole new identity, Starlena felt she could too easily lose that identity which was the very essence of herself.

To a certain extent, she had gone along with Miss Elizabeth's teachings. She had improved her reading and writing – pastimes which Starlena greatly loved. She had learned how to sit patiently at a dining-table, while po-faced and stiff little figures waited on her. She had known the luxury of never being hungry, of bathing in hot soapy water followed by lazy pampering, when the huge white towels were soft as silk against her skin, and afterwards there were always evocative perfumes which made her giddy from the scent. She had her pick of no less than eight of the fastest and finest thoroughbreds ever to grace a stable. Miss Elizabeth had taken her on exciting shopping sprees – the results of which were arrayed in a wardrobe bigger than her mammy's old wagon; clothes to cover every occasion from riding to sleeping, every shape, style and colour – each and every one having cost a small fortune.

The deeper she had been immersed in this new and privileged lifestyle, the more Starlena found herself confused and afraid. Often, when lying awake at night, she would ask herself why it was that fate had taught her the free and wandering ways of a gypsy then, when she craved no other life, wilfully uprooted her and cruelly plunged her into the wealthy aristocratic values once denied her. The conflict wrought within her was such that often she would cry herself to sleep. At other times, when a mood of great anger and longing for the gypsy way came over her, she would wander away to sit alone in the woods, with only the moon above for company. Here, she would contrast one existence with another. What did it matter if she could bathe in hot soapy water, when the cool sweet waters of a moonlit lake overhung with heady-perfumed flowers were far more romantic and invigorating. And how could a silk-soft towel compare to the warm whispering embrace of a gentle breeze against your skin? To gather the harvest of nature, prepare it yourself and barbecue it over an open fire – was this not far more enjoyable than sitting upright to attention at a long lonely table where, scrutinized by Redford Wyman's one unnerving eye, you stayed, most uncomfortable and conspicuous, to be served by people who had no love of such work, and who made no bones about their resentment of it. And oh! to rear a horse in the wild, to feel at one with its free and bold spirit was surely one of God's most precious gifts. Gypsy horses were like in nature to gypsies themselves. They disliked pens, stables and a strict regime of routine. They lived for the endless, winding open roads, along which they could meander without hurry, without purpose, without being fettered by sense of destination.

Starlena never stopped questioning and as yet she had not discovered any answers to satisfy her – only more questions. What did a gypsy need with fancy clothes which must be changed for every event? What use were silken sheets when hung out to dry on a bramble-hedge? As long as there was kindling from the woods, with which to keep a body warm, as long as there was water in a brook to quench a body's thirst and, as long as Nature kept on supplying its plentiful source of food, there wasn't a life more satisfying or fulfilling than that of a gypsy. All of these things and more Starlena pondered on, yet still she was left in a great dilemma – all the more frustrating because it was not of her own making. Whether lady or gypsy, Starlena was first and foremost a woman. It was the unique feminine instincts that were being tortured and torn apart. And other instincts even more powerful were being brought into play – the instincts of a mother. For it was not only herself who must be considered here. There was little Ronalda, grand-daughter of Edward Wyman and therefore an intricate part of the heritage he left behind. Of all the different facets of Starlena's dilemma, this was the greatest. Choosing for herself would not be easy, she knew. But making the choice for another still unable to make her own decision would be that much harder. Were she to make the wrong choice, there might come a day when her own daughter would turn against her because of it. Oh, Starlena agonized, if ever she needed God's help, it would be when Kathleen, her mother, was released from this earth. Beyond that, she dared not think.

'Starlena, lass . . . it's miles away yer are!' Her mammy's voice broke into Starlena's thoughts, 'I asked, if yer not content, lass . . . then, what's to be done about it?'

There was no need to think on her answer, for hadn't she mulled the very same question over, time and time again? 'There's really nothing to be done about it yet awhile, Mammy,' she murmured, her great eyes staring absent-mindedly into the fire, 'Only do what I promised Kathleen . . . keep the baby close to her, and watch over them both.'

'Yer a good, warm-hearted creature,' smiled Rona, herself feeling more content than she had done for a long time. There was no more need of running, she'd promised herself. At last she could rest her weary old bones and draw breath more easily. She had been long convinced that it was Edward Wyman who, before his change of heart, had sought to kill Starlena. Now, with him gone, somehow that persistent fear in her heart had gone with him. Yet Rona was no fool and she was not blind. It was plain to see that Starlena's battle was still going on deep inside her. The lass had said nothing, but Rona knew that very soon there was a choice to be made – perhaps the greatest test of her true loyalties that Starlena would ever be called on to make. For her and the babby *both*! There was no question in Rona's heart but that when the time came, she would stand by the lass, whatever she made up her mind to do. Because, there were many things on God's lovely earth which she passionately loved. But none as much as she loved Starlena. And there wasn't a night which passed when she didn't pray to the Lord to give the lass strength and to help her to do the wisest thing.

'How's Kathleen been today, lass?' she asked. Only once since they had arrived here had she set eyes on Starlena's real mother. On that one occasion, seeing Rona strolling towards the woods with little Ronalda in her arms and Starlena alongside, Kathleen

382

had been watching from her sick-room. It was only afterwards that the nurse had told Starlena how, on seeing a shawled gypsy with the child clasped in her arms, she had become most agitated at the sight, protesting that 'the gypsy's taking my baby!' Eventually, the nurse had quietened her down and got her back to bed, where she slept a fitful sleep – waking with a demand to have her baby brought to her. Only then did she become content. Since that day, Rona had been sure to stay well out of sight.

'She knows me, lass,' she told Starlena, a measure of guilt in her voice. 'She remembers that night when I made off with you, Lord 'elp us!' And, in the face of Kathleen Wyman's ongoing suffering, both she and Starlena were more resolved to do what they must, in order to make her last few months a time of joy. Starlena was glad that little Ronalda was not answerable to two names, for Starlena called her only 'my baby' – as though in uttering those words, she gave herself a great deal of comfort.

'The doctor came to see her this afternoon,' Starlena told Rona quietly.

'Aye? An' what did 'e 'ave ter say?'

'That she was an amazing woman. That he was astonished at how she kept going – her whole constitution was weaker, her mind failing and her heart giving out all the time.'

'Hmh . . . well, none o' that's surprisin' is it? Not when yer 'ave ter consider what the wretched woman's been through. A lesser woman would 'a gone under *years* back!'

In a quiet voice, Starlena murmured, 'Why is it people have to be so cruel to each other, Mammy?' Rona knew she was thinking of her late father, Edward Wyman – a man she had never forgiven for his part in this tragedy. A man whose funeral she had adamantly refused to attend. And, if Rona knew Starlena – and she did, like the back of her hand – a man whose inheritance she would never touch.

'All manner o' things can mek a body turn cruel, lass. The two most known reasons being love and hatred, an', often, when the two o' them go hand in hand, well . . . they mek a powerful persuasion on a body, that's fer sure!'

'What do you think of Redford?' Starlena asked. She had stayed as far away from him as possible, for in spite of his bursts of outward charm and consideration, there was something about him that gave her the shivers. And it wasn't just that piercing dark blue eye of his – although inwardly she shrank from it, more so when it was smiling. No! There was something else. Something hidden beneath the surface of his 'brotherly' affection, which had the effect of putting her on her guard. Also – to her knowledge at least – he had not yet paid a visit to his mother's sick-room. That in itself had set her wondering about him.

'I ain't seen the fellow but twice,' replied Rona, recalling the image in her mind, 'once stridin' towards the stables, an' the other time when 'e were tearin' the men off a strip by the far fence.' Here she stroked a finger over her chin, her brown eyes thoughtful. 'Can't say 'e seems a pleasant fella . . . surly an' bad-tempered if yer ask me. But y'know, lass . . . I've a strange feelin' as I've clapped eyes on that one afore. Oh, 'appen I'm imagining it. Me ol' memory ain't what it was, d'you see.' She gave a little laugh, 'You don't care fer the fella, do yer, eh? Well, if yer not inclined, lass . . . brother or no brother, yer 'ave no need ter 'ave owt at all ter do wi' 'im.' She suddenly gave a long yawn, 'Hmh! Seems I'm ready fer me bed earlier an' earlier these days!'

Starlena had not noticed how late it was becoming. The little clock on the mantelpiece told her that it was way past Ronalda's bedtime, although judging by the way she crawled and explored across the floor, there seemed little sleep in her. 'I'll be away to the house, Mammy,' she told Rona, getting to her feet and gathering the child in her arms, 'I'll look in on Kathleen . . . then I'll put the baby to bed. Goodnight, Mammy.' She bent to kiss the upturned face.

'Goodnight, God bless the pair on yer,' Rona replied, rising from the chair. At the door, she reminded Starlena, 'Yer sure yer don't mind me not comin' on our usual little jaunt in the mornin'?' When Starlena reassured her, she went on, ''Tain't so bad when it's warm, lass . . . but 'tis gettin' a bit sharpish o' late, an' me ol' bones 'ave a tendency to seize up.' She gave a laugh. 'D'yer see

384

'ow livin' atween four walls an' being pampered meks a gypsy soft, eh?'

'Away with you!' retorted Starlena with good humour. In a more serious tone she asked, for the umpteenth time, 'Will you change your mind, now the winter's not far away, Mammy? Will you move into the big house with me and little Ronalda?'

'I will not! I've bent as far as ever I'm goin' to . . . oh, look 'ere, lass. I know you've no choice at the minute, what wi' Kathleen wakin' in the night an' sneakin' into yer room for a peek at the babby . . . an' I know ye'd rather be 'ere wi' me, than in that gurt dark place, but I'm only a few steps away, an' nowt's spoilin' fer the time being, is it? Eh? . . . eh?' She dug Starlena playfully, her brown eyes reaching up to meet Starlena's shadowed gaze with an encouraging smile.

'You're a wise old mammy and no mistake,' Starlena laughed, going out of the door and quickly making her way back to the house before the darkness got too thick.

''Ere! You mustn't forget there'll be fellers prowlin' about in them woods wi' shotguns the morrer!' called Rona.

'I've not forgotten!' returned Starlena. 'Anyway . . . they'll be way off towards Dinglers Dell by the time me and Ronalda show our faces.' Just like her mammy to find something to worry about, smiled Starlena to herself.

Some time later, after she had satisfied herself that Kathleen was sleeping peacefully and little Ronalda was also deep in slumber, Starlena made her way down the great staircase. Her intention was to settle herself in the library where she might browse through the book-shelves and maybe pick up one of those red leather-bound volumes which Miss Elizabeth had taken down on one of her frequent visits some days ago. It was a book of sonnets by a man called William Shakespeare. There was one which Miss Elizabeth had read to her and it had affected Starlena greatly. Now she was in the mood to read it for herself, in privacy, where she might dwell on those beautiful words a while longer.

The library itself gave Starlena little pleasure, for here she sensed that Edward Wyman, her late father, must have spent many a long hour. It was a square room, large and high-ceilinged. Every wall was lined with shelf upon shelf of books, bound mostly in leather of many colours, the predominant colour being brown with exquisite gold lettering to the front and spine. At one end of the room were two windows, some fifteen feet high and made up of tiny little panes, through which, in the daytime, could be seen a fragmented view of the gardens beyond. Situated towards the centre of the room was a highly-polished desk of gigantic proportions and pulled up to it was a deep-buttoned chair of finest leather. By the fireplace, in which still glowed a cheery fire, there were positioned two comfortable armchairs, of plum-coloured leather.

Going straight to the shelf where she had seen the book replaced and quickly locating it, Starlena came to the fireplace. She sat in one of the chairs, with its front towards the windows and its back to the door. And, turning to the page where Miss Elizabeth had left a blue embroidered marker, she settled back into the chair and proceeded to whisper the words aloud. She was always grateful to Miss Elizabeth for having taught her to read, among many other things.

When in disgrace with Fortune and men's eyes,
I all alone beweep my outcast state,
And trouble deaf heaven with my bootless cries,
And look upon myself, and curse my fate,
Wishing me like to one more rich in hope,
Featur'd like him, like him with friends possess'd,
Desiring this man's art, and that man's scope,
With what I most enjoy contented least;
yet in these thoughts myself almost despising,
Haply I think on thee, and then my state,
Like to the lark at break of day arising
From sullen earth, sings hymns at heaven's gate;
For thy sweet love rememb'red such wealth brings
That then I scorn to change my state with kings.

Starlena closed her eyes and dwelt on the sonnet's meaning, keeping the book open on her lap, the very touch of it giving her comfort. Miss Elizabeth had gone to great pains to explain how she saw the meaning of the words and now, having read them and savoured them herself, Starlena also came to know what it was the poet was saying. She marvelled at the profound and romantic nature of such a man. The words were truly beautiful – telling as they did of a soul's craving to experience the material riches of life and to have as many friends as his neighbour possessed. It spoke of the beginnings of dissatisfaction and greed, of coveting that which belonged to others, despising yourself because of it, yet not being able to resist such temptations. It spoke of all those intolerable and crippling emotions. Then, rising above it all, came a stronger, more worthwhile and lasting emotion – that of the love between two people. And it mattered not whether you were rich or poor. To have everything in the whole world at your fingertips, yet to be without the love and affection of another, was the true loneliness – the real deprivation of any human being.

How strange that these exquisite words should echo her very own sentiments exactly, thought Starlena. She had also been curious about the ways and means by which she might live the life of a lady. She had been foolishly mesmerized by their grand carriages and fancy clothes. Yet, when at first hand, and through matters always beyond her control, she had come to experience these things, they had left her dissatisfied.

A feeling of weariness suddenly washed over Starlena as, sinking deeper into the chair, she murmured again one particular line which stood out in her mind – 'For thy sweet love rememb'red such wealth brings'. With the words came an overwhelming sensation of loneliness and longing, bringing also the clear tormenting images of two men – Anselo and Jackson. If she *had* known 'love', then it was because of these two. Each, in his own special way, meant a great deal to her. Oh, but this was no time for remembering long lost loves, Starlena sharply reminded herself. She had other matters playing on her mind. But she could not forget a particular stud farm near Boston, America. Oh, how very happy she and her mammy had been there – what a sanctuary that wonderful place had been! Starlena didn't fool herself that she might not have been half as happy there, had it not been for Jackson Grand. How very strong was his presence in her mind – that slow deliberate voice and those thrilling dark green eyes, which struck at her very being whenever they gazed on her. And how could she not recall time and time again in her deepest loneliest hours, that one time during Danny's illness when he had kissed her so deliciously? Her heart had been laid bare to Jackson whom she still loved most deeply. Yet Starlena knew that he had made the only choice he could. In his position she would have done the very same. Jackson had been strong then. *She* must go on being strong in her determination to forget him and what might have been.

Anselo was another who often crept into her most private thoughts. There was a great deal of affection in her heart for that laughing, handsome gypsy. She had been sorry when her mammy told her of Jemm's passing for she knew how much Anselo loved his father. Now there was only him to care for Celia, his adopted sister. Starlena knew – expected even – that the two of them might by now have wed. That would be good for them both she thought; Jemm's passing would bring them closer. Such things always did. If the two of them found solace and love in each other, that was a wonderful thing she told herself. Why did the thought give her small comfort?

'My! My! Sleeping Beauty!' The harsh intruding voice gave Starlena a fright, it was so close behind her. In an instant she sat bolt upright in the chair, her dark eyes following Redford Wyman as he strolled round to confront her. 'Skulking in dark little corners, is it?' he teased, at the same time plucking the book from her lap. Opening it wider at the page she had been reading, he swiftly scanned the verse. 'Shakespeare, indeed!' he grinned, withholding the book from Starlena and, in a most unnerving fashion, raking her from head to toe with his one blue eye.

'Hmh! Elizabeth Judd taught you well.' Now his lips were drawn tight across his white even teeth as he continued to stare down at her, 'Tell me, Starlena. Do you have the true instincts of a lady? Or are you even more of a gypsy than the old one in the cottage?'

There was no mistaking the arrogance in his voice. It was there also in the bold upright stance of his thick sturdy body and the wide-apart positioning of his booted legs. In the firelight's glow he made a peculiarly handsome yet grotesque figure – the one side of his face bearing a crimson eye-patch beneath which could be seen the top and tail of a sore and jagged scar. On the other side of his face – the side most eerily illuminated by the fire's flickering light – the features had an aristocratic bearing, the one deadly yet beautiful eye sparkling in brilliant facets of first deep sapphire then coal black. Suddenly, Starlena became acutely aware of how sinister dark was the night beyond the windows and how in the room's dim light Redford Wyman's presence seemed almost to suffocate her.

But Starlena knew his little game and would not be intimidated. She remembered the old adage, 'The best form of defence is attack'. So, bringing her loveliest smile to bear on him, she replied, 'First, explain two things. What do you see as being the "true instincts of a lady"? Then, tell me, Redford, do you consider yourself to be a gentleman?'

The sly half-smile never left his face, while Starlena continued to look up at him in readiness for his answers. The answers were not given, for at that moment there came a knock on the door. Upon Redford Wyman's authoritative instruction, 'Come!' the bustling figure of the housekeeper swept in, carrying a small silver tray laden with coffee pot, sugar and milk jug – all in exquisite Georgian silver – and the daintiest blue china cup and saucer.

'Oh!' she gasped, laying the tray on the desk and catching sight of Starlena. Quickly switching her gaze from Starlena to Redford Wyman, she asked with seeming embarrassment, 'Shall I fetch another cup, sir?'

Not surprised that the woman had addressed her brother rather than her, Starlena stood up, saying, 'Don't bother on my account. I'm about to go to my bed.'

The housekeeper still did not look at Starlena. Instead, she nodded subserviently to Redford Wyman, 'Thank you, sir. Goodnight,' making a hurried exit from the room.

Redford Wyman smiled with some satisfaction at Starlena. 'I don't suppose you fancy a small brandy?'

'I would not,' returned Starlena, reaching out to take the book from his hands, 'I'll take this, though.' Then, in a superior voice which caused his smile to deepen, 'perhaps I'll enjoy it more in private in my bedroom!' Starlena flinched as he took a determined step towards her, but she kept her hand stretched out to receive the book, her black eyes raised in defiance. When he gripped hold of her hand and bent his head closer to her face, saying, 'Wouldn't you rather enjoy me more privately … in your bedroom?' she kept her eyes fixed on that one piercing light in his devious features and, drawing back her free hand, she brought it against his face in a resounding slap, which caught him off-guard and sent him off his balance. When the book fell to the floor Starlena made no effort to retrieve it. Instead she swung away, telling him in a low furious voice, 'If that's the wrong way for a lady to react . . . then, forgive me if I make no apologies for the gypsy in me!'

All the way up the stairs, Starlena was inwardly seething. Her mammy's instincts about that one were true enough, she thought. From now on, he would see even less of her than before.

Lying in bed a while later, Starlena mulled over the events of the evening more closely, reflecting on not only Redford Wyman's obnoxious character, but also the behaviour of the housekeeper, whose attitude was well in keeping with that of the rest of the staff at Bessington Hall. Yet Starlena bore them no ill-feeling. She could understand their embarrassment – and even disapproval – of her. After all, they no doubt saw her as being on an even lower social level than themselves. If it was hard for *her* to accept and adapt to the situation, then how much harder it must be for them. She might be a Wyman by birth and consequently a mistress of this household – but by nature, upbringing, and by heart, Starlena was a gypsy.

Just before she closed her eyes, Starlena was alerted by a movement at the door which joined this room to her mother Kathleen's. Hitching herself up on one elbow, Starlena recognized the painfully slim figure as it came into the room on slow careful steps, the cream silk nightgown shimmering in the moonlight. There was a gentle breeze coming in also through the windows, for Starlena could never sleep unless the curtains were drawn right back and the window partly open.

The sight of Kathleen creeping into the room after dark was a familiar one to Starlena. Her own sixth sense always alerted her to it. She watched now, her heart filled with compassion, as her mother tiptoed to little Ronalda's cot – here, to reach her hand inside and, with a gentle lullaby on her lips, to stroke the infant's dark sleeping head. It was at times like these that Starlena thanked the Lord for allowing her to bring that gentle tortured soul a measure of contentment and love in her failing years. And though her own love for her Mammy Parrish was as fierce and devoted as it ever had been, Starlena felt also a deep and loyal love for her true mother. Kathleen Wyman was one of nature's tragic victims, as she herself was, and Starlena felt a close kindred spirit to her. It made her shudder whenever she thought back to Kingston Asylum and to the agonies her mother must have endured all those terrible wasted years. Now, as her dark quiet gaze followed Kathleen from the room, Starlena gave up a little prayer to God. Then, on seeing the joy on her mother's face as the door was gently closed, she knew in her heart of hearts that her purpose here at Bessington Hall was, without doubt, the right and only one. She fell asleep with a degree of contentment in her heart.

Downstairs, Redford Wyman smashed the empty brandy bottle into the fireplace, his face twisted with rage. 'Bitch!' he murmured, over and over again, 'Gypsy bloody bitch!' After a while, he fell back into the depths of the armchair where less than an hour before Starlena had been. Suddenly he began writhing about, his two hands caressing the chair arms and on his face the beginnings of excited rapture. With his one eye closed and a faint groaning issuing from his trembling, open mouth, his movements grew greatly agitated. Until suddenly his eye opened with a secret smile. After some considerable effort he struggled to his feet, then with unsteady gait, he left the room. Once outside he leaned against the wall, his wide open eye looking beyond the great staircase to the narrow door which led to the servants' sleeping quarters. Giving a devious chuckle, he set off on that particular path which he had followed many times before.

As he fumbled his way along, two thoughts were uppermost in his befuddled mind. One being that his craving must be satisfied, and quickly! The other was the morning's shoot, for which he must be sure to rise early. 'Have to be ready . . . and waiting!' he snarled under his breath. Then, gingerly touching his fingers against that part of his face which still stung, he added vehemently, 'Oh, yes! I'll be waiting all right dearest sister, for both you and your gypsy brat!'

There was always tremendous bustle and excitement at Bessington Hall whenever a shoot was on. The gamekeepers were always the first away – making ready to release the pheasants, so lovingly cared for in previous months. In the first light, the sound of hunters arriving – some on foot, others on horseback and those from farther afield in noisy, grandly polished motor-vehicles – signalled the whole household to be on their toes. In no time at all they were warmed by a measure of brandy or port and their silver hip-flasks were duly refilled to arm them against the long cold hours when they tracked their prey. Finally, looking resplendent in their high boots and deerstalkers, with shotguns safely broken under their arms, off they would go – like a creeping wave, into the far woods, with the unmistakable figure of Redford Wyman leading the onslaught. On this particular morning he was especially keen to make a start, in spite of a powerful hangover which gave him an even sorer head than usual.

Starlena watched from the window of Kathleen's bedroom where, in the background, little Ronalda was giggling and squealing from the tickling she was enjoying. When the last of the figures had been swallowed up by the trees, Starlena turned her attention back to her mother and Ronalda. It was good to see them indulging in each other's company in that joyful way.

'Well, they've gone!' Starlena said, coming to sit on the edge of the bed.

'You don't like them out shooting, do you, Starlena?' Kathleen paused in her playing, as she looked deep into Starlena's troubled gaze, her own afraid and, as always, a little confused.

Starlena saw that she had disturbed Kathleen by looking so downcast. At once she took the woman's frail hand into her own and, in a warm strong voice, assured her, 'No! No! . . . It's all right, Kathleen. I was just interested to see them away, that's all.'

Kathleen was right. Starlena didn't like the idea of helpless birds being used as targets. Far from it being a sport for gentlemen, she saw it only as a barbaric and cruel activity. Her mammy had always said she thought more about the creatures' welfare than she did her own. But Starlena could not help her feelings on the matter. Out there in the wilds of nature a gypsy might be forgiven for catching an animal or two, that was a means by which they survived. Rearing birds, only to be shot down once released, was another thing altogether. It was just one more revelation which made her wonder about the 'civilized' behaviour of the rich and privileged.

Seemingly satisfied with Starlena's answer, Kathleen sank back into the pillows, her once-lovely features shadowed by weariness, her large dark eyes beginning to close as she murmured, 'I'll sleep awhile now. Mind my baby, won't you?'

'Don't you worry. Your baby will be here when you awake, Kathleen,' Starlena promised, collecting Ronalda into her arms. The nurse was at the door with Kathleen's breakfast tray. 'Will you have some breakfast before you sleep?' she asked but already Kathleen was slipping into her uneasy slumbers.

'Never mind. She'll be all the hungrier when she wakens,' smiled the nurse, her kindly features homely and pleasant as ever. She brought the tray into the room, picked up a slice of hot buttered toast and began nibbling at it – offering Starlena the remaining slice, with the remark, 'No use letting it go to waste. She won't want it cold, will she?'

Laughing, Starlena declined, thinking what a fortunate choice this dedicated nurse had been. 'That's just what Mammy Parrish is always saying . . . waste not want not!' she commented, going out of the door, 'I'll not be taking Ronalda quite so far this morning.

393

We can't go through the woods, so we'll take a gentle walk across the lawns and skirt the path alongside the brook. We should be back before Kathleen wakes,' she called behind her.

'Fair enough. But don't hurry yourself. It's a lovely morning and should bring a bit of colour to both your cheeks,' the nurse pointed out, between eagerly picking at the food on the tray.

It *was* a lovely morning. Indeed, as Starlena began pushing the perambulator along the drive, she thought the sun was exceptionally warm for November, although there was still a fresh nip in the air which made her glad of the warm fur-collared coat she was wearing. Ronalda too, was snuggled up against the fresh air, looking quite cheeky in a thick white jacket and matching bonnet, lovingly crocheted by Rona some few weeks back, and already beginning to look a size too small.

'You little scamp!' Starlena teased the infant, who loved these daily jaunts as much as she did. She was sitting up confidently in her straps, stretching her little neck every which way in order not to miss a thing. 'I swear you grow by the minute!' She laughed out loud, causing the infant to laugh also and to clap her hands together in glee. It was in moments like these that Starlena's joy knew no bounds.

She was so engrossed in her child that Starlena was blissfully unaware of the figure skulking just inside the woods ahead. Shotgun at the ready and carefully training his sights on her, the closer she came, Redford Wyman had considered his plan well. He must wait until she and the brat were at the point where his powerful shotgun would do the most damage, and where it would be most likely to seem like an unfortunate and tragic accident. He had doubled back from the main shoot and he would rejoin the party by the swiftest route and, upon the news of the 'accident', be even more surprised than they!

If Starlena was unaware of the skulking figure, there was another who was not. Kathleen Wyman had snoozed badly, being for some reason, particularly restless. When her patient had wakened with a raging thirst, the nurse had quickly taken herself off to the kitchen for a fresh breakfast and a pot of tea. In the few moments following the nurse's departure, Kathleen had got from the bed, moving on unsteady steps to the window where, just over an hour before, Starlena had watched the shooters disappear into the woods. Her attention was quickly caught by Starlena and the perambulator – a familiar sight and one which did not alarm her. If anything, such devotion to her baby moved her with love for Starlena, whom she believed to be a dear friend.

Kathleen longed for them to return, when she might take the child into her arms and hold it close to her. Now, something took the gentle smile from her face – a movement, a figure creeping about on the edge of the woods, his shotgun pointed at Starlena and the perambulator as they veered left almost out of sight. Kathleen gave a gasp, then a scream of terror as she glimpsed what seemed to be an eye-patch covering a large area of the man's face. Some incredible force deep within her surged into every corner of her being, as she stumbled from the room, crying out that he meant to harm her baby. 'No! I won't let him!' she sobbed, rushing headlong down the stairs. That man! She knew him! He was bad and he meant to harm her baby, she was convinced. Distorted images attacked her confused mind – images of a night with violence, terrible, terrible violence when a man was stabbed and another blinded. That was the man out there! The one who stalked her baby with a shotgun. That was he – the one blinded on that terrible night of violence.

Screaming for her baby, Kathleen ran onto the lawn. The nurse returning with the tray saw the delicate creature so frantic and unprotected against the sharp air and called out a warning to the servants busy in the other rooms. Then, clattering down the tray on the nearest surface, she too rushed from the house, still calling and afraid for that desperate creature, who, oblivious to her own plight, cried loudly for her baby as though she thought it in mortal danger.

Starlena stopped in her tracks on hearing the shouts and seeing Kathleen coming towards her dressed only in her flimsy nightgown, as though driven by some unseen terror.

Redford Wyman also heard and saw. And, afraid that he had been somehow detected, he went quickly into the woods and back to the shooting party – making all haste before he was seen by others.

Starlena had come within only eight feet of Kathleen when the exhausted woman sank to the ground. Leaving the perambulator, she went to gather her mother into her arms, a shock running through her as she felt the coldness of the thin frail figure against her. Quickly, she stripped the coat from her own back and, wrapping it about Kathleen, held her close until one of the manservants who had rushed to the spot collected the woman into his arms, saying quietly to Starlena, 'All right, miss. She'll be all right.'

But she was not. Some two hours later, attended by a doctor and the nurse who had grown fond of her, Kathleen Wyman left this world for what Starlena prayed was a better one. She had sat beside her mother during those two hours when she slipped further and further away, and when, in the last moments, Kathleen had taken Starlena's hand, to say in a soft and intimate voice, 'I love you,' Starlena had wept unashamedly. In those dark and wonderful eyes which gazed serenely into hers, she had seen the torment fall away and in its place had come such understanding that, just for a moment, Starlena thought her mother must have recognized her own daughter at last. It was a most humbling experience, a moment of glory filled with the most profound emotion. It was a moment of tender realization between two people – a moment which Starlena would never forget. Not as long as she lived.

Chapter Twenty-five

On the 20th of November 1920, Kathleen Wyman was laid to rest in a picturesque and sheltered spot beside her husband. The churchyard was one of Accrington's grandest and, besides the landed gentry who had come from far and wide to pay their respects, the pews were filled to overflowing with people motivated more by curiosity than reverence. The story of the wealthy Wyman breed had spread from one end of Lancashire to the other – its intriguing and fascinating details having infiltrated all levels of society, from the bars of the local ale house, to the corridors of greater power in the city of London. So the curious and the morbid were all drawn here today, alongside the genuine mourners and the immediate family.

Throughout the long service, Starlena had felt their eyes prodding and prying in her direction. Some tried to disguise their avid curiosity. Others were more blatant as they stretched their necks to stare at the two remaining Wymans – the surly-faced and authoritative son, Redford, and his mysterious and ravishingly beautiful sister – the one they called Starlena, the one who had been brought up as a gypsy by the old woman who now stood protectively close to her, a small stooped figure swathed from head to toe in a long black-fringed shawl, which showed only the hem of her long flowing skirt, her bright new boots and above, a tiny face, wizened with age and lighted by two shining brown eyes. Mostly the eyes were puzzled and staring across the church at one particular woman by the name of Freya Judd.

Starlena showed little sign of her gypsy upbringing, dressed as she was in an expensive black woollen coat with deep revers which reached down to the waist, there to be caught together by an enormous shiny bone button. At her neck was a fine dark scarf. Beneath the plain basin-shaped hat which came down to cover her ears and whose outwardly-turned brim framed the perfectly shaped face with its extravagantly beautiful eyes, the rich black hair was secured in tight upward coils, with only a wayward clutch of wispy curls escaping to flatter her face. She wore dark stockings and dainty black-strapped shoes, and altogether presented a most striking figure.

Anselo, learning of the demise of Starlena's mother, had come to the church with the idea of consoling her. When he saw her, looking so grand and prosperous, and surrounded by figures of apparent wealth and superiority, his courage deserted him. Starlena had come up in the world to be in such company; beside them he felt small and insignificant.

He wasn't to know that as he rode swiftly away on the gypsy cob, Starlena had caught sight of him and, her heart lifted by it, had run after him, calling his name and entreating him to return. Then, when he was gone, she returned to where her mammy was waiting, to be assured, 'Never fear, lass. 'E'll be back.'

Starlena hoped so, for in the back of her mind was Celia, the gypsy queen, and some deep instinct warned her against pursuing them. It must be Anselo who came to her.

The next day was bitter cold, with cloud-laden heavens which threatened to send the full weight of winter down any minute. There was a shrill wind which howled like demons through the trees and in amongst the chimneys. On such a day, Starlena found the most loving company in her mammy's cottage.

'She's at rest now,' Rona said, whenever she caught Starlena gazing out of the window in quiet mood.

'I know, Mammy,' Starlena replied, making a deliberate effort to focus her attention on little Ronalda, who was up to all manner of mischief. Saddened as she was by her mother's passing, it was over. That phase of her own life, also, was over and whether she was ready or not, the time had come when she must make that decision which had tortured her all these long months. Her mind was already half made up, but she needed just a few more days to make that important decision irrevocable.

'What else is ailin' yer, lass?' Rona sensed the deep despair in Starlena, and it bothered her so.

'Oh, it's all manner of things,' Starlena replied quietly. Recently her thoughts had dwelt long on Jackson Grand. She wondered how he was. Did he ever think of her? Was he happy? Was there love in his heart for her still? Or was she far from his mind? Of a sudden, and much to her surprise, Starlena found herself speaking out loud of her innermost feelings.

'Don't you ever think of America . . . and Grand Farm?' she asked. And if she thought that wise old woman would be surprised, it was not the case.

'Aye, lass. I do.' Rona peeked at Starlena from behind curious narrowed eyes, 'Yer *loved* that fella, Jackson, didn't yer, lass? Yer love 'im still don't yer?'

Starlena had to answer, 'Yes. I love him still!'

Rona drew her lips together in a tight little circle, her expression one of regret, 'I *knew* it,' she said softly, 'an' there's no denyin' 'e's a fine fellow. Oh, lass!' her voice fell low, ''twere me as dragged yer from 'im, I know.' She shook her grey head, 'But 'e's a *married* man! An' there's nowt but 'eartbreak to come fro' such a thing!' Now her gaze fell to the floor, 'I am sorry, darling.'

Starlena changed the subject, 'Why is it that some folk feel the need to make money their god?' she asked in such a quiet voice that she might have been talking to herself.

Rona was also glad of the opportunity to change the subject, saying heartily, 'When did you say that solicitor fella's comin' ter see yer, lass?' She would be glad when the whole blessed thing was settled one way or the other. Yet she would not interfere in Starlena's decision. Whatever road she chose to go down, it must be of her own choosing.

'Next Tuesday,' Starlena replied.

'Aye. It'll be to talk about Kathleen Wyman's share o' the inheritance – comin' ter you, if I've the story right, eh?'

'You have it right,' confirmed Starlena, 'but stories can change their endings, and a lot can happen between now and next Tuesday.'

'Still at the big 'ouse, is 'e – yon solicitor?' asked Rona, more to stop Starlena brooding on Kathleen, than for the need to know.

'Yes. There were quite a few stayed over . . . mostly business folk from London.'

'An' did yer not want ter stop an' talk we' 'em, lass?'

Starlena had played her part as a dutiful hostess. Well into last evening, with Miss Elizabeth by her side, she had talked and mingled with those stiff authoritative men and woman, whose range of subjects included such issues as the state of the stock market, the latest fashions and – the most heated debate of all – the Representation of the People's Act which, less than two years before, had given the long awaited vote to all women over the age of thirty. Starlena had little interest in the matter, being not yet thirty and having few political inclinations to speak of. The longer she had stayed in the company of these men and women with whom she might have been comfortable had she been raised with them, the more Starlena realized how very little they had in common. In their presence she felt distinctly self-conscious – almost an oddity. There had been times when she had come upon a close-knit group who, before her arrival, had been engrossed in busy whispering, and came to an embarrassed stop once she was perceived to be within hearing distance.

Throughout the evening, right up to the late hour when she and Lester departed for Whalley Grange, Miss Elizabeth stayed close by, intervening tactfully at awkward moments and giving constant encouragement. Starlena had been most grateful to her friend. But she was never comfortable – not for a single moment. There were many things which Miss Elizabeth had taught her, for which she would always be grateful, but Starlena was convinced that there were other things one could never be taught by others. They were born of instinct, or were inculcated into a body's teaching during the formative years when they were being raised in a particular way. Saddened already by her mother's passing, Starlena had become even more distressed at the indisputable fact that, however she might try and fight it, she had *two* identities – each one as far removed in character and harmony as night from day. In her own being, there was neither peace *nor* harmony; she felt torn in two and beset by so many conflicting emotions. Until she had committed herself finally to one way or the other, there would be no harmony, no peace in her soul and, no progress at all. She knew that. She knew also that her decision must be made soon, for the benefit of Ronalda more than for herself. When it was decided there could never be any going back. Never!

'I'll be glad when they've all gone back to London, or whereever else they've come from!' There was bitterness in her voice. 'Not one of those faces were familiar to me. To my knowledge, none of them came to see Kathleen when she was ill, so why turn up at her funeral? Morbid curiosity, and a chance to take a peek at "the gypsy girl". They all think I'm some sort of specimen to be gawped at.'

'Now, now, my gel! It's not like you to talk that way!' Rona chided, yet she was fully aware of what Starlena was going through, for some of those sentiments were her very own. If it hadn't been for the fact that she believed her own act in abducting Starlena those many years ago had contributed to Kathleen Wyman's tragic life, wild horses would not have dragged her to that church, amongst all those stiff-necked strangers.

Here, Rona's brown eyes grew troubled and a frown creased her forehead. There had been one particular woman who had greatly intrigued her. She had been already installed in the front pews when Rona was brought into the church, and Starlena had kept her mammy so close afterwards that there had only been time to catch a glimpse of the woman on her departure. Yet there had been something about that prim and proper figure, so upright and full of itself. And those eyes, which just the once had fleetingly and contemptuously swept over Rona's face. Green, they were – small and green, like a snake's eyes. Cunning too! Oh, *where* had she seen them before? Where had she come across the figure that belonged to them? Rona had asked herself the same questions countless times since yesterday. Now, in the first opportunity since then, she asked Starlena, 'There were a woman at the church yesterday, lass. Stiff little body, with a fox-fur round 'er neck and one o' them silly little 'ats perched on top of 'er 'ead.' She saw Starlena studying the image, then added, 'Tight-lipped sort o' face, wi' little sharp green eyes . . .'

'That's Freya Judd!' From her mammy's description, there could be no mistaking Lester Judd's sour-faced sister.

'*Judd*, y'say? What? . . . relative o' Miss Elizabeth's?'

'Freya Judd is her sister-in-law, Mammy . . . Lester's older sister. She brought him up after they were orphaned. Oh, she idolizes him, I tell you! Almost frightening it is, the way she clings to him every minute.' Starlena pulled a wry face. 'Can't say I like her at all. She's a strange one and no mistake. If you ask me, Mammy, there's a bit of badness in that one. Did you know that she was once a parlour-maid at Bessington Hall? Seems she rose in favour suspiciously quickly after Kathleen was put away . . . grew to be someone of importance, so Miss Elizabeth said. She must have blotted her copy-book though, because some years back she was flung out on her ear by Redford Wyman. Hmh! She wasn't flung out no pauper, though! Seems she's fairly well taken care of in terms of money.'

Starlena had also been curious about the aloof Freya Judd. When Miss Elizabeth had revealed what she knew about her, it was soon obvious to Starlena that there was no love lost between the two women. As for herself, she had no wish to make acquaintance of Freya Judd, nor apparently, did she with her.

Suddenly, Starlena became aware of her mammy's great agitation. All the while she had been talking to her Rona had sat, eyes closed and finger and thumb rubbing hard at her forehead, as though in an effort to extract a bothersome thought from within. All the while she rocked her chair back and forth, back and forth, with increasing agitation. Now, she brought the chair to an abrupt halt and sat bolt upright, her brown eyes wide-open and startled.

'The maid,' she said in a strange voice, 'she was the maid!' Now she swung her gaze to look on Starlena, 'Freya Judd! Lord 'elp us! *She* were the one as gave you to me. It were *that one* as snatched yer from yer father's arms an' told me yer mother was dead. Oh! What a vixen . . . to tell such a lie, an' ter play such a devious part in it all!' She was beside herself and, clasping her two hands over Starlena's shoulders, 'Oh, don't yer see, lass . . . if I'd known yer mother was *alive* . . .' Here, she bowed her head and covered her face with her hands, 'Oh, I don't know, lass!' 'Appen 'e would'a strangled yer . . . 'ow can I tell?'

The whole nightmare was too much for her, as she thought on Starlena's mother, lying there in that churchyard. Then another memory caused her to shudder. She spoke her thoughts out loud, 'Some'at else an' all.' Taking her hands from her face, she lifted her gaze to where Starlena knelt on the floor, so obviously shocked by her mammy's tearful revelations. 'That one . . . the one yer say is Freya Judd, she's sunk deeper than ever in this 'ere business . . . 'cause it were 'er as followed us to 'Merica! It were 'er as came lookin' fer us at Jackson Grand's place. I saw 'er! That's why we 'ad ter run, lass. 'Cause of 'er!'

For Starlena, already in a sorry state of mind, it was one shock after another, 'If Freya Judd *was* the maid who was there at my birth, why would she follow us to America, many years later?'

'I don't know, lass. But I'll tell yer one thing fer sure . . . she's a bad 'un! There's things been going on that 'appen only *she* can tell!'

Ghosts from the past had reared up to put a great fear in Rona. Of a sudden, every instinct she had since coming to this God-forsaken place would not now be denied. 'Oh, lass!' she cried, looking about her as though afraid some stranger might be listening, ''Appen *'tweren't* your father as wanted yer dead after all? Oh! I'm afeared fer yer safety!'

'My safety?' Starlena was at a loss to understand her mammy's thinking, 'What makes you say such a thing?' Yet she was so moved by Rona's anxious face that Starlena instinctively grabbed her wandering child close to her, 'Away with you, Mammy! If Freya Judd came looking for us, I expect it was on Edward Wyman's express instructions to fetch me home again, and we fled in ignorance of it. It's a fact, isn't it, that he was smitten with guilt and desperate to make amends? The solicitors made it all very clear. So

don't you worry, Mammy. It's all over and done with long ago.'
She shook Rona gently, 'It's all done with! Do you hear what I'm
saying?'

Rona seemed easier and nodded her head, making the remark,
'Aye. As yer say, lass . . . all done with.'

Not convinced, Starlena put the impatient child to the floor and,
getting to her feet said, 'I'll make us a strong brew, then I'll be
away to get Ronalda washed and ready for bed.' Bending to kiss
her mammy's face, she added, 'I've a mind to stay here in the
cottage with you, darling. But I've a feeling that once I've had a
long talk with Mr Sanders, we'll be making plans of a more
permanent nature, you and me, and the little one.'

Starlena saw little sense in uprooting the infant and throwing
everything into chaos for the want of a few more days. She told
herself this most fervently, hoping that was the only reason for
choosing to stay on in the big house. But there had evolved another
reason. She would be better placed to keep her eyes and ears open
– if what her mammy had said was true – and Freya Judd not only
bore a greater responsibility for her predicament than either Starlena
or anyone else had known, but also was 'sunk deeper than ever' in
what had transpired at a later date.

Starlena was both intrigued and angry. What devious part *had*
Freya Judd played in all of this? Why had she traced them to
America? And why had she kept so very secretive about it all? For
Starlena was certain that neither Lester nor Miss Elizabeth were
aware that Freya Judd had been so involved in the Wyman tragedy.
Her anger growing the more she thought on it, Starlena found it
hard to forgive that woman's cruel act, in first convincing Rona that
Kathleen Wyman had not survived the child-birth, then persuading
her to take that woman's newborn from its rightful place. Starlena
could never regret a single minute in her Mammy Parrish's loving
care, for whatever else might be shifting and insecure in her life,
now or in the past, the deep devotion she felt for that sweet old
gypsy was true and strong. It would be so for ever.

Now Starlena wondered at Freya Judd's motives for her sly and
cunning actions. How had it come about that a penniless and

orphaned parlour-maid, with the burden of a younger brother, had been so swiftly elevated to a far more lucrative and superior position in the Wyman household? On explaining how her sister-in-law had come to stay with her – and not being truly welcome – Miss Elizabeth had also expressed her surprise at the fast and furious promotion of one so young and inexperienced in matters of household management.

One thing was sure, thought Starlena when some time later she watched her mammy sipping thoughtfully on her tea. This Freya Judd had the answers to a lot of questions that puzzled both Starlena and her Mammy Parrish. There were ghosts to be laid alongside Edward and Kathleen Wyman and it was time this Freya Judd was made to give up the secrets which she had kept to herself for so long. And she would! On the very next day Starlena intended to confront her.

The opportunity came more quickly than Starlena had hoped. Early next morning there came a message from Miss Elizabeth. It asked whether Starlena and Rona, together with little Ronalda, would like to come and spend the day at Whalley Grange as it was David's birthday. With Lester in London on business, Miss Elizabeth and her son were feeling somewhat lonely and nothing would cheer them more than the company of such dear friends.

'The mistress asked me to wait in case you'd like to come at once.' The black-suited chauffeur stood cap under arm, awaiting a reply to Elizabeth Judd's note.

Starlena smiled warmly, saying, 'Oh no! It wouldn't be fair to keep you hanging about here. It'll take an hour or more to get ready. Please go back and tell Miss Elizabeth that we'll be there shortly. Jarvis will bring us. Oh, I hope it's all right if I bring Nurse Reynolds – she can help keep the children amused, eh?'

She gave a little laugh and playfully touched him with the note in her hand. His serious face broke into a smile. He liked this Starlena. She wasn't stuffy like others in this household and the way she referred to his mistress as 'Miss Elizabeth' . . . well! Starlena could be one of *his* kind, that she could!

'Very well, Miss Wyman . . . er . . . Parrish.' It seemed strange calling her that, he thought. She was a Wyman after all and since her poor mother's death, mistress of this great household. Oho! It was common talk that the repulsive Redford was suitably reduced in rank and importance. Common talk and commonly applauded by one and all, for there were none, to his knowledge anyway, who had any liking for the fellow.

On the stroke of eleven, following a good deal of rushing about in great excitement, the little party was loaded into the car by Jarvis, Edward Wyman's old and trusted servant, who had been retained by Redford and who executed a number of duties about the grounds and stables, chauffeuring being his main occupation when the need arose.

'Y'know, lass, I'd jest as soon not go.' Rona gripped the small of her back as she was bundled into the back seat, 'Me ol' bones is that stiff this mornin' . . . they'd be best suited to a spell a front o' the fire in me rockin' chair.'

'Aw! Away with you, darling!' exclaimed Starlena, in mock chastisement. 'It's just an excuse and I'm wise to your old tricks! Look, darling . . . I know you've no love for big houses and being one of a crowd, but it's David's birthday and Miss Elizabeth wants us there. *All* of us! Right?'

'Aye, all right then, ye bugger!' Rona reluctantly conceded, grabbing the infant from Starlena's arms and placing it on her lap as she grudgingly sat down. 'I s'pose I'd best come along an' keep an eye over the pair of yer, eh?'

She turned to Nurse Reynolds, who was seated alongside. 'Nowt but a bloody bully she is, wouldn't yer say? I expect ye'll be glad when yer week's up an' yer away fro' this place, eh?' she asked.

'Not at all,' Nurse Reynolds only wished that Starlena would take her up on her offer to stay and look after little Ronalda. She had grown used to Bessington Hall and, given the opportunity, would gladly stay when her week's notice was up. 'I've already made it known that I'll be very sorry to go.' She chucked the baby under the chin, smiling up at Rona to add, 'I'm a bit old in the tooth to keep making changes.'

'Hmh! Me an' all!' retorted Rona. 'Both on us past us best, an' bein' roped in as childminders, eh?'

At this, the two of them burst out laughing. Glad that it was settled, Starlena would have clambered into the car, but she was alerted by the sound of urgent shouting coming from the side of the house. Straightening up again, she was surprised to see Tim, one of the stable-grooms, come running towards her, his face red and excited, his whole attitude one of panic.

'It's Misty!' he yelled, as he rounded the house and caught sight of Starlena, 'she's down, an' badly!'

Starlena hurried to meet him, greatly concerned. Of all the horses in the stables, Misty was her favourite – the one she had chosen for her very own. Although Starlena could afford little time to concern herself with other matters regarding the estate – spending her time between her mammy's cottage, looking after Ronalda and gladly giving many hours to Kathleen's comfort and well-being – she had spent every spare moment in the stables. She loved it there and, having supervised the covering of Misty by one of the Wyman prize stallions, she had followed the pregnancy with great enthusiasm.

'Calm yourself, Tim!' she said now, her voice firm and authoritative. 'She's down, you say?'

'Aye! Looks badly an' all.'

'Who's with her now?' demanded Starlena.

'There's nobody wi' 'er, Miss. Mr Fairley's miles away up top meadow. He's setting the men on clearing them ditches . . . an' the other lads are out exercising the 'orses. I've just been in for Mr Wyman, but 'e's . . . the 'ousekeeper can't waken 'im!' He was so frantic he would have continued to gabble on, if Starlena hadn't stopped him.

'It's no use trying to wake Mr Wyman,' she told him, 'he's probably roaring drunk!' Starlena was disgusted and she didn't care who knew it. Now she took the lad by the shoulder and turned him about. 'Look, Tim, go back to the house, hurry! Ask the housekeeper to ring the vet, tell him to come quickly. It's urgent! *Urgent*! You make sure she tells him that. I'll go down to the stables. Quickly, now. And hurry back, I may need you!'

Once he'd started running, Starlena came to the car, 'Explain to Miss Elizabeth, Mammy. Say I'll be along the minute I can . . .'

'Hey! I'm not goin' wi'out *you*! Nurse can go on wi' the babby . . . I'll come to the stables an give yer 'and.' Rona began shifting Ronalda onto the other woman's lap, but was stopped short when Starlena insisted.

'I've no time to argue, Mammy! The days are long gone when you're fit enough to tend a full-grown horse, and well you know it. *Please*, Mammy! I promise I'll be along the minute I can.'

'Oh, well, 'appen yer right. I'd probably get down an' not be able ter get up again. Oh! I know what yer sayin' yer bugger! That I'd be more 'indrance than 'elp, eh?' She leaned forward to speak to the chauffeur.

'Go on, Jarvis, ol' sunshine . . . let's be off.'

As they passed Starlena, who was already running full pelt towards the stables, she shouted out of the window, 'Don't you leave me stuck wi' these bloody toffs, my gel! Foller me quick as yer can . . . else I'll fotch mesel' back sharpish!' Rona would have had a word to say if she'd seen the hearty smile on Jarvis's face at her outburst.

In the stable, the mare was down on her side, legs kicking out in spasms and deep pitiful groans emitting from her mouth, which was speckled with foam. Straightaway, Starlena diagnosed it as a serious bout of colic – the worst attack of which she had seen take a full grown and hardy stallion like he was a helpless newborn foal. With Misty being herself big in foal the chances of her surviving without help were painfully slim.

'Hold on, darling,' she said in gentle voice, falling to her knees and tenderly feeling the area of stomach which had grown hard, 'I'll take care of you, don't worry.'

'Vet's on 'is way, Miss.' Tim crept in through the door and knelt beside Starlena, 'What d'yer reckon?' he asked, nodding towards the unfortunate animal.

Starlena studied the horse for a minute then softly, so as not to alarm it, she answered, 'It's either a bad bout of colic . . . or there's trouble with the foal.'

'Shall we try an' get 'er standing?'

'How long will the vet be?'

'Twenty minutes or so . . . said 'e were leaving straightway.'

If the mare hadn't been in foal, Starlena might well have agreed to struggle it to its feet. If, however, there were complications with the foal inside her, standing her up might be the worst possible thing. 'No . . . we'll just keep her calm, make her as comfortable as we can.'

The lad nodded his agreement, 'What can I do?' he asked. When Starlena told him to first fetch a bucket of clean cool water and a sponge, then to go back to the house and get the housekeeper to make sure the vet *had* left, he lost no time in doing both. He left Starlena soothing the feverish horse and swabbing her down with a sponge, and soon returned with the welcome news that the vet's wife said he'd left straightaway and should be here in no time. And did Starlena know that Freya Judd had turned up at the house in a pettish mood and, at this very minute, was brandishing a sharp tongue at Mr Wyman – who, according to the housekeeper, was still drunk as a coot, and calling Freya Judd all the names under the sun.

'I don't think it's right for you to be gossiping like that,' Starlena told him, though not unkindly, at the same time wondering what had brought Freya Judd here. Even after Kathleen's funeral, she had not come to Bessington Hall with the others. Obviously she had business with Redford Wyman – but Starlena was not aware of any business between them. She was intrigued and, not forgetting her mammy's words last night, her resolve to confront Freya Judd about her calculated and secretive part in the complex circumstances of the Wyman tragedy was doubly strengthened. Even the thought of that woman being in the house made Starlena shudder.

Some twenty minutes later, the vet assured Starlena of the mare's pending recovery. 'Colic! No doubt of it,' he told her, 'aggravated of course, by her condition. But, I've dosed her . . . it'll take a while, but she'll be all right.'

Ten minutes after that, she was already showing signs of recovery. Her breathing was less laboured and she began visibly to relax. Starlena also began to breathe more easily. She loved that mare and it would have broken her heart to see anything terrible befall her.

'Stay with her till I get back,' she told the stable lad after the vet had gone, fully satisfied that the mare was out of danger, 'talk to her . . . keep sponging her down. I won't be long.' She wanted to catch Freya Judd before she decided to cut short her visit. It would be far better to broach the subject here than at Whalley Grange, for she still wasn't certain how much Miss Elizabeth knew. She didn't want to compromise that dear soul.

Being covered in straw and carrying bits of horse-muck on her shoes, Starlena thought it best to enter the house from the rear. She brushed herself down in the vestibule, coming into the kitchen bare-footed and decidedly dishevelled. Learning from one of the kitchen-maids that the master was still in the library, and his visitor with him, Starlena suggested that the stable-lad should be taken a hot drink and a sandwich, then said, 'Ask the housekeeper to ensure that no-one disturbs me. I'll be asking Mr Wyman's visitor to join me in the drawing-room.' After which she went, still on bare feet, towards the library, where Freya Judd was reported to be in the company of the unlikeable Redford Wyman. Starlena was most curious to know what those two might have in common – especially since she'd been told by Miss Elizabeth that Redford Wyman had once thrown the woman out in no uncertain way.

Starlena's curiosity regarding Freya Judd was soon satisfied in a cruel way she would rather not have experienced.

Advancing towards the library door, Starlena was silent as her shoeless footsteps hurried her along the polished wood floor. Now, with one hand on the doorknob, she gently tapped with the other, at the same time edging the door open. She would have pushed it all the way open had she not been riveted to the spot by the spitting remark made by Freya Judd.

'If *I'm* a conniving bastard, Redford Wyman, then you're a bigger one!' Here her voice fell a shade quieter, but not so quiet Starlena didn't hear the foul accusations she made. 'I've my own ideas as to why your mother ran out screaming . . . so terrified she almost fell dead of a heart-attack!' She gave a little laugh, 'She was a sick woman, Redford Wyman! So what terrified her so much that she found the strength to do what she did?'

'Bitch! Out with it . . . what are you getting at?' Judging by the slur in his voice, Redford Wyman was still heavily under the influence of the immense quantity of booze which he had downed the night before. Even for him, the indulgence had been excessive, giving those who had little knowledge of him the idea that he might be grieving for his mother. When in truth it was more in the nature of a celebration – although there *was* a measure of regret in that the execution he'd planned had come about in the wrong order. But no matter, he had consoled himself, the end would always justify the means.

'You want me to spell it out for you, eh?' suggested Freya Judd in a teasing superior manner. 'Well, what would you say if I was to tell you that I believe the poor woman saw something . . . or someone sneaking about in the trees. Somebody armed with a shotgun? Oh, but not for shooting pheasants or the like! Oh, dear me no! More for ridding themselves of a thorn in their side, eh? A man, with his shotgun poised to rid himself of his prodigal sister, would you say? A foolish, hot-headed man, so intent on his target that he forgot to hide himself more securely? Now then! That's my theory . . . what do you think of it, eh?'

There followed a hushed silence, during which time Freya Judd awaited his answer. Starlena was astounded by these frightening revelations and, recalling her mammy's warning, 'I'm afeared for your safety', she too waited for his answer.

Slouched deep into the armchair, his mind not so befuddled that he didn't know what he was being accused of, Redford Wyman asked himself how the blasted woman could come so near the truth without herself having been there! Made bolder by his conviction that she had not been there, he said confidently, 'What do I think? I think you're a crazy bugger . . . but I've *always* been of that opinion. You tell *me* . . . how did you come to conjure up such a clever little plan, eh? I'd never have thought of such a devious plot!'

'I'll tell you how I came to conjure up such a plot then . . . because I know how your cunning mind works. You forget, Redford Wyman . . . you and me, we think alike! We always have.'

There was a pause when Redford Wyman gave out a volley of abuse at which she laughed.

'What is it you're after in this house?' he roared, struggling to his unsteady legs and cocking his head on one side in his peculiar fashion, as he pinned her with his one staring eye. As he moved his head he caught sight of the door being held slightly ajar and trembling from someone's nervous hand. Whose? he thought, with a clarity which belied his condition. Whose hand held open the door? Whose ear was pressed to every word he said? Ah! His beloved sister, that was who! Looking to see what villainy could be put on him, eh? But he was no fool to be caught out by a woman . . . no! Nor *two* women neither.

Not for a minute betraying his discovery, but cleverly using it for his own sly purpose, he demanded of the unsuspecting Freya Judd, 'Is it blackmail you're after? Looking to fleece me dry in the same way you fleeced my dear departed father all those years?' He sounded so genuinely hurt that for a moment Freya Judd fell silent. Then, when she gave out a laugh, he went on in the same hypocritical voice, 'Oh, don't think I haven't pieced it all together, you vixen! Don't think I don't know how you made his life a misery – forcing him to pay handsomely for the "secret" between you. A dark secret and no mistake . . . taking a newborn from its mother and handing it over to a gypsy. Why! You're an accomplice to child abduction! Oh, if I'd only known earlier, I would have searched far and wide to bring my sister home . . .'

'What are you saying you drunken fool?' Freya Judd could hardly believe her ears, 'You would have brought her home! I'm sure you would. In a coffin, you'd have brought her home!'

Quickly now, before she could truly incriminate him, Redford Wyman shouted her down with thunderous voice, 'You're an evil liar! Don't judge me by your own standards, Freya Judd! Recall if you will, how it was *you* who got rid of my sister . . . *you* who blackmailed my father and schemed with him to get my poor

412

mother locked away! Oh! Had I but known before it was too late. I don't forget how you came to me with plans to have my sister murdered. All the while hoping to gouge money out of me. I showed you the door then, and I intend showing you it now.'

He began pushing her and, having recovered from his startling attack, Freya Judd pushed back, yelling obscenities at him. But not yelling loud enough to be heard over his more robust and vehement accusations that, 'I may be drunk, I may not be as honourable as I should be . . . or as industrious! But, God forbid I should ever be as black-hearted and vicious as *you*! Now get out of this house! Out! Out! Out, I say! Leave a fellow to his mourning! And consider yourself fortunate that I don't have you arrested!'

Her peace of mind totally shattered, Starlena leaned for a while on the door jamb, her heart numbed and an overwhelming sensation of nausea pressing down on her insides. All intentions of confronting Freya Judd fled with a great surge of horror. Hearing the clumsy footsteps issuing towards the door, she rushed away from there, across the hall, out through the back of the house and past the tack room adjoining the stables. She ran to the nearest stable, which housed Redford Wyman's own black stallion – a fast and furious beast, which no-one other than he had been able to handle.

'What're you doing, Miss?' Tim had come dashing out of the mare's stable on hearing the whinnying of Redford Wyman's ill-tempered mount. 'Yer can't ride that one! He's a killer!' He glanced down at her bestockinged feet, 'What! With no boots . . . no saddle!'

Ignoring Tim's adamant warning, Starlena swung herself up on to the stallion's bare back, thankful that in readiness for a carefree day at Whalley Grange she had chosen to wear a full and more casual dress. Even so, as she rode away at daring pace, Tim was for a moment held spellbound by the length and beauty of exposed thigh, until, flicking the skirt over her knees, she called back, 'Look after Misty, Tim.' Then, hearing his assurance that the mare was already on her feet and looking well, Starlena kicked her mount on to neck-breaking speed. What she had learned just now couldn't be contained. Miss Elizabeth would have to know the nature of the

413

viper she was sheltering and her mammy also deserved to know that she had been right in her fears. The next thing was to decide how best to deal with it all. Certainly, that woman had a lot to answer for and no mistake! Whether the authorities should be brought into it though, well, that was another matter altogether.

All the way to Whalley Grange, across country, over ditches and hedges – long hair blowing in the wind – blue-black as the stallion she rode – and her skill as a rider keeping her to the stallion's bareback, Starlena couldn't get out of her mind what a scandalous criminal Freya Judd was. Evil and corrupt! There was no other description for her.

When, breathless and shaking, the story tumbled from Starlena in Miss Elizabeth's shocked presence, her reaction was the same.

'God help us!' she exclaimed. 'I knew it! I just knew it!' She then launched into a long and angry explanation of how she should have done something about Freya Judd – how she should have insisted that the woman be thrown out of Whalley Grange long ago! 'Oh but . . . I was never *sure*!' she told Starlena. 'All this while, I've tolerated her because of my own doubts as to how even she could be so wicked . . . Being the clever person she is, Freya Judd has always taken great pains to be on her best behaviour in this house. And, of course, there was always that deeper reason for giving her the benefit of the doubt . . . Lester. As a rule, he's such a wise and shrewd man, but where those he loves are concerned, he sees only their goodness.' Now, running her two hands up and down her skirt with great agitation, she asked Starlena, 'Will you stay here, at Whalley Grange, until Lester returns this evening? He shall have to be told, and he'll know how best to deal with it.'

Starlena could see that Miss Elizabeth didn't want to be alone in the house with Freya Judd. 'Of course we'll stay,' she said.

'She *what?*' Lester Judd could hardly believe his ears. His own sister a party to child abduction! Blackmail! And Lord only knew what else, if what he'd just been told was the truth. 'Where is she?' he demanded.

'She came in and went straight up to her room, like she always does.' Elizabeth had waylaid her husband on his return in order to tell him of Starlena's discovery without the others present. Now, as he stormed away upstairs to confront his sister, she shuddered nervously and, tutting quietly with a shake of the head, she made her way back into the drawing room where Rona and Starlena were waiting – young David and little Ronalda being allowed the privilege of a late bedtime and, in the company of Nurse Reynolds, playing games in the morning room.

Rona came to meet Elizabeth, shaking her fist and declaring, 'Fotch the police why don't yer?' Suddenly, remembering her own part in it and feeling all of her considerable age, she stumbled to the nearest chair, and falling into it she said, in a softer and more weary voice, 'Aw, Starlena, lass! I rue the day we were ever forced back ter these parts.'

'Calm yourself, Mammy.' Starlena came and sat on the arm of the chair and taking Rona into a warm embrace, she said, 'It's all out in the open now, eh? No more secrets.'

'Lester will take this all very badly,' Elizabeth murmured, staring ahead and wringing her hands, 'he's never suspected anything of Freya's real character . . . or, if he has, he's never betrayed it to me.'

Starlena was concerned at how anxious were Miss Elizabeth's kindly blue eyes. Leaving her mammy's side, she crossed to where her dear friend stood, obviously close to tears. Taking hold of Elizabeth's hand, Starlena led her to the settee, and sat down alongside her. 'Forgive me,' she said quietly, 'perhaps I shouldn't have brought the news to your door. It was the first thing that came into my head . . . the *only* thing I could think of . . . get to Miss Elizabeth's house. It seemed so right that you should be warned about her.' Starlena was beginning to wish now that she'd stopped to think before racing here.

'No! No, Starlena. You were *right* to come straight here. Your family was here and Freya Judd has gone her own wicked way for far too long.' She patted Starlena's hand reassuringly, then in a thoughtful voice added, 'I know it's a terrible thing to say, but, try as I might, I can't take to that woman, you know.' She gave Starlena a long quizzical look, before asking, 'And you say your brother knew nothing of this until recently?'

'Not only that, Miss Elizabeth, but he expressed great anger at what Freya Judd had done. He actually intimated affection towards me and . . . was deeply saddened by Kathleen's passing. Like you, I was most surprised.'

'Do you believe what he said?'

'I'm not sure, Miss Elizabeth. To tell you the truth . . . I don't really trust him.'

'You do know that it was his mother . . . *your* mother, who blinded him?'

'*Kathleen*! It was Kathleen who did that to him?' Starlena was shocked. As was Rona, who suddenly sat upright.

Quickly, Elizabeth told what she knew. How, on the night of the big ball, there had been a dreadful scene in one of the bedrooms, the ferocity of which was heard all over the house. Nobody was certain as to what really happened, but Edward Wyman was viciously attacked and Redford Wyman was stabbed in the eye. 'It was said, though, that two things were deep-rooted in the whole business . . . one being your father's blatant affair with Freya Judd; the other being your mother's constant belief that her baby had been stolen from her. Oh, Edward Wyman vehemently denied it, saying she was mad to think such a thing. No-one knew the truth, you see.' Here, she bowed her head, 'We know different now though, don't we? *She* knew! Freya Judd knew. And, because it suited her, it seems she watched that poor woman slowly lose her mind.'

Rona was deathly quiet all the while Elizabeth was talking. When she had finished, Starlena had hate in her heart, 'And Redford? Did he know?' she asked.

Elizabeth shook her head, 'No. Not till your father relented when he knew his health was failing fast.'

Starlena wondered, then, whether her mistrust of her brother was unjustified. It would certainly be splendid to think so. But, somehow, her instincts would insist on warning her otherwise.

After what seemed an age, Lester came through the door, his

416

face drained of colour and a deep weary stoop to his shoulders, 'It's true,' he said in a dejected voice, 'it's all true.'

'She *told* you?' Starlena had believed that Freya Judd would deny it to the bitter end.

'No. She confessed nothing. She didn't have to. Nothing she could have said would have condemned her more than her absolute silence. She's guilty all right . . . guilty of all you overheard, Starlena. And probably more.' Saying this, he cast an appealing glance at Starlena. 'I can't tell you how I feel about all of this . . . the agonies you've been put through,' he switched his glance to Rona, '*both* of you. The more I think about it, the easier I can see the truth of what transpired. The sudden influx of money . . . Freya's unexpected rise to importance at Edward Wyman's side. Then, when she was told by Redford Wyman to leave that house. Oh! What a blind fool I've been. There's no doubt in my mind that she could have exerted her influence in your favour at any time . . . and possibly, in your mother's favour. Instead of which, it paid her not only to guard the conspiracy, but to deepen it . . . possibly even to the extent of attempting murder!' The despair in his hazel eyes was painfully evident to Starlena, as, giving her a direct look, he told her, 'You'd be well within your rights to prosecute.'

When Starlena was quick to assure him that she had no intention of taking any steps that would bring more scandal down on them, Elizabeth rushed to hug her, saying, 'Oh, Starlena! How could *anyone* ever want to hurt you?' She was grateful for Starlena's decision, for it was obvious that Lester had suffered enough. Going to him now, she asked, 'What's to be done about your sister, then?'

Lester's attitude visibly changed. Bringing himself up to his full height, he looked at her with grim, serious eyes, his voice vibrant with emotion as, in a soft voice more telling of his feelings than if he had shouted, he said, 'She is no longer a sister of mine! She has my instructions to depart from under this roof within the hour. I never want to see her again. *Never*!' There was a desolation in his voice as he went on, 'Why in God's name are we so *blinded* by love? Why is it that we can never really see the faults in those we truly care for? No . . . I never want to see her again.'

However, he did see her again. They *all* saw her as, at that very moment, she came to within four feet of the doorway, where, having heard her brother's final words, which struck her to the heart, Freya Judd took a firmer grip on the handle of the portmanteau and without a word, turned away towards the front door. As she did so, her small green eyes alighted on Starlena's face; remaining motionless for a moment she continued to stare into that black defiant gaze, which never flinched.

Her mouth drawn tight, head upright and whole countenance unyielding, Freya Judd took stock of the woman who had driven a wedge between her and her brother. A wedge which had lost him to her forever. At that moment, Freya Judd's heart had never been so filled with loathing as she drew into it the image of Starlena. Starlena! Heiress of the immense and powerful Wyman fortune. Starlena! Daughter of the once great and feared Edward Wyman, who in his last years had shrivelled to a man whose strength had been eaten away by remorse.

All of this careered through Freya Judd's mind as she looked on the woman who, in spite of her stockinged feet and dishevelled appearance, presented a sight which to others might have been captivating. But Freya, who was now more than ever a sworn enemy, saw her contemptuously as a gypsy – always a gypsy!

For a long moment the two of them faced each other in that inner struggle for supremacy – Freya Judd a prim stiff little figure with hard chiselled features and penetrating eyes. Starlena, small of build and seeming smaller by her lack of shoes, long black hair still wild and unkempt as the wind had blown it on her ride here, her large black eyes magnificent in their challenge of the other woman. Outwardly, Starlena betrayed no sign of fear, yet inside it was taking all of her courage to stand her ground. The hard green eyes all but devoured her in their glowering hatred, before, with a last lingering look at each and every one in the room, Freya Judd went quickly from the house.

All the while his sister had stood there, Lester kept his gaze to the floor, lifting his eyes upwards only when he heard the resounding slam of the front door. In the wake of her departure, Freya Judd had left her brother both miserable and ashamed, Elizabeth quietly trembling, Rona sinking more deeply into years gone by. Starlena wondered how it would all end, for some anxious voice inside her warned that all was not yet finished.

'You bastard! You knew that bitch was listening! You *knew*, didn't you, eh? . . . That was why you threw all the blame onto me. I should have told them everything! Oh, but you'll pay, Redford Wyman . . . if I've to start a new life and a lonely one, I'll see it has its rewards, and it'll be *you* who foots the bill, my friend!'

Up to now, Freya Judd had kept her voice to a sinister low, facing Redford Wyman across the inn table and spitting out her hatred of him so that only his ears were wise to it. Now she grabbed up the glass from which she had been drinking and, with a swift movement which caught him unawares, she flung the whisky in his face. 'My own brother's turned on me, you swine! I ought to kill the *pair* of you . . . you *and* that damned gypsy!' she yelled.

'Quiet, you fool!' For once, Redford Wyman was sober, choosing instead to ply Freya Judd with enough drink to feed her loathing of Starlena to such a pitch that she would do *anything* to get revenge on her.

Angrily wiping the wet stain from his face and clothes, he leaned intimately across the table, saying in a low voice, 'It wasn't *I* who told Lester, was it? It was her, Starlena. *She's* the one. If it wasn't for her, you'd still be safe and secure in Lester's house, isn't that right?' When, steely-eyed, she nodded, he went on, 'And *I* would be in full possession of what's rightfully mine . . . isn't that so?' When again she nodded, he looked about furtively to ensure they were not overheard then, with a sly smile and with that one deep blue eye peering at her, he put it to Freya Judd that, 'It would suit *both* of us to see to it that she pays for what she's stolen, isn't that right?'

Now, his smile was met by one equally as cunning, 'Oho! Yes . . . I *would* say. The sooner the better.'

Turning to draw the innkeeper's attention and surreptitiously signing for another bottle, Redford Wyman's conspicuous eye-patch drew the attention of two others who had innocently overheard Freya Judd's threat that she ought to kill not only the one-eyed fellow but some 'damned gypsy' along with him.

Scratching one of his large ears, Jack the poacher made himself more comfortable by undoing the buttons of his green and black checked jacket. 'Seem a likely pair, don't you think, Abe?' he said, casting an amused glance in the direction of Redford Wyman and the inebriated woman with him.

Abe gave a little laugh, taking off his trilby and placing it on the table in front of him. Fidgeting with one of the handsome fishing flies which decorated the rim, he said, 'Hmh! Wouldn't want to meet *either* of 'em on a dark night!' At which the two of them burst out laughing, finished off their ale and, bidding the landlord a good evening, they collected up the sack which contained the tools of their trade and sauntered off into the night without a care in the world.

Their destination was by way of the woods surrounding Bessington Hall. This time of the year there was little game to be had but, from past experience, they just might bag a likely catch if they kept patient for a night or two. There were plenty of customers willing to pay a pretty penny for a juicy pheasant – them as believed there was never anything as tasty as a prime bird for Christmas especially if it was first left to hang a few weeks till it fell so rotten the stink met you a mile away. All the same, there was no arguing that in such condition this didn't make a pretty sight!

Two nights later, the two enterprising poachers came upon another scene that made even less of a pretty sight than a strung-up rotting pheasant.

It was the worst November weather yet, with a sharp nip in the air that sliced right through a body's bones. Jack and Abe had set a trap or two and, with a while to kill, they favoured the idea of catching a kip in the relative warmth of the big old barn in the grounds of Bessington Hall.

''Ere! Some bugger's beaten us to it!' observed Abe with some indignation, rubbing his hands together and blowing his warm breath between them.

'Ssh, man! You'll 'ave us hung drawn and quartered if we're caught.'

By this time Abe wasn't paying too much attention to what his partner in crime had to say. He was too busy ogling through the grimy barn window at the antics of the pair inside. 'Lord love us, Jack!' he whispered, his eyes wide open and a look on his face that told his surprise and amusement at what he'd just seen. 'Come and have a look at this.' He bent his head and gave a little snigger. 'It warms me up just *watching* 'em!'

Coming on tiptoe to peer in through the window, Jack also grew wide-eyed at what was going on inside, and he too had to smother a fit of laughter as he clapped his two hands over his mouth and in a muffled voice, spluttered, 'Bloody hell, Abe! I've seen some things in my time . . . but I can honestly say I've never seen owt to top that!'

They stretched up to peer through the window where, side by side, with mouths open and eyes popping, they took great interest in the flurried and frantic activities of the one-eyed man and the woman with him.

'Ain't they the pair as were arguing in the bar the other night?' asked Jack, without taking his eyes off what was reaching fever pitch in there.

'Aye, thar right. Although the woman looks a bit different with her hair down loose . . . not so stiff and starched, eh?'

Jack couldn't help but laugh as he remarked, '*She* may not be so stiff and starched! But, I don't reckon you could say the same for *him*!' It was all he could do to keep his laughter under control.

And as for Abe, he nearly collapsed from the effort, saying, 'By, 'e's going at her like a bull to a red rag!'

'Oh, but just look at the pair of 'em!' snorted Jack. 'Ain't there something particularly nauseating about the sight o' two middle-aged folks, stark naked and rolling about in the straw, eh?' He turned to look at his pal, an expression of disgust on his face, the sight of which threw Abe into such a fit of giggling that he fell to his knees on the ground.

'Oh, Jack!' he laughed, 'it's more than disgusting . . . it's downright bloody *comical*!' At which Jake also fell about laughing. And when from within there came a shout, 'Is someone there?' they scrambled to their feet and, still roaring with laughter, headed back to the woods and safe camouflage.

Inside Bessington Hall, the housekeeper was contemplating what *she* had just innocently witnessed. First, there had come the sound of raised voices like two lovers arguing – he insisting that she was making a great mistake and should do as he suggested. And she protesting that it was the most important decision of her life, and she must be sure to make the right one. As to the subject of the argument, the housekeeper had little idea – except to strongly suspect that it was a matter of the heart. It was only when she saw with her own eyes that Starlena was afterwards lifting her face for Lester Judd to kiss it, that the housekeeper was both astonished and disgusted. Fancy! Those two! Behind that nice Miss Elizabeth's back! What *was* the world coming to? Well, there was no doubt in her mind that the argument between them was whether the two of them should go away together. Thankful to be turning out most of the lights and retiring for the night, she bustled about, wondering why it was that the morals of the day were so loose and shameless. A *married* man, pressing his attentions on another. And she, having raised his hopes, seemed now to want rid of him. Such a dreadful, shameful thing!

In the drawing-room, Lester gave Starlena yet another hug, saying, 'You're a very lovely and forgiving person, Starlena. I only wish *I* was blessed with such compassion, but I'm afraid I meant every word I said. I have disowned her . . . completely!' He moved away from Starlena, saying in an altogether different mood, 'This idea you're considering . . . I can't change your mind?'

She smiled, telling him how he had done enough, 'Each of us is as stubborn as the other, and still not in agreement over the matter.'

He laughed. 'At least we didn't come to blows,' he chuckled.

Starlena walked with him to the door and opened it wide, giving him a warm smile which, because of the turmoil within her, was tinged with sadness. 'I haven't finally decided,' she said, 'and I won't – not till I've discussed it thoroughly with Mr Sanders.'

'Well, for what they're worth, Starlena, and however strongly I may have expressed them, you have my thoughts on the matter.' He waved a hand to encompass the whole luxurious room. 'All of this is your inheritance and, one day, Ronalda's. Please don't be rash in making any decisions. Promise?' He leaned down towards her, his hazel eyes both smiling and anxious. 'You could regret it for the rest of your life.'

Laughing gently, Starlena replied, 'No rash decisions. I promise.'

'Good! I hope you didn't mind me coming to talk with you about it. After all that's happened . . . well . . . when Elizabeth told me what you were thinking of, I felt I had to come.'

'I'm glad you did, Lester. But, like I said, it wasn't entirely because of what your sister did. I had already been thinking along certain lines, and, to tell you the truth, I've known very little happiness since coming to this house.'

'Your Mammy Parrish still won't move in here?'

Starlena laughed, 'If you knew Mammy Parrish, you wouldn't even ask. When her mind's made up, there's no shifting it. No . . . she'll bide in the cottage, at least for as long as I bide in this house.'

'And your brother?'

'I see little of him. He complained of feeling unwell today and has retired early.'

'Hmh! He's a strange one and no mistake.' Seeing how tired she looked, Lester bent to kiss her swiftly on the forehead, 'I'll be off, then, Starlena . . . let you get to your bed.'

'Oh! I still have a most enjoyable duty to perform before I take myself off to bed,' Starlena declared, her dark eyes alight at the thought of it.

'Oh. And what's that?'

When Starlena explained how every evening, before retiring, she went down to the stables to satisfy herself on Misty's condition, Lester at once chided her on the foolhardiness of wandering the grounds so late, 'There are poachers and all manner of criminals abroad at such an hour,' he warned her. 'Don't your stable-grooms keep a close eye on the mare?'

Starlena assured him that they were most conscientious, with one in particular as fond of the mare as she was herself. 'Tim sleeps in the adjoining stable. He's a very capable lad.' She felt the need to defend him, 'It's just that I like to see her myself each evening.' Starlena laughed at her own soft emotions but made no apology for them, 'It makes us both feel better,' she said, 'me and the mare!' Upon which Lester insisted that as it must have been his keeping her talking which had made her nightly visit that much later, he would accompany her. Starlena gladly accepted – blissfully unaware of the horror which awaited in the pitch black of that stable.

Lester had taken the lamp from Starlena to light their way along the path. Now, on reaching Misty's stable, boldly identified by the elaborate painting of her name on the door, he lifted the lamp high. Quietly, so as not to disturb Tim next door, Starlena fumbled to release the lock. The stables were always secured, as many of the Wyman horses were extremely valuable animals, particularly a pregnant mare such as this one.

Of a sudden, there came a slight noise from inside the stable, followed by the mare's gentle snorting – always a sign that she was nervous. Instantly, Starlena was on her guard. 'Something's disturbing her,' she whispered, turning to Lester and seeing in the dim cast of light the anxious look on his face.

In a quiet voice, he told her, 'Careful now! Open the door gently – then step away. I'll go in first.'

This she did. Lester eased the door back, saying in a soft warning voice so as not to alarm the frightened horse more, 'Who's in there? Show yourself!'

There followed a nightmare of noise and confusion, so terrible and with such speed that, even when later gently questioned by the police and later still more aggressively interrogated, Starlena could not recall with clarity every single detail. What was indelibly stamped on her brain was the firm warning given by Lester to the intruder. Whereupon, in the same moment, there came from inside the stable what she could only vaguely describe as 'a kind of astonished gasp', following which the horse threw itself into a fearful panic – kicking and thrashing herself into a frenzy.

Starlena made to rush in there, in a bid to soothe the terrified animal. But Lester gave a cry, pushing her back as the horse careered out of the stable, sending him staggering to one side and causing the lamp in his hand to fall crashing to the ground. Starlena, assured that he was not hurt, rushed into the stable. It was pitch black, save for a hole in the rear wall through which a shaft of moonlight reached in – this hole no doubt made by the thief as he made his escape. But she thought wrong. As she turned to reassure herself that Lester was recovering from the glancing blow which had sent him reeling, there came a flurry of noise from behind her. Before she could cry out, a hand was clamped over her mouth, and a voice, so near to her face that she felt its warm breath, warned in an urgent whisper, 'Quick, you fool! Get out!'

Immediately a second figure was silhouetted against the moonlight as it sought to escape through the hole. Starlena surged forward, at the same time sinking her teeth deep into the hand which sought to gag her. There followed a cry of pain as the hand swiftly withdrew and straightaway Starlena was grappling with the figure just retreating from the stable. It was all over in a minute. She felt the first intruder brush past her as he fled out of the bolt hole. As she frantically struggled with the other, there came between them the hard and unmistakable shaft of a shotgun! Of a sudden, a deafening explosion rent the air! There came a cry of anguish, the intruder fled, and Lester, already coming to Starlena's aid, fell to the floor, a look of astonishment on his face, and the white of his shirt splattered with crimson.

By now the whole household was roused, with people running and shouting, all converging on the stable and all horrified at what they saw there. Tim was the first out of his straw bed next door, then Mr Fairley from the Lodge – quickly followed by the two remaining stable grooms and, last of all came the household staff, tumbled from their beds, to gather round, mouths gaping open, eyes bleary as they stared first at Lester's shattered body, then at Starlena, who stood some distance into the stable, sobbing hysterically. The shotgun was in her hands, pointing directly towards the door where they all stood. Only one voice spoke out. Holding her lamp high above the others, the housekeeper said in little more than a whisper which became a thunderous echo in the shocked silence, 'She's *killed* him! The gypsy's *killed* Mr Judd!'

Some way beyond the stables, the two sinister figures who had escaped were still running fast towards the outer fields – frantic with fear of being discovered. Breathless and trembling, they crept into the hay inside the big barn, blaming each other for a well-laid plan having gone desperately wrong, and their heated argument finishing with the more cunning of the two instructing the other, who was in a state of shock and liable to get them captured, 'You stay here a while – till I come back. Don't move – do you hear? – or you'll get the pair of us strung up!'

For a long while after the man had departed, the two poachers lay still and silent – afraid to move, afraid almost to breathe. Then, when the terrified voice in the far corner began praying out loud, they signalled each other to move out in the direction of the big door – so slowly and silently that it was the most desperate and agonizing thing they had ever done.

Once outside and away into the woods, it was a while before either of them spoke, so astonished were they by the event they had just witnessed. It was Jack who spoke first, 'God Almighty! . . . There's been a murder!'

'And happen we're the only two as know who the murderers are,' breathed Abe, almost afraid to whisper even.

After that short exchange, only one other thing was agreed between them. For their own safety and peace of mind they made a grim pact. They agreed that when they were about their own criminal activities they had seen nothing – not a thing! For in these parts there was only one thing worse than murder, and that was poaching. There was many a poor poacher rotting in a cell and valued less than the game he'd bagged. Well, these two poachers knew nothing about any murder. In fact, the quicker they made their way out of this area the better for, by the sounds of it, there was not a minute to lose.

* * *

'Ssh! Not a sound, Maisie!' Redford Wyman put a careful hand over the maid's mouth, 'just tell me what's going on.'

The timid little maid described how Mr Judd had been shot, saying, 'Your own sister was still holding the gun when they found her.'

Redford Wyman began stripping off every inch of his clothing. When she went on to explain how the police had been called and were even at this minute questioning every single member of the household and estate staff, one after the other, he put a question to her, 'Tell me, Maisie, dear. Have they asked anything of *you*, yet?'

'No, sir. They're still talking to your sister. Parlour maids and kitchen staff were told to wait in their rooms and not to leave the house at all.'

This pleased Redford Wyman. 'So . . . for all they know, *I* could have been here all the time, isn't that so?' he asked slyly, slithering into bed beside her.

Giggling a little, the girl told him that yes, she supposed so, for they hadn't searched the house. In fact they had only just this minute past returned from the stables.

'Well, now. It so happened I had so much to drink last night, that I didn't hear a thing.' He kissed her full on the mouth. 'Why! I've been here, in your bed . . . the whole night. Isn't that so, Maisie?' When she nodded, he gently laughed. 'And if you're the clever little thing I take you for, you'll find it very easy to bring me a clean set of clothes.'

'O' course, sir. I'll be quiet as a mouse.' It wasn't her place to question the master's motives.

'That's right. Then, afterwards . . . us little mice can play a game or two, would you like that?' His hand began groping at her beneath the bedclothes, before with a nervous giggle she crept from the bed, then from the room like a shadow on the wall.

In the early hours of the morning, Starlena was arrested and charged with the murder of Lester Judd. The evidence appeared overwhelming against her: she had been caught red-handed with the murder weapon still in her hands and pointing at the victim, and they had been furtively creeping about the stables at that hour of night. The housekeeper voiced her indignation at the affair which was going on between them and at the shameful manner in which they had betrayed Elizabeth Judd, 'such a nice, respectable woman!' And on top of all that, there was the evidence given by the timid little maid, Maisie, that she had heard Mr Judd and Starlena Parrish in full fling of a heated argument only that very evening, while clearing away the supper things.

All of these things Starlena vehemently denied, wondering how in God's name such a dreadful picture of lies had built up against her and why. But when the scales were put to the test the lies badly outweighed her truth.

As they bundled Starlena away, many hours after the murder, her heart wept for the little shawled figure who held the child Ronalda close to her breast, her crying pitiful to hear. She was also deeply saddened at the thought of Miss Elizabeth – so cruelly robbed of the man she idolized. Oh, why was it, Starlena thought, that no-one believed her when she described how someone had escaped through the hole in the back of the stable? Suggesting even that *she* had arranged it so? How could they believe that she and Lester were having an affair? And why had that maid told such blatant lies?

Redford had promised that he would secure her the finest lawyer in the land, so Starlena prayed the whole truth would come out and she would soon be freed.

All the same she felt trapped and desperately afraid. Yet again her life was in the hands of others. Not for the first time, Starlena was forced to ask herself who were her friends and who were her enemies.

Chapter Twenty-six

Two weeks after Starlena's arrest, Jackson Grand received a letter which shocked him to the very core. The letter was from Mrs Elizabeth Judd and it read,

Dear Mr Grand,

I am writing to you at the request of Rona Parrish, who, along with Starlena, worked for some time at Grand Farm. It seems that Rona is of the opinion that you might be of considerable comfort to Starlena, in her most desperate hour.

My own dearest husband died in tragic circumstances and, because of certain evidence which leads the authorities to believe that Starlena is the guilty party, they have arrested her and have resisted all attempt of bail. Her trial is scheduled for January the fourth. The charge is murder.

There is not the slightest doubt in my heart that she is totally innocent. There is much more that you do not know – including the fact that Starlena has inherited a vast fortune. Unfortunately, she also has secret enemies who would see her hanged for a crime she did not commit. If, as Rona assures me, you are a true friend, can you find it in your heart to give Starlena the support and encouragement she so badly needs? At present, I am very much afraid that Starlena's friends number very few.

Your sincerely,
Elizabeth Judd.

'I know how ye feel, sure I do!' Paddy Riley was also shocked by this dreadful news. 'But look . . . ye're still in mournin' yersel', sure ye are!'

Jackson Grand lifted his eyes from the letter still trembling in his hands, and bringing his dark green gaze to rest on Paddy, he said in resolute voice, 'I must go to her, Paddy. Jesus, man! Can you imagine how Starlena must be suffering?' He got to his feet and, crossing to the window, looked out over the area where in his mind's eye he could still see Starlena's lovely presence. He could see her in the stables tending a foal, in the field taming a stallion, or lunging a colt. He could see her riding like the wind, or leaning on the fencing, with one foot on the bottom rung and her long wild hair lifted and teased by the warm breezes. And how deep in his heart was the image of her as she had been when Danny was close to death – when she had gone without sleep, and holding the boy to her heart had sung a gentle lullaby to him, bringing him love and comfort. Now it was she who needed love and comfort.

'There is no question,' he said, turning back into the room, 'I'm going to England on the first available ship.' His voice grew softer as, coming to the Irishman, he put his two hands one on either shoulder. Looking down into those familiar bloodshot eyes, he said, 'You know I did right by Deandra. Now the mourning is over. Will you take care of the boy while I'm gone?'

'O' course I will!' Paddy replied with his broad toothless grin. 'You be gone. And God go with ye.' He gave a sly grin, 'An should ye get the chance, will ye pass on me felicitations to that grand o' gypsy woman?'

Knowing Paddy's fondness of Rona, and of his regret at her going from Grand Farm, Jackson gave his assurance most willingly.

But as he hurried about making arrangements, his only thoughts were for Starlena. In spite of the fact that on their last meeting she had publicly declared her commitment to another man, he had never stopped loving her. It had been Deandra's worsening health that had prevented him from searching her out. Yet Starlena had made no attempt to contact him. From this Jackson had to deduce that she had forgotten him altogether and wanted him to have no part in her life. But now Starlena needed a friend and he would not let her down.

Rona hugged the child to her as though afraid some dark unseen hand might reach out to pluck it from her should she relax her hold. 'I *know* it's that brother of 'er's! *'E's* the one be'ind it all, I tell yer . . . I can feel it in me bones!' She rocked back and forth in the chair, with such violence that Elizabeth Judd and Jackson Grand felt uneasy watching her.

Now, shaking her head and looking in despair at her guest, Elizabeth walked from the drawing-room. Casting an anxious glance behind him to where Rona sat deep in thought and greatly agitated, Jackson followed. They entered the morning room and Elizabeth sat in the deep floral armchair by the fire where on a small circular side-table had been placed a tray of refreshments. Jackson went to the window. Gazing out at the snow-covered lawns, he asked quietly, 'Rona *will* stay here for the time being, won't she?' He wouldn't quickly forget the devil of a job he'd had that very morning persuading Rona of Starlena's wish that she and the baby vacate the cottage and stay at Whalley Grange – at least for the duration of the winter, which, judging by the recent violent snowstorms, promised to be bad.

'Oh, I think she'll stay,' Elizabeth replied. 'I can't thank you enough for bringing her from the cottage this morning. It was so cold in there . . . no place for either Rona *or* the baby.' Her voice fell softer. 'Starlena's mind will be at rest now her Mammy Parrish and the child are here.'

Coming from the window, Jackson sat down opposite Elizabeth, his voice sad when he told her, 'What a good loyal friend you are, Mrs Judd. And you only recently losing a husband in such terrible circumstances . . . These suggestions that he and Starlena were planning to . . .' He couldn't bring himself to say it.

'Starlena is my dear friend. And the circumstances you mention were never of her making . . . you know that. Whatever they say, I will never believe that. *Never*! That Starlena killed him in a rage of passion. That Lester and she were lovers. Jealousy! Revenge! That they fought and she wanted to be rid of him! Oh, how foolish and blind are these people. It's lies, all of it … monstrous lies. You *do* believe that, don't you?' she asked Jackson.

'I do! Oh, I do! Yet, at the same time, I feel so very helpless. They're saying it was a lover's quarrel . . . we know different. But how to prove her innocence? How?'

Of a sudden, Jackson recalled Rona's words. Leaning forward a little, he asked, 'What do *you* make of this brother of Starlena's . . . this guy, Redford Wyman?' He was most interested to know.

Passing her guest a cup of coffee, Elizabeth considered for a moment. Then, a frown working its way deep into her forehead and the blue eyes clouding over, she said, 'I don't like him. Not at all!'

'How so?' Jackson was not unsympathetic to the great sorrow in Elizabeth Judd's countenance. She so obviously adored the husband lost to her. It was there in the unhappy stoop of her black-clad shoulders and in those delicate blue eyes, which were stricken with so much pain. He hated having to question her on so many matters pertinent to Starlena's desperate predicament. But he had little choice if there was any hope of discovering who it was that had killed Lester Judd and afterwards left Starlena to take the blame.

Elizabeth was keen to help in every way possible. Since his arrival yesterday she had taken an immediate liking to this American, who, in her opinion, was every bit as wonderful as Starlena had recently described to her. So she relayed to him her distrust of Redford Wyman and also her deeper distrust of Freya Judd. She revealed the extent of Freya Judd's involvement in Starlena's tragic life-story and the beginnings of it. Not a snippet of information was withheld.

At the end of their long conversation, Jackson Grand had made up his mind to visit both Redford Wyman at Bessington Hall, and Freya Judd at the Accrington inn, where she was presently staying.

As they had done earlier, when bringing Rona back to Whalley Grange, Jackson was transported to Bessington Hall by horse and carriage – the lanes being not yet clear of snow-drifts.

Some time later, after being told at Bessington Hall that, 'The master is not at home,' Jackson arrived at The Horseman's Inn, on the outskirts of Accrington. Here he lost no time in locating the woman called Freya Judd who, with a gentleman friend, was seated in the bar area and by the looks of her had been there for some time.

The first thought that crossed his mind when setting eyes on Freya Judd in such a dreadful state with her blouse unbuttoned immorally low, her hair loose and unkempt about her head, was that she was obviously inebriated; the woman looked demented! His second impression, when she lifted her eyes to ask, 'Who the hell are you?' was that those small green eyes were familiar to him. In spite of her disorderly appearance, which at first had thrown him, Jackson knew at once that he had seen this woman before.

Convinced now that she was the very same woman who had visited his farm in America soon after Rona and Starlena had fled, he leaned forward to spread his hands on the table, and to answer her question with another – at the same time repelled by the stale smell of booze which enveloped both her and her friend, who was lying flat out across the table, head in hands and obviously the worse for drink.

'We've met before, I think,' he said, keeping his eyes fixed on hers. 'You paid me a visit, didn't you? . . . I'm Jackson Grand. Do you recall when you came to my farm in America?' He watched her closely. 'You were looking for an old gypsy woman . . . and the girl with her, Starlena.'

At the mention of Starlena's name, two things happened. Freya Judd recoiled in fear and, grunting, the man raised himself up from the table and to Jackson's astonishment, stared straight at him. From Elizabeth Judd's description, there was no doubt that Freya Judd's drinking companion was Redford Wyman – Starlena's brother!

For a long uncomfortable moment not a word was spoken. In the silence, Freya Judd began to tremble when she saw that it was the American she had questioned about Starlena, yet her mind was so befuddled with drink that she could not be sure. Redford Wyman continued to scrutinize the stranger with his one seeing eye then, in a voice like thunder, he ordered the stranger to, 'Piss off!'

Jackson Grand thought he had never in his life seen a pair so steeped in debauchery. They were as guilty a pair of conspirators as he was ever likely to see.

Leaning closer to them both, he warned in a low voice, 'There's something bad here. Something I mean to get to the bottom of, if it's the last thing I do!' Looking straight at Freya Judd, he said, 'You are the woman who came to America looking for Starlena, I know it!' When she vehemently denied it he ignored her and, turning his attention to Redford Wyman said, 'I'm *not* convinced that you're doing all you can to clear Starlena. After all, Wyman . . . you must want to get your paws on Starlena's share of the inheritance.'

'Liar!' Redford Wyman made an unsuccessful attempt at struggling to his feet. 'What right have you to say that?' he blustered. 'She's my only flesh and blood.' Suddenly his eye grew darker and a look of evil came over his features. 'I don't know who you are, but you're not welcome in my company! Like I said . . . piss off! And if I catch sight of you within a mile of me or my property, I'll set the bloody dogs to tear you limb from limb!' Then he fell back in a most ungainly fashion and lifting up his tankard to drain away its last drop, he began mumbling to himself – every now and then raising his voice to repeat his instruction to Jackson to 'piss off!'

Before turning away, Jackson let his gaze linger on Freya Judd who, inspired by Redford Wyman's example, told him defiantly, 'You're wrong. I've never seen you before in my life. As for Starlena . . . she killed my Lester! She's a murderess, and she'll hang for it!'

She grew agitated when, seeing he would make small headway there, Jackson turned away in disgust, thinking there might be better opportunity to get at the truth were he able to speak to the woman when she was less drunk and preferably alone.

'She'll hang, I tell you. Starlena will *hang* for it.'

434

Part Seven

1921
Starlena Accused

'I will maintain until my death
I could do nothing, being sold'

Muir

Chapter Twenty-seven

In her cell Starlena could still hear the words which Freya Judd had yelled at her from the gallery. She had been cleared from the court, but her words stayed to fill the air and to weigh heavy in Starlena's heart. And now, in spite of Jackson's desperate attempts to save her, she could see Freya Judd's prophecy coming true. Oh, what a grand effort Jackson had made, she thought, yet all for nothing. His suspicions that her brother and Freya Judd were hiding something had done nothing to help her. Without evidence to the contrary, that was all they could ever be – suspicions. The authorities insisted that it appeared to be an open and shut case of murder. And even those defending her gave out little or no hope at all. Those who had lied were sticking to their lies – covering up for who? Starlena wondered whether Jackson was right in his suspicions that Redford was behind it. Somehow her deepest instincts told her it was possibly true. But, if so, Redford had been clever in covering his tracks, for there was not a single shred of evidence to suggest he was anything but innocent. On the other hand, there was more than enough 'evidence' to damn her to hell.

Yet there must be *some* members of the jury who doubted her guilt, thought Starlena. Here it was, dark enough for her light to be switched on and still they had not returned a verdict. Ah, she told herself, there must always be those who were hesitant to send a creature to the gallows. Their long deliberation gave her little hope for she believed that in the face of the evidence put before them they must eventually return only one verdict – that of guilty.

At that moment the door clanged open and Starlena was led to a small adjoining room. At the far end of a long narrow table Jackson waited, the love in his eyes painful to see. In the presence of the vigilant officer he told her that the jury was being retired overnight to a secure establishment and would be recalled in the morning.

Starlena felt drained and devoid of emotion. Only her dark eyes conveyed the tragedy of her situation. Being forbidden the pleasure of his touch and numb in her heart, Starlena could not find the words to speak of her love for him, and for her friend Elizabeth and her darling baby and Mammy Parrish. She could only look into his beautiful green eyes and hope he could see what was in her heart.

'We won't be far away, sweetheart,' he assured her. 'Close by, at the inn. When the morning comes, we'll be near you . . . to pray, and to give you strength . . .'

He broke off, his voice faltering and his heart so full that he could not stop the tears welling up into his eyes and spilling down his face. And, on seeing them, Starlena also silently cried.

It was at this point that the officer stepped forward and the two of them were parted, each to be isolated in their own great sorrow and never ceasing to pray for that miracle which even now, could happen – if God willed it.

Tucked down a country lane not four miles from the inn where Starlena's loved ones were preparing an early return to the courtroom gallery, there were others also making ready and whose hearts were heavy with thoughts of Starlena's terrible plight.

All night long, Celia had lain awake, wrestling with her conscience and praying that what she must now tell Anselo would not be the means by which she would lose him. She had not forgotten his torment since Starlena's arrest – nor the visits he'd paid her and the prayers she had heard him murmuring when he thought himself alone. She knew only too well how much he still loved Starlena – even though she herself had begun to believe that she was winning a deal of his affection for herself.

'Celia! Why didn't you tell me this before?' Anselo was frantic. Here was a glimmer of hope for Starlena – only a glimmer perhaps, but it was *something*! And Celia had kept it to herself. 'It's true, you say? These poachers *know* who killed the man, Judd?'

''Twas the ditch-digger who said so.' Celia hadn't deliberately kept the news from him. It was just that she needed the time to weigh all the consequences of it before passing the information on. 'Anyway . . . even if they can prove Starlena's innocence, you'll never get them to set foot inside a court of law. Why, they'd be sent down for years. How can you expect them to come forward to free her, when they'd be putting their own heads in the noose, eh?'

'They're her only hope, don't you see that?' Anselo began fastening a halter about the cob's head. 'This fellow from America . . . I'll go to him! He's the one been turning over stones, asking questions and desperate to prove Starlena's innocence.'

Anselo had known from the first that the fellow was a rival for Starlena's affections. But this was no time for bearing grudges. '*He'll* persuade these poachers . . . happen even get 'em off the charge of poaching.' As he swung himself up on the cob's back, he asked urgently, 'Quick, Celia! Tell me again the ditch-digger's description of the poachers.'

Riding like a thing possessed to the Manchester inn where the Judd party were staying, Anselo relayed both the news and the poacher's description to Jackson who was in the company of Elizabeth and Rona.

It was Rona who cried out in excitement, 'I *know* them fellas! . . . They're Jack an' Abe . . . as found my darlin' Leum an' our babby . . .' So many memories came rushing back that Rona clasped her hands to her face and began sobbing.

'There's no time to waste!' Jackson had heeded Anselo's warning that the poachers might not be persuaded to come forward. But, equally determined that they *would*, he entreated Rona, 'Where will I find them, Rona? Think hard, quickly!'

'If their habits are unchanged over the years . . .' Rona said in tearful voice, '. . . you'll 'appen find 'em through the landlord o' the Dog an' Duck, on the Blackburn Road. Time was as they'd sell most o' their bag to the customers there.'

As Anselo and Jackson rushed from the room, Rona called after them – something she hoped would tug at the poachers' heart-strings and loosen their tongues – 'You tell 'em to remember a night many years back . . . when they came upon a terrible accident. Remind 'em of 'ow they carried a young man an' a small bairn to their last resting-place. Tell 'em what Rona Parrish 'as ter do wi' all this business now . . . an' mek sure they know as Starlena's all I'ave left in this world!'

'Right . . . and *you* make sure that barrister guy is told where we've gone . . . and why,' returned Jackson. 'See if he can get an adjournment or something.'

Jackson was curious about Rona's first words – was this a part of the story he had not yet been told?

Rona nodded her head as she watched the two men go quickly from the room. Then, turning to Miss Elizabeth, who looked close to collapse, she asked, 'Are ye ready, lass?' adding in weary voice, 'we'd best be away to see what the good Lord 'as in store.'

Like the wind, Jackson and Anselo rode in search of the poachers – Anselo urging the horse faster and faster, over ditch and dale, with Jackson mounted behind him hanging on for dear life. Two desperate men in love with the same magnificent woman, two rivals drawn together by that same love and driven by one single purpose – to secure Starlena's release.

When, breathless and windswept, they dismounted outside the inn referred to by Rona as the Dog and Duck – and confirmed by the swinging sign outside – Anselo took a moment to tether the sweating horse, while Jackson lost no time at all in bursting into the bar.

The two poachers were well-known hereabouts and at that very moment were tippling back a jug of ale in the adjoining saloon.

Jackson and Anselo quickly told their business to the wide-eyed and astonished poachers. But their reply sent Jackson into a fury. For Abe declared in a strong clear voice, 'I'm afeared ye've wasted yer journey. Wild horses wouldn't drag neither me nor Jack 'ere a front of any court 'fficial.'

Here he stepped back a pace, as though fearing he might somehow be dragged by the scruff of the neck to such a place – willingly or otherwise. Turning to his mate for moral support, he asked, 'Ain't that right, Jack?'

440

To which the other fellow nodded most vehemently, 'Aye, be buggered!' he rejoined with great enthusiasm. 'Fellas such as us ain't got no rights in such tirrible places. Oho! Fellas the likes of us, well, we spends us life *avoidin'* such divilish places, so we do!' He gave a long shivering moan, for the image of himself standing with bowed head before any bewigged official started him trembling uncontrollably.

Devastated by their attitude and desperate to persuade them otherwise, Jackson began soft-talking and cajoling, then when it became painfully obvious that it was having no effect whatsoever on the two men, he once more put the fate of Starlena before them. 'An innocent!' he pleaded, 'who'll surely be put to the gallows if you don't come forward. Jesus! You're her only hope!' he told them.

But their response was as before, and even Anselo's pleading brought no better result. 'We *saw* nothin'!' they both insisted. 'We *know* nothin'! And, if ye'll excuse us, we'll be goin' about us business.'

It was when the one called Abe brushed past Jackson with the intention of leaving, that he suddenly saw red. In the grip of frustration and anger at their unbelievably selfish attitude, he launched himself at the fellow, fixing his hands about that scrawny neck and warning him in a low and terrible voice, 'I swear – if Starlena swings, then so will you, my squeamish friend. So will you!'

He had the inclination to throttle him there and then – and might well have done so had not Anselo stepped forward to draw him away, saying, 'Let the rats go back to their hidey-holes. They're not worth the effort of good men!' His voice was scathing, in his dark eyes a look of utter disgust, 'We'll find another way,' he told Jackson. 'There must be others who saw or heard something that night. We'll find them – we must.'

'Oh, but never in time!' Jackson protested, his emerald eyes smouldering as they continued to rake the faces of the poachers before him. 'Let's get these guys there one way or another,' he said in a quiet controlled voice.

A chorus of protest came from the frightened pair, 'The story's the same whoever we tell it to! We saw *nothin'*! We know *nothin'*!' They were visibly trembling.

Now Anselo reminded Jackson that unless they came forward willingly and told freely everything they knew, they would be useless to Starlena. At this late stage only a strong detailed eye-witness account which pointed the finger away from Starlena and in the direction of the guilty party would suffice.

Reluctantly Jackson knew that to be the truth. As he turned away, he cast a long condemning look upon the two men, telling them coldly, 'Rona Parrish must have you yellow-bellies wrong! She was of a mind that it was you two who helped her when her husband and child were killed in some accident years ago.'

At this, Abe and Jack exchanged glances. And when, Jackson went on to say, 'Couldn't have been you two who carried her family to their last resting-place . . .' Abe stepped forward.

'Tell me,' he asked softly, 'Rona Parrish, you say? What has all this to do with her?'

The question raised a derisory snort from Jackson, who had no wish to converse further with such cowards.

From Anselo came an answer, given with a forlorn look as he told them, 'Starlena – the innocent woman whose life we would save – well, she is the only family left to Rona in the whole world. The only one.' Whereupon, he followed Jackson outside, where they mounted the horse and without delay made all speed back to the court house, where even now the trial was in its last throes and where the two sorry men hoped there might yet be worked a miracle.

As they rode away, they left behind two fellows deep in thought, stricken by the news that tragedy seemed to have struck poor Rona Parrish yet again. Was it not enough, they asked each other, that the Lord should see fit to take her entire family *once*? It did seem particularly spiteful to rob the wretched creature of her only loved one for a *second* time.

'But it ain't *our* fault, Abe!' wailed Jack, putting down his jug of ale on the counter, seeming to have lost his thirst altogether.

'Mebbe not,' rejoined Abe, his face a study of discomfort, 'but that don't make me feel no better. No better at all!' This delivered with a deep frown and a vigorous shaking of the head.

It was time! The court was brought to order and the grim-faced jury was ready to bring in its verdict. Further adjournment was refused and the prisoner sent for.

When Starlena was quietly ushered into the dock once again, it was to see before her a sea of serious faces. In the depths of her heart she sensed that all was indeed lost. Now, when her dark tragic eyes lifted to where Jackson and Anselo were seated, the fraught and terrible expressions on both their faces spoke volumes. Hope, and the heart, sank within her.

In that moment before the judge made his entry, there fell over the entire court a deathly hush. In the midst of that awesome quiet there came a disturbance from the back of the court-room. When Rona saw who the fellows creating the disturbance were – one being a court official and the others being Jack and Abe – she rose from her seat and, in a cry of relief, she called out, 'God bless you!'

Whereupon, Jackson was on his feet and making a hasty exit from the public gallery – all in the space of a minute.

There came a shouted warning that the court would be cleared forthwith should order not be instantly restored. This had the desired effect of subduing everyone. At the same time the court official had delivered hand notes to both defending and prosecuting counsel who, in turn, were summoned before the bench by a most irate and offended judge.

Following this came an urgent meeting in chambers where this startling new evidence was studied. It was all the more astonishing because it was given by witnesses who, in doing so, had confessed to the serious crime of poaching – thereby putting themselves in the hands of the court.

They testified in graphic detail how on the very night that Lester Judd was murdered they had seen a certain man and woman on no less than *three* occasions. The first was when they appeared to be engaged in a hot-tempered argument at the inn. Then later, when they were stripped naked and cavorting about in the big barn situated in the grounds of Bessington Hall.

'The last and worst time we had the misfortune to clap eyes on 'em, sir,' Abe said in a fit of nervousness, 'was in that very same barn some hours later. Me an' Jack 'ad crept in there a while . . . to shelter from the cold, d'you see? Oh, 'twas the very same pair, yer honour! Sayin' as 'ow they'd meant ter do fer this 'ere Starlena. An' how the two on 'em had lain in wait in that stable – wi' black murder in their 'earts!'

'Aye!' interrupted Jack, also nervous, but sure they were doing the right thing, because if he lived to be a hundred he would never forget how he and Abe had collected up the broken and lifeless bodies of Rona Parrish's family some twenty-three years ago. And if that poor woman had since found a creature to love – the same as now faced the gallows for a crime she didn't commit – then there'd be no rest for him in this world nor in the next if he didn't help to point a finger in the direction of the guilty pair.

'We saw the buggers all right . . . scared as two rabbits at what they'd done. The woman he called Freya cryin' out 'twas she who'd squeezed the trigger – killing her own brother. The other one – the one with an eye-patch – the one she called Redford . . . well, that one told her to shut her mouth or she'd be hanged, sure enough. Told her to keep hidden in the barn till he came back to fotch her!'

'If yer ask me, yer worship,' Abe added with a respectful nod at one and all, 'them two had been planning that terrible murder earlier on at the inn . . . 'cause me an' Jack here, we clearly heard the woman say they ought ter kill the pair of 'em . . . an' that damned gypsy. Oh, what an evil packet them two are.' He clamped his mouth shut when it was obvious by the looks he received that his own opinion was not required.

The two poachers looked at each other, thinking what an ordeal this lot had been for them. Yet, thanks to their courage and forthrightness in coming forward, Starlena's ordeal was at long last over.

Events followed swiftly. There were due arrests, the Attorney-General was informed and, on his issue of *nolle prosequi*, the trial was aborted. At long last, truth and justice won the day.

Chapter Twenty-eight

'I love you more than words could ever say.' Jackson held Starlena's small hands in his own and, leaning so close to her that she could feel the warmth of his breath on her face he asked in a voice trembling with emotion, 'Come back with me? Marry me, sweetheart?'

Filled with joy at his words, Starlena raised her head to look up into those beautiful green eyes which had the power to mesmerize her. She could never deny the emotions which trembled in her heart at that moment. It was true she had loved Jackson from the first moment she'd set eyes on him; the night when she had danced on the streets of New York and he had come to her rescue. She had loved him when they had worked together on his stud farm. And she loved him now – loved him with all her heart and with such intensity that it frightened her.

'Please, Starlena. Be my wife,' he implored, his eyes brimming with love and his gentle voice caressing her soul. 'You'll never know what agonies I went through when I couldn't find you. After I heard that O'Malley had been killed and, later, when the story emerged that he was already married, I didn't know what to think. I didn't know whether in fact you had married the guy, or whether you'd changed your mind. There were so many conflicting stories . . . and the more I questioned people, the less I knew.' He took her two hands to his mouth and gently kissed them. 'Oh, Starlena! It seems I've loved you all my life. And . . . you love me, I know it. We'll be so happy together. I know it won't be easy. You have so much to keep you here . . . you're a very rich lady, with land and a magnificent home in which to raise your child. I don't have the right to ask that you leave it all behind and come to live with me in America.'

He half turned away, as though unable to look into her dark eyes, as he murmured, 'I could no more give up my country or my home to come here to live.' Turning back to look pleadingly at her, he said, 'There has to be a way we can work it out. There *must* be!' Bringing his face closer to hers, he asked, 'You *do* love me, don't you?'

'Yes. Oh yes! With all my heart,' Starlena whispered, at the same time sliding her hands from his. She was torn by so many strong and fearful emotions which made her tremble when he gazed at her so. At this very minute she wanted to melt into his arms and be pleasantly suffocated in his embrace. She wanted to taste again that strong attractive mouth – the memory of whose kiss she had long cherished. To be his wife would be so wonderful she dared not think on it, yet life was never so simple. There were other things she must now consider, other people who must come before herself. Of a sudden, life had thrust so much responsibility on her that the weight of it was crushing!

'You know I love you, Jackson,' she murmured now, keeping her distance, but her dark unhappy eyes never leaving his face. 'Can you be patient with me a while longer?' she pleaded.

He sat up straight, then stood to look down on her, saying grimly, 'I'm sailing for Boston the day after tomorrow. If I don't hear from you by four in the afternoon on that day, I'll have my answer.' Striding quickly away, he turned just once to tell her tenderly, 'No man could ever love you the way I do, Starlena.'

Then he was gone, leaving his words echoing in the room and Starlena feeling devastated.

Having seen Jackson's serious and unhappy face as he left Whalley Grange, Miss Elizabeth told Rona that David's nanny would mind little Ronalda while she went into the drawingroom where Starlena might need her. 'She has been through so much, my heart bleeds for her,' she added, bravely ignoring her own loss and heartache.

When Rona came upon Starlena it was to find her quietly crying. 'Oh, lass . . . lass!' she said softly, sitting alongside her on the settee and gathering her up into her arms. 'Life never gets easier, does it, eh?' She began lovingly stroking the wild mass of deep black waves which hid Starlena's face from her, 'I know 'ow yer sufferin', lass . . . I *know*! Yer torn i' two, ain't yer? What ter do that's best fer the babby, eh? . . . an' whether yer ol' mammy might stay or go . . . am I right?'

Starlena stirred in the old gypsy's loving arms and, lifting her tear-stained face, she said bitterly, '*Why* is life so cruel? I do love him, you know, Mammy . . . I love Jackson so very much.'

'Then what? Tell yer ol' mammy, sunshine.'

Wondering how she could explain to her mammy all that was in her heart, Starlena spoke for the first time and, as she unburdened all the fears and anxieties which had grown to plague her, she began to feel much better of heart and to see all the problems in a clearer light. She told of how it would be wicked of her to sell Bessington Hall and its acres and, what of the tenants in the cottages? Now, with Redford coming up for trial on a charge of murder, the responsibility lay on her, as the only remaining Wyman. Was it not her *duty* to accept that responsibility? And if she stayed as mistress of Bessington Hall, would her mammy also stay, or would she take to the roads again, leaving Starlena and little Ronalda behind? And what of Ronalda. She also was a Wyman. What of *her* inheritance and, did anyone have the right to decide such an issue on her behalf? How then, could Starlena turn her back on it all and walk away forever?

'Aw, lass. No wonder yer all churned up inside,' Rona told her lovingly. 'An' don't think I'm makin' light of all that yer say . . . because nobody could do that. Look! First of all, let me set yer mind at rest on one issue anyways. Yer ol' mammy will not go wanderin' off. Wherever you an' the babby are . . . well, that's where yer ol' mammy will be, will *allus* be . . . till the good Lord calls fer me, eh?' She gave a laugh and hugged Starlena. Then, holding her at arm's length, she went on, 'As fer being duty bound to carry on the Wyman tradition, only yersel' can decide on that.

447

An' only you can decide whether yer deny Ronalda her inheritance. Y'see, lass . . . yer ol' mammy's the very last to give advice on that, because a long time ago it were *me* as took yer from what were rightly yourn. That were bad . . . an' from one bad thing came another, an' then an avalanche. I can't tell yer now whether yer ought ter tek yer own child from what's rightfully 'ers . . . it's *you* who must mek up yer mind on that, me darling.'

Listening to Rona talk had calmed Starlena's fear that the old gypsy would go her own way, rather than stay on at Bessington Hall. Along with that thought had come another. She would first put her idea to Miss Elizabeth, who was more acquainted with legal and business matters. Then, if Miss Elizabeth thought it a possible solution, she would go straightaway to the solicitor, Mr Sanders.

Not only did Miss Elizabeth applaud Starlena's idea as an excellent one, but she offered to accompany Starlena to London that very hour, and she would arrange for Mr Sanders to be waiting to receive them.

'Are you quite sure this is what you want to do?' Mr Sanders had been astounded at the proposition, never having come across such a thing in all his legal experience. 'You want to renounce your inheritance?'

'That's right, Mr Sanders.' For the first time in a long while, Starlena was looking forward to the future with a happier frame of mind. 'I don't want a single penny of it. The entire fortune to be in trust for my daughter, Ronalda, until she reaches the age of twenty-one. Then, she must decide for herself what she wants to do.'

'Very well.' He was shaken at the thought of how immense would be that child's inheritance after twenty years or thereabouts. Having seen how some people could be affected by great riches, he couldn't tell whether in this instance it would be a good thing or a bad thing. All would depend on the beneficiary's character when she came into such a vast fortune.

'However,' he went on, 'although your appreciation of Mr Fairley, the General Manager, is to be commended, I'm afraid he simply does not possess the necessary experience. Such a thing must be considered most carefully . . . executors and the like to be appointed. After all, the Wyman estate is quite considerable. And, of course, there will be a number of meetings to decide on policy, overall management, investment of funds . . . that sort of thing.'

'Miss Elizabeth has kindly offered to represent me on all issues. Is that all right?' Starlena had no head for all this business and legal talk. And, unlike Miss Elizabeth, she never enjoyed it.

'Of course. Of course, that's perfectly in order. I'll have the papers drawn up.' What a unique character this lovely woman is he thought. If her daughter grew up to be as forthright and trustworthy, there would be few problems this fortune could bring. It was the Redford Wymans and the Freya Judds of this world who brought the wrath of heaven down on their heads. God forbid the child should grow up to mirror the likes of them.

Chapter Twenty-nine

It was early morning on the day of Jackson's departure. Starlena headed the horse in the direction where she suspected Anselo might be camped and when, some ten minutes later, the horse carried her over the rise away from Whistledown Valley, there, nestling by the spinney which skirted Dinglers Dell, were the two wagons.

When he saw Starlena coming, Anselo hurried to meet her. Helping her down, he grabbed her into his arms where, for a long moment, she was content to be. After a while, they strolled along the rough path which led down to the brook. Here, they sat on the low stone wall, looking at each other and seeming lost for words.

Presently, Starlena's handsome dark eyes smiled into his. Taking his hand, she said, 'How can I ever thank you?'

'Don't thank me, Starlena,' he told her softly, 'it was the poachers you should thank . . . and your guardian angel,' he added with a small laugh. 'They were lucky to get off with a heavy fine . . . although their honesty did serve them well.'

'When you see them, Anselo, will you pass on my heartfelt gratitude, and tell them I've left instructions that they must *never* be prosecuted for poaching the grounds of Bessington Hall.'

Anselo smiled at that. Then, looking more serious, he took hold of her hand and gently stroked it, saying, 'You've come to say goodbye? I knew you would.'

Starlena nodded, but said nothing for her heart was full.

'I love you . . . you believe that, don't you, Starlena?'

Again she nodded, before saying in a small voice, 'And I love you, Anselo. You were my very first love and you'll always have a special place in my heart.'

'But not in your future, eh?'

Starlena's heart was heavy and the tears bright in her eyes as she asked softly, 'Forgive me, Anselo?'

'Forgive you!' Anselo smiled, and gently touching her face he said, '. . . there's nothing to forgive. We none of us can dictate what our hearts feel. I know you can no more help loving this American than I can help loving you.' He turned to glance at Celia whom he guessed had followed them and who was now standing a short distance away, the look on her face so pathetic that it tore at his heart, '. . . or that Celia can help loving me,' he finished.

'And you, Anselo . . . can you love her?' Starlena hoped he could. Back came the answer, 'I think I already do!' With a warm laugh he added, '. . . it sort of crept up on me,' and Starlena knew he would not be lonely.

Leaning forward to brush her lips against his mouth in a loving and grateful gesture, Starlena got to her feet. Drawing the horse's reins in, she quickly mounted and inclining her head to the spot where Celia watched them intently, she told him, 'You know, Anselo . . . Mammy Parrish has always said that you and Celia were meant for each other. It looks as though she was right, eh?'

When, smiling he nodded, she went on, 'Love her Anselo, as she loves you. I know in my heart you'll never be sorry.'

For a long moment their eyes met in memory of a certain night when something so beautiful happened between them that they would never forget it. Now there was nothing more to be said. The past was gone, the future waited. It was as it should be.

When, from a distance, Starlena looked round, it was to see Celia and Anselo hand in hand, drawn close to each other and a look of contentment about them. The picture did Starlena's heart good. As she rode away, Starlena was convinced that the two of them would find great happiness in each other. And she was glad.

'Hurry, Starlena, or we'll never make it!' Miss Elizabeth ushered the little group into the car – Rona in a new long frock and grey

451

shawl, Ronalda desperately trying to wrench the pretty white bonnet from her dark curly locks, and Starlena, looking magnificent in a dark-blue full-length coat with extravagant fur collar and blue woollen hat, which Rona had teased 'Looks like a puddin' basin upside down!'

Now, with the luggage also secure, Miss Elizabeth climbed in beside the chauffeur and pulled young David onto her lap. 'It will be a miracle if we ever get there before the ship sails,' she tutted.

'Well, at least you had the foresight to get the tickets beforehand, Miss Elizabeth,' laughed Starlena. Oh, but she felt wonderfully happy!

'Huh!' Rona intended also to have her say – simultaneously fighting the baby for the bonnet which little Ronalda would have off. 'If yer weren't so soppy as to insist on this blessed "surprise", Jackson would be here, to give us a hand.'

'Oh, but it's a *wonderful* surprise, Mammy!' Starlena said. 'He'll love it!' And he did. The ship pulled out of Liverpool docks and, feeling desperately lonely and unhappy without Starlena by his side, Jackson leaned on the railings, his eyes drawn back to the shoreline and his heart aching for his lost love, wondering whether he would ever see her again. After a while he turned away, a look of despair on his handsome face, to see Starlena standing before him as though the lovely image in his heart had taken form.

'Do you really love me, Jackson Grand?' she asked teasingly, her large black eyes moist with happiness.

Jackson took a step forward, then paused, gently roving his soft green eyes over her lovely face. 'Let me look at you,' he murmured. 'For as long as I live I won't ever forget this moment.' Now with a cry he rushed forward to grab her into his arms, 'Oh, Starlena! My lovely Starlena! Do I really love you? Oh, yes! Yes! For every day of my life, until I'm old and grey!'

In his arms, Starlena trembled, so wondrously happy in his warm and affectionate embrace. In her heart there was a little voice which told her that, at long last, the bad things in her life were gone. Only the good and wonderful things waited for her. Things that mattered in life – love, family, loyalty and friendship. And sharing the struggles and triumphs together. These were the treasures of which dreams should be made. She had her mammy, her darling baby, a life ahead on the stud farm where she had been so very happy. And, most wonderful of all, she had Jackson. Her American dream!

Epilogue

'Ye're enough to try the patience of a saint sure ye are!' The irate voice of Paddy Riley sailed out of the kitchen and into the paddock, where Starlena and Jackson were making all secure at the end of another glorious September day.

'Would you look at that!' Jackson laughed, as he drew Starlena close to his side, 'they're at it again!' He pointed to where the Irish fellow was charging from the kitchen, waving a vicious-looking ladle and sending three bodies fleeing out of his kitchen as fast as their legs could take them. First was Rona, her long skirt drawn up and filled with freshly-baked scones. One hand secured the skirt into a safe little bundle, while with the other she pulled along a dark-haired mischievous girl child whose mouth was covered in jam and who chuckled heartily at these fun and games. Bringing up the rear was Danny, now a handsome, healthy looking boy, who was also giggling.

Starlena burst out in a fit of laughter at such a comical sight. 'I swear Mammy Parrish has more energy than all of us put together,' she said, 'and how old Paddy puts up with her antics, I just don't know!'

'Well he must love her, sweetheart,' laughed Jackson, 'else he'd never have married the woman!'

The two of them watched Rona and the two children disappear into the cosy little home which Rona still insisted on calling a shack, but which, since she and Paddy had taken up residence in it, had been given a facelift. Fondly now, Starlena thought on Rona's recent words, that she wanted nothing more out of life than to be always near Starlena and the child Ronalda, 'An' if it means never seeing old England again . . . then after what we've all been through, that's all right wi' me an' all.'

Later in the evening, when Danny and Ronalda were abed, when Paddy and her mammy were together in their love-nest and she with Jackson in theirs, Starlena got from the chair where she had been lovingly observing her husband, thinking how very handsome he was and how extraordinarily happy they were. Coming to kneel on the carpet beside him, she peeped over his newspaper, all her love alive in the softness of her voice as she told him, 'Jackson Grand, I love you!'

Lowering the paper just enough for him to see her face, he whispered, 'Oh, you do, eh? Well, have I told you, Mrs Grand, that I positively *adore* you?'

Smiling up at him, Starlena patted the growing bulge beneath her skirt, 'Four more months,' she said, 'and there'll be another little soul to love.' At this Starlena saw the smile slip from Jackson's face and in its place there emerged a look of such precious longing that it made her heart almost stop. Placing the newspaper on the arm of the chair, he put his two strong arms about her and, drawing her closer, he gazed into those dark and wonderful eyes with such intimate searching that Starlena thought she would surely blush if he did not stop.

Brushing his face against hers, he touched her lightly with his mouth – softly kissing her skin, her ears, her neck, until with a small cry of passion, he kissed her full on the mouth, causing Starlena to quiver deep within herself. In all of her eventful past, she had barely dared to dream of the happiness she felt at this minute – and which, God willing, she would have for many years to come. Starlena felt she had already lived a lifetime packed with experiences and adventures which most people would never encounter in *twice* the number of her years. But if, at times, her despair had been intense, then so now was the exhilarating joy she felt. And the love of those dearest to her heart was more precious and a greater fortune than anything this world could offer. She prayed also that, when the day came for Ronalda to make a choice, it would be the right one.

As Starlena and Jackson left the room to go upstairs, the draught from the door caused the newspaper to fall to the carpet. The flickering firelight showed that it was an English newspaper dated 12th September 1921. Halfway down the page and taking up considerable space was an article circled in red by Elizabeth, and reporting that the sentence passed on Freya Judd and Redford Wyman, both convicted on a charge of murder, was duly executed on September 11th. All the facts were reported in a cold and precise manner.

What was neither cold, precise, nor reported was the feelings of another who, at that very moment, was reading the same article. This man had never forgotten how, because of Redford Wyman, it might have been *him* swinging from the gallows for the murders of a gypsy woman and the girl, Starlena. Neither had he forgotten how, later, when he was desperate, that same villain who had hired him to do the deed, had thrown him from Bessington Hall, with the dogs baying at his heels.

As he screwed up his beady eyes and stroked his thin moustache, the fellow laughed out loud. How ironic that now, even though he was still a poor man, he was better off by far than Redford Wyman, for he was warm and alive, was he not? In a quiet voice trembling with hatred, he screwed up the newspaper and threw it to one side, saying, 'Rot in hell, Wyman. I'm sure you will, for the devil's got his due!'